Cary J. Lenehan is a former trades assistant, soldier, public servant, cab driver, truck driver, game designer, fishmonger, trainee horticulturalist and university tutor (among other things). His hobbies include collecting and reading books (the non-fiction are Dewey decimalised), Tasmanian native plants (particularly the edible ones), the SCA and gaming. He has taught people how to use everything from shortswords to rocket launchers. He met his wife at an SF Convention while cosplaying and they have not looked back.

He was born in Sydney before marrying and moving to the Snowy Mountains where they started their family. They moved to Tasmania for the warmer winters and are not likely to ever leave it.

Looking out of the window beside his computer is a sweeping view of Mount Wellington and its range.

Warriors of Vhast Series
published by IFWG Publishing Australia

Intimations of Evil (Book 1)
Engaging Evil (Book 2)
Clearing the Web (Book 3)
Scouring the Land (Book 4)

Warriors of Vhast Book 1

Intimations of Evil

by
Cary J Lenehan

Intimations of Evil

Book 1, Warriors of Vhast

All Rights Reserved

ISBN-13: 978-1-925956-41-2

Copyright ©2018 Cary J Lenehan

Second Edition V1.1

Printed in Times and LHF Essendine font types

IFWG Publishing International
Melbourne

www.ifwgpublishing.com

Acknowledgement

I would like to thank the many people who have read this book as it has evolved from notes written while sitting in a cab waiting for fares to what it is now. While most have been polite and said they liked it, sometimes the readers have not enjoyed it and have been kind enough to say why, which has often told me things about my writing. Some have also offering some amazing insights that have led me to change sections and the way I write. In particular I wish to thank Pip Woodfield who has read so many iterations of the text that she may know it all better than I do.

None of the characters are based on real people, but feel free to ask how they came to be.

A glossary of terms used in this novel can be found at page 311

This is book is dedicated to my mother, Eden and my beloved wife Marjorie, both of whom have shown incredible patience with me over the years as I have followed my dreams. I hope you both enjoy it and are proud of how it has turned out.

Preface to the Second Edition

In between finishing the series of books and having written over forty Vhast short stories (so far) for my Patreon followers (*Cary J Lenehan is creating Books, stories, recipes, drawings, maps, characters and cosplay*), my writing style has changed. Thankfully IFWG have allowed me the chance to have this second edition to bring the first book into line with everything else before it goes into bookstores.

There is no need to panic over the changes, as there has been no change to the plot at all. I have moved from third person more to first person in the narrative and fixed the annoying errors that crept in somehow. Now the short stories extend from well before the books start to well after they finish (and they do have a definite finish). The books give the central story and are not dependent on the stories at all. The stories are merely the garnish that explores other aspects of the world and backstory for some of the characters, for instance, why the people of The White World call Astrid 'Mathanhaɪ feɑd'.

I hope that you enjoy what has been written.

Cary J Lenehan
March, 2018

Prologue

From dark deep lands above
Far flung beyond dark sky
Winged lords of light wove magic vast
Built up lands and mountains high
Eldest gods in sky-borne homes
Weave in place our fates so fell
Fetched forth from earth and water
Races many come forward to dwell
Bring the Dragons; bring the Dwarves
Among the peaks, find who is bold
Then do Seven beget the slaughter,
Old and dire, find who will hold

Tales of the Beginning
Paarlakmugaani,
Bard of the Cenubarkincilari Hohgoblins

All events have a beginning.
There is always some incident which people can look back at and wisely say to each other, "If this single thing did not happen then our history and our world would look different."

Such a beginning may not be sufficient—other things may have to happen as well—but it is necessary and all else that happens flows from this single point in time.

What follows here is just such a beginning.

Chapter 1

Basil

For Sergeant Basil Akritas the decision to leave Ardlark was easy. *The Strategos Panterius has called me in to his musty office and asked for my badge. I am surprised. My amulet-badge is what I hold as a member of the secret police, the Antikataskopeía. It is the one that enables me to be easily found and that marks me as one of many in the organisation.*

Basil asked no questions. He almost never wore a uniform and spent far more time seeking criminals and potential traitors than wielding a bow like his Kichic-kharl great-grandfather or waving a sword like others of his family, but he was still a soldier.

"Follow," the Strategos Panterius said, and without further word his superior left the room.

With Basil trailing behind, they entered the vast building that was both a military base and palace to the Empire.

They made their way through the maze of cold corridors, passing from the strictly functional granite of the castle inwards to the more civilian corridors of marble that made up the palace itself. They went through corridors and up stairs and around corners, places that Basil had never seen before. Without his head turning or otherwise betraying interest, his eyes flicked around and noted everything he passed.

Islamic subjects have obviously built one corridor; my soft boots make no noise as we walk on the tiled floors. The walls are covered in friezes of bright geometric design and an ornate plaster ceiling. His eyes filled with wonder. Through marvellous arches another corridor opened to a secluded garden with a fountain. A cold breeze blew bringing with it the aroma of flowers. *A second passage shows its Christian building style with painted plaster walls and mosaic murals depicting the business of the Court. One mosaic shows*

3

the God-King Hrothnog seated on a throne in the vast ceremonial audience chamber buried deeper in the palace, receiving homage from the various races of the Empire.

Yet another corridor was clearly of Kharl workmanship; the polished black basalt floors almost slippery but making a surface that would allow an impressive sound to echo around with hobnailed boots. This corridor also had white plaster panels on the walls, and on each, painted scenes of battle. Above them were old banners of tagmata, and possibly even countries long vanished, their memory perhaps only preserved here by these fragments.

They passed doors of different timbers and sizes, and more corridors, small and large. These themes repeated themselves in a hodgepodge of styles as they moved further inward and climbed up several more stories. Eventually they came to a pair of large well-polished wooden doors tall enough for even one of the giant Insak-div to pass through without stooping. The smell of rich cedar oil lay around the area and tickled Basil's nose. The doors had large shiny brass handles and the Strategos grasped one, which opened silently as he ushered a very nervous Basil inside. *Where are we going?*

The room looks over thirty paces wide in each direction; its floor covered in a thick carpet, with rugs and tapestries on the white smooth-plastered walls. Silence seems to radiate from it and there is an underlying scent of sandalwood. Three glazed windows in one wall light the room with natural light. At the rear of the room is a single door as wide and equally tall as the one we have walked through. It is made of one of the jungle timbers from near my home. I am not a carpenter so I am not sure which, but I have seen its red colour and grain before in the doors and furniture of the south.

A desk and some leather-covered chairs are in the centre of the room. A Human male sits behind the desk dressed very conservatively in the Islamic fashion. A handsome young man and a very attractive young woman also sit on chairs near the desk, each in baggy purple silk trousers and golden jerkins, gathered with golden sashes at their waists; embroidered on them, over their hearts, are the Imperial symbols.

Strategos Panterius gestured to Basil to sit then spoke to the man behind the desk. The man glanced at Basil, nodded and gestured at the seated servants. The girl rose, listened for a moment, and moved silently across the room. She opened the single door and went through, closing it behind her without a sound.

After a couple of minutes the girl emerged.

"Come," she said in a mellow contralto, and gestured to the Strategos, who in turn, impatiently waved for Basil to follow. They went through the single door and entered an odd-shaped room that had three walls made almost entirely of huge sheets of glass. The view from this end of the palace was over the public buildings and administration, the Circus, the docks, and over indeed most of Ardlark.

In the centre of the room are a desk and chair and coming around them is the God-King Hrothnog himself. Being a Christian I don't accept the God part of the title…although close up it is a very different proposition. Hrothnog is clad in a purple silk tunic. It is a far finer and softer-looking silk than his messengers outside wear, with designs worked in gold, possibly even real gold, on the breast. He has breeches of a lighter purple tucked into deep purple leather boots and wears a ring on each of his fingers—they are like a rainbow with the variety of colours. Each will be more than a decoration, holding enchantments, or at least serving as the focus for a casting.

It was the first time Basil had actually met his ruler close up. *I am not sure what terrifies me most. It could be the piercing golden eyes that glow, even in this well-lit room. It could be the resonant bass voice. It turns my knees to jelly when he speaks. Possibly it is the hands and face; desiccated as a body found after years in the desert; belonging to a dead man rather than a living one.*

I am not sure if what I see is real, or if it is an illusion. Even more, I don't want to know. I don't even want to think about it—after all Hrothnog probably knows what I am thinking and to offend my ruler is unthinkable. That movement of the lips—is it the rictus of a corpse or is it the ghost of a smile? Damn, I am thinking again. Basil's face was immobile and showed nothing of what went on behind it, as befits a trained intelligence officer, but his mind was running everywhere and letting his God-King know everything. That had to be a smile on the face as he turned from the Strategos to let his gaze fall on Basil as he tried to still his mind.

"I have a task for you," Hrothnog intoned. "It may take you all of your life and still not be finished when that is ended. If you accept you will leave Darkreach and might never return. It is possible that you may never see your family again. You might not ever be paid and you will only have the instructions that I give you to guide you. For these reasons you can decline the task now and there will be no mention of it again and you will have a normal career in your field.

"If you choose to go you must tell your family you are going away on my orders. If you do accept, the circumstances of your family will improve dramatically for all of time. That will be your payment. Do you accept?"

I am a soldier, I have agreed to give my life for the Empire, and now the Emperor is asking me personally to live it for a task. Not much of a choice really. He swallowed. His voice did not seem to want to work. "Yes, sir," he eventually managed to croak out.

Hrothnog nodded. *I am sure I heard Panterius sigh. I must have been personally recommended by the Strategos. It must be important to the*

Strategos that I agree to accept the task.

Hrothnog, to Basil's discomfort, looked him up and down again. "My great-great-granddaughter Theodora left the palace several days ago disguised as an Insakharl Kataphractoi mage. She is leaving Darkreach behind and thinks that her departure is secret. Despite her taking some time to leave, I have decided that I do not believe she is prepared for the outside world. You will report to the Strategos at dawn tomorrow with two saddlebags of personal effects. The rest will be supplied to you. You will have two tasks: to keep Theodora alive—even if it costs you your own life—and to act as her servant wherever she goes." He paused and looked at Basil as if expecting to see him refuse.

Basil was full of a mix of curiosity and a still-quaking stomach, but he said nothing.

"You will be transported to Dochra where you will pose as a servant whose master has died. She cannot care for herself, but she believes that she needs to leave and be independent. For my own reasons I think that she may actually be right in this and, what is more, I think that she needs to believe that she is on her own with no support from me."

I am not sure if I want to hear my Emperor explaining his thoughts to me in what I am sure is meant as a confidential tone. He kept his attention focused.

"Until you have left Darkreach well behind, you cannot tell her who you are, or that you are under orders in case she rejects you and leaves. You must always be a servant who just happened to find her when she needed you. After you have left, whether you tell her or not, is up to you. Is this clear?"

Basil nodded—*I don't quite understand them, but at least I have orders.*

"Then go."

At this dismissal Basil and the Strategos bowed, withdrew a couple of paces, and left the room. The servant girl messenger was still behind them and she opened the door for the two.

Basil found that they were retracing their route from Hrothnog's room with the Strategos motioning Basil to silence. On reaching his office the Strategos told his staff that they were not to be disturbed and closed the door. He briefly checked something, *I cannot see what, but it is in his desk drawer*, and motioned Basil into a soft chair at the side. *It is one of a pair that have always been there but I have never seen used.* The smell of leather rose around him as he sat.

The Strategos poured them both a goblet of red wine from a bottle in a cupboard before sitting in the other chair. Basil took a sip, savouring the aroma and the flavour. *It is a far better quality than I am used to.*

"This is a delicate matter," Strategos Panterius said. "The Emperor is quite concerned. I wish that we could do more, but nearly the only resource we can give you is money. Here are a set of saddlebags." He rose and strode over to where a set of good quality, but old and well-used saddlebags sat in a corner, and lifted them up on the desk. "You will see that they look mundane but, if you look here you will see hidden pockets. There is a supply of imperials, sesterces, denarii and numismata, not just in our coins, but also in currency from other realms. Spend it wisely. We cannot give you any magic items that you would not have as a servant. Theodora is a powerful mage and she will sense any magic you are carrying. This is about as far as we can go." He handed Basil a small oak wand the size of a little finger that was in a pouch that would slide easily onto a belt. "Up to eight times a day, on being grasped and given the command 'light', it will produce a flame that will last long enough for you to light a fire. At least you will not need a flint and steel." He handed it over.

Basil lit it and commanded it to go out, before putting it in one of his larger pouches. *Useful, and not just for cooking.*

"Without magic or any other support, you will have to rely on your cunning and experience. You are one of our fittest agents available; you can run fast, track and hide in the city or the field, and are used to dealing with people and finding things out. In addition, and this suits you most for this mission, you have worked extensively as a servant. You can cook and are experienced in treating wounds. As well you can speak a few outland tongues and look much younger than your twenty-five years. People expect you to be a youth with a youth's lack of experience. They underestimate you. All of this is why I selected you for this task." He paused and sighed again.

Basil was still savouring sitting in the Strategos' office and enjoying the rich wine.

"If you do manage to discover anything of importance to Darkreach, write it down and seal it with this." He pulled out a small cloth bag. *In it is a small green cylindrical seal with a complex and unfathomable design on it. I am used to seeing these magical seals with high-ranking officers.*

"Hold it in your hand until it goes cold."

Basil did as he was told. It didn't take long.

"Once it is sealed hand it to any of our merchants headed back here. You can promise them a good reward when they hand it to me personally. Tomorrow we will provide you with some good quality weapons, no armour of course. Do you have any questions?" *I have many questions, but none that I feel that I can actually ask.* Receiving no queries, the Strategos followed on, "Good. Now take your saddlebags home and pack. Say farewell to your family. Remember you are just going away on orders. You may tell them that it will be for a long time. Return here to meet with me at dawn."

"I hear and obey." Basis brought his right hand up in a salute with his fist—thumb on top, over his heart. Putting his new sigil carefully away in a pouch, he picked up the saddlebags and slung them over his shoulder and headed for the door. As he was leaving he paused.

There had been a question floating in the back of my mind. Whatever it was has escaped me. He shook his head and returned home to pack.

*I*will take my own weapons now. If I like those they offer me I will leave these behind. Mine are all of reasonable quality and I am used to their feel.* He spent time saying goodbye to his brother and his sister-in-law, whom he lived with, and wrote a note to his parents to be sent to them in Southpoint. Like many part-Kharl families, his was career military, in Basil's case in both his Human and his Kichic-kharl lines.

His brother still had the incisors of his ancestors. All that Basil displayed was a faintly reptilian and greenish-hued scaled skin on his chest and back and arms—that and his in-family name. To them he was Kutsulbalik—'Holy Fish'—the name taken by his great grandfather when he was told that he had to become a Christian to marry his wife to be.

Basil currently had no woman and no other ties. *It had not been mentioned, but I suppose that also suits this particular mission.* Taking his brother quietly aside, Basil told him that all of his other possessions and money could go to his nephews if he didn't return, or no word came within two years. He wrote out a note to this effect, in case of complications.

That night they drank heavily and reminisced about their life growing up in the hot and steamy jungles at the southern edge of the Empire, where their family were posted when Basil was young.

In the morning, in the deeper darkness that comes before dawn, after only a few hours sleep, he dressed. Basil went downstairs and said goodbye. *Even the youngest are up to say goodbye.* He picked up the saddlebags and headed off to the palace.

Despite his nervousness about the mission, he was expected and ushered straight into the Strategos' office as soon as he appeared. Despite the early hour, the office was already busy, but then it always was. *Some of its most important work is done at night.*

As the first glimmer of light appeared over the sea to the east, Strategos Panterius met Basil with a brusque, "Good, follow me." *It is obvious that the Strategos has to be more used to late nights than to early mornings. After all, he wouldn't be losing sleep over the mission, would he?*

He led Basil to a room in the stables. There was laid out a set of gear that a servant might have packed: a sheet of canvas, cooking gear, food supplies, two bags of bandages and salves, some healing berries, rope and so on. It was all good quality, and well used.

"Is there anything that you need?" a supply sergeant asked anxiously.

"More salt, pepper and seasonings. I do not know when I will get more. Is there anything my subject particularly likes in the way of food?" he asked the Strategos.

"She has been eating Arabic food since her cousin left," was the reply.

"In that case I also want a steamer, pine nuts, asafoetida, mountain rice, pistachios, currants, dates, date sugar, and both rose and orange water. As well we want a small supply of ready-pulverised kaf, a goodly supply of kaf beans, a small mortar and pestle, and an ibrik to make it up in." He ticked these off on his fingers as he spoke. This was the signal for frantic activity and a hand of waiting servants were sent running. *It is gratifying, but worrying, that my word can send so many people springing into action.* When all was as Basil wanted, the servants packed everything into two waiting horse packs while Basil was led away to another room to look at some weapons.

Laid out on tables are a goodly selection: six short swords, three sets of throwing knives, eight daggers with different styles of hilt and blade. and four long quiver-pouches for the belt, each with six heavy martobulli in them. Proudly presiding over them all was the mottled brown-green figure of a senior Alat-kharl sergeant. *By the size of his arms and chest and the scars from burns on his hands, a blacksmith as well as a soldier. At the end of the room is a target.*

For half an hour Basil tested weapons for feel and balance under the approving gaze of the other sergeant. As he made his selections he laid them aside. *Both of the shortswords and the belt dagger that I have chosen are a matched set.* He strapped on the smooth oiled leather of their harness, smelling the oil before silently drawing the shortswords and going to guard and then replacing them. *Yes, they feel good in my hands.*

"A good choice, sir," said the sergeant. "As you can see, the blades are pattern-welded. They also have a minor charm to enhance their bite. Expensive for a servant perhaps, but your master may have been generous or, seeing that they are of an older pattern, they could have been an inheritance."

He left the throwing knives but chose a quiver of martobulli. *The heavy throwing darts have sharp points, a nice balance, and, if used at close range, are often more dangerous than a sword if the user knows how to throw them well.*

Basil strapped on his new weapons in place of the old. His own familiar weapons he laid aside regretfully, asking the Strategos to see that they were delivered to his nephews. Once he was equipped, Basil was led to the stables where three grooms each held a horse. *Two are riding beasts, each with saddlebags; one is hung with weapons as if it is waiting for its rider to come out from a bathhouse. The third is a sturdy looking chestnut pack animal and it wears the packs I saw earlier.*

"The extra beast is that of your supposed dead master," said the Strategos. "If you successfully meet up with Theodora then you are to leave him at the army post at Dochra with word for him to be returned to me. That will be a sufficient message. Theodora will probably head there. We know that she is disguised as Insakharl Kataphractoi. Are these horses suitable?"

Basil looked over the two that he would have with him. *I expect that any horse selected for this mission will be perfect, but I will go through the motions anyway. I can ride one at need, but I am not an expert on horses. Without taking them for a ride, I cannot tell. They look fit and have no blemishes.*

"They appear more than suitable."

"Good. Now follow me."

Basil went to take the horses. *The grooms will not let go. I am supposed to just walk on after the Strategos.* He quickly caught up and discovered that, rather than heading to a gate out of the palace, they were heading further inwards. At the rear of the stables they reached a large door that, when a groom opened it, led further inside and could be seen to slope up. *How this will get me to Dochra and ahead of my subject, I am not sure. I will just trust and follow.*

A corridor that was of a size meant for horses led inwards and then, moving outside, circled around the palace under the battlements. *I have never seen this before or heard of it; or if I saw it, I did not realise what I was seeing—it was now after midday. The air lies heavy and hot around us—waiting for the sea breeze of the afternoon to lend its cooling balm to the city.*

Eventually they reached the palace roof and all became apparent. *Laid out in front of us is a large and a small magical diagram. Someone is standing in the smaller one. The diagrams look to be worked into the stone of the roof itself and are clearly well used. This is obviously a source of part of the Empire's reputation for always having agents on the spot when needed. They can be dispatched anywhere given a powerful enough mage.*

Basil gave a start. *The person in the small diagram is Hrothnog himself. The mage will certainly be powerful enough.* Without a word the grooms delivered the horses to him and one pointed to the larger figure. He led the horses inside, trying to make sure that none crossed or broke a line. A groom hurriedly swept up some horse droppings.

The pattern is easily large enough for several more beasts. I wonder happens next. The grooms, experienced in this, started running around, lighting incense and placing things on the diagrams. Objects of metal and wood were placed at key points. Hrothnog started reciting a spell in a language that Basil didn't know. *His voice is again resonating in its deep and awesome tone. It is not a short incantation and only someone of Hrothnog's power could cast such a long and obviously powerful spell—a spell that will send so much weight so far away safely—I hope it is safely.*

The smell of the incense mingled with the salt smell of the sea as Basil held tightly to the horses. *Damn—I must have blinked—a view from a hill overlooking The Great Plain has replaced the view to the east and over the sea.* There was no sense of movement, but now the arid heat of the inland replaced the relative coolness of the coast. *I have arrived in the middle of a cleared circle near the top of a hill, a place obviously prepared for such travel.*

The horses showed their uneasiness at their translation by whinnying and pulling at reins and leads. Basil settled them down and gazed down a road as it circled what must be Nu-I Lake with Dochra to the west of it. *To the east is the dot of a solitary horseman. The dot is the only object moving on the road that is coming from the east. This could, should, be Theodora.* He decided to move down the slope away from her and onto the road.

He took some dried food from his bag and ate it. *It will be a few hours before she arrives below me and it will not take me long to come down from the hill. Broken as the terrain is, there is a path to follow if you look for it.*

Picking his way down and onto the road he went over the story that he had decided on. *I will move slowly and allow her to almost catch me so that it will be apparent to Theodora that I am a new arrival as well.* As he left the searing heat of the open road and entered the cool of the oasis around Dochra and its palm groves, he was able to use the sudden transition from light to dark to look back unseen. *My timing is perfect. Whoever the rider is rides only a few hundred paces behind.*

Chapter II

Theodora

*E*ver since my cousin, Miriam, fled the confines of life in the Darkreach Court, I have felt isolated from those around me. I am both lonely and bored. I blame the Granther and the other elders. Hrothnog's descendants may live for a long time, a very long time, but they have few children and all of the others of her generation were male; caught up in military interests or cloistered away in dry and dusty research.

Without Miriam beside me the games are less fun, the endless suitors who seek a night of pleasure or more are harder to avoid, and I have no one to talk to without being dragged into incessant and meaningless games of prestige and intrigue. What do the endless rounds of court politics matter when the Granther has lived for well over twelve thousand years, which I knew of for certain, and shows no sign of ever relinquishing his role as a seemingly immortal God-King? There are even so many great aunts and uncles and other granthers and granmers that there are no interesting jobs left that I am allowed to do. The accident of my ancestry prevents me from doing anything outside a very narrow range of jobs, and most of these are already taken. All the others that are left are really boring.

For the sake of appearances I am not even allowed, by the family, to learn or do anything that is considered 'beneath me', anything that may bring disrepute on the House. With my gifts, I can train as a mage, as a military officer or as an entertainer, but in the last I am a performer who can only amuse my own family. I have done all of those but can see none of them leading anywhere for me. I have looked at my aunties and uncles and cousins. Some throw themselves into sex and other pleasures, some into hobbies like gardening. Most seem to be happy.

She had tried to follow them and had ended up bored and as boring as she thought them to be. *Each pathway has ended with me throwing an epic tantrum. I am not proud of them, but I just feel so frustrated. Sometimes I think that the collective granthers who run most of the house affairs are far too conservative. Barring killing myself, at one hundred and twenty years of age, I have at least another five hundred years ahead of me, if not a thousand.*

Anytime I look at those around me it is as if they are on the other side of a very thick pane of glass. I can see them and faintly hear them, but it is if I am cut off from them; isolated and stranded. I am the only one left alive in a vast mausoleum of golden-eyed golem.

No, Miriam has made good her escape, arguing to the Granther that her marriage to the Caliph's third son will both help heal a long-standing war as well as to introduce the bloodline of the Imperial House to the Caliphate. It didn't hurt that she is in love—even if it is to a short-timer and cannot last. To top it off she has even managed to have a child by her husband already. That particular experience Theodora was not yet ready for, but the rest of her cousin's life she envied.

The final straw was a birthday party. Several of the family have a birthday every single day and most were ignored even by the person who had them, but Granmer Kale had reached the round sum of six hundred years, an auspicious age, and a hand of centuries. She was fit and healthy and didn't look a day over thirty, but a party was the name for such a celebration.

Funerals are usually more fun than this. The scent of orange water may have filled the air instead of that of burning frankincense, but the party in the hall has the same food, near the same music, the same people, and the same conversations as every other house gathering had had for the last hundred years. Nothing changed—ever.

She was ready to scream after an hour of the event. Mercifully the speeches came early and she fled immediately afterwards toward the more secluded part of the palace, ignoring the servants as if they were one with the decorations. She swept through corridors filled with rich tapestries and artwork that she had seen a thousand times before, fingers unconsciously brushing against the smoothness of silk and the coarser warmth of wool.

The swish of silk as her blue under-dress and shorter gold over-dress rubbed against her legs, was the loudest sound of life to be heard. Theodora paid no attention to where she was going except that it was away from the party.

She eventually found herself in one of the quiet and secluded gardens hidden in the dips in the roof. She couldn't see out but from where she sat she could watch as the water played and gurgled in a small fountain and smell the flowers as a breeze played through the diminutive courtyard gently stirring the plants. As she sat her body relaxed. *The relief of being out of that room is amazing. Light played on the folds of the soft, golden silk of my over-robe that contrasts so well with my thick jet-black hair.* Theodora rested and allowed quiet signs of the world to wash over her. *If it is that much of a relief to be out of a room, what would it be like to be out of Ardlark, perhaps out of Darkreach itself? No longer would I be stifling within a box. I could have a chance to breathe, freely, and to finally be myself without asking permission of anyone.* She began thinking about this idea, turning it over in her mind and then, perhaps even without a conscious decision, she began planning.

It is quickly obvious that I cannot get what I need to take with me at the palace. There are far too many servants around and too many relations with too little to do except to be curious about anything odd or out of the usual. I don't own very much that will be useful in the wilds outside Darkreach. I am not even sure what I will need or even how to buy it. That is what servants are for. I will have to just try things and see if they work.

At least I can be inconspicuous while I do it. Ever since Miriam married the Muslim man, face veils have spread and become popular with the wealthy of all religions. Between wearing one of those and my spells of illusion, hiding and misdetection, it is possible that no one will notice what I am up to. That is unless Hrothnog himself suspects something—my spells will not prevail against his. At least money is easy to get. I am sure that I have a lot in my room and, if it runs out, I can just go to the palace purser and ask for more and most likely no one will question me. With money, I will be able to get the rest of what I need.

A mixed feeling of excitement and trepidation began to creep through her. *I am going to actually do something; something that my family will not approve of. Firstly, I will need a base—a place where I can collect the things I need and disappear to for short times so that people become used to me being absent. It cannot be in the palace, but it has to be somewhere that I can get access to easily. To actually escape will be marvellous. Even this planning is exhilarating.* Her heart began to race like a small child expecting gifts.

Early the next day Theodora dressed in her plainest riding clothes; the sort of thing she would wear in the country when there were only close family about and no one to impress. She chose a green divided skirt in fine wool. *I can feel my fine cotton chemise smooth against my skin and my light-green embroidered dark-green waistcoat holding it tight to show my figure.* She wore matching jewellery from her collection of magical rings and amulets and put on her veil.

After checking outside her rooms and seeing no one was about she left. She hadn't bothered checking a mirror, she would have seen through her own illusion. *If anyone sees me they will notice a beautiful girl wearing a veil, eyes the black colour of a part Kharl, my raven blue-black hair now a dull braided orange, moving towards the palace gate and out into the city through the main doors.* But she had taken more precautions than a simple glamour of appearance and, as she moved through the palace, servants' eyes seemed to avoid her. As she left the building, the keen-eyed guards didn't notice her passage out of the wide public doorway. She had to duck away and hide a few times as she saw relations who were also mages, lest they sense her and grow curious, but otherwise she had moved quickly through the palace.

Not being accustomed to being outside on foot and alone, I have to work out where to go. Under my feet I can feel the smooth and uneven roundness of cobblestones, but they tell me nothing. I have entered a world that is totally different to that I am used to. Although the streets were still spotless, due to the sewers and the constant presence of street sweepers, they were also teeming with humanity, and with other races.

The various Kharl races, many Insakharl, Boyuk-kharl and others, and even the occasional giant Insak-div with skin so dark-green it was almost black, went about their business in a riot of colour and confusion. Even the Humans had three groups visibly distinguished by dress: the Christians, the Muslims, and the military. Among the Kharl, off-duty Kichic-kharl with light-green skin from the missile and reconnaissance units contrasted with darker green and much larger Isci-kharl infantry, while mottled green-brown Alat-kharl, their tusks often inlaid with metals and gems to show their wealth, moved around engaged in their trades. Musky sharp smells competed with the pungency of dung and the wafts of various perfumes as the breeze swirled gently through the plaza.

Around Theodora, on the tree-fringed edges of the wide streets, street entertainers juggled, twirled fire, told stories, and played music as they competed to eke out a meagre existence while adding to the cacophony. People, of various races, moved in and out of the buildings around the street.

She looked around with new eyes. *This close to the palace the buildings are all made of stone—black basalt, creamy sandstone, and blinding-white limestone. Some have bright-painted bands and friezes around them or as panels. Several are up to six stories high and house the administration of the city and the Empire in magically lit rooms that are busy, both day and night.*

Ardlark, as a city, has a larger population than many of the so-called nations west of the mountains and it takes an army of clerks to run both it and the Empire it rules. There are other buildings: courts, libraries, and the university. They have massive colonnaded fronts facing the long avenue.

She left the palace and moved right towards the columns of the law courts. These were five stories high and were designed to make anyone entering feel very small and insignificant.

People kept bumping into Theodora and looking confused afterwards. *I am still wearing my 'don't notice me' ring. A man just glared at me—he must be a mage to sense me.* Quickly she moved down the stairs again, ducked behind a tree and removed the ring. *Taking it off in public would have drawn more attention to me—the reverse of what I want.*

Still unsure of what she wanted, apart from 'a place to hide things', Theodora walked down streets at random, peering into taverns and inns and looking on public noticeboards. She passed the Circus Maximus with its notice boards depicting the attractions in various languages of the next big games a month away. *The stones around here are worn smooth with the passage of thousands of feet. For several of the condemned it is their last fight before being pardoned so a good crowd will be guaranteed. There is even a beast fight promised with a whole group of vicious lizard pack-hunters. I wonder how many will be matched against them. The betting will be interesting, depending on weapons and numbers. Intent as I am on my own task, I am becoming enthralled by the details and prospect of the combat. How much more will people be interested and side-tracked on the day of the combat itself? The distraction it provides will make that a good time to escape. Can I organise everything that I want to do in thirty-six days?*

The scents of the city came and went as she wandered the streets. At different times Theodora could smell cinnamon, salt water, roses, cooking, horses, camels, oxen, and people. Sometimes they were distinct and sharp and sometimes all mixed up together, and making her nose pinch.

Theodora turned a corner, the saltiness in the air said that it must be towards the docks, and she saw an inn. *I have been looking into many of these, but they have not seemed right for various reasons. Some have just felt wrong, but some have smelt badly of spilt beer, with a couple of the inns having had men in them who looked at me far too eagerly and inappropriately. Another had women in it who wore far too little in the way of clothes and who sat on the laps of men. All of the women at that inn had glared at me and the men had just looked greedy.*

This one, the 'Grey Doe', is different. It had a Human female guard on the door and a sign, in the usual several languages, which said simply, 'Admittance to Ladies Only'. She went across the street to a kaf shop and ordered some of the sweet, thick brew and some sticky pastry. She seated herself where she could see the inn while remaining inconspicuous. *The people who go in and out of the inn are all prosperous looking and all female, or at least appear to be; it is sometimes hard to tell with Kharl.* Under her, the woven straw seat was getting uncomfortable as she finished her second cup of kaf, now a bit cold. She got up and went across the road and into the inn.

The taproom is not like any of the others I have seen today—it is more like a quiet sitting room. There were still cards being played at a table and alcohol, and a girl playing a dulcimer and singing in Insakharl, the half-Kharl language. *This inn is much more civilised than the others I have been in. It also feels more like a relaxed room in a hunting lodge.* She approached the bar and with some trepidation addressed a woman who seemed to be the manager.

"Is there a room and stable space here that I might rent?"

The woman behind the bar looked her up and down. *She is dressed in the Muslim indoor style of loose and baggy trousers and a baggy undershirt, both in pale yellow, and a thigh length sleeveless flared jacket in brown. She wears a matching headscarf and a veil that does not cover the eyes.*

"We may," she eventually said in Darkspeech. "How long would you want it for?"

"I think around six weeks." *The next games will set my time limit.*

"Why?" asked the innkeeper suspiciously, eyeing the fine fabric of Theodora's dress.

*I can see the woman looking me up and down. Think quick*ly. "My family have plans for me that I do not wish to follow. If I cannot change my father's mind I may have to hide for a while. He has a suitor in mind that is both old and particularly ugly. My father only cares that the man is rich. I could live with either old or ugly, but not both at once."

The innkeeper is smiling at this. It is a common story, at least according to what I have heard servants gossiping about.

"I need a place to prepare in case I have to run away. I cannot do this at home; the slaves will report what I am doing to my father." Her voice had fallen into sounding more like a pleading little girl instead of that of a grown woman. She was falling into the role she had given to herself. "Please let me have the room. I am sure I will be safe here."

"We have had some girls like you here before," admitted the innkeeper. "I am Maryam bint Suliman and I will let you stay here if you follow my rules. I am strict on these. You may not break them. No men are allowed inside the main building, not even relations or eunuchs. If you must see one, there is a small private sitting room over there," and she waved vaguely, "that can be used briefly. There is no admittance after the tenth hour of the night, without having made a prior arrangement. Breakfast and an evening meal are included in your rent—regardless of whether you eat them or not. Your rent, one hundred and two nummus, is payable a week in advance. There will be another charge of one hundred and seventy if you have a horse. Do you accept these terms?"

"Gladly." *I hope that was not too eager. I have no idea whether that is a reasonable amount or not, but that is beside the point. Money is not something I actually pay much attention to.* "Let me pay you for a month now. That way I will not accidentally miss paying you because I cannot get away. When may I see my room, and occupy it?" She felt in her purse, the coins unfamiliar by touch, hoping that she had the amounts right, then quickly handed over four silver sesterces and a numismata, all of them freshly minted.

Maryam looked at them suspiciously but pocketed them. She went to get some change but Theodora waved that away. Maryam shrugged and went behind the bar, removing a key from a hook. "Follow me," she said as she led the way. "All our doors are trapped and opening them without the right key will have consequences. It makes our lady guests feel safe. We are also be-spelled against mice, rats, and insect vermin," she added in a satisfied, businesslike, tone.

They climbed a set of stairs—*the carpeted floor is almost familiar in feel—* and gone along a corridor before ascending a much narrower second set of stairs, and entered a second corridor. *Another set of stairs is visible going to the third storey at the end. It is obvious from the spacing between the doors that the rooms on the first floor are much larger than those on the second.* Maryam stopped and opened a door.

"This will be yours," she said.

Theodora looked inside. *I wonder how small the rooms are on the third floor. This room is smaller than my clothes room in the palace. It contains a bed—just large enough for two if they are very friendly—a washstand, a chair, and a clothes chest. A rail across one corner provides some hanging space. The air smells clean and fresh and I can see no dust. The servants have done their work well.*

"Umm…thank you." Theodora put her hand out for the key. She only just stopped herself from giving a tip at the same time. *The woman is not a servant. She probably owns the place and could be offended. I might have done the wrong thing by refusing change to start with. I have much to learn. I have never lived away from the palace and have only ever been outside it with servants and often with guards as well.*

Perhaps tonight will be a good time for me to start my absences from the palace. This room is mine now, and I have started my escape. However, I cannot just leave the palace. In a sense, I now only own what I stand up in and my purse. She looked at the room with its plain cotton quilt over the bed. *Still, the sun is still up.* "When is dinner and where may I get some things?" *Was this the right thing to do?*

"Do you know your way around here?" asked Maryam.

It sounds like Maryam already knows the answer to the question. Theodora shook her head ruefully. *I might have lived in Ardlark all of my life but I have realised, in the short time that I have been wandering the streets around the city, that I only know where a few things are—and those are places you can easily see from the windows of the palace. I have ridden in sedan chairs or carriages, usually with the curtains down, and servants and slaves take care of where you were going; it is not something you need to know.*

"Umm…not too well."

"Then I will send a girl with you. Tell her what you want and she will get you there and have you back in time to eat."

The next two hours were spent under the animated charge of an eight-year-old called Saidah. They *have been a very educational two hours.* From the expression on Saidah's face when she was purchasing anything she soon learnt not to take the first price she was offered for an item. *It is lucky that none of my first purchases are major ones. I am sure that the rumours of my gullibility are spreading quickly through the market, even if I am starting to get items at around half the first price I am offered. Shopping can be fun. I am sure that I can get the prices lower if I really try.*

Theodora had also worried about what was wrong with her money. After Maryam's reaction she noticed that, even though it was all good new coin, gold denarii and imperials and silver sesterces and numismata, people looked at them strangely. It was only after she had received a fair amount of change she realised what the issue was. *People are not used to so much new money at once. Some of the change I am getting is so well-used that it is hard to make out the writing and even the pictures on it. My handfuls of bright new-minted coins stand out.* Some of the tiny copper follis coins she received back were so bent from use that they looked more like thimbles than discs. *I need to, where possible, give out more valuable coins for small items simply to get less conspicuous coins.*

She had only collected a few things: combs, toiletries, and a bag to put them in, as well as a nice set of indoor wear, similar to Maryam's but of better cut and of a smooth and cool silk, as well as some slippers, when she discovered that her time was up. *Saidah is steering me back to the inn.* After tipping her a numismata she retired to her room to change into her new clothes. This turned out more of a production than she thought it would. She was not used to dressing by herself and was a little later for dinner.

She arrived and began eating, and soon discovered others were watching her. *There is nothing malicious about their gaze, but I am sure I have become a source of some humour as my attempts to eat and keep my veil unfold. I am also sure it is becoming obvious to everyone in the establishment that I am not what I am pretending to be—a Muslim woman seeking a way out of a misalliance—however the women appear happy to tolerate my pretence.*

I think they have decided I have some sort of trouble with a man, not necessarily what I first said, and do not wish to reveal to anyone who I really am. It seems they all are including me in a female conspiracy where perhaps all women are sisters in the face of all men. The women let slip they thought she must be of a very high ranking. *I suppose my inexperience with so many things makes it obvious.*

By the end of the meal, as the tavern returned more to being a tavern, several of these business-like women had made it obvious they were not going to play games and were going to openly coach her on how to live away from home. *They may not know why I am running away, or what I am running from, but they make it clear they will help me if they can.* Theodora felt a surge of relief.

The smell of kaf and other food and drink, and the feel of the leather and material on the seats lulled her, so that by the end of the night it was all becoming comfortable.

In the morning Theodora asked Saidah to help her find the rest of what she would need. *I will concentrate on clothing first.* She tried to avoid buying the best things she saw, even when she wanted to and tried to buy cotton instead of silk, even buying something that was made of what she was told was hemp. She looked at Saidah loaded down with purchases. *The young girl is overloaded. Unless I obtain a real servant, I should be carrying some of these things.* Despite the inconvenience, she was soon carrying most of what she bought. *How tiresome this part of buying things is.*

As Theodora left the Doe she told Maryam that she was not sure when she would return, but if anything came for Salimah al Sabah it should be put in her room. *Time to return to outside the palace and put on my ring before going to my room.* The door closed and she emerged as herself.

The next few days passed with Theodora fielding questions as to where she had been. *I will try to leave people with the impression of having a lover without being definite about it.* As she waited she made a listing of what she would need. This turned out to be the first of several different lists. The initial list, made while sitting in her window-seat with pen and an inkwell she had unearthed from when she had last needed it some time ago, would have needed a pack train to carry everything that was on it and a string of servants to care for it all.

She started collecting money, trying in particular to get used coins. *I had never noticed it before but, although as a member of the Imperial House I have ready access to funds, it is always mint coinage. I wonder why. Is this deliberate?*

As she was making one of the lists Theodora realised she had never paid any attention to geography. *If I am going to flee and at least temporarily make a life outside Darkreach, I need to know what is out there.* She went so far as to make her own map using those that she hoped showed the most recent information on outside towns.

Looking at what she was copying from, often maps drawn on fine smooth vellum and beautifully illustrated, hers was not a very good map. *Some of the squiggles I have used as symbols need my own interpretation, but I am pretty sure the rivers and towns are in the same places as they are in my sources.* To her annoyance, she was starting to get ink-stains on her fingers and having to use pumice to clean them off.

It took several days to draw the map, and she was still not very happy with her account of the mountains. *The different maps I am using as sources have somewhat different ideas on where some mountains, and indeed some ranges, are. Outside Darkreach most of the rivers and towns are the same from map to map, but not all. I wonder if the Granther, who everyone supposes knows everything, has a better copy of these maps kept somewhere else. I dare not ask.*

*I*t has been a week of list-making and map-drawing. It is now time to go back to the inn.* She tied up her best sword, shield, bow and arrows, all of good quality and magically enhanced, and made them into an ungainly package with the rolled map. Once they were held together she wrapped them with rough calico that she had found in a nearby room where it had been covering new furniture.

I am proud of myself for having thought of that, rather than just getting someone to bring me something suitable. She searched her room until she found a mana storage device made of teak inlaid with copper and amethysts that she had made many years ago. It held twice the mana that she had available in a day now and, having made it long ago as an exercise at school, she had discovered that her palace life gave her no real use for it. *It has lain discarded in a drawer until it is needed. It goes into my pouch with more money.* She donned her throwing knives and dagger, put on her ring, and left the main imperial building.

The vibrant smell and noise of life outside is now familiar, a contrast with the muted aromas and silence of the palace. This time I have to dodge people even more as the bulk of my package gets in my way. I miss not having a servant. Once she was out in the street, and had quickly moved behind a tree, she again removed the ring and headed off to the inn. *I am passing many other professionals and merchants. They all have servants to carry their goods. I am the only person of substance actually carrying anything. As it is, I am just a wealthy woman carrying a large and decidedly odd-looking package, not even worth a second look except in humour.*

However, if someone else carries it, the contents will be all too obvious to them and they could talk. In Darkreach, if someone talks, someone else is listening. Everyone knows that the Granther's secret police, the Antikataskopeía, are very good at their jobs. The power of his magic is only one reason that he has ruled for so long.

Having reached The Grey Doe, she went up to her room, unpacking the package and folding the calico before putting it on a shelf to take back to the palace for later use.

She studied her room. *All of the things I bought last are still sitting on the bed.* She got to work and put the shopping and her weapons out of the way on shelves, in drawers or on pegs. When finished, she stood back proudly and surveyed her work, before looking at her hands. *Perhaps for the first time in my life I need to wash them because of work; and still with faint ink stains on them as well. There is a jug and bowl in my room.* She washed them and went to the common room. Being still very early in the afternoon, there were not many women present, but she greeted and was greeted by those she knew before leaving to look for Saidah.

"Now—I need a horse." The search for a horse continued into most of the next day. It was late in the afternoon that she rode back to the inn, Saidah seated behind her, full of excitement and nervousness on a large, and fairly ugly black warhorse with feathers around her feet called Esther. *According to the trader, the horse's last owner had died. I know that very few people are willing to try and win the loyalty of an older animal, but I am an expert rider. I think that it is worth the risk.*

Esther had seemed to accept her, and through this to tolerate Saidah. *Being older does not mean that Esther is a cheap purchase. The dealer asked a lot more, but she ended up costing fifty-four thousand nummus.* Theodora removed a stack of thirty gold imperials from her pouch and counted them out in front of the dealer. *I am aware that they are all shiny and new, but there is nothing I can do about it.* This display of wealth left Saidah gasping at the transaction. *After all, such an amount is more than twice what most well-to-do families earn in a year.*

Theodora now had to work out whether to armour Esther or not. *A battle steed without at least some protection cannot take its place in a charge.* Like all of the members of the Imperial House, she was trained as one of the Kataphractoi, the heavy cavalry. Although, being a little lazy she was not as strong as she could be, she could at least use a lance more than competently. *This might be of more use to me in combat than my magic. After all, I am a mage of madness and illusion, not of battle. I can throw air bolts and even make wands to throw them, but I lack the array of destruction that a battle mage usually employs. Even the most potent magic that I know only hide things away and this is rarely needed in the heat of a battle.*

I am not the mightiest person. I am only of average strength, but I can at least competently use the weapons I have, if not as well as many. I will buy at least some light armour for Esther, and this means that I will need a set for myself as well. It follows that if I am getting armour, I may as well get a lance. I will look odd without one. It will try my skill at concealment to hide myself fully as I leave, but if I ride out openly like this, people will see a cavalry rider rather than a runaway mage from the Imperial House.

Saidah is not much use at shopping for armour beyond pointing out the right part of Ardlark to go to. However, I am used to having her there while I shop and the girl's reactions to my purchases and spending are valuable to me as part of my learning how to bargain better.

They took Esther with them and it was just as well they did. *The horse is hard to fit. She is both tall and broad.* In the end, they found an armourer who had a complete set that fitted her well. *It is intended for a horse in the front rank of a heavy unit and consists of a padded drape for both front and rear with a bronze chain covering for the rear and tempered bronze alloy lamellar for the front, including the neck, with a single plate for the face. It is all good quality work and brand new.*

Theodora thought about the purchase and decided in favour. *Esther will not be moving fast in a charge, or at any other time, but she will be nearly unstoppable. Once again Saidah gets to see the depth of my purse as I count out six platinum crowns—nearly three times the cost of Esther herself. Her eyes are huge.* She bade Saidah keep strict silence before relenting and making Saidah promise to be silent for at least three weeks after Theodora left. *Then she can tell everything and not feel guilty about it. From the slightly guilty expression on her face, Saidah would soon have not been able to contain herself. Her face has changed to relief.*

Now I need armour. The horse armourer quickly indicated a cousin who might be suitable and had his apprentice run ahead to direct their way. Theodora steered Esther after him. *People are giving us far more space on the street now than they did when the two of us just walked.* Esther showed her teeth and snorted at anyone who came too close.

It turned out that the cousin specialised in armour for mages. *I had not realised before, but this part of my secret appears obvious to the people that I am dealing with.* She looked at a set made of magnesium alloy (her metal) but declined to buy the beautiful armour, as a fire mage's spells would have a dreadful effect on it. She finally obtained good quality padding and a full set of bronze alloy lamellar, inlaid with magnesium stars, for a further four crowns. There was also a matching helm for another crown and, unconscious of what she was doing, Theodora whipped off her veil to try it on. *Saidah's eyes have grown as round as kaf cups — my hair — my eyes.* She quickly turned her back on the dealer, who appeared not to have noticed anything. *Saidah has distracted him with a question. She will get a much better tip today.*

The helm was a smoothly rounded cone with a solid neckpiece and a mail drape hanging around it, and coming down over the face and all around extending down to the chest and part way down the back. The drape was heavy as the cold metal slid over her, but it was designed for safety and could be held up at the front by a sliding nasal. It was her last crown, but she managed to get the merchant to add a small metal shield, really a buckler that could hang off her belt, for no extra charge while she changed again. *I am glad I have no more major purchases. Even though I think that it wouldn't be noticed, I don't want to draw the attention of the Logothetes tou trapeza basilikē, the accountant of the Imperial money, to me if I can avoid it. These ones I obtained some time before to go towards the purchase of a chariot and team, a purchase which, luckily, never eventuated.*

The workmanship on the armour was superb, but it had obviously been designed with Insakharl tastes in mind. *It is amusing to see that some of the engraving on it is writing in Insakharl praising Hrothnog.* Having made the purchase, she asked for it to be delivered to the inn under her assumed name, the same as she had done for the dealer in horse barding. They headed off leading Esther to seek a lance and saddlebags and the other necessities. Along the way, Theodora saw a kaf shop and she looped Esther's reins over a nearby hitching post, telling the horse to wait and without even thinking about anyone stealing her, taking Saidah aside and heading towards a corner filled with plump cushions while ordering some kaf and a plate of sweet sticky pastries.

Theodora seated them and checked that no one was near. "You now know why I hide my face. My eyes tell everyone my family."

"They really are gold," said Saidah eagerly. "I thought it was just a story, but they really are gold. You are so beautiful without the veil hiding your face. And your hair changed as well. Are all of the other stories true?" She went on to ask with all the lack of tact that the young can muster.

"It depends which stories you listen to." Theodora let Saidah see and feel her arm. "I have no hair anywhere on my body except what you can see on my head. That much is true. I am already one hundred and twenty years old and, barring accidents of battle will live another six hundred at least, even many more, which also is true. However, when I attack young girls it is only to tickle them," she suited action to words, provoking a fit of giggles, "and not to drink their blood."

They continued with their shopping on a new and lighter note. *Now that she has such a big secret Saidah is acting as if I am her big sister, one who does not know her way in the world.* Theodora reciprocated. *Not since Miriam left have I had so much fun, and never in my life have I had so much enjoyment from such innocent pursuits.*

L ater, that night at the inn, while still wearing her veil, Theodora entertained the other women. *I may have training in this art but, so far, have only performed for my teachers and family. It is something a woman is supposed to be able to do, at least within their family.* Tonight she danced, told stories, poetry, and sang.

This should confound any rumours, even if what I am wearing is not what a normal dancing girl, or indeed any other entertainer, can afford to wear. At least no one will expect any girl of the Imperial House to entertain commoners in a tavern. Despite my inexperience at working in public I must have done fairly well. When she finished her first set, Saidah, without asking, went around the room and collected a fair amount of money. *It has dirhams and other small coins in it, but a quick glance shows there are at least five numismata among them.* She was going to indignantly refuse the money or at least put it in drinks for the room. *I am going to have to pay my own way in the world outside, and this might be how I do it.*

After that, every night that she was at the Doe, she entertained. So as to not get the regular entertainer offended, she included her music in her act and shared the money with her. On discovering Saidah beating rhythm on a pot she bought her a doumbec and included her in her act as well. *As a self-taught drummer, she is a natural.* Each day Theodora worked hard at fitting in, at seeming to be just one of the inhabitants of the inn. *Slowly the purse that I keep is beginning to get fatter and fatter instead of losing weight.*

Alternating a few days at the Doe with a few days at the palace enabled Theodora to bring down all her magical supplies and her jewellery. *My magic supplies, now wrapped in my calico, are a bit bulky and Esther will have bulging saddlebags. There is a light carpet of woven kapok that has my pentagram on it and woven with the significant signs of an air mage of the month of the Bird and the Year of Air Bird, ten cycles ago. This will be rolled up inside my bedroll and slung over Esther's withers.* There were a few other items as well, bits of Demons to use the Law of Contagion on as well as herbs, medallions and other items needed to cast spells under the other air signs of the Butterfly and the Monkey. And the one thing she could not bear to leave behind.

At the bottom of one saddlebag is my favourite formal dress and under-dress of silk, my best heavily jewelled superhumeral and my favourite coronet. Theodora rationalised the decision to take these useless things with her by thinking you never knew when you might need to dress up. She had also created a new spell on an earring amulet that obscured her nature from observers. *When I wear it I appear to have the black eyes of an Insakharl and the same hair colour of such. I have woven this into the veil's spell.* She started wearing it at the Doe and leaving off her veil. *At least that makes it easier for me to eat and drink.*

One day, she came out of the palace early. *Today is the day. I have not been noticing the change of smells and sights and sounds as I transform into Salimah anymore. I am ready to leave. I feel at home outside now. Everything is packed and ready. I have settled my accounts with Maryam, and the Circus is on today.*

As she moved towards the Doe, the excitement on the streets was quite evident. *I was right. Today is a good day to leave.* She dressed in her armour and made sure that everything was packed, then made her farewells, tearful and full of hugs, to Saidah, giving her presents: jewellery and clothes that would not fit in her bags and that Saidah would have to grow into.

She rode away. *I can hear the calls of people betting. I can see the crowds moving towards the arena.* Raucous cries punctuated the buzz of an excited crowd. The sweaty smell of excitement blended with perfumes in the air. Esther lacked a smooth stride at the slow rate she could travel in through the crowds and her walk jolted Theodora, and the horse huffed and made more noise than usual. *The crowds make my horse nervous as she tries to watch all around her.*

The usual crowds made today a gala day full of excitement for many, but the excitement that was shared by Theodora was for a different reason. Her mood didn't last long.

While Esther has grown happier, and is snorting less, I seem to be the only person heading out of the largest and most vibrant city in The Land. Around me crowds are kicking up dust I can smell, even from the paved roads, and it is hot in my armour. It is a long time, a cycle or more, since I needed to wear armour all day and I am already itchy. Sweat trickled down her back and went places that made her uncomfortable. *I am sure that I will smell when I take it all off.*

I have an uneasy feeling I am being watched—I fear breaking free of the confines of my family has been too easy. She made herself keep going, occasionally looking back to see if anyone followed. She rode through the fields and past many small settlements. *I am sure that I have seen these places many times, but I have never bothered to learn their names.* She headed southwest towards The Great Plain.

The crowds dwindled and Theodora shared the road with only a few traders with creaking carts. Their horses steered clear of her; with a wagon train from the Platys Dromos, the Imperial haulage, full of iron ore, trailing red dust; and with some late farmers with produce to sell in a festive city. *All of them are headed the other way.* Early in the day she even had a tagma of several hundred Isci-kharl, with Insakharl officers, headed into the city and marching hard, go past her. *They are singing one of their marching songs as their drums and pipes play to a quick beat that even has me tapping my finger against the saddle pommel. They must be hoping to arrive in time to see some of the fighting in the games. Despite my vigilance, I can see no one travelling at the same pace as me, even in the far distance.*

As part of the military machine of Darkreach, the roads had all of the items necessary to help travel and Theodora was able to stop in the middle of the day for a meal and a rest for Esther at a military way station. Being military in appearance she could get a meal but, lacking written orders, she had to pay for it herself. She sat outside in the hot sun to eat. *After a morning riding, the bench is hard beneath me.* In front of her was rough fare, well below what she was used to in both quality and variety, and she started to just pick at it, but it was filling and she was hungry, so she quickly finished it.

That night she slept in another way station. The bed had rough blankets and sagged in the middle. *Who knows how many have slept in it? At least it seems clean. Unlike the inn there are no servants at these way stations, and very little privacy. At least there are places to bathe, even if I could not get my clothes washed. I need a servant. I am useless without one. I will be more likely to poison myself, than to cook a good meal.*

C easelessly looking back, she settled into a routine of travel and break by the time that she passed the turnoff that led north to Metal Hill— the largest source of iron in The Land and, in essence, one of the sources of Darkreach's military strength. *I remember from school many years ago, that we have more iron in Darkreach than in all of the other nations put together.* Coming down the road in the distance was another Imperial caravan of the Platys Dromos carrying iron ore—*hundreds of swords waiting to be made.* Soon after was the road heading south towards Jade Mountain. This was a strangely inverted rocky massif, clinging to the upper slopes of which were verdant oases complete with taverns with lacquered timber walls and secluded gardens. *The rocks of the massif yield jade, in its many colours, but that is not why I am here.* Wistfully, Theodora cast her thoughts back and reminisced. *I spent a very pleasant month there with a few lovers and friends.*

As Theodora travelled along the firm roadway, gradually getting herself and Esther used to each other, she could see the land beside the road was growing drier and farming was giving way to pasture, and then to dry lands, almost desert, where only at the rare oasis was farming possible. Looking down she noticed that a layer of dust was starting to coat her and Esther. *It is a long dry road that I am following and even reaching Nu-I Lake is no relief. This year it is largely dry and the road borders a hard-baked surface of mud with occasional remnant pools of salty water. The air smells dry and has a bitter tang. I am glad of the dryness though. I am sure that, despite the unfamiliar sensation, I am sweating far too much and, by now I am sure to smell more than a little off to an observer, something else that I am not really used to doing. Each morning the effect of bathing is gone in far too brief a time and I dare not attempt to wash my clothes as I have had no idea how. I have to get a servant.*

Images of trees and a town that never seemed to arrive hung in the air ahead. *Eventually—I can see a patch of water in the distance that does not disappear. It is slowly growing into the permanent water that enables the existence of fields of plants and the village of Dochra. I know that it is fed from below in aquifers. Some say by water that flows underground from the mountains thousands and thousands of chains to the west. Also, ahead of me, for the first time in my entire trip, is a single rider going the same way that I am. At least it is not someone who has been following me. I am not moving fast, but the other person is moving slower. Whoever they are they ride one horse and lead two others behind them, one a pack animal and the other a riding animal without a rider in its saddle.* The stranger ahead led her into the palm groves and fields of maize and peas that surrounded Dochra by a few hundred paces.

Chapter III

Basil

As he rode, Basil looked over Dochra. *I have been here before and it still seems to be an incomplete town. Three rows of adobe houses on a low slope form the three sides of a hollow square facing the bubbling spring and resultant small stream that feeds the only source of water, the lake.* He gazed over the large square which was several hundred paces across and looked to be well used by caravans and army units to camp in. *From the prints and the floating dust and, despite the best efforts of the local sweeper, it still has hanging over it the faint sweet smell of animal shit.*

The small military post on the side closest to the lake along with buildings that, among other things, housed a stable, an inn and a hall. *I guess that the post sees more messengers than anything else.* There was a rail outside to hitch horses onto and a wooden watering trough. By the time Basil had reached the post, the rider behind had well and truly emerged from the palms, and by the time he had his horses tied up, they were beside him.

Now that I am closer, a quick glance shows it has to be Theodora. She is equipped as an Insakharl Kataphractoi. The horse must have good stamina to still be moving so well in the heat with all the armour it carries. What is more she not only rides in full armour in the safe heart of the Empire but has the mail drape of the helm worn over her face to hide her features. The armour is nice work, but looking over it, the saddle, and the rest of the tack, I can see it has not been cared for properly. No one who has been through officer's school would allow that. He itched to get to work. *It doesn't take long, even in this heat, for sweat drops to form rust and to weaken the leather and cause it to break.*

Despite the lance and the other usual weapons, the armour is obviously that of a mage, albeit one who expects to see combat. It is high quality, inlaid with mystic symbols and very expensive. This is confirmed by the roll over the withers, obviously not a tarpaulin, so it is most likely a rolled-up casting pattern. Basil fussed around with the horses for a bit longer so that she entered the post first. *I want to be seen as being with her.* He hung back at a servant's distance as she approached the desk.

"I am Salimah al Sabah," she said in a musical, and very sexy, voice. "I am on a tour of the Empire before I must join my unit. Do you have accommodation in the post?"

It sounds like a practiced line. She must have been using it for several days at all the posts from Ardlark.

"I am sorry ma'am," said the Human sergeant behind the desk. "This is a very small post. All of our travellers here, even the ones on duty, use the inn and stable at the other end of this row." He sounded regretful as his hand waved in that direction. "I am sure that they will have accommodation for you and your servant."

"My servant?" she asked looking around puzzled. "I don't have a servant."

That is my cue as a young man out on his own and alone. "Do you need one? My master was hunting when he was bitten by a snake and has died. I have just buried him up on the knoll near town and I am free to take other work. I can send his horse back to Ardlark from here with a note to his unit. That's all that would be expected of me. I am not in the army and so am not obliged to go myself. He would prefer me to gain work rather than go without."

'Salimah' is thinking. "What makes you desirable as a servant and what makes you think that I need one?"

"If Milady will pardon me, your clothing under your armour shows that it needs some attention that would be beneath you. I am a good cook. I have served as an officer's batman and am competent in caring for most wounds. Alas—unless I have a potion, I have no skill in dealing with poisons. I can care for Milady's clothes and know how to wash and mend. I have worked in both the field and in garrisons. Is that what Milady seeks?"

She seems to realise that she really needs a servant. She is glancing down at her armour. It is new, but has she noted the flecks and spots on it? I can see sweat stains on the parts of the clothing that can be seen under the armour and, to be frank, she can be smelt from some way off. I can see her mind working away. Surely, she will realise—

"I will give you a trial," she finally said. "I have never really employed someone before. What do I pay you?"

"We will work that out when you decide if I am suitable. I am called Basil Akritas, Milady, or as my employer you can call me by my family name of Kutsulbalik." She smiled at this. *She does not realise that a junior Insakharl officer, such as she claimed to be, even if they are a mage, would have corrected me and demanded to be called 'Ma'am' even if they are from a noble house.*

"I will be leaving a horse tethered outside," Basil dropped his voice to the post sergeant, trying not to be overheard "It belonged to my late master. There is a note in a saddlebag. Apart from feed and water nothing needs to be done with the beast. Please arrange for the horse to be sent to Strategos Panterius in Ardlark." *The sergeant is suddenly paying more attention to me, but 'Salimah' shows no reaction. That confirms that she is not who she says she is. Any soldier of any rank should know the name of the head of the Antikataskopeía.*

"Of course," said the Sergeant and saluted Basil with a fist placed over the heart. *Luckily Salimah has turned away.* Basil frowned disapproval at the sergeant, who quickly dropped his hand.

"Milady, shall we see the inn?" Basil ushered her out the door and gathered his two horses and hers before following her a few doors along. *Hers is a battle steed and it is taking all my skill to get it to cooperate with me. 'The Old Lobster', its sign showing a Kataphractoi in full armour, is actually better than I had expected but, from the expression on my new mistress' face, a bit of a disappointment to her.*

Once they were shown to their rooms, a large one for her with a much smaller one next door for him, they found them clean and comfortable. *The rooms she has taken are well beyond the means of a junior officer on tour, but 'Salimah' does not seem to notice.* Basil installed their saddlebags, unpacking hers and hanging everything that needed it.

After he had lain everything out he went to the stables to check on the horses. *On returning to the main house the Islamic clothes have gone from where I hung them and the travel clothes worn under the armour are in a pile at the foot of the bed and in dire need of attention.* After bundling them to be washed and dried for the next morning Basil returned to the room and brushed, cleaned, and oiled the armour before neatly arraying it on an armour stand. He had a look at her weapons as well and cleaned them. Soon the room smelt of neatsfoot and mineral oils. Then he went to the stables and did the same with her tack. *Luckily the stable hand has already done the horses.* Basil grinned. *He must have danced nimbly to have done that horse with its hairy stomping feet.*

Having finished his tasks, Basil returned downstairs to find the inn in full swing. *'Salimah' is sitting in a corner, watching everything and, despite her Islamic dress, drinking a glass of wine, sipping it under a veil. It is possible that she is just not very observant of the laws, but then, why the veil?*

When it arrived, the meal was in accord with the inn: plain but well prepared and tasty. The food was in the fashionable Islamic style. Very few were eating, but once the meal was over the inn's function as the local social centre became obvious.

The locals are all Human, mostly Islamic, but with a few Christian families. One group is drinking kaf and sitting at hookahs, fragrant-scented tobacco or other herbs burning within; another drinking the local red wine. Typical of any village in the Empire, they mix and share conversations and pipes. With so many different people in it, Hrothnog cannot afford to have religious or racial strife in his domain and making sure that it does not occur is one of the main duties of my corps. I fear that it will be different outside and I, as a part Kharl, could suffer problems from their ignorance.

After they had eaten Salimah surprised Basil by starting to sing to the people in the inn. She went on to tell a story and then some poems and then back to songs. Basil found an older local man in a headscarf pondering a chessboard with a vacant seat beside him and settled in there for the night while the locals enjoyed what was obviously a rare treat for them. *This will be how 'Salimah' will be able to pay for rooms and such that are beyond her means. She is actually quite a good entertainer. I have heard many people that are far older than she appears to be and who have a lot less skill. This could be an interesting trip. I wonder what other skills she might have.*

Chapter IV

Theodora

Theodora looked at the little man beside her at the desk. *At first glance he seems to be a very plain and ordinary youth, but I am used to looking beyond what a first glance shows; after all, I am one hundred years older than I look. At a second appraisal, he seems more certain than a youth should be. Still, I really do need a servant. A man may not be ideal, but he is here and might have what I need.* As they walked back to the inn she could sense the magic he wore. *It all appears very minor, but I cannot pin it down. It seems to focus on his waist, probably something on his weapons and something else in a pouch. He looks neat and tidy, far tidier than I do, and seems to have good manners. He says he can cook; presumably he can care for horses. Maybe he can even sew. All of these are areas where I have grown very conscious of my lack of training or experience as one who has been brought up in the palace. Yes, he will have to do.*

When they reached their rooms her last impressions were confirmed as he acted the same as every maid she had ever had when she'd stayed overnight at a strange place. He went straight to hang things up and to lay out her toiletries. After he left to check on the horses Theodora gathered some clean clothes and went to the bathhouse. *It is clean and the water is hot.*

She luxuriated in the clean house clothes from The Grey Doe before heading downstairs to wait for food. The cool cotton and silk of these clothes on her freshly washed body made her think. *Should I start entertaining again? Instead of being in an army post, I am back in an inn, presumably a fairly normal one, the kind I will see a lot of. At least I can test my skills with the sort of people I will be seeing all of the time before it becomes vital to earn money this way. It might look a little strange to Basil, but anyone who has a family name that is so obviously both part Kharl and yet Christian as 'Holy Fish' should be used to at least some small amount of whimsy.* When Basil joined her downstairs he did not blink at her house clothes. *The deception seems to be working perfectly.*

The best that can be said of the meal is that it is not Army food. I hope that Basil can cook better than this. The couscous and lamb lack all of the delicate flavours and fluffiness that I am was used to and the pilaf is just—plain. The baklava and rakis lacoum are acceptable after the main meal and the kaf at least is thick, hot and sweet.

Afterwards she approached the landlord. *He is happy to have someone entertain his clients. The village is too small to have a regular bard, although some of the villagers will be able to make some music for local events.* She settled in for the night, eschewing any court music and stories apart from the most fantastic. The veil got in the way, but she left it on. Gradually, as word spread, the whole village seemed to gather around. *Basil is sitting in a corner sharing a hubble-bubble pipe and a game of chess with a local Islamic elder. Good, if he can play chess I will have to find a place to buy a board. I wonder if he can beat me? It is unlikely, but I can always hope. It is becoming harder to find good competition, even in the palace.*

The night went well. Some locals disappeared for a while and then reappeared with instruments. *Even a garrison sergeant, an Alat-kharl, is joining in, on of all things, a hammered dulcimer. I have never seen a Kharl play more than drums or sometimes horns or pipes before. He must have made it and taught himself to play as well by the sound it makes. My band will never play at the palace, but they are at least enthusiastic.* Money started to appear in front of them, which she left sitting, only drawing from it for refreshments for herself and the band.

A local mage must be water-based in his work. It is the only way they can have cool drinks this far into the Plain—with ice even. Theodora began to enjoy herself. *People are coming up and bidding goodnight. It must be late. There is time for one last song, perhaps about sleep, ah yes, 'Sohab's Dream'.* She divided up the money with the band, thanked them for their efforts and, finally, went to bed. *Basil is following me upstairs close on my heels. He is very attentive.* After she had gone into her room and locked the door, Theodora heard him testing the lock and rattling it. *It seems that he takes his charge seriously.*

Basil

*S*he *is pretty good.* He had positioned himself so that he could see all the entrances to the room as well as having the 'stage' in view whenever he looked up. *Not that I have much chance to look up. I had better think of her as Salimah to avoid mistakes. I suspect this oldster, a mage by his belt pouches, that I am playing chess against is far better than me, but at least if I concentrate I have a chance.* Every time he looked up a new instrument seemed to have joined in on the small stage. *Apart from my charge, there is not much skill in evidence, but the whole village seems to be here and they are all enjoying the fun. Even the garrison has joined the party. My presence as a bodyguard seems to be uncalled for, so I can enjoy myself and just keep watch out of habit.* He takes a sip of wine. *The locals obviously do not really believe in aging their local wines for very long when only they are drinking them. Still, I have drunk much worse.*

Eventually the common sense of farmers took over and everyone decided to head to bed. *I have ended the night only two games down to the oldster. He thanked me profusely—far more than I think I deserve. It is obvious that the man doesn't have a lot of competition here.* Basil followed Salimah upstairs and checked her door, once she was inside, before checking the horses and leaving word with the innkeeper on when he should be woken up.

*T*he *worst thing about being a servant is the early starts.* Basil shivered a little in the chill of the desert dawn. He collected Salimah's clean clothes and a tray of food and drinks and started back upstairs. When he reached her room, what started as a quiet tap on the door, ended up as a persistent pounding. He was just thinking about getting his lock picks and letting himself in when the door opened. *Salimah has opened the door only a crack, but I can see her golden eyes uncovered and, as she opens the door further—I recollect that I saw no night attire when I unpacked. Salimah's eyes, black hair, and hairless naked body is the final proof that she is in fact Theodora.*

Without batting an eyelid, he greeted her, "Good morning, Milady. Here are your travel clothes and something to eat. By the way, Milady, it is best to check who is outside the door before opening it. One never knows."

Theodora

*P**ounding, pounding. Drums in the distance...the door...that is what it was, the door, not drums at all.* Theodora jumped out of bed, roused from a deep sleep, unlocked the door and—*it is just my servant—Basil—I smell kaf. He has food and clothes—clothes! I am naked. Basil seems oblivious to my nakedness. That is a good sign. My eyes are bleary with sleep and I don't have my charms on so they are their normal colour, my hair as well.*

His eyes were casting around for a place for the tray. *He must not have noticed or he would have reacted.* After quickly donning the ear charm she reached for some juice. *It is probably best that he has seen me naked anyway. I now have the final proof that he is a real servant. That total lack of reaction to what their masters wear, or don't wear, takes years of training.*

After he had laid out her travel clothes, Basil let himself out. While drinking kaf and eating—*at least they can make good pastries here*—Theodora dressed herself. It was only when she turned to where she had dropped her armour that she realised. *It has been cleaned and put on a rack. It smells faintly of oil and it shines. The marks that had been starting to appear on it are gone. Some fruit and more kaf and I am now ready to face the world. Put on my other jewellery and then another knock on the door and Basil is letting himself back inside to pack. He already has all of his things with him.*

They reached the stables. *The horses are already waiting and ready to leave. What time did he wake up? Has he slept at all? Has he eaten? He is even ready to help me into the saddle. The inn—I haven't paid for breakfast. He must have paid for that as well.*

"Before we leave I want to see if I can buy something here. Have we paid our bill?"

"Yes, Milady," he replied.

"In that case I need to give you expense money." She fumbled in her purse and handed Basil some coins without really looking at them. *I know that you have to trust servants. If you don't, then they became untrustworthy.* "Tell me when you need some more." She started walking down the row of buildings, past the army post. The door guard saluted her and she nodded back. *I am looking for the store that deals in goods that come from outside this area. Every village, no matter what size it is, has at least one of these.* Theodora found it, entered and discovered Basil had followed her. *He must have already tied the horses up.* The shopkeeper, *a Christian by his dress*, came to greet her with a warm smile on his face. *He must have been at the inn last night.*

"I want to buy a small chess set. *Last night I had a band. I don't now.* She turned to Basil. "Do you play any instruments?"

"No, Milady," he replied. *For an instant, I thought I saw a flicker of surprise cross his face, but it is quickly gone.*

"Never mind. You can learn. I may need some backing." Turning again to the shopkeeper she added, "And a small dombec or a tambour or some other type of drum."

The shopkeeper fussed around for a while looking through boxes and under counters before unearthing a small board, which he apologetically wiped some dust off. *It is suitable for carrying in a saddlebag and made of some sort of inlaid timber with two small drawers containing pieces for chess and draughts with the pieces being made of ebony and ivory.* Theodora looked critically at it. *It is still fairly new, perhaps even unused. It is not as good as something you find in the palace, but certainly good enough for a hunting lodge.* The drum was easier to find. *He has several of them on hand.* Theodora selected two tambours of different sizes that would fit one inside the other. *They are of timber and have goatskin laced over them.* She also chose a small beater for the drums.

She turned. "Is there anything that you need?"

"No, Milady. I was prepared for a long trip away from towns," he replied.

"Then let us go." Theodora bought the items. Carefully counting out the money, she ended up handing over a golden imperial, four gold denarii and the same of silver sesterces and several silver numismata. She turned again to go. *Even though he is trying not to show his disapproval, Basil's face looks a little like that of Saidah when they had first started to shop. I must have paid far too much.* The shopkeeper effusively ushered them out into the street conveying his sincere wishes that they visit him again some time.

Basil

It was still quite some time before they left. Basil helped Salimah up onto her horse. *She is not as accustomed to this as she should be. She needs the help. It is obvious that, although she wears heavy armour, and seemed used to wearing it, she is only of average strength. Most Kataphractoi are more accustomed to the weight they carry every day and grow much stronger over time. Today she is wearing the camail on her helm raised. I can see that her eyes are again black and a stray braid of hair shows as orange. The quicker I get her away from this village the better. It seems that this is going to be a long assignment in so many ways. Salimah is obviously intent on making me into some sort of musician, adding another task to a daily list of duties that already looks long.*

As they rode along Salimah asked Basil to come up beside her, then starting quizzing him about his past. Their ride was comfortable along the road, the main artery of the Empire, and the horses would almost stride along it naturally while they talked. *Luckily, I have done enough of my work acting as a servant to be able to mention names that she may have heard of and so satisfy her curiosity. In the process, I am finding out more about her than she is of me.*

It turns out that I have seen more of the Empire than she has. I was born in Ardlark, but I have been mainly raised in the far south among the jungles that surround Southpoint. I have been to Mouthguard in the only gap in the mountains that are both the defence of Darkreach and also its barrier to expansion. I have seen the fabulous eternal flames in the island-town of Antdrudge and even briefly been to the snows and frozen seas around Cold Keep in the far north. I think that I deflected attention quite well by implying that I was at most of these places as a military servant. It seems that Salimah has only seen Ardlark and the coastal towns as far as Axepol in the west and Silentochre in the south.

Salimah is always letting information slip. She made these visits in one of the great dromonds of the navy. Even the nobility do not get to use these as pleasure barges. You have to be from the Imperial family to have one of these made available to use for a leisure trip. At least, in her defence, she may not even know that. In so many ways she is truly an innocent to the world, she acts like a little girl out on an adventure.

At lunch, he produced fare he had obtained at the inn; cold meats and salami, feta cheese, pickled vegetables, olives, and dates. Salimah shocked Basil by demanding that he sit beside her to eat, and then insisted that he use some of the break to start practicing beating time on the drums. And then, they were on their way again.

That night they stayed at a military post after the long, hot, and dusty ride. It was a lot less comfortable than The Old Lobster. Basil's decision to help the caravanserai cook to prepare the meal turned out to be a good idea. *I actually know far more what to do with the spices than the cook does.* After eating, the post commander tried to get him to stay permanently, much to the indignation of Salimah. Once again Salimah entertained. Now it was the post commander's turn to be scandalised at the behaviour of this supposed officer. The troops, half of them Kichic-kharl foot archers and the others Human Kynigoi, light patrol cavalry, loved it. They particularly enjoyed Basil's learning attempts to provide rhythm as they hit their table tops with hands and with the butts of their knives along with him roughly in time. *At least I choose to interpret their laughter as enjoyment. The troops want us both to stay.*

Theodora

When the pair left the next morning, they had a cavalry escort. It was setting off for a routine patrol to the west and shared the first part of the day on the same route. The heat grew heavy and the dust rose around them. Sweat trickled and the horses' heads began to droop. After lunch the escort cheerfully waved Basil and Theodora goodbye as they turned to continue their patrol into the arid lands to the north, leaving the pair to continue west.

Except for the quality of the food, which varied greatly depending on the skills of the post's cook, the next few days went similarly. *So much for adventure—I am getting bored. It shows when I get excited over a caravan or a small group of travellers coming the other way.* Only once did a military courier, one of the Oxys Dromos, appear from the mirage behind. *He is riding at a much faster pace than we are and ignores us totally as Basil has already taken us off the road to allow him to overtake us. It is not long before he disappears into the heat haze ahead.*

On their breaks, Theodora discovered that she was a much better chess player than Basil, but still got a little confused over draughts. *I have never played it before. At least, over the days, Basil is getting better at beating out simple rhythms for me.*

After lunch on the fifth day they saw ahead the vast plateau on which stood Deathguard Tower, holding its vigil over the ancient barrows that dated from a time before the founding of Darkreach. About the same time, Basil discovered that their packhorse had developed a loose shoe and a stone had lodged inside it, threatening to lame the horse.

"I am sorry, Milady," he said apologetically. "I swear I checked them this morning and there was naught wrong with them then." *His voice has more than a touch of chagrin in it.* "We cannot risk laming the beast so we will have to travel very slowly. This gives us a choice of what to do next. Should we camp now and go on tomorrow, or do we go on further today and reach Deathguard well after dark? They don't always let people in after dark. We may end up camping anyway, and in the dark."

The place has a foul reputation, but the Granther is supposed to have the unquiet dead under control with strong barriers placed around the barrows.

Either course should be safe, but I am filled with unease over the choice. I wish that I had some skill at foretelling but, lacking that option; I will toss a mental coin and decide to camp now. The nearest barrow is over an hour's travel distant and it is still daylight.

I should feel relief. Basil is capable of making a camp out of very little. The magical item in his pouch turns out to be just a firelighter and he soon has a fire going. The sweet smell of burning dung, mixed with herbal fragrances of the dried shrubs, smells that tease at the nose, rose into the air. He used the fire to make kaf while he boiled some rice and, in another pot, some dried things taken from the horse packs. He stirred these into the rice and handed Theodora a bowl and spoon where she was seated on a saddle before serving himself and moving to sit a little way away.

"Why are you sitting over there?"

"I am your servant, Milady. It may be suitable for a roadside stop to sit beside you briefly, but it is not right that I should eat a proper meal with you," was his fairly prim reply.

"I suspect that we are going to be together for quite a while, and a lot of that time we will not be in towns. You cannot treat me as if this were a one-night hunting party."

He moved to sit opposite her on the ground. *His eyes are still not watching me, they are scanning the plain that stretches towards Deathguard and the hill.* "You look as if you are expecting trouble."

"I do, Milady…always." *His eyes do not stop looking further afield.*

"Does that mean that I should be looking as well?" *I feel so innocent. We are still deep inside the Empire, not out among the lawless wildings. It is supposed to be safe in the Empire. I have not seen the faintest risk of trouble at any time in my life and have scarce heard of any.*

"Yes, Milady. We are far from the city or any other help. Wild beasts prowl out here, and even occasionally criminals. Think about where we are. The dwellers in the barrows have broken loose many times before. I am your servant, so it is part of my duty to keep you safe. It makes my job much easier if you are also alert for danger."

"So, you think that we might be attacked tonight?"

"It is always possible, Milady," said Basil. *That sounded diplomatic.* He rose and took her empty bowl. "Would you care for some more kaf before I put out the fire?"

"Why put out the fire? I thought that you would build it up. Don't we need its light?"

Was that a stifled sigh from Basil? "It is about to get dark and a fire will make it hard for us to see any distance at all beyond its circle. We are not a large and strong force and so our best defence is simply not to be noticed." He began laying out her sleeping roll.

"In that case, I also have preparations." Theodora went over to her gear and pulled out her rolled up magical diagram and unrolled it on the flat ground near her where her bedroll was. From the corner of her eye she noticed that Basil scarcely glanced at it. *Unflappable, he is looking to be the perfect servant. Maybe I should tell him who I really am. No, I will not do that until we have left Mouthguard behind and he cannot easily back out. Still, there is something I can do to bind him closer to me.* "I think that you should call me by my name, Salimah, at least when we are alone."

"As Milady wishes," he said. After kicking dirt over the fire Basil had driven two stakes hard into the ground behind them and away from the plateau, which he joined by a piece of rope. *Now he is watering the horses and tying them with lead ropes to the rope on the ground.*

Theodora corrected him. "Salimah."

Basil

"Yes, Salimah." *Our camp is ready for the night, now for my last duty before she suggests it.* He softly practiced for a while on his tambour until darkness started to fall.

"Salimah, I suggest that you should get some sleep."

"What are you going to do?" she asked.

"I will be watching."

"But shouldn't you get some sleep?"

"Tomorrow will be a short day. Once we reach Deathguard I can catch up."

She nodded and removed her armour, leaving it in a heap. *It is so obvious from the unconscious way she does this that she is accustomed to servants doing everything for her. She has taken her boots off but kept her clothing on and curled up under her blankets.* Basil sighed and picked up her armour, dusting it down as much as he could in the dark, and neatly stacked it near her head.

Having that horseshoe come loose is vexing. I am not an expert horse handler so I made sure that I took particular notice of everything to do with the animals. I inspect their hooves every night and morning, even when there is someone else to brush them down and look after their other needs. None have shown the slightest sign of coming loose. But then, I suspect it is not anything I have done to cause the loose shoe.

There is nothing to be done about it now. A night in the open should not hurt us too much. I am sure that we have more ahead. I can see, from the expression on her face that Salimah does not like the prospect of just lying down in the dirt on a blanket. Like the spoilt young girl she sometimes seems to be, she needs to realise that life will be a lot harder than what she is used to if they do, indeed, leave the Empire. It is best if she finds out now.

I will spend the night on my feet, a bit of relief actually after several days in the saddle. Although I am a competent rider, lately I have been more used to being closer to the ground. He walked around the campsite, occasionally stopping, and dropping low to examine the horizon, hoping that the contrast between earth and sky might reveal anything that approached. He saw some animals avoided their camp, mainly smaller pouched hoppers, but once there was one of the giant animals, twice the height of a man, with a tail thicker than a man's leg, which grazed on low trees not on grass.

Chapter V

Basil

Around midnight the stillness of the night was broken by an odd noise. Basil had his back to Deathguard at that time and spun around to discover the source of the sound. He smiled. *It seems that, when she sleeps on her back, Salimah snores. Softly, but she snores.*

By the stars, it was around three in the morning. The chill of night lay on them with the faint dampness that grows on the skin. Basil had been concentrating on the early autumn chill that he felt on the tip of his nose and in his fingers. He was brought to full alert by another distant sound. *It is like the sound of a galloping animal, only somehow wrong.* He peered through the night. *Three dark shapes are coming from the direction of the plateau ahead. They are still maybe a bit over a couple of hundred paces away, but they are moving quickly towards us. I don't think that they are likely to be friendly.*

He quickly moved to where Salimah slept, grabbed her foot in the army fashion and shook it hard. The snoring stopped abruptly and she sat up. *She already has a dagger in her hand. Something is coming out of her mouth.* It may have been, 'What's happening?' or 'What are you doing?' Basil didn't wait to find out.

"Wake up Salimah—Get into your circle—We are about to be attacked."

She is mumbling something else—but at least she is moving and awake. After seeing her disentangling herself from her blankets and springing barefoot to grab her weapons belt he turned and put himself roughly between her and the approaching shapes, keeping to one side in case she would be casting spells.

It is dark near the start of the month with both moons very thin, but the lack of clouds in the night air allows the stars to give us some light. Basil peered into the darkness. *I can see there are five approaching shapes. Each is a black mass atop a skeletal horse. Black formless shapes mean either Wights or Wraiths.* He shuddered. *One touch on the skin from either of these will drain some of my life force and I will have to be very close to them to strike with my weapons. Luckily both are magically enhanced and thus can actually damage them.*

A wind—passing me by. He turned to see Salimah standing on her casting rug, pointing a wand at the approaching undead. Turning back to the front as more gusts passed him, he saw the undead horses staggering. *She is an air mage and at least she has some offensive magic in her arsenal. That is a relief.* One horse fell, and then another. Their riders rose up and continued moving. *They are far slower now that they are on their own feet.* He compassed himself and began muttering a prayer.

The last to be unhorsed is only a few paces from me, with others strung out behind it. It carries a sword and shield and wears a hauberk of chain link. Although it has a bare skull, it seems to be more substantial than a mere skeleton, as if there is a man still inside the armour—definitely a Wight. Its eyes glow balefully in the dark as malevolent points of white. At least this one is not likely to touch me if it relies on its weapons. My opponent holds its sword in its right hand. Basil, who could use both his hands equally well, cross-drew his blades, and stood to favour his left, to give himself a slight advantage. They closed and Basil was soon concentrating simply on defence.

This Wight must have been a formidable swordsman in life to keep so much skill when he is one of the less dextrous undead. The creature's mail is hanging in rusty festoons and proving more of a hindrance to its wearer than a protection—but a second Wight is growing closer—and it has no weapons. It will try and grasp me and drain my life force. I have to do something.

His opponent chose that moment to rush him. Basil sidestepped to his right, his opponent's shield side, turning and stabbing across his body into its shield. The point stuck in and he dragged the shield down as he thrust into the skull with his other weapon, piercing the glowing spark in the eye socket. His point hit the back of the skull and pierced it.

He wrenched his blade free. *The skull is impaled—I have removed the head from the creature—Its body is falling at my feet, thrashing in the throes of its second death. Oh well, my instructor always said to use a shortsword to get your point across.* He gave a short bark of nervous laughter.

I still have my second shortsword stuck in the shield. This forced him to lean down and put his foot on the shield in order to pull out the blade. The second Wight reached for him and he desperately swung a blind cut towards its hands with his free hand. The skull flew off the end of the blade and, as luck would have it, struck the second Wight full in the face causing it to flinch.

Basil's shortsword continued its wild arc, clipping the tip off one of its six bony fingers as its grab missed. Basil leapt back and came fully to his feet, facing the creature.

I have two blades to counter the two hands of the Wight, but my two blades can cut as well as thrust. If I make my defence so that, when I can counter my opponent with an edge, rather than a flat, I can perhaps damage it and trim it back gradually. As he fought, Basil began to say a prayer of thanks for his blades. *Their enchantment for extra damage is converting my defensive strokes into attacks. It may be slow, but by concentrating on defence I am destroying my opponent. I hope that I can do this before my next opponent arrives.*

The second Wight, at last, fell. Basil looked around. *As far as I can see there is no one and nothing ahead of me. I can hear the heavy breathing of someone who has been fighting hard and who is not used to it, but no sounds of fighting.* Scanning the horizon, he turned around. *Salimah is standing looking at me, her sword is hanging down to the ground on one side and her buckler against her leg on the other. She doesn't look either composed or steady.* He finished looking around and moved towards his charge.

Theodora

I am running, running hard. I am not sure what from, but I have to run. All of a sudden, the earth shook, and someone called out. *Not to me, but to someone called Salimah—but I am Salimah as well. I am in danger. I am dreaming.* She woke up grabbing her dagger from under the saddlebag she was using as a pillow. *Basil is shaking my foot. Why my foot?*

"What is going on?"

He said we are being attacked. "Kutsulbalik?" *We are being attacked? Who would attack us? I am a Princess.* She felt confused. Still struggling with the effects of sleep Theodora reached again under the saddlebag and grasped two wands before leaping to her feet and grabbing her weapons belt from where it lay beside her with her small shield hanging off it. She struggled into it, trying to come alert before running to her casting pattern. *This is where I need to be.* A stab of pain ran through her foot as she trod on something. "Damnation." *Try and ignore the pain.*

She stood in the centre of the rug. *I hope that I am not getting blood on the pattern of the rug.* She looked ahead. *There stands Basil looking quite small between me and some approaching riders. It seems he thinks they are a threat. He is a servant and probably cannot take them on alone. What was I told in class about times like this—oh yes.* She pointed a wand and began to cast from it, aiming at the lead mount first. She kept up the casting until one went down and then another. *I need to keep count—that wand was empty and I was still trying to use it.* She tossed it aside and continued casting using the other.

Damn. I must have been well asleep not to realise it before. These are not just bandits. They are undead, probably Wights from the barrows. Again, she felt confusion. *The Granther is supposed to have them all safely contained. What if he has found out about me leaving and disapproved so much that he has sent them to stop me?* Another mount fell. *The mounts are undead as well—keep casting. No, he would have just sent soldiers, or even had those in one of the posts attend to me. I have not seen any signs that he has noticed or had me followed, and I have been watching for them.*

A fourth mount fell, and then the fifth. *Its rider is just in front of Basil. He continues standing there, placing himself between me and five Wights. I cannot hit the last two riders to lose their mounts; they are too close in line with Basil.* She aimed at the third. It fell as the second wand became exhausted. *Now I have to cast my own spells.* She summoned the phrases of a more powerful bolt than she was able to put into a wand.

Concentrate—I wish that I had time to grab items from my saddlebag to aid me. I must sleep with my spell adder in future. Its mystic combinations of metal, number, gem and shape aid my casting—Don't think. My teachers warned me about that. Focus and concentrate. Repeat the phrases. Summon the mana. Let go. She felt the almost orgasmic rush as spell was released. The fourth Wight fell. *The same spell again. If the Granther has not released the Wights, then someone else must have. His wards would not have failed accidentally and he will not have forgotten to renew them. Concentrate. Repeat the phrases. Summon the mana. Let go.* The fifth Wight staggered, but did not fall. *I have reached the limit of my mana. Do I dare risk going over my limit to hit it again? No. It is too risky. Failure will mean that I could be unable to defend myself. How about getting another wand out of my pack? No, there is no time.*

Basil has disposed of one of his opponents, but he is hard pressed by the second. If the fifth attacks while he is occupied, and currently has his back to it, he will die. No, I have to use my weapons. She unhooked her buckler from her belt. *It is so much easier to use this than my large teardrop for a charge. I am glad that I bargained for it*—and ran forward to Basil's side. *Under foot is dry dirt and grass. I feel dust and sand, but no more stabbing pain. So occupied is Basil, that I am sure he doesn't notice me.*

She saw why he was so hard-pressed. Except for a few arena games fighting to first blood, she had never had to fight seriously. *It has all been for fun. If I make a mistake now I could die. I am fighting for my life. My opponent has a sword in one hand, one that looks dangerously unmarked by age, but its other hand is empty. I have to avoid that one. The sword can probably only cut or pierce.* Sword clashed with sword as she tried to fend off the Wight with her buckler held out in front. *I wish that I had more practice.* The Wight closed on her and was inside her shield. *I can feel its bony hand touch my neck. It is brief, but there is a coldness spreading through me.*

Its eyes briefly glowed more strongly in an intense coldness. *I feel weaker.* Panicking, she backed up. It followed even faster, dropping its sword, eager to grapple her and steal more of her life to add to its own. She tripped over something on the ground and fell on her back. It was following her so fast that it fell too. Theodora flung up her arms instinctively to ward it off, but it landed on top, driving her arms down. She struggled to get clear. *Lord preserve me—I am gone—I will die like this—from its cold touch—but where is the cold? Where is the loss? All I feel are bones, rotting cloth and dried out parchment skin.* She rolled free, sneezing from the dusty mould that now covered her, grabbing for her sword. *The Wight is impaled on it. When I threw up my arm I pierced its body. I must have weakened it enough with my last air bolt. It died, or died again, or was unmade at least by this last wound.* She shuddered. *That was far too close.*

She looked up to see Basil still fighting a nearly armless opponent. *He seems to have been chopping bits off it so it is harder and harder for the Wight to touch him. It is now defending only—hard to do when you only have stumps for arms—and attempting to avoid the whirl of two short blades.* It closed on him to be met by the classic shortsword stroke coming up from below the waist to where its stomach should be and continuing to enter the chest. *On a person, the blow ends in their heart. On the Wight, the blow just ended its existence.* It folded up and collapsed in a pile of disconnected bones at Basil's feet.

Basil quickly moved to calm the horses, which were at most twenty paces from the last fight and had almost pulled their pickets loose, one to attack, and the others to run. He then sat Theodora down and bandaged her foot where she had trodden on a sharp rock, using one of his healing salves while he did so.

It is unusual to actually have to do this for real. Under direction, she bandaged the cuts he had received from his first opponent.

"You must go back to sleep now, Milady," he said. "You have used all of your mana and will have no more until you are rested and we do not know what will happen tomorrow. As well you admit that one touched you and removed some of your life force." *He shudders as he says that.* "That, in itself, will weaken you."

Theodora was glad to comply. *I am shaking as the exhilaration of combat wears off. It is taking me a while to calm and get back to sleep. I am not sure that I will. Sex would have been a good release. As it is there are pebbles on the ground under me and they dig into me, whenever I move around.*

Chapter VI

Theodora

She woke up to the smell of kaf. *A small mug of the hot sweet brew is beside my head. This time my sleep had been undisturbed by dreams.* Basil hurried over. *He is fussing over me as if I was an aged relative.* She bade him leave her alone and he returned to his relit fire to heat a pan and pour something into it. She had just finished the kaf and her eyes had started to focus properly when Basil came back with an omelette and an ibrik with more, sweet kaf in it. As she breakfasted Basil saddled the horses. Theodora started to don her shoes and then her armour. *Basil is again helping me as if I am an aged aunt who has had an accident. One look at him, with the dust of the plain all over him and tousled hair after his fight and a sleepless night and I think that I should be helping him—although I am not sure how.*

While Basil was checking the horses, Theodora went to examine the bodies of the Wights. She put some bones in one of her endless supply of small pouches, in case she needed them for a spell, and was about to turn away when the sword of Basil's first opponent caught her attention. *It fairly glows in my senses. Its inherent magic impinges strongly on my consciousness.* She picked it up and looked at it. *It has a pommel shaped in a fashion that I have not seen before. The flat base has five lobes rising from it. Even I can see that the weapon is well made and still new-looking after perhaps an age in the grave. On the blade there are words of some sort, inlaid into the steel in gold or bronze.* She held it up to catch the light. *It is in the script used by the Dwarves and the Greydkharl, the underground-working Kharl. I can speak and read all of the Darkreach tongues, and some others, but this one is a mystery. Dwarven is similar to Greydkharl in some of its words, so it is unlikely to be that. The individual letters make sense, but what they spell does not. I will put it in a horse pack until I have time to work it out.*

They started off; travelling slowly so as to not fully cast the loose shoe. *The packhorse walks better after the rest, but Basil insists on stopping frequently to make sure no more stones become lodged under the shoe.* As the sun rose and the day warmed some little dust devils swirled around nearby in temporary funnels. *Even with the halts we are circling around the plateau towards Deathguard before noon.* Soon they were climbing up the slopes towards the grim rectangle of the tower. *The temperature is rising as we climb.* Fine dust eddied around them and tickled their noses.

To their right in the north and west they could see the expanse of the Great Bitter Lake. Unlike a normal lake, it was a body of water that was far saltier than the ocean itself. *Nothing can drink of its waters and I have floated on top of it with no effort.* To the south lay the dry rolling grasses that covered the top of the plateau and, dotted over it, could be seen the barrows that held captive the unquiet dead of past millennia. Unlike any other garrison town in Darkreach there was little in the way of a civilian presence at the tower. They had passed only a few fields of vegetables, and a little grain, on their way up the slope and the few animals kept by shepherds looked to be brought inside the tower at night along with any passing caravans. The grim keep, itself a long rectangle known to have the tallest walls in the Empire, had only two functions; to house the garrison tasked to watch the undead and try to control them if they escaped or to at least give warning if they did so in numbers too large to be held.

Upon arriving at the keep they split up. While Basil headed off with the horses, Theodora took herself off to pay her respects to the duty officer. *I need to tell the garrison what happened to us. The soldiers stationed here have to find out whether the Wights had escaped their confinement or were released. They also need to send out a patrol to gather the remains and take them back to their barrows to re-inter them. Once a body has been raised, it becomes easier and easier to do so and, allowing the bones to sit in the open is an invitation to the malicious—and this would not be good.*

Her news threw the garrison into turmoil and the duty officer sent a runner to fetch the castle's Kentarchkos to the room. *I should have expected that to happen.*

Basil

B asil unloaded and unsaddled the horses and then sought out the blacksmith. *Not only do I want that packhorse re-shod, but I also want all of the others checked over thoroughly.*

The news from the blacksmith is alarming. The nails in the loose shoe have not worn down or been broken. They are actually missing, as if someone has pulled them out entirely. I checked those horses myself in the morning before setting out. No-one else has been near them since then and no one at the way post could have done this. That only leaves magic as a cause. I know bugger-all about that, but I suppose that it is possible. Mages seem to be able to work out ways to do all sorts of odd things. He shuddered at what that meant. *If it was magic that did it, it meant that someone wanted us delayed out there and spending the night in the open without support. It means that the attack on us was not a mishap. It was deliberate. It was not an accidental escape of the unquiet dead, someone wants us...well her at least...dead.* Having supervised the re-shoeing and made sure that the horses were comfortably ensconced he hurried off to tell Salimah.

Theodora

T heodora was in the cool duty office talking to several officers when Basil returned and drew her aside.

"Someone sabotaged the horseshoe," he said. "Remember that I said that checked them and they were fine? Well, they did not break; they did not lose their head. Somehow someone removed the whole nail, even the part that is bent over through the hoof. Could magic do that?"

I cannot now, but I am sure I can work out how. She nodded.

"That means someone wanted us delayed out there," he said. *That was definitely a flicker of concern that crossed his face. Even in the keep he is concerned.* "That attack was not an accident. Someone wanted us to be out there when the Wights came."

She looked out the window. *In the courtyard, a large patrol is assembling. Kataphractoi and the skirmishing scouts of the Kynigoi gather with packhorses, mounted mages, and a Christian priest. A company of Kichic-kharl are already heading out the gate and it looks like they have one of their priests running along with them as well. Anything I say will only excite suspicion and I can imagine the Kentarchkos in charge here asking why someone would want to kill her. No, everything is being done that can be. They don't need to know what Basil has deduced.*

By the time they had finished talking, Basil was swaying slightly and Salimah took him off to find a place to sleep. The keep had a hostel used by the passing traders. Basil consented to go to bed after leaving instructions to be woken for the evening meal.

Theodora went to the battlements to watch the cavalry riding down the road they had arrived by, while the infantry inspected the barrows as they moved along the edge of the plateau.

Events took several hours to unfold and, by the time they happened they were so distant that all of the actors were mere dots. Suddenly the dots that represented the Kichic-kharl archers converged on a barrow. After a short while, a small group detached and moved to the edge of the plateau. After another while, a group could just barely be seen moving up the slope, becoming more visible when they reached the grassland. They joined the first group. *The larger dots of this group have to be horsemen. The combined group are headed back to the barrow. I cannot be sure, but it looks like some dots disappeared into the barrow for a while.* After a time, the dots joined up and headed back towards Deathguard Tower. *The dots stay together. They will return a little after dusk.* Theodora kept watching until it was time to go down and eat.

It is important that we leave tomorrow, even if we are still tired. Although the barrow is now sealed, the Granther will probably want to come himself to be sure. It could be a while, but I don't want to be here when he arrives. To minimise, if possible, the attention that is paid to us, I won't entertain tonight.

The next day they left early on the road to Sasar. They travelled for six more hot, dry, and dusty days and slept five more nights at army posts—those that had good permanent water starting once again to develop small hamlets around them. The dread plague of The Burning had subsided a few years ago, and many places had lost almost all of their people. Theodora had been told that entire settlements had been lost or destroyed. Seeing it, she now understood how the whole of The Land would be slow to recover from its impact.

They overtook caravans and passed others going towards Ardlark. Sometimes they kept company with army patrols. *Once again, I am beginning to feel the ennui of slow travel in a flat and boring land—not that I want to face more Wights.*

What can I remember about Sasar from school? It is a vital town to the Empire. It sits in front of a mountain and has one of the two good mines providing the iron that is used in Darkreach.

Sasar also serves as a crossroads of the main east-west and north-south roads that bind the Empire together. She sighed. *It may be important, but it doesn't look it. Its oasis is small, far smaller than that at Dochra. I may not know much about farming, but I am sure that it cannot support many farmers and to support a proper town you need lots of food. Unusually most of the residents here are Kharl, all of them Alat-kharl or Greydkharl, rather than Humans or even Insakharl. They play a lot of Ball.*

The village is only a scattering of houses, more barracks than houses, around a vaguely cross-shaped pair of streets. The ground, and the houses, and even the trees, are all coated with a fine red dust from the mines. She kept brushing herself as she noticed she was getting a layer of it all over her. *I can even taste its bitterness in my mouth. Basil is spitting and washing his mouth with water.*

The dust coated the entire town and made everything look the same. *Where is an inn? Ah—Basil is pointing and urged her there.*

Despite a good response to the music, in terms of money, Salimah and Basil were both glad to leave the dusty town the next day.

After Sasar, five more days of travel will bring us to Nameless Keep. Where will we go from here? Theodora reviewed what she knew about the place. *It is the main army base for the west of the Empire and stands on the eastern end of the Darkreach Gap on a basalt ridge. Its walls are not as tall as those of Deathguard, but are much thicker, being carved directly out of the ridge that the citadel stands on. A rumour, which I know to be true, has it that the black walls are magically strengthened.*

The Land has gradually grown more fertile after Sasar and is now far better than the Great Plain. I may not know much about farming, but I notice that grasslands are spreading around us as we ride. The bare dusty ground alongside the road has disappeared beneath tussocky and dry-looking grass some time ago and it gets greener as we travel. There are hoppers everywhere. Occasional creeks and rivulets splash down from the mountains and I can see small hamlets spreading around the Keep's imposing bulk. From where I sit atop Esther I can see six of them, a full hand. It is here that the, still rare, caravans taking part in the new trade to the west, trade that my cousin's marriage has signalled, form up. I hope that there will be one for us to join as guards as an excuse to head further west. At least that is my plan.

Habib is selling. I notice that it is getting harder and harder for him to fend them off without upsetting them.

They set out through the keep to the other side of the river early the next day. *For the first time since setting out from Nameless, we have the road completely to ourselves. It was also the first time that any of them had seen the forest west of the mountains. The maps I saw in Ardlark said that this forest runs in an unbroken sweep from the ocean to the south of The Land to the frozen north, changing as it goes from jungle to endless pines. This forest is unlike any I have seen in Darkreach.*

The trees here are mostly deciduous; giant oaks and yews, and some broad-leafed conifers. There are also patches of occasional gums and a profusion of brambles and shrubs in the clearings. Even the smells here are different to me. The air is damp on my face even in the middle of the day and it is quite cool under the trees. She looked around. *To my left runs the Methul River and to my right are the ramparts of the mountains. The road seems to snake over the foothills, seeking the easiest path and running from ford to ford.*

It isn't really a road, not as we know them in Darkreach; merely a collection of tracks travelling in the same direction as each traveller has chosen the path they think best suits them. It is all dirt and mud underfoot. The paths narrow and come together to cross small rills and to ford larger creeks. None of them are bridged as they flow down to join the river. It is a different world to that we are used to; much less orderly; much less safe. Basil rode well out to the front and he and Kraznik, who stayed at the rear, kept looking all around them. *I stay near the pack animals and try to look around as if I know what I am doing. All I see are trees and birds—and I see the birds only when they fly off or land.*

That night they camped on the far side of what her notes told her was the Duvel River. *We forded it in the gathering twilight as it begun to rain. I am a little worried that I have the most knowledge of where we are going. Even Habib has only a very vague idea. Seeing that I knew the name of the river everyone looked to me for guidance. How am I going to know how high it might rise or if it would perhaps have trapped us on the wrong side in the morning if we had not crossed?*

Basil cooked for them all, lighting his fire under a huge expanse of oak, where it was at least partly dry. They set up their camp under the branches for it promised to be a dampish night. They set watches, exempting Habib. "I am not used to being outside a city and am useless with any weapons at all."

After extinguishing the fire Basil took first watch, then Theodora, then

Kraznik. Before trying to sleep Theodora was careful to lay out her casting rug near to where she would sleep *and to leave my boots on, although I find it uncomfortable. It is not a good night, not only are there pebbles under me, but I feel damp in my clothes. At least it is quiet, except for the drip of water from the leaves.*

The next two days to the Yuggel River went the same way. *Apart from some animals and endless birds, glimpsed through the trees and some of them very noisy, we may as well have been all alone in the world. The drifting showers of early autumn are gradually soaking through my clothes and trickling down my back. I feel damp all the time. I am not used to this privation and not even being able to change my clothes. It makes me feel uncomfortable and dirty and even Basil, fussing around me, can do little to help.*

In the middle of the next day Basil called out softly. *There ahead is my first village outside of Darkreach. Despite the tales of trade opening up the world, I am nervous. According to my map the name of this village does not help my apprehension. It is called Kharlsbane and is a Dwarven settlement.*

Kraznik had already made it clear that he wanted to avoid it completely and strike west through the forest towards Evilhalt, *itself not a propitious name, both names reflecting the ignorance of the outside barbarians.* Habib, however, had been adamant that they follow the road. "This is not Darkreach, it is a lawless place, and these woods are probably filled with outlaws and wild tribes, and are certainly filled with wild beasts. At least the Dwarves are supposed to be friendly at present." *I am now nervous enough to think about going back and siding with Kraznik.*

Basil and I are passing through a few small hamlets and the surrounding fields, looking around as we go. The other two are following a hand of hands behind. I admit to feeling nervous. I can see that some of the farms are worked by Humans, but mostly they are tilled by Dwarves looking like strange distorted Kharl with bearded Human faces. They all seem to have a weapon handy and no Dwarf females are visible. Maybe the rumours are true and they really didn't have any women and just grow the next generation somehow. However, at least they are looking at us more with curiosity than enmity.

We are getting closer to Kharlsbane and it is trying to live up to its reputation, at least in appearance. The village exists within walls carved from the living rock of a hill, vast ramparts of granite with towers topped with ballistae. It is Nameless Keep but built to a different plan. I can see a massive gatehouse adorned with grimacing faces carved out of the stone. There is little I can do if they don't like us. Now I have to cross a dry moat on a wide drawbridge, pass through an ironclad gate and two portcullises. Between these the roof is fretted with murder holes for pouring boiling oil and water on unwanted guests. I am not a siege engineer, but I am sure that this fortified village could break an army.

Despite this war-like appearance they were greeted warmly at the next gate by a Dwarf clad in mail and an axe at his side. In a torrent of accented Darkspeech, he gave his name as Bjarni the Talker, asked their names, what they had to sell, how their journey had been and whether they needed a place to stay, all the while smiling broadly and seemingly without drawing breath.

Theodora stood back and let Habib talk. *He has only managed to introduce us and get to 'liquid fire' before this Bjarni held up his hand, made his grin even wider and turned to call over a young Dwarf nearby. He said a few words in what has to be Dwarven to the youngling who ran off quickly.* Bjarni turned back to them and gestured to Habib to continue.

By the time he had finished, another Dwarf was moving down the street towards them. *This one wears a houppelande of dark green velvet with a hat with a long liripipe wound around it to match. The mace at his side is almost invisible in the expanse of thick rich cloth.* He approached speaking fluent, if accented, Darkspeech, and greeted a stunned Habib as if he were a long-lost brother. The Dwarf steered the trader further up the street and was already offering to buy his entire cargo while Theodora and Basil fell in behind. Habib may have been startled, but he had immediately fallen into negotiation. *It is obvious that liquid fire is truly precious here and that Habib's profit will be large. I am listening to how he does it. I wondered if I will ever be able to bargain like that.*

Theodora looked up. *There is sign there in the trade tongue and Darkspeech, and with runes that probably say the same in Dwarven, proclaiming the inn to be 'The Delver'. The building is, like all I can see in the village, carved directly out of stone and then ornamented.*

Kraznik took Habib's mount and gestured to Theodora and Basil as he led them off to house the horses. Once this was done they entered the inn. *I can see that the building has only a few narrow windows, almost arrow slits, and, even in the middle of the day, is lit by mirrors reflecting the sun from above and some enchanted lights. It seems that, even when they live above ground, Dwarves like to feel that they are under it.*

Habib found the other three where they had been seated. "It seems I need go no further. Kraznik and I can return and get another cargo. I still owe you your accommodation here and this is yours." He held out a pair of small purses.

Basil took them. *We are being paid.*

"I contracted you to go to Evilhalt, so it is also for another five days of travel. I can be generous. I like this place. They have paid me in these." He opened a pouch and poured out a fortune in emeralds. *Those are rare stones in Darkreach.*

"They mine them here. I will be coming back to this village, so this means that I will need to have guards the whole time. Do you want to sign with me permanently? Most of the trip will be in Darkreach, so it will be easy work."

I need to pretend to give the offer some thought. Habib is right. If we were what we are pretending to be, then it is a very good offer.

"We thank you for the offer, but no. We are now outside, and this has long been a dream of mine. The barbarians and their squabbles have long fascinated me. Now I have a chance to find out what they are really like."

Habib is looking at Basil with an upraised eyebrow. Basil still says nothing and shows no emotion, he is just glancing at me and giving a little shake of his head. Habib sighed. *Even I can see that he looks more than a little disappointed.*

"Oh well, the young are always curious. I hope this curiosity does not kill you. We may yet meet again and you may wish for a nice easy job as a guard."

The rest of the night they relaxed. *Although I do not speak Dwarven, I am going to entertain with what I have, and Basil is again going to help.*

From the money we are getting, I think that it is obvious that the local talent is well below my skill level and the tavern is quickly filling. From the amount he is taking out of his upturned second drum, so is Basil's purse.

The night went on as the tavern filled with smoke and the smell of beer and spirits. *Finally, being outside Darkreach makes me feel as if I am more alive somehow. I am free and, despite the incident with the undead, there is no sign of pursuit or even of the Granther's intelligence people dogging my path and looking for me. Once we are free of Habib's presence, it will be time to shed the protection of the amulet and the awful orange hair and let Basil in on my secret. Out here, in my new-found freedom, I can finally be myself and not one person of all of those around me will know what my golden eyes mean.*

Chapter VII

Thord

Thord smelt the richness of the late autumn pasture and felt the coolness of the soft breeze play and ruffle his beard. *With what I have, life should be almost perfect, but it isn't.* He sighed. *I'm not bored. I am busy every day and I love what I do, but I want more and I feel that I am destined for something greater. As it is, I am a shepherd. Of all the work that does not involve mining or making, this is one of the most prestigious vocations for a Dwarf. It means that, not only do I look after sheep, goats, and cattle, but also, I am one of the few Dwarven cavalry. Admittedly I ride a sheep, but it isn't small and brainless like the herd beasts. He is the size of some ponies: agile, smart, and fierce as well.*

The smell of wool grease is on me always, but I can ride Hillclimber using only my knees down a steep hillside while still firing my bow. In a charge, I know that I am deadly. But do I get to see any combat? No, the wild tribes are quiet. Do I get to travel? No, nowadays our town doesn't send out traders, traders now come to us. My family lives at Kharlsbane, a fortress of solid rock. It is a crossroads and yet all I see are my herds and, from the high pastures of summer, over the forest of trees, visions of a distant and freer world; one where adventures happen to other people.

The legends say that once, well before The Burning, Dwarves occupied all of the mountains. You could not travel for more than a day without seeing my people and their works. In those days, Dwarvenholme, now long lost, was the home of the Dwarven chief, the Mountain King. The legends tell of its beauty and of its size and of its wealth. Surely one city could not hold more people than all of the Dwarves now alive, but some say that it did.

The tales say that, at a time of strife, one day people just stopped coming, and anyone who went in did not come out. Armies were sent. They didn't return either. As a final straw, long after the last Dwarf to visit there had died (and we are a long-lived race) all of the records about its location were lost in the madness of The Burning.

Some now regard Dwarvenholme as just a tale. Others set out to find it. Perhaps some do find it, as they don't return. This might be due to whatever doomed the city, or it might just be due to the normal hazards of the wild tribes: Gnolls, Hobgoblins, Ogres and even The Dragon of the mountains. Dwarves breed slowly and so many Dwarves have not returned from their questing that the Elders eventually banned anyone from seeking it. Despite this, some still sought it under the guise of trying to find new mines, always a respectable quest for a Dwarf, and some still did not return.

I also want to seek Dwarvenholme, but I will be content with just seeing the world before coming back and finding a partner. These are dreams, and perhaps more than dreams. I have a feeling that everything so far is leading up to something. Maybe something big.

It all simmered in his head unremarked until one night, when Thord brought his flock in to Kharlsbane for the autumn cull, he went to the tavern. *There is a small group from Darkreach who have obviously made a very successful trading trip. They have clearly been on the trail for some time and the ring of empty tables around them and their aroma made it apparent. To me, however, they smell of travel and of excitement. They smell of destiny come calling.* He looked around. *I will take one of these empty seats. I cannot understand a word, but it is obvious that some of them are parting with the merchant.*

Maybe I can leave with them or with the merchant.

The Human guards left the other two behind, returning some time later washed and changed. *The woman now wears more normal clothes, as if she were from the Caliphate, although she still wears a sword, but then everyone else in the tavern has a weapon at hand. Dwarves always carry arms with them.* After talking with the innkeeper, the two started to entertain the customers. Songs were sung in a variety of languages. *The only one that I understand is in the Trade tongue of the brown-skinned Human southerners of Hind. One of the languages the girl sang in is very soft and flows around the ears like honey. It is very fair and beautiful and, although few seem to understand it, the song tugs the heart and, by the time she finished people are trying to hum along with her. The next song is totally different. The words are harsh sounding and urgent. It has the sound of a march and the small man is beating time on a drum, not very well. It is obvious that he is only learning.*

The Kharl is singing along loudly. Many of the Dwarves are also singing along in Dwarven, using words that sound something like the chorus but, from the broad smile playing on the face of the Kharl, almost certainly are not related. As they play, the small man's eyes keep scanning the room the whole time. She looks to be in charge, but he might be the more dangerous of the two.

Again, the girl sang in the fair language. *This time it sounds very sad, and again tugs at my heart even if I cannot understand the words, and it is very long. Old Thorgrim, the best mage in town, obviously knows the tongue. He is staring blindly at the girl and tears are running down the crevices of his cheeks to get lost in his beard. Who would have thought that he had even a single tear in him? These are the songs of the world outside. Why isn't it possible for me to go to these places and hear the people talk these tongues?*

After a bit more time sitting and drinking the bitter beer, *Thord could* became *Thord would* in his head. By the time everyone was ready to pack up for the night, Thord had made plans.

It is easy for me to find my parents. They, along with many of Kharlsbane's people, have drifted into the inn to see the rare excitement. Thord went over and let them know what it was that he wanted to do. *My mother does not want me to go, but I know my father thinks that a young Dwarf should see the world before settling down to responsibility.* Thord smiled. *I know what will come next.* In his youth, his father reminisced, even with The Burning raging he had left his home and visited all three of the surviving Dwarven areas, even going to the mountains far away to the southwest across the plains. Once his father had said this, his mother glared. Thord left his parents 'discussing' the matter while he went to pack. *For once my father will surely prevail in this discussion. After all, it was while he was away on his travels that he had found my mother.*

It was late in the crisp morning before Thord woke, later still by the time goodbyes had been said to the family and neighbours and his sheep, Hillclimber, was led down to the inn. There Thord discovered that the pair that he wanted to follow out into the world had left some little time before. Scrambling onto Hillclimber, Thord trotted briskly out between the carved gate towers of the town, waving goodbye to family and friends, and setting out on the long road to adventure.

Chapter VIII

Theodora

In the morning light, after saying goodbye to Habib and Kraznik, Theodora and Basil parted company with them. The trader and his guard would return to the south down the flank of the mountains and into Darkreach ahead of them. *For the first time in quite a while I feel clean. Basil has gotten my travel clothes cleaned overnight and they even smell fresh and faintly herbal; eucalypt certainly, but other scents linger as well. Everything is almost as good as it had been new and feels nice to put on.*

Theodora allowed Basil to take the lead as they left the village. *We are heading west to cross the Methul River on an ancient long stone bridge that is just visible ahead across fields and through the trees. I checked everything on my map. Once it leaves this last bridge the river wanders to the north and eventually arrives at the cold sea at Wolfneck. The road that I am riding on is more like a road than the one that we entered Kharlsbane by. Our horses' hooves make little noise on the firm dirt that is packed down by generations of regular travel. Very little dust rises to mark our passage and what there is soon settles.*

They were well on the way and Basil was already checking all around them. *He wants me to look back—Coming out of the village, now far to the rear of us, is a Dwarf mounted on the strangest animal that I have ever seen. It looks like a sheep, but not the kind of sheep that normal shepherds would want to see anywhere near their flocks. For a start, it stands nearly as tall as a small pony. Its rider is making it move along smartly as if to catch us and now I can see that it has the same sort of horns that a normal ram would have, except that these are clad in metal. On its brow is borne a metal chamfron with a spike coming forward. As it comes closer, I can see that the eyes on the beast have a malevolent cast, as do those of many wild rams, and its head in its armour resembles some form of demented unicorn. It has the thick, coarse, and matted fleece of a wild sheep, pulled down around its waist by a saddle and girth.*

Hurrying up to them, its rider held up his hand. "I am T'ord t' Shepherd," the Dwarf said in a heavily accented Hindi, addressing Basil.

Theodora looked at the sight before her. *If that is the shepherd, I am not sure I want to see the rest of the flock.* Her nose wrinkled as it came beside her. *The sheep smells strongly as well—I am not that familiar with live sheep, but that must be what old greasy wool smells like.*

Thord continued, "I ha' long wanted to see more of t' world. Last night, listening to you," *he nods towards me*, "I made up my mind to go with you. I ha' consulted with my family and t'ey're not agin my plan."

How different he is to me.

"I don't a know where you're a going, but I want to go with you. 'll you take me with you?"

Basil is looking at me. It would sometimes be nice if his face gave some clue as to how he thinks. The Dwarf is following his gaze. What do I say?

"Why don't you go with Habib? He wants a guard and will pay you well. He is going back into Darkreach where few outsiders have been and he will come back here again."

"I've t'ought of 'at," said the Dwarf, replying with a serious tone, "but with t' money 'at he made here, he'll do this trip for so long he'll have a home at both ends. He'll be like migrating bird, always travelling, but always seeing t' same sights. I t'ink t'at I be fated to see more of t'Land 'an 'at. I want to see flat lands 'n' jungle 'n' t'ocean. Can I join you?" he asked eagerly. "I can take orders 'n' am used to outdoor life 'n' Hillclimber," he patted the giant sheep, "'n' I work well together." *He is looking from me to Basil again. He seems to be unsure which of us is the leader.*

Theodora looked the Dwarf over again. *He, I presume that he is male; I have heard that one never knows with this race, is clad in mail. He has a long-handled war-hammer at his side and a round shield on his back. A recurve bow and two bristling quivers of arrows grace the sheep's flanks on top of well-worn saddlebags. Who had ever heard of a sheep archer before? This close I can sense that he has items of magical interest on him. His armour has a charm on it, perhaps quite a strong one, as does his hammer.*

"Very well," she said. "I am Salimah and this is Basil. I won't promise you anything after Evilhalt, but you may travel with us until then as long as you do what you are told." The Dwarf nodded in agreement and wheeled his mount and formed up to cover their rear. Basil now moved well away to look ahead. *He keeps checking back. I suppose that I should do the same.*

I *can see that the road we are following towards the southwest is better made and flatter than the one to the south of Kharlsbane, but I think that the plants around it are the same and the animals I see look the same as well. I see glimpses of hopper, of deer and rabbit and even the occasional giant lizard browsing on treetops or shrubs. Thord wants to hunt.* "Unless you need food, there is no need to kill and it will slow us down."

Thord looks disappointed, but he obeys without question.

Tonight I must deal with what comes next. When they reached a campsite for the night, she asked Thord if he could gather some firewood away from the camp as she had something she needed to say to Basil. Thord looked from one to the other before finally nodding and telling them not to go near Hillclimber as they may be attacked. He then went over to his pack and unstrapped a small hand-axe before moving away.

Theodora waited until the sound of his axe could be heard. She turned to Basil. *He is looking at me.*

"I am going to trust you with a secret. Even if you decide to leave me afterwards—" she held up a hand to forestall Basil saying anything, "I ask that you tell no one voluntarily." She paused. "I am in disguise and am not what I seem." Again, she paused.

I wish that Basil's face gave something away of what he is thinking—no, nothing. "It is true that I am a mage, and I am not entirely Human, but the rest of my makeup is not a Kharl heritage. Most of my story is made up. This will explain much." She reached to her ear and removed the amulet that hung there, allowing her eyes to turn to their normal dark luminous golden colour and her hair to turn raven black. *For once Basil's face shows expression. His eyes widen and he looks a little surprised.* He started to bow until she stopped him. "My name is not Salimah, but Theodora. As you can see, I am from the Imperial family and I felt the need to run away from home. I was once worried that the Granther, sorry Hrothnog, sent those Wights to stop me, but I don't think so now." She paused again. "Knowing what you now know, do you still want to stay with me?"

"It is every servant's ambition to directly serve the Imperial family," he declared proudly. *That is a relief.* "If you will still have me, I will be honoured to serve you."

I had not realised until now how worried I was that he might decline to stay with me. It is a huge relief and I feel lighter. I need my practical servant and, what is more, while I want to leave it all behind, while he is with me I can feel that I have not entirely abandoned my home.

"I suggest we tell Thord you have run away from an arranged marriage at home. You had your eyes and hair disguised as they are your most noticeable feature and part of the description that your father would send out." Basil paused. "Milady, are you really a Kataphractoi as well as a mage, or is that also part of your disguise? I need to know this."

"No, it is not disguise. All of our family train in at least two areas. Remember that I have training as a bard as well. After all, you have to have something to do to fill in the time when there is nothing to do. I may look young, but I am over one hundred years old." *Basil again looks surprised.* "Please though, do not call me 'Milady'. I said to call me by my name. I still want you to."

"Yes Sal—Theodora," replied Basil. "Now, let us set up camp."

By the time Thord returned to camp the horses were unsaddled and hobbled and Basil had a fire going. Theodora gave Thord the explanation that Basil had suggested and, although Thord was startled by the change in her appearance, and particularly the colour of her eyes, it was obvious that he did not realise their significance and seemed to accept them.

That night Theodora took the first watch, then Thord, and finally Basil, who could then start breakfast while he finished his shift. The night was a little bit chilly, although uneventful, and the colder weather, along with the unfamiliar stirrings and noises in the bush, kept them alert. *I will have no trouble at all sleeping with my boots on tonight. They will keep my feet much warmer.*

Five days of uneventful but fast travel followed. On the third day Theodora allowed Thord to kill a deer as their supply of meat was running low. The deer had fled as soon as it saw them. *Basil says that is a sign that people are well known around here. Thord proved skilled as an archer and his strange mount shows itself to be agile in the forest.* On the fourth day they passed a caravan of light carts heading the other way.

"Food coming up to our towns," explained Thord. "We give 'em metal 'n' gems 'n' t'ey give us dried, smoked 'n' pickled foods—'n' especial fish." They exchanged greetings with the traders, all of them Human, as two groups in passing do, and both moved on without pause. On the end of the fifth day they saw ahead of them the river with the small keep nearly across it that marked the ford that led across to Evilhalt.

Chapter IX

Ayesha

A *polite invitation to take kaf with the Princess Miriam, brought to you by a well-dressed and deferential slave with a guard, is not one you can easily refuse.* As she went, thoughts whirled through Ayesha's head. *The princess is—indirectly at least—my patron, even if I have never met her before. The Princess has argued against the traditions of the Caliphate that restrict our sex and has said that more use should be made of its women.*

That caused the tongues to wag and some of the older and more conservative men to rant and rail against it. I have heard them talking angrily to my father on the subject. That the Princess had been able to do this was only possible because of the ambiguity of her position due to her foreign birth outside of the mountains, her diplomatic marriage into the Caliph's family and her ability as a mage. That she is the granddaughter, or something—no one seemed sure exactly what, of the ruler of the vast empire to the east didn't hurt either. Even the most zealous Mullahs are reluctant to disturb the recently made peace with Darkreach by calling her a blasphemer.

All know that a new prosperity is blowing through the Caliphate and now the blood of its sons need no longer run as freely as it once did to keep the Caliphate independent. Now the Dar al-salaam, the house of peace, could grow as the time when over half of all men died in Al-jihad al-Akbar, the Great Struggle, was finished—at least for now. It could, after all, be only a pause.

My current life is partly as a result of this—at sixteen I am the first fully-fledged female religious soldier in a culture where most prosperous adult women are kept secluded and seen only by their relatives. Despite the opposition of several of my teachers I have taken the vows and am now pledged to serve the Faith and the Caliph as its voice, to the death in any capacity that is demanded of me as a Ghazi, a Holy Warrior. Apart from that I am free to act as I will—including the right to freely move about the Caliphate and beyond. This right is something that few women have, especially high born ones such as me.

I always wanted to break out of the restrictions imposed on me as a woman by custom. Now I have done it.

So, it comes to pass that I am now being led through the palace by a female servant. I have to resist the urge to stop and stare at the rich carpets on the walls and the marvellous mosaics and carved plaster around them and on the ceilings. My senses are open however. Cool marble under foot, occasional scents of sandalwood, of orange and rose, deferential servants—I am in the Alhambra; the palace, after all.

Everyone in the Caliphate has seen beautiful carpets and prayer rugs, there are many in my parent's home, but the ones here are marvellous and beyond compare. She was led past the public rooms and through a pair of huge bronze doors guarded by grim-faced men, one of whom she recognised from training. They exchanged greetings by finger language as she was taken through the door.

There was an immediate change in the atmosphere. *Even more than before, my nose is soothed by the smell of rose, orange, and other scents and the furnishings have become even more luxurious, if that is possible. The sound of small children and women's voices tells me where I am.* She felt her feet disappearing in rugs that now covered the floor as well as the walls. She heard songbirds trilling in cages. Small tables of precious woods and polished brass stood around. Cushions of silk could be seen in rooms to the side through rich hangings. Servants moved silently.

I am in the private women's section of the palace. All the women that I can see have bare heads and uncovered faces. Ayesha reached up and dropped her veil and pushed back her headscarf. She was led onto a veranda looking out over the city of Dimashq. *It has a filigreed wall so that the women can look out and the breezes can come in, but no one on the outside can see in. On the veranda are two low couches covered in silk and sitting on one of these is a woman who must be the Princess.*

The tales told of her do no justice. She is easily the most beautiful woman that I have ever seen. She has very pale blonde hair, almost white, and eyes of brightly burnished bronze. In the shade of the veranda they seem to glow as if they are made of molten metal. Ayesha salaamed and the Princess motioned her to sit on the other couch. She clapped her hands and two servants appeared, one bearing kaf and two cups, and another bearing two trays covered in rakis lacoum and baklava, each one with a finger bowl, followed her. In turn, a faint increase in the general aroma of roses and oranges followed in their wake.

Three other servants followed with small tables of wood. Each of these had designs inlaid in them done with metal, ivory and semi-precious stones. Two tables were placed in front of the princess and Ayesha, and the third put between them where either could reach. They were served, then the servants inclined their heads and left without a word.

Ayesha waited. *The Princess is looking at me as most people would look at a horse before buying it, measuring it to see if it is capable of the tasks you need it for. This makes me nervous. The Princess keeps looking at me over the cup as she takes some kaf and sips.*

"Eat and drink, these are not here for decoration. You are here as my guest," said the princess, finally, in a musical voice. Ayesha took a cube of the lacoum, its pink jelly coated in fine sugar and starch dust and smelling of roses. She took a nibble. *It is delicious. As expected, the cooks of the Caliph are so much better than those of my father.* Next, she sipped some kaf. *There is the faint scent of cardamom and a hint of a peach aftertaste. It is far finer than even I am used to.*

The Princess spoke again, "How was your training?" she asked.

"Hard, O Illustrious One, but nothing that I could not learn. I was the best at many of my classes. My instructors found it hard as well but, like me, they learnt." *I may sound a bit smug about that.*

"How have your family taken your choice?"

"They are torn, Most Illustrious. My mother and grandmother would like to see me with a husband, even as a third wife as I was previously destined, and raising children. They worry that I might never find a man to marry me now or that I might die or never have children. I point out that it will occur as Allah wills, even if I were to marry. My brothers are all dead and my father does not know whether to be ashamed that I have rejected tradition by being allowed to choose as I have and rejecting a woman's role, or proud that he has raised a Holy Warrior. I think that perhaps pride is winning. He has no sons to take over from him as Sheik of Yāqūsa and his brother, my uncle, will succeed him. Like my sisters, I would have just been a minor wife for someone. Instead I have managed to break away from that and now I think that he is starting to see me instead as the inheritor of his legacy although I am but a woman."

"And yourself?"

I must keep eyes downcast and voice demure. "Before Allah the Wise, I am very humbled and thankful for this chance. I am happy and eager to perform my work and to do whatever the Caliph, the Voice of Allah on this world, requires of me."

"I am very glad to hear that." The Princess paused and changed her tone to a less conversational one. "I cannot say how, but it has come to my attention that my beloved cousin Theodora has left her home in Ardlark. I believe she will leave for the west to seek adventure. If she comes in this direction, I can look after her, but if she goes elsewhere, I cannot. The Granther, whom you call Hrothnog, may decide to accept her leaving or he may decide that she can tell Darkreach's enemies too much and decide to eliminate her.

"I asked for your services, and the Caliph has graciously consented. I want you to find her and protect her from any harm, including from our joint ancestor, if need be."

Ayesha shuddered inside at the idea that she could be set in a personal battle against the infidel mage-king. *My training does not allow my fear to show. I have been taught to think of him as the immortal servant of the Seytanyi, and yet his grandchild sits before me and has accepted Allah, praise to his Name.*

"I think she will most likely leave Darkreach through the Gap and go to Evilhalt. You will go there as fast as I can get you there. I have decided that you should pose as an escaped slave and become her close servant. I think that she will accept a woman without question more easily than she will accept a man. This is a very dangerous course. You can tell no one you meet of your real nature and you will be in constant danger." The princess sounded pleased with herself and her scheme.

Of course she is pleased. She won't be the one in peril.

"If any of our people hear of your cover tale they will, of course, most likely attempt to capture or kill you. However, I think that it is also the best way to gain Theodora's trust. She will not be looking for an escaped servant, a slave, to be a guard set after her." The Princess paused. "If she does not reach Evilhalt within a month of you leaving here you are to return through Kharlsbane and the Darkreach Gap, seeking information of her and her fate." She paused again. "Are you willing to do this?"

"If it is the Caliph's will, the choice of the Voice of Allah on this world, then it is my will." *I wonder what will come next and how I should adapt to such a role. I am skilled at disguise and trained as a medic and an alchemist dealing with killing and curing potions. The skill with disguise should suit me for work as a lady's servant as I know well how to skilfully use makeup to effect. As well as what I have learnt growing up, I have also been coached even further as an entertainer. Now I can sing, dance, tumble, juggle and tell stories as if I am a professional. It has always been thought that this is where I can best serve, concealed under a possible target's eyes as a tavern slave, so this part of the deception will be natural to me.*

"Good," the Princess said, in a settled tone. "Here are some instructions from the Caliph to give to the armoury," she handed over a note to Ayesha. "Now then, let us enjoy this food and kaf and talk more of your training before you return home. Enjoy what little I can give in thanks to you. You must say farewell to your family, as you may never return. Tell your father that, if you do return and you choose to leave your service and marry, and the man you want cannot raise a suitable mahr, then I will pay it, whatever it may be. Tell your mother and grandmother they can make any arrangements they wish and I will support them and remember that, should you so choose, the Caliph has another son as yet unwed. He is young and could do with a strong wife and there are no suitable obvious ones. He is a lot younger than you but..." and she shrugged.

It sounds like I could be away for some time. The two spent the rest of the afternoon talking and eating.

For a short time, under the prompting of the Princess, Ayesha became a young girl. *Something I gave up to enter my training.* Her fingers were often sticky with the little rosettes of baklava, sweetened with imported sugar rather than the honey of the common people. She ate the rakis lacoum, flavoured with roses and oranges. *The princess encountered many of the same things I did; trapped within a traditional upbringing, not able to do what she wanted until a chance had opened up and she seized it. I need to keep my thoughts to myself, but I am saddened that, while I was able to gain a vocation, the Princess has only been able to escape her fate through marriage, even if it is one she welcomes. I am, however, glad that at least the princess has used her background to bring change to her adopted land.* Feeling full of sugar energy, she was eventually left to prepare. Ayesha had until the next eve to select what she would take and to say farewell. *I am lucky that my parents are currently in Dimashq. At least I am able to see them to bid farewell.*

Once she left the Princess, Ayesha took the note straight to the armoury. *I am being deferred to in a manner I am not accustomed to.* Her training naturally made her proficient with the weapons of stealth, so she selected an array of throwing knives, which she could also juggle, and several daggers, all different in shape and purpose. All of these had worn sheaths and were not new themselves, none were too good a quality, but all were enhanced for additional damage. *Knives are an assassin's weapon, but they are also those of a servant and they are the type of thing that a servant might steal before running away.*

I hope that none will see the special blades that I have selected to go into the bottom of my pack until I need them. She also selected a plain horse mace, its grip rough and not likely to slip within her hand, a recurve bow in a belt case and a belt quiver of fifty shafts. *If I am fighting openly in more than self-defence, I will most likely be on a horse—the getting of which will have to wait until I arrive at my destination.* She added two thumb rings and a few spare strings. None of these were magic but all were of competent workmanship. *It is hard to turn down some of the items I am being shown, but they will not fit with my cover story.* For the same reason, she took no armour.

Going back to her parent's house in Dimashq, she sought a meeting and told them that she was going away on a secret and important mission under the orders of the Caliph. *Naturally they ask no questions, but I can see that pride has definitely won out in my father. The old man's beard cannot conceal his smile.* She also conveyed the Princess' instructions about her marriage prospects. *They both reacted badly to the idea that a Sheik's daughter might need help in finding a marriage, until I mentioned the Caliph's as yet unwed youngest son. My mother has not been thinking of anywhere near that good a connection and her eyes are wide.* She took her leave as her parents began an animated conversation as if she had already returned home as a victorious hero and decided to forsake her career. She did not disabuse them that she had no plans in this direction at all, but simply left them to their happy musing to go and pack. They scarce noticed her leaving.

Packing is easy. I am an escaped slave travelling on foot. Just a worn set of travelling clothes to wear, a warm over-robe and my dancing and performing clothes will complete my main packing. Throw in a small medical kit, a spoon, bowl and cup, my finger cymbals—zils, juggling balls, a supply of travel food, including dried fruits and nuts and cheese, and some water skins, and my backpack is nearly full.

She tied a length of old and strong rope to the outside. At the last moment, she added a supply of powdered kaf and date sugar and a battered old ibrik. *I have many useful skills, but cooking is not one of them and I will have to rely on food bought along the way, but at least I can have kaf.* Thinking of the Princess, she placed some rakis lacoum in the ibrik where it would not get squashed and went to say a perhaps last goodbye to those of her sisters and half-sisters that were available.

The next evening, upon again meeting the Princess, Ayesha was given a purse. *It is made of plain leather with a brass ring on a loop to hold it closed. Smooth and worn, dark green, once good, not too fat and with a good supply of old coins such as could have been saved or more likely stolen. Now—I have been wondering all day how I am supposed to start my journey.*

She became sure when she was taken by the Princess to the loft over the Caliph's stables. *I am to be delivered by carpet.* Being the daughter of a sheik, admittedly near the last one and from his third wife, she had, of course ridden on one before, but only to make lazy circles in the sky around Yãqũsa. *This time, from what I remember from maps, I will be travelling for most of the night.* She was introduced to the mages who would take her—one for the trip there and one for the trip back. The instructions she was given by them were simple: stay in the middle of the rug unless told otherwise; secure your baggage to yourself so that it would not blow off and to warn them if she felt ill. She quietly bade farewell to the Princess and obediently mounted the carpet.

The trip itself is—interesting. The mage in charge is guiding the carpet by a means I cannot see as we go north over the Caliphate of the Believers. He is obviously following an agreed path, as the second mage sometimes consults an object in his hand and leans forward to correct his colleague's direction. Despite my beauty and the importance of how I am being sent, both looked at me with some distaste and neither one will talk to me. It seems that either they do not like women, or at least do not like them taking the work that they think properly belongs to a man. I have met many of both sorts before.

Mountains are slipping past, initially just on the left, but then on both sides. I am wishing that I brought warmer clothes or a thicker robe with me. The chill of the mountains is made worse by the wind created by our passage through the air. I am surprised. The carpet, a large military one with upturned ends, travels much faster than the small one I was on for my previous short trip, and is very solid. With no give in its fabric, it is like sitting on a mat on a stone floor. At least it is a feeling I am very familiar with from my training and I am quite relaxed sitting there.

We travelled through the night. It is at least two hours since we departed and I presume that is the ridge south of the Darkreach Gap looming in the distance far ahead. The second mage made a major correction to their direction and they took a wide turn to the left and began slowly descending through the mountains. The landscape below them changed from mountains to hills to forest. To her left there was visible a twinkle of light where, in the middle of the night, a large fire burned. *We are too far north for it to be the Swamp. That must be from one of the hidden Bear-folk villages.*

A hand of hours passed and Ayesha could see the flat expanse of Lake Erave reflecting the moons ahead of her as the carpet moved down almost to the level of the treetops, its mages seeking the trail north from Haven and a spot to alight. A break in the trees appeared ahead, then a clearing below. They moved slowly forward to veer off when the light of a fire revealed that it was occupied. *A meeting with traders while alighting from a carpet will destroy the secrecy of my mission.* After circling around they continued up the road. *The next clearing is seemingly unoccupied. The mages are consulting something in their hands—they are nodding to each other in confirmation.*

On reaching the ground Ayesha removed her gear and said goodbye to the mages and thanked them. They merely nodded brusquely at her words. *Because of the role I have chosen I am used to this behaviour from many men, if they do not behave worse.* She sighed. *I wonder if things will be different among the Kāfirūn, the Unbelievers.* She moved to the side respectfully. The mages changed positions and, without a backward glance, word or gesture the carpet lifted and headed back towards the mountains.

Suddenly I feel very alone. Around me the noises of the forest night, which I hope are normal ones, are heard. As she moved away from the clearing, she felt the fallen leaves soft underfoot. *It is not a good idea to just curl up on the ground as food for any passing carnivore.* Ayesha started to climb a tree. Her weapons and pack made this awkward, so she stopped and tied them to one end of her rope. The other went around her ankle. This time the climbing was easier. She had selected an old oak and, with the aid of her daggers she was soon up in its lowest and widest branches. She pulled her gear up with her and was soon snugly nestled into the junction of branch and trunk, falling asleep. *The cool night air of the lowland woodlands is positively balmy after my earlier passage through the chill mountain air.*

A yesha awoke to the sound of birds singing and a pale autumn sunrise, which laid dappled patterns through the turning leaves. She waited a while, just listening. *Apart from the birds there is nothing to be heard.* She peered down at the ground and around. *Nothing is to be seen.* She lowered her gear on the rope and, throwing the other end over the branch descended to the ground before reclaiming and coiling her rope. After praying, she donned her weapons, ate some food, and headed north along the track, walking briskly along with bow in hand. *My senses are alert. They need to be. I am a single person, moving alone in an unknown land.*

After a while she came upon a couple of men with a packhorse. *From their dress and weapons, they are probably hunters. They are similarly alert and a single armed Muslim woman on the track to their town is obviously not what they are accustomed to seeing.* Although they had pale skin, they greeted her politely and well enough in Hindi and she answered in the same tongue. They were happy to tell her that Erave Town was only a three hour fast walk away and she would come on the first hamlet, where they lived, very soon. *It is a bit of a shock that, despite their surprise, the Kāfirūn men are more polite to me than the mages who brought me here.*

The village proved to be very different from the places she was used to.

For a start, there is no wall around it. The houses appear to have timber frames with dirt packed into them and then painted, instead of solid stone walls. Lastly, the roofs are covered in straw rather than slate. They are easy prey to any attackers here. Raiders or someone with The Burning still running through their body could set fire to them so easily. There are also both men and women visible. Most of the women wear dresses with no trousers underneath and have, at most, straw hats. Many are working bareheaded. They are looking with curiosity at my hijab and veil as if I am the odd one.

Still, they don't appear unfriendly. The small children stared as she drew near, but no one drew them back and some even smiled at her. She nodded her head back at them. *To my left, I can see a broad river. It has to be the Rhastaputra, which flows down from the mountains and the lake to Haven and the sea. Ahead of me is more forest.* As she kept walking the forest proved to be only a narrow belt of a hand of six hundreds of her small paces of trees. *Beyond it are grasslands and then fields and then Erave Town standing on its peninsula where the deep green-surfaced lake flows into the river. Boats are clustered in the river in the lee of the town.*

Ayesha walked in through the fields where men and women worked together. *Their skins are mainly brownish, but whether this is natural or from the sun is hard to tell, although the pale hair on some gives an indication.* She went past a low wall and then a caravan campsite, which had a large assemblage of wagons and a few horse lines. Then she went over a deep dry moat that looked, from the thick wooden gates at its ends, as if it could be quickly flooded if need be.

The town walls were solid stone and mounted ballistae and the entry was through a stone arch with metal clad doors. *Armed guards are at the gate. They look curiously at me, but on stopping me only ask, in Hindi, if I know where I am going. They do not seem very concerned that a single small woman could be a threat to their town, despite my arms.* "I would be most grateful if you honoured men could direct me to a place to stay." They sent her down a street, past an unbeliever's temple, and turning left towards the docks to find the Fisherman's Arms. *I remember that it is often said, mainly by fishermen, that Allah does not deduct from a man's span the time that is spent fishing.* Thinking about this and the speculation that the people in the town are perhaps long lived brings a smile to her lips. The first floor of the inn is good solid stone, but the next two above it are timber, and it looks as if there are even rooms in the roof.

Ayesha took this in and, with an appearance of timidity, entered the inn and asked to see the owner. A large smiling man with a thick black beard and black hair with brownish skin, this time with a descent that was at least part Havenite, appeared wiping his hands on his apron as he approached. He introduced himself as Anani Roy.

"Oh Venerable Sir, I ask blessings upon your house. I need a place to stay the night and have little money." *His smile just tightened—now to sell myself before he denies me out of hand.* "I can pay for a night if needed, but I am a skilled entertainer. I can sing, tell tales, juggle and dance the dances of my people."

His smile just broadened again. "I was hoping, oh munificent one, that I might trade with you a night's entertainment in this most noble establishment for a bed and some food?"

The innkeeper is thinking. He is looking me up and down, trying to gauge how shapely I might be under my travel clothes. "Do not worry. I have been told that I am most comely and I dance well and men will pay attention to me."

The innkeeper nodded. "Very well," he said. "If you draw in enough business from the caravans and the boats then I will find you a bed and food. If you do not, then you must pay. Is that fair?"

"It is, oh Patron of the Poor. I thank you profusely. However, I dance best if there is music and something to give a beat. Is there anyone in this most magnificent town that could do this small service for me?"

"Actually, there is. Hamid is our cobbler here and he comes from your land. He plays a stringed instrument and his son plays a sort of drum. I will send a boy to see if they will come here for this. They don't drink, so they rarely are seen in my establishment, but they usually do not mind playing there if they are asked by someone."

"Thank you, oh Most Magnificent Solver of Problems. I cannot dance in these clothes. Is there somewhere that I can change and safely leave my things?" Ayesha indicated the weapons on her belt.

A girl was called over and she led Ayesha up two sets of stairs before lighting a lamp and pulling a concealed rope that revealed a ladder that rose into the roof. She was led to a small room, obviously one that was meant for a servant. *The bed is small, but it looks clean and the air smells like clean straw. There is no smell of mould or of unwanted animals. A huge feather quilt covers the bed. This speaks much on the temperature in the roof in winter. There is also a small table with a jug of water on it and just visible under the bed a pot.*

Ayesha thought hard about how to dress tonight. *If I were to dance in public at home I would wear something on my head and a small bodice over a light gauze shirt. However, I suspect that this audience will not be used to the subtleties of movement that people would watch for at home. I will be daring and leave off the shirt. This leaves me in a low pair of loose trousers and a bodice with a lot of bare skin and, while I have sometimes danced in this way before women, I am nervous about doing so before men.*

Will they think that I am a fallen woman? I have to be prepared to reject any unwanted advances. She also discarded her headscarf but kept her veil. *I am not going to doff that yet.* Her brown hair she gathered loosely in a clip at the rear of her neck. After washing and prayer she outlined her eyes in kohl. She then put on her belt of silver bells and picked up her pack, now with only her zils, knives and juggling balls in it. With a swish of the hips and a faint jingle as she walked, she returned downstairs.

Anani Roy introduced her to Hamid and his son. *Hamid's eyes widen at my appearance, but his son shows no reaction, beyond appreciation. He must have been born outside the Caliphate and does not understand how a decent woman should dress.* Her face colouring, she profusely apologised to Hamid and explained her clothes. He looked around and nodded and introduced her to his son, Ibrahim. "I am a favoured freed slave who has been given leave to see the world and bring back some new entertainment." *Hamid looks dubious, but we are soon involved in preparing to show our combined skills to the unbelievers.* Hamid played an oud, its long, bent neck rising from a timber base with a rounded back. Ibrahim had a riq; a small hand drum with cymbals built into it that could provide a more varied range of sounds than just a simple drum.

Ayesha opened on the tiny stage with a dance. By the time she had finished it, caravaners were scurrying back to their campsites to return with others. As the evening wore on Ayesha displayed all of her skills, even bending backwards to stand on her hands and walk about on them. Money clattered as it started to appear on the small stage in a corner of the main room. *There are 'chinking' noises as coin is hitting coin instead of just timber. We three Muslims are the only ones that seem to be imbibing water in the whole room. Anani, presiding over a rowdy chaos, which only goes quiet when I sing or speak, has a grin that grows broader as the evening wears on. That I will have a free place to sleep tonight is sure.*

Discovering that one caravan was from the Swamp, she sang a bawdy song in Faen. *They respond with the tinkling applause of much more money hitting the stage.* Seeing that a couple of guards were obviously Khitan with topknots, long moustaches and shaved heads, she sang a song of the plains and the tents in their language. *They are nearly crying.* Most of the songs and stories she sang or told in Hindi as everyone there seemed to understand it to some extent, and it was the tongue of the town. She juggled balls and knives and all of these activities went well, but the best response was to her dancing. She received several offers for 'private' dances, but these she declined so politely that the makers did not object.

By the time the caravan masters had driven their animal tenders and guards back to their campsite and the boat owners had removed their sailors and rowers, the three entertainers had collected a sizeable amount of money and Anani had brought them all large platters of food without asking for any money. *I am sure that what is before me is not halal, that is going to be impossible out here, but at least it does not seem to contain any forbidden meats—at least that I can see. Hamid and Ibrahim are eating heartily.* They divided the money and Hamid was so dazed by the amount that he had received that he started discussing with Ibrahim and Anani whether they should entertain more often at the inn and indeed whether Hamid's wife could teach his daughters how to dance. *Tonight they have made more money for the family than Hamid usually makes in several days making shoes.* After thanking both father and son Ayesha left them to their discussion and retired to bed. That night she slept soundly.

Ayesha was woken by a knock on the door as a serving girl told her that breakfast was ready. After prayers she dressed and packed her few belongings before finding a large breakfast. *and, wonder of wonders, kaf,* waiting for her. Anani was there and tried to convince her to stay in Erave Town and to work for him, but Ayesha declined, without closing the door completely, saying that she may be back some day, 'Inshallah'.

After eating she was on her way. *I even have some extra food for the track. Even though I can easily afford to take a boat, I will walk. Despite the danger of travelling alone in an area I do not know, it fits my cover story better to walk and I can more easily pretend to be poor this way.*

Two days of travel followed in the still woods filled with dappled light, many of the leaves turning orange around her. She stopped only to attend to nature, pray, eat and sleep. She did the last in a tree of course, one that was near a watercourse. She overtook a trader with packhorses and slowed to walk with him for a while and they passed three groups of carts going the other way as they went. *It seems that this road is well travelled and so should present few problems.*

The second night on the track, at some time after midnight, her senses woke her. *Something is moving below me, moving quietly and trying to be stealthy, but not trained in how to do it correctly. Most people would not have heard, but I am trained to be alert.* She looked down to see two figures moving around. *Both are Human shaped, but they are black, hard to see, despite the moon. They are not black as the dark skin of the people from the southern isle are supposed to be, they are black—the colour of night. They are sniffing the air—searching.* One said something to the other. *I can see moonlight reflected from a mouthful of teeth. These are not real people but Deodanth—eaters of men—children of some ancient evil.*

In the light of the fullness of Terror, the larger moon, I see the two shapes casting around. She ran through what she remembered from her lessons. *Deodanth are solitary, use weapons when they can get them, never wear clothes, have very tough and completely hairless skin and eat their victims raw—often while they are still alive, removing choice bits to snack on from a pinioned captive. At least they are supposed to die as easily as men, if you can hit them—but they are fast moving and good with weapons. Each of these has a sword and shield and both are naked. It is very bad luck to find one, let alone two of them together.*

Ayesha thought on her situation. *It seems impossible to just stay still. The Deodanth are searching around and it is simply a matter of time before they include the branches of the trees. Trying to string my bow will make far too much noise and they will be up the tree to get me before it is done and I can fire.* Circumstances let Ayesha make a decision. The male was moving underneath her perch, while the female was ten paces distant and facing away. Quickly she drew two throwing knives and threw them at the female's sword arm as a distraction. Without waiting to see the effect, although a bestial scream told her that she had hit something, Ayesha drew two more daggers and, as silently as she could, dropped behind the male. *I hope that his kidneys are in the same place as they are for Humans.* She struck home with her blades. He had sensed her landing and was just beginning his turn as she struck. Both daggers drove home, plunging their full length in his vitals as Ayesha twisted them around before pulling them out. The Deodanth spun around, his legs already wobbling as Ayesha raised her left dagger to parry his blade. It struck weakly and as she tried to bind it with her left-hand dagger, she closed and thrust up under his chin with her right-hand blade. His scream ceased as the point grated on the bone inside his skull and hot blood gushed over her hand. He collapsed at her feet, almost carrying her blade with him as he did. A metallic smell filled her nostrils.

She had just pulled her blade clear when she saw the female approaching. *She has thrown aside her shield and now grasps her sword in her left hand. Her right arm is hanging limp at her side. It has my blades still in it. I must have severed something in the limb with my cast.* The woman's jaws gaped as she approached. *Allah, the Strong, aid me. Inside are multiple rows of the white pointed triangles of her teeth, strong and ready to rend. She is making a noise that may be a language or may just be a scream.*

Ayesha stepped around slightly, reversing her blades to lie along her arms. *The male's body is now a minor impediment to the female's attack.* As the female closed Ayesha feinted forward and then moved back, hoping to upset the female's timing. *It worked. She has tripped slightly on her mate's body. That is enough.* "Allāhu akbar." She leapt forward, trapping her opponent's blade with her own two and driving her knee upwards hard into the female's groin before carrying the sword away from her to her right. The creature howled and winced. This move freed Ayesha's right dagger to slash across the female's throat before reversing her movement and bringing the blade back to plunge deep into the muscles at the junction of neck and shoulder.

The scream stopped, turning into a gurgle as blood gushed from the wound. *It is obvious that she is dead. It is not obvious either that she knows this, or that she wants to accept it. She is trying to make her damaged shoulder work, to free her larger blade and to strike at the same time.* Ayesha withdrew her blade from the shoulder, changing her grip again to a blade-forward style and plunging it towards the Deodanth's heart beside her breast. The female's efforts grew weak and her eyes glazed and she slumped to the ground, almost on top of her mate.

It is the first time that I have actually had to fight outside of training and my knees feel weak, but now I know that at least my training has worked. Once I made the decision to throw and drop to the ground everything happened so quickly that I have not really had time to think. Everything was done on reflex and now two opponents, each one of them more powerful in a fair fight than I am, lie dead at my feet. The smell of blood is strong in my nose. The rush of combat is wearing off. I can sense my pounding heart. I have been liberally coated in blood and it is already starting to go sticky on my skin.

Recovering her throwing knives, Ayesha headed down to the nearby stream and, removing her blades, sheaths and belt, found a pool and immersed herself in it and began scrubbing. *The water is cool, but not as chilly as the mountain streams that I am used to.* She kept her eyes moving around in the dark—*there could be more.*

Feeling cleaner, but very wet and with no means to dry herself, she regained the rest of her gear and began to clean her blades, drying them on her robe before oiling and donning them. *I could try and go back to sleep again, but doing that while wet, even though the breeze is only light, is a good way to catch a chill.* Ayesha strapped the swords from the dead pair to her pack, strung her bow, and set out into the night. Hoping to dry off and to warm up at the same time, Ayesha walked a little faster than she normally would. *I need to keep my senses alert to anything that might approach me.*

Apart from the normal noises of a forest at night, it was quiet and it was not long until daylight. *I will keep going through the day.*

By the end of it Ayesha was feeling very tired. *I am going to camp early.* This time she selected a tree that was harder to climb, however the extra precaution was unnecessary as her sleep was uninterrupted. Except for traders on the road and, once, a pair of hunters, the next two days passed uneventfully as she passed through unfamiliar forest. Late on the second afternoon she began to come upon assarts, and then upon a hamlet with its fields. *It is in an earthen ditch and has an encircling mound. A wooden stockade is being built on top of the mound. The enclosure is old. It must have been meant for a much larger settlement that stood there before The Burning and it is only now being reclaimed for use.*

As the sun was nearing the horizon she came upon the fields east of Evilhalt, the river that protected the town, and then the strong stone walls of the town itself. The whole image was softened by the red light of the setting sun behind it. *I had forgotten that I have to ford the river and that I will be entering the town wet.* Bundling her weapons so that she could carry them clear of the water, she crossed. *The ford is wide and made of laid stone slabs so that the footing is good and even. Luckily the water only comes up to the top of my thigh, and I am not tall. It is a wide crossing, almost a bow's range across and the current is strong.* Eventually she began to rise out of the water as the ford rose to meet the first gatehouse on a small island.

Here Human guards speaking the language of the town, Dwarven, greeted her. She returned their greeting fluently. *They seem surprised.* She asked directions to the inn. Rather than supply them they called over a small boy, explaining that he had just brought their meal to them from the inn and would guide her there. *Their gaze lingers on my wet clinging trousers and outlined legs. I will ignore the embarrassment and just thank them and follow the boy. First, we go over a drawbridge and then through a smaller guarded gatehouse and into a long wide courtyard, walled on both sides and a death trap for invaders, before going through a third gate and, only then, into the town itself.*

It is a small but substantial town, one built largely of stone but with timber and plaster upper floors. However, the stone is left plain, and the timber and plaster are painted in plain black and white. There is a lack of the decoration that I am used to. No gardens and no fountains are visible and I cannot hear any water cascading behind walls. There are only the sounds of hammering and of people at work. She sniffed. *The village could also do with a street sweeper working in it.* Men and women walked around together and small children ran around and between them, all dodging animal waste in the streets. *The streets are sloped towards the centre where there is a stone ditch. It seems that the streets here are only cleaned by rain. I will have to be careful where I tread.*

Both the men and the women carry weapons. Looking around it seems the entire populace either wear a weapon or are close to where one has been leant against the wall of their shop or on a hook. I think that even a surprise attack here would likely fail. There is no sense of the imminence of attack— this preparedness seems to be just a normal part of the life of the town. She was led straight down the central street and past an infidel place of worship, then escorted into a substantial building on a corner and taken to see a large, bearded man.

The boy introduced her to the man in Dwarven, "Master Nobah, t'is be Ayesha. She be from t' Caliphate and wants a room."

The innkeeper is looking hard at me. *He sees a short and slender woman, veiled but well-armed, somewhat of an anomaly. His eyes flick to my mace and bow and they look out of the door at the hitching rail. He has realised that, while I am equipped to fight on horseback, I have no horse with me.*

"I do not just seek a room, Master. I also seek work."

The innkeeper's eyes widen slightly at my grasp of Dwarven. My accent might betray my origin, but the words and grammar are correct. What does he think Caliphate women are—uneducated?

"I have some money, but I am an escaped slave and must make my way in the world. Do you have entertainment here? My master had me trained in this."

"What do you do?" asked Master Nobah.

"I sing, I tell stories, I juggle and, in particular I dance our dances. You may have heard of them. I have been told that I am very good." She swayed a little as she said that and batted her eyelids.

He noticed and grunted, perhaps in some amusement. "Let me hear you t'en," he said. *Now to try hard to impress.*

Ayesha launched into a song in Dwarven about the defeat of Darkreach at this town.

After a few verses he said, "T'at be good, but we do not sing it now. We get too much trade from t'ere. Let me hear another."

Ayesha tried one in Hindi about love.

Master Nobah held up his hand stopping her. "Now tell me a tale."

I know just the short tale. She told a short funny story about a possibly mythical man called the Mullah Nas-ru-din and an inheritance and seventeen horses that had the innkeeper screwing up his face in thought as he followed it. When she finished Master Nobah laughed briefly at the solution.

"Now juggle."

Ayesha produced throwing knives from several unseen places and started to whirl them through the air.

Again, a hand was held up. "Enough. I'll give you a bed and meals for t'night and you'll work in t'tavern. We'll see if you attract customers. You get to keep all t'at people give you and after tonight we'll talk again. Be you happy with t'at?"

"Yes, most munificent Master. I have one request. Do you know of anyone who is skilful with a hand drum of any sort?"

"Yes, why do you ask?"

"Because, oh provider to the poor, it is hard to dance without one. You have to keep the rhythm in your head, and no one else can hear it from there. Also, almost all songs sound better when a beat is added behind them."

Master Nobah beckoned to a serving girl. "Take Ayesha up to one of t' top rooms and let her unpack and t'en take her to see Howard. If he be not busy, and I don't t'ink that he be, t'en tell him to get his bodhran and to do what she tells him to do."

Chapter X

Hulagu

Hulagu stood still and drank in his surroundings. *The sky is pale blue and clear, rising as a dome above the flat grasslands that lie beneath. Wisps of smoke rise from centre of the ger, the circular hide and flannel tents of my people, and a subdued babble of children, sheep, goats, chickens and, indeed, everything else in the camp can be heard. This is the day that marks me having seen seventeen years come and go. I have been initiated into the tents for a full five years. Now it is time for me to leave my tuman and set out on my Year of Discovery, my wanderjahr to go where chance and curiosity lead me, and so find out more about myself—perhaps even to visit the clans with which my own has blood feud. Rather than just wander the plains, as most do, moving from one tuman to another and often finding a partner, I have been feeling a pull to the east—to see the mountains and the forests.*

Standing on a rise above the camp with an ovoo, a shrine of stones, beside him, Hulagu looked around. *I have already left the blue cloth of a traveller on it and circled it three times. The wind that I feel on my cheek can be seen bowing down the ample grasses of the plains, carrying my prayers with it. Below, in a sheltered shallow dip in the plain, the ger of my tuman spread around the start of a small creek. It emerges bubbling cold and crystal clear from a spring in the rise I am standing on and falls rapidly down the short slope to form a small stream that winds away between the low swellings of ground. Wisps of smoke rise from the cooking fires of dried dung. They show that the evening's feast is being prepared. Spread out around the camp the children are cheerfully riding home from a day spent looking after the tuman's herds of fat-tailed sheep, long-horned and shaggy cattle and tough horses. A chorus of bleating and lowing rises from them and mixes with the cries of the children to mothers and siblings.*

Some carry buckets of milk from the mares and cows while others have bags of dung slung over the withers of their mounts. Although only children, all are armed, with a bow or sling at least, as the yearly truce for the Festival of the Dragon has not yet started. Raids aside, the plains still offer many non-Human predators which enjoy a plump sheep as much as the tribe.

Around the camp and sometimes stalking alongside the riders—oft near as tall as their ponies—stride the occasional dire wolf; the totem animal of our clan. Riding out to replace the children to watch the flocks at night are the young adults—a job I did myself until last night. Each is dressed warmly and is fully armed. Some wave and call out jests and greetings as they pass me by. They will miss out on the festivities tonight.

Overhead a soft blue sky trails pale pink clouds as the smaller moon, Panic, shines wanly in the east. There is a promise of a cool night, just right for mid-autumn. To the south, the very top of the vast bulk of the sacred Dagh Ordu, known to outsiders as The Rock, just shows itself on the horizon as a faint dark line. The ancient ruined city that crusted the top is invisible, as is The Dragon, which lives in a vast cavern there. It still slumbers contentedly. The time for its awakening at the autumn equinox has not yet arrived. It will then be roused and fed the herd of panic-stricken offerings that make up the heart of the festival, and are a part of the pact all of the tribes of the Kara-Khitan have with the gargantuan creature. Once fed and appeased it will return to sleep and think until the next year or until all the tribes agree on a need to wake it for its role as the destroyer of armies—the last defence of the Khitan.

In the legends, it has only been used once in this way. Because of The Dragon, Freehold, while still disputing the matter of grazing rights, no longer tries to spread its cities and towns into the domain of the Khitan. They no longer built new settlements to bind and choke the open grassland of the tribes but stay next to the rivers, and even then, they have their limits. Not even when the hordes of Hrothnog had pushed out of the Darkreach Gap had The Dragon been called, although it may have come to it if his armies had not been broken at the river and ford where was built the town that is now called Evilhalt. The Dragon has no name that is known to men. Well, to be honest, it probably has one that some of the elders know but it is, as befits the largest and oldest of its kind and even to its face, reverentially referred to in the third person.

I wonder if the new army of traders coming out of the Darkreach Gap will cause the townsfolk to change their town's name in deference to the increasing prosperity that the traders bring. Evilhalt has long been the key link for trade between the scattered northern and southern villages, strung along the coasts like beads, the Dwarves of the mountains and hills, the Khitan, the richness and arrogance of Haven and the fat complacency of Freehold. It has just assumed a new importance lately. Maybe the town will keep the name that it was given long, long ago as a constant reminder to the new and more peaceful invasion that trade is the only way that it will allow itself to be entered.

According to rumour, the inhabitants of the area around the ford spend even more time watchfully under arms than the Khitan do. Soon I will have a chance to find out as I intend to make Evilhalt the first town that I visit on my wanderjahr. The stories also say that if one searches hard in the woods you can still find many items left over from that great battle over two and a half thousand years ago. Sometimes the finders have to contest with the former owners over possession and sometimes it is with other dangers. Maybe I will spend some time searching the woods myself. I have a year to fill up after all and I am eager to start.

The bards tell tales of the frozen north where, although free, the people speak the speech of Darkreach and hunt with spears for fish that are many times the size of a ger. The tales say that these fish can swallow men whole and that the men can continue living inside the fish. The fish hunters are supposed to do this hunting in seas of ice mounted on hollow trees. I have heard tales of the lost city of the Dwarves. Lost twice it is, once to some fell beasts and then, during the plague century, even its location disappeared from memory. I have heard tales of the land to the east and the south, buried in the Swamp lands, where plants walk and anyone who ventures into their realm is hunted and eaten by them. Much has happened since the Great Plague, whole cities were burned as a part of the madness, most everyone had died, new creatures, or at least forgotten ones, are still being found in the wilder places and the world is almost born again. However much I love the tales, I refuse to believe in walking plants.

By the custom of the tribes, I now have a year of four hundred and thirty-two days, twelve full months of thirty-six days each, or two hands of months, each of which is a hand of hands of days ahead of me to find out how many of the tales that are told about the lands around the grass sea by the bards are true—if any are. In that time, I should be able to cover all of the lands west of the mountains that cut Darkreach off from the rest of The Land. I might even get into that strange land if I am lucky.

If trade is coming out, surely some should go in the opposite direction. After all, the Khitan are always popular with traders as guards. The town dwellers might sometimes think that our customs are odd and we try to keep away from their bad spirits, but we are the only people that all trust, if we have given our word, to fully keep it.

As the first notes of music and singing drifted up towards him, Hulagu took a last long look around the seemingly endless horizons that were the familiar home range of his tribe. He looked up at the darkling sky and headed down the slope to the ger of his family for his farewell feast.

Hulagu stepped into the well-trodden area between the ger, brightly lit now by all the means the tribe used; braziers smelling the pungent-sweet smell of dried dung, lights glowing heatless with magic, and even by smokily flaming torches soaked in tallow. He was greeted in turn by his adult family members, while the children played games around the edges.

Firstly, there came to him his adult cousins, aunts, and uncles, each with words of encouragement and tales of their own wanderjahr. Most gave him something to drink, mostly kumis, sometimes wine or a stronger drink plundered from Freeholders or traded from the villages far to the south of Dagh Ordu where the sea of grass met the emptier vastness of the bitter-salt sea.

I wonder if my travels will take me to that. All my life the most water that I have seen can be ridden across or, rarely after heavy rain, floated across clinging tight to my horse. I have heard that people travel on this water in giant hollow trees, bigger even than those used in the north but, much as I want new experiences, I am not sure that I am ready for that. With a horse under you, you know where you are going and what you are doing. You can even sleep on a mount and it will keep travelling. If you go to sleep on a floating tree, who will direct it and keep it afloat?

His mind was still wandering as he gave responses to his well-wishers, kissed aunties and girl cousins, hugged and joked with the younger men, agreed to follow the advice of his uncles and, back to his aunties again, promised faithfully not to take as bride someone they would not approve of. *The younger members of the tuman have already started beating drums, playing flutes, harps and dirge pipes, and begun dancing well before I have spoken to everyone.*

Eventually he reached Nokaj. *A familiar figure all through my youth, Nokaj is not only the senior shaman of the tuman, but also my grandfather. Age has him stooping a little now, with his long, once black hair now bound back in a grey pigtail from the top of his head. Amulets and magic talismans hang about him and a single green dragon is embroidered on the right side of his leather jacket and on each of his boots to mark his rank.*

Hulagu was surprised by how his grandfather greeted him. *Instead of the happy face of an elder seeing a younger off, he has a surprisingly grim expression as he speaks.*

"Hulagu, I must now tell you what I have seen in the wind and in my dream-trance," he said. "You must consider these words tonight and then reach a decision. You know that it is our custom that when a major decision must be made you must decide it both when drunken and when sober. The signs say that this is such a decision, not just for you, but also for the tuman, the tribe and possibly for all of the tents."

The Spirits have signs for me? "But, Grandfather, I am young and just setting out on a wanderjahr as the youths of the tribes have done ever since we were created by the sky spirits and set down on the plains. How could anything I choose to do be so important? Many have set out who are better riders than me, better trackers, mightier warriors, more in touch with the gods."

"My grandson, you know that you are the youngest child of my youngest child. Know also that you are the seventh son of a seventh son, all born living. Some regard this to be an auspicious birth. I know not why I have had these visions, but perhaps this is the reason. One way or another, this is a destiny that is fated for you. I just know that I have to tell you today your choices. You may choose to ride directly to a walled village on a river, which I believe to be Evilhalt. If you choose this path, then you are to brook no delay. You should also know that you may yet meet a person along the way, one who will be meant to join with you on your journey.

"The signs are unclear on this. Once you are there you should join a group of other young folk, from all over The Land, each of whom has left their people to travel, as you do. Do not despise them as folk of the walled places for, if you do accept this fate then you, as a group, will be the subject of many tests, as each member of the tribes must do when they become an adult, but different. Like our tribe members, if you fail the tests, then you will die. If you undertake this path and fail these tests, then I have a sense of great foreboding for us all. Eventually you will face a dire challenge and it is on the success of this that your geas will be fulfilled. This challenge is a great evil. I know little of it, but I do know that it somehow threatens to overwhelm us all." He paused and thought a little before continuing.

"You may also meet a woman, not of the tents, fall in love with her and marry her, but the signs are unclear on this. The dreams sometimes present us with forks in our paths. I have such a fork for you. If you do not choose this first path, I have also seen that you will live a long life both as a tribesman and as a father, without note and without being distinguished in any way, but happy. I am not sure that this way is the best for the tribes, but it is the safest for you. The choice is thus clear for you, you may have a geas and danger or you may have safety. What you decide to do is up to you. If you choose the first path, I think you should not reveal the destiny ahead to the others you meet until you fully trust them not to flee their course." He paused and looked around.

"Now you must go and see you parents, they have tokens of wandering and other things for you and only hold back out of deference to my age and to the fact that I speak so seriously to you. Remember, that you must get drunk tonight, that should be no problem, it never has been on such a night, and you must make one decision. I will speak with you tomorrow for your second choice." With these words Nokaj smiled and hugged his grandson fondly before he turned and went into his ger.

Hulagu next turned and saw his mother and father, and he was looking at them with fresh eyes. *Sparetha is tall for a Khitan woman. Her mother had been a thrall taken in a raid who had become a leman of a tribesman. Her still slender build conceals her strength. She is still a master archer and almost unsurpassed as a rider. Today, in concession to the formal leave-taking, she has put aside her normal riding leathers and wears a low-cut divided dress of dark-red silk with an embroidered waistcoat of golden dyed linen. The waistcoat has garnets sewn onto it, and a ruby hangs from a chain on her forehead with other rubies mounted in a network of fine golden chains around her throat and dangling into her cleavage. Her skin is lighter than is usual in the tribes, despite a life spent outdoors. Her eyes are green and straight, rather than the far more common dark and slanted eyes of the rest of the tuman.*

In her hands Sparetha holds the woven design of a ten-spoked wheel done in the twelve colours of magic. Each arm of the wheel denotes one of the tribes and, looking closely, one can see the totem animal of each tribe embroidered along its arm. As is traditional the top-pointing arm has the motif of a dire wolf done larger to denote the home tribe of the wearer.

"My son, here is the cover for your shield, so that all the tribes may know of your wanderjahr and make you welcome and give you immunity unless you should choose to remove it. Here also is a band marked the same to bind about your forehead. You are my youngest child and now, with your leaving, your father and I can relax and become ancients."

A mischievous smile played on her lips and her eyes twinkled to show her amusement with the idea.

She laughed. "What I really mean is that now you are all moved to your own ger, we can have ours to ourselves again." She batted her eyes at Hulagu's father, who grinned and patted her bottom as Hulagu blushed.

Parents should not be thinking about such things. It is wrong.

Togotak is shorter than his wife and his rolling gait and slightly bowed legs speak of a life spent in the saddle. Few riders are better than Sparetha, and Togotak is one. He has often joked that the only way that he could win her was to out ride her and Sparetha has never contradicted him in this. Togotak wears baggy golden silk trews of our Khitan pattern, standing the crotch comes down to the knees for its comfort under you in a saddle. His equally baggy shirt is red raw-silk and his waistcoat is made of white walla. Like me and most of the men around, his head is shaved, except for a braid coming from the top of his head and hanging down over his left ear. His cheerful face bears a scar down the left cheek from a sabre cut and the tip of his right ear is missing. This may be the last time I see my father look so happy.

"My son, you have always shown that you are more interested in the world outside the camp than in the camp, and its people." He held up a hand to stop Hulagu protesting, leaving him with an open mouth. "Do not say anything. This is often the case with our greatest hunters and warriors. Maybe while you are away you will add to the legends of the tribes. Your mother and I wished to give you something to mark this time that would best help you."

Here he reached behind his back, as if expecting something to be there. *It obviously isn't.* He clicked his fingers and Sparetha gave a start, lifted a cloth lying on the ground to uncover something and put it in Togotak's hand. Bringing it around the front he presented it to Hulagu.

"Take this. It is time you had a newer and stronger bow. Nokaj and I both crafted spells of accuracy into it and it shows some of your Uncle Tolan's best work in its construction. Your mother made you a full quiver of arrows to go with it."

The bow is a beautiful curved sinew and horn horse bow around a pace-and-a-half long. It has the typical long straight blackwood arms extending from its re-curved shape and when fully drawn would be only half-a-pace high. Many of the town dwellers cannot use these bows. In particular, they cannot master the thumb draw that enables a much higher rate of fire than can be had from their longer, single piece weapons that are near useless on a horse.

Hulagu took the bow. *Its grip feels right in my left hand, the waxed string is smooth and new.* "Thank you my parents. This is a beautiful gift and I will treasure it and remember and thank you every time that I use it. May I try it now?"

"Boys and their playthings," said Sparetha. "As they get older, their games just get deadlier. No, it is time for your leave-taking celebration. You will have enough time to try it as you set out. Besides, you should first use a horse bow when you are mounted."

"Yes," said Togotak. "Besides, I believe that Nokaj has set upon you a task. Go now, enjoy yourself and think on it."

Hulagu smiled and touched his forehead with the first finger of his right hand in respect. "You speak wisdom my parents. As always I obey." With that he bowed and, still carrying his bow to show it to his relations he went towards the others. He first sought out Tolan, a master bowyer, and thanked him for the workmanship. He then proceeded to display it until all had seen it, then unstrung it and put it away.

Hulagu enjoyed his celebration feast and got marvellously drunk but, just before dawn, while dancing in a circle with the other men, he paused. *Much as I love my family and their way of life, I have always wanted to see more of the world and what it can give. If I have a possible destiny ahead of me, I should take the chance it offers. Most people are never given the opportunity to have the bards sing of their adventures and I have this prospect in front of me.* Having made this decision, he threw himself into the celebration with renewed vigour. *It may be my last chance to enjoy myself this way with the tribe.*

He was nearly the last to collapse among the other bachelors—sleeping well clear of the ger on rugs, as was tradition in such cases.

A fter only a few hours' sleep he awoke to the warmth of the autumn sun with the feeling he was drowning. Spluttering and gasping for air he struggled to stay afloat to discover that he was on dry land. *Sparetha is pouring water on my face.*

"It is now time for you to break your fast and pack what you wish to take with you. This should sober you enough to make your second choice," she said. "Hurry though. Nokaj has been hopping from foot to foot waiting on an answer since dawn."

Even through the fog that was filling inside his head, Hulagu smiled at this unlikely thought and moved off to begin preparing to leave.

I could end up anywhere in this year and so I have to be prepared for the heat and dampness of Haven as much as for the bitter cold of the northern forests. As he was packing he thought on his decision of last night, the packing going almost automatically. By the time he was done, his saddlebags were bulging with items tied outside them and a pair of sacks tied across his horse as well. *I am starting to regret not having spent my money on getting a packhorse, but it is too late for that now.*

It was not until he was leading his horse towards his grandfather's ger that Hulagu realised he had already made his decision. *By choosing practical gear that will be useful away from the plains, instead of an array of fine clothes for showing off around the tribes my body has chosen to take the path of destiny instead of that of safety and comfort. It is now up to me to carry out what my body has already accepted and wants me to do.*

Nokaj was sitting cross-legged in the sun in front of his tent. *He has been smoking a pipe of Somniofulgio brought from Haven. The aromatic smoke still drifts sweetly on the air teasing the nose. From the smile on his face and unfocussed eyes it is obvious that he is in a trance—conversing with the spirit world.* Hulagu cast his horse's reins over its head, confident that the well-trained horse would stay nearby browsing, and sat down, with the patience of a shepherd, cross-legged opposite his grandfather to wait on his return. *It is dangerous to disturb someone whose soul is wandering. The shock might cause the body to lose focus and the soul may not be able to find it again.*

While he waited, the sounds and smells of his people around him, Hulagu reviewed his decision in his own mind. *Every way I look at it, I am comfortable with the decision that I have made. My way is clear. Now I wish that my head would stop pounding and that the light from the sky were not so bright.* He closed his eyes and waited.

The sun had nearly reached the zenith when his grandfather's eyes began to focus and he shook his head. "Ah Hulagu, you are here to tell me that your decision is to go on the quest are you not?"

"Yes grandfather."

"I was soaring as an eagle over the next few days," continued Nokaj, almost without noticing that Hulagu had spoken. "Something happened last night along your path. It is a terrible wrong and I must rouse the tuman to deal with those who committed it. It will not directly affect you, but as a result you will meet friendship and you will meet enmity. I cannot see in what form these will come to you, but they will come. It will not be from the same people. The friendship and the enmity may indicate that the first is one who is on the same quest as you—although they may not know this. The second is probably implacably opposed to your quest and may, indeed be the first test you will face."

"Do you know how many people I will meet? What tribes will they be from? I mean will my enemies be Bison?" The questions came tumbling out. The natural reticence of the Kara-Khitan tribesman to discuss the real spirit world when in the shadow world was overcome by what Hulagu was seeing happen in front of him.

Nokaj's powers as a seer are legendary but, even with him as my ancestor; it is overawing to see them practiced in front of me and, not about a general tribal matter, but specifically about myself and my future. It adds to my conviction that the choice I have made is the right one and increases my eagerness to be off—even if I am starting to feel myself unworthy of such an interesting future and just a little nervous.

"I can see little else," continued Nokaj reluctantly. "Something or someone, perhaps among the sky spirits, is casting a veil over time and fighting my efforts to see. In fact, there are two forces fighting. One is determined to twist things in its own path, but is not necessarily hostile. It just wants to hide what it does, but does not seem to have much ability in this. The other is definitely hostile and evil and responsible for most of the fog. It knows what it is doing and it actively fights any attempt to see its actions.

"Its presence is like a thick blanket over the streams of time. I can sense the shapes under the blanket, but I can see no detail. I should have seen what happened last eve well before now. It is in the lands of our tribe and so it is our responsibility. However, the people who committed the acts that I sense have travelled through the lands of other tribes and no one else along their way has even caught a glimpse of their evil or of the evil that has sent them. I was only able to see it briefly now for the blanket could only be lifted for an instant. It seemed that the attention of the power that blankets and smothers vision was elsewhere for a brief time.

"Now go and say your goodbyes. Do not head straight for Evilhalt. You must head north until you meet what you must meet and only then should you turn north and east to Evilhalt. I will try and keep track of your destiny through the thickness of the blanket. If you meet me in your dreams I will have words for you to heed. Now I must rouse the tuman." With that Nokaj unfolded himself and rose, hurrying to the hetman, Ordu's, ger. His body shows little effect from the herbs that he has smoked — they have all been burned up in his getting of this vision.

Hulagu touched his forehead and then rose and led his horse, Kurghiz, to where his parents waited by their ger. He told Togotak and Sparetha of his decision to follow his more dangerous destiny, come what may, and exchanged embraces with them both before respectfully taking his leave. *I may be nervous, but it is time to mount and ride away to the north.*

Hulagu looked back after a few paces. *Are those tears on my mother's face?* Togotak took her hand and leant over and said a few words to her.

He looked back from the first rise, near the ovoo. *The camp looks as if it were an ant's nest that has just had hot water poured on it. People are running everywhere, gathering horses and donning armour ready for combat. In the centre of all of the turmoil, my parents still stand silent watching me go.*

Having again circled the ovoo, Hulagu was soon swallowed up by the vastness of the plains. The seemingly endless grasslands rose and fell, as if subject to very long and very slow waves. *On a crest it seems like you can see forever; the horizon is broken by only the occasional tree or small clump of wattle or other shrub.*

The next crest may only be the height of a mounted man, but it takes half an hour of hard riding to reach it. Sometimes there are small outcroppings of weathered rocks and some shallow valleys have creeks or still ponds. Sometimes there are patches of olive trees, wattles or some other tree, sometimes a patch of mallee or blackberry or some other small shrub. Of people, there is no sign, although one who knows how to read the indications can see occasional signs of their passing.

Feeling tired from the night before, Hulagu decided to camp early for the night and take advantage of a nearby small creek and a patch of acacias, to give him cover. He unsaddled and rubbed down Kurghiz, giving him a small handful of grain and putting on his hobbles. He looked around his grove and laid a few snares before laying out his bedroll. Once this was done he climbed the nearest crest, making sure that he did not silhouette himself against the sky. He took a long look around, checking also the birds above and looking at the sky itself before going back down. *I see neither friend nor foe.*

Once at his camp he prepared a cold meal before wrapping himself up in his blankets and going to sleep, his weapons beside him, but with his bow unstrung. Hulagu was used to sleeping on his own when out hunting or tending flocks. *There may be people actively wishing me harm, so I should try to sleep lightly.* Light or not, his sleep was undisturbed by intruders or by dreams from or of his grandfather.

In the morning he awoke soon after first light when a squealing announced that one of his snares had caught a victim. While he was hurrying off to see what it was, a further noise announced a second snare had been successful. Finding a rabbit in each, Hulagu dispatched them and gathered his snares. As he went around the traps he saw the prints of many small animals, as well as the prints of a rare meerkat, which had avoided his sleeping area. *A look from the rise shows nothing visible moving on the plains around me. The air is crisp and clean and the sky cloudless.*

Returning to his camp, he packed up and cleaned his catch. After a light breakfast, he set out again. *It should be another quiet day on the plains.* He was not disappointed. Apart from the tracks of animals and old signs of other Khitan, the day was without event. He kept his bow strung out of habit and occasionally took a practice shot at different ranges, recovering each shaft he fired and only breaking one. *My father is right. I am ready to handle the extra pull of the new bow. The spells wrought into the bow make it more accurate, particularly at long range. My old bow and indeed all other bows normally lose accuracy when they make a long shot, my new bow doesn't seem to. This is an advantage.*

Each shaman has a limited number of charms that he can learn and use and this is a new one. I am sure that my grandfather or my father must have just developed it. I have never heard of either of them using it before. Admittedly it will be used again and again, but it is quite a complement to think that one of them has done this first for me.

The land rolled along under Kurghiz's hooves with the grass sea below parting before, and occasionally bowing to, the light breezes. Above all a light blue sky was peppered by an occasional puff of cloud scudding along from the southwest.

Changes in the light signal the approaching advent of dusk. *Some way ahead, there are two riders outlined on a crest. Interesting—they first appear to be looking for tracks or something on the ground, but on seeing me they have started moving towards me. They may either be friends or enemies, or indeed one of each.*

Hulagu grunted. *With two of them I have to put myself in a position to gain an advantage if they mean me ill.* Digging in his heels he sped up and rode faster towards the point where he had decided to spend the night. It was a place known to him as a common campsite, and there was usually a supply of fallen timber to burn there, as well as fresh water.

As I enter the low valley of the campsite I lose sight of the two. It is deeper here than the usual dip and rise and the trees in it cannot be seen from the nearby crests and the creek it contains is on the way to becoming a real stream. He rode up beside the brook's bed quickly towards the area of the fire pit, looking up at an ovoo on the skyline and checking the hills and looking for tracks. *The fire pit is long disused, although wood stands ready near it. It seems that I am the first person to visit here for well over a week. The rare grove of trees that runs up the hill from the campsite and provides the firewood seems to be free of movement, but I cannot be sure. I feel no sense of threat from it at any rate.*

After dismounting and tying his horse to a small tree branch, Hulagu stretched his body a few times to loosen the muscles that had been made tight by his ride. After that he had just enough time to innocently start looking like he was setting up a camp when the two riders rode into sight atop the low ridge ahead of him, less than a hundred paces away.

I have made sure that my preparations are more cosmetic than real—at need I can just jump on Kurghiz and ride him away without leaving anything important behind. Neither of the approaching riders show any sign of their tribe—something that is unusual on the plains where all proudly display their totems.

As the first at the campsite, by tribal custom, Hulagu became the host and it was up to him to either welcome the newcomers or, by not mentioning it, to force them to move on. *I am tempted to take the second course of action but, if the riders are simple travellers, then it would be needlessly offensive. Even worse, if they are those who may be my friends then I might destroy the friendship before it has a chance to form. On the other hand, if they are to be my enemies, a great Kha-Khan of the past, Khirghat, had supposedly once said that one should keep one's friends close, but keep one's enemies closer and it is better to know where they are than to risk them creeping up on me while I sleep. I notice that they are still looking around as they approach. It is as if they want to see if they are alone with me or if there are any others nearby. This makes me even more suspicious of their motives.*

I have misgivings, but I should go through the formalities. "I offer you the gift of hearth and water and may your sleep be safe and restful here. I am Hulagu of the Dire Wolves and I am on my wanderjahr."

The two men look somewhat surprised and there is an exchange of glances and a moment of hesitation before the older man speaks.

"I am Kitzez of the Bison, and this is Koyunlu, also of the Dire Wolves," *again there is hesitation before Kitzez states Koyunlu's tribe.* "We accept your hospitality and thank you for it. May prosperity attend upon you and yours."

I hear that, although his words are correct, he has spoken them hesitantly, as if he has not used them for a long time and they do not sit easily with his tongue. Luckily for Hulagu, both men immediately started to dismount. *I can master my surprise. Not only have I never met or heard of a Koyunlu who matches the one before me, but also the Bison and Dire Wolf clans are in a feud at present over some 'lost' stock and a few other matters that has continued for a few generations from when their lands had met. It is only a minor feud as our grounds do not meet now, but it is still sufficient to make it unlikely that two members of the different clans will travel together.*

All three began to unsaddle and make moves to set up camp. *I need to dissemble and seem less than I am. I will slow my speech a little so as to seem a little slow in the head.* "You are far from your tribe."

"We have been hunting and living for some time in the forests far to the east," said Kitzez, "and have only just decided to return to the land of the tribes. We travel slowly so as to find out what has been happening while we have been away."

That is an unlikely tale. Hulagu just grunted. *Wait—they have manoeuvred me to be standing almost directly between them.* He reached for his shield hanging from its place on the saddle. *Taking advantage of my main attention being on Kitzez's words, Koyunlu is half-turned and drawing his sword.* Hulagu was only just able to grasp and swing his shield around in time as the sabre lashed out at his neck. It made a meaty sound and his arm jarred as the sword lodged through the woven cover into the leather beneath that clad the shield and then into the timber at the core. Hulagu twisted the shield to try and keep a cross-pressure on the blade to keep it lodged where it was as he danced back away from the suddenly skittish horses.

I wish that Kurghiz were a warhorse to fight at my side. I am outnumbered and have to draw on all my skill against two older, and probably more competent, men. Koyunlu gave a hard jerk as Hulagu backed away quickly and the sabre wrenched free, unbalancing Koyunlu in the process. Kitzez is still drawing his blade and grasping a shield. *I can back up and draw my weapon. Because it has a long shaft so it can be used from horseback, my small-headed mace, as well as my slightly greater height and reach gives me a range advantage over the other two. I need it. Being back against the trees means that, if I am careful I will not have one of them attacking me from the rear.*

However, he was soon in the fight of his life. *Both of the pair are obviously more experienced in combat than I and, despite Kitzez cursing Koyunlu for acting too early, it is clear that they will eventually prevail. Their tactic is obvious. As in their first attack their object is openly to try and attack me from two sides, making me confront one of them while the other finishes their work. Despite my best efforts, it seems that they are about to succeed in killing me, and I still don't know why I am being attacked.*

Chapter XI

Bianca

While the rest of the trade caravan set up for the night, Bianca went out into the open plains looking for some Guthog's Blessing to make a wash to get rid of the fleas that were on a couple of the pack animals. *Saint Pandonia, lend me aid. It is supposed to be a common plant, but it is hard for me to find in the wild with my lack of the necessary skills. One grass, when growing, looks to me much like another and I am still learning to find things for myself out in the world. I am experienced at using them, but I am too used to buying my herbs at the apothecary's shop, usually dried.*

I have moved far from the camp in my search. The light is starting to fade. I am over a long bowshot away from the camp and have circled right around to the other side of it. It is only now, with the light going fast, that I am returning with an armful of the grass that I have found.

The attack came when she had been away for an hour or more and there was a rise between her and the others. *I hear a shout, screams, and the noise of fighting.* Bianca felt surprised at this. *We are only a small caravan of three light carts and a dozen pack animals, but we are well protected, with six experienced guards. As well, the traders and the other drivers and handlers are well-armed and experienced. No one expects any real trouble. The Khitan prefer to trade if you are peaceful and non-threatening. A good watch was to be kept. It has apparently failed us.*

This is my first trip away from Freehold and, while most of my sixteen years have been spent working with animals or in taverns I know that I lack the experience of the rest of my caravan. I am the apprentice. I just have belt daggers and the sling that is knotted around my waist so I want to hide in the low scrub, but there is no one in sight and I need to find out what is happening.

Bianca dropped the grass and moved cautiously to the top of the rise to see. Upon getting to the crest she peered through a small bush, hardly bigger than her head, trying hard not to be seen. As she did this the sounds of combat ceased, although yells and then new screams soon arose in a female voice. *The raiders are raping at least one of my companions—no it is two of them. Several of the other animal handlers and drivers, and one guard, are women, but I cannot tell who is being assaulted from here. Everyone else seems to be dead. Most of the attackers are already searching the carts and horse packs and seem to be looking for something. They break off what they are doing to take turns with the women. Saint Ursula lend me aid.*

One Khitan stands on the rise opposite me—peering in the direction that I left the camp. This made her crouch lower and she kept very still, the grass tickling her nose. *He turns around. He is closely examining the horizon and looks to be listening to the wind. It seems to me that he is familiar—he is one of the guards, Mongtu. I don't like him. He is always leering and I think he spies on everything I do. I have a strange prickly feeling when he is anywhere near me.*

It seems that my hunch has a deeper root than I had realised. He is close with another guard, Giacomo, who I have the same feeling about. The two joined the caravan at Toppuddle at the last moment when two other guards fell sick and the local priests were unable to pray them better. Bianca looked down again among the other brigands. *There is a man, one who is dressed like Giacomo, standing up from one of the rapes, adjusting his clothing and armour.* Bianca marked him down. *I am not sure how I will do it, but I swear to God and Saint Ursula that I will somehow avenge his victim. The Khitan may be a pagan, but Giacomo is supposed to be a Christian and above such things.*

About half of the brigands are Khitan. The others are mostly clothed in the fashion of Freehold although one wears the dress and has the brown skin of Haven. Yet another is a Dwarf. It is hard to tell, but all look to be male and they appear to be working to a plan.

How they have managed to make it into the centre of the Khitan lands without being destroyed I do not know. The Khitan do not like armed groups moving around the plains attacking people and they look to be outlaws, subject to instant execution whenever caught.

Curiously calm, Bianca said what she could remember of the prayers for the dead and the dying, asking the Lord to look after their souls. *Surely, seeing that they have died fighting evil men, I hope that it will do something to lessen their time in purgatory.* Bianca had always paid close attention in church and, if being a foundling and not having any dowry at all had not been an impediment, she would have liked to have become a nun. Keeping watch, reciting as much of the funereal mass as she could remember and then silently rubbing her wooden rosary helped keep her mind off the screams and cries as they subsided down to muffled and pained sobs.

It was obvious when the brigands found what they were looking for. A Freeholder in a steel back and breastplate and greaves worn over a multi-coloured slashed tunic and leggings ran to the Dwarf. *He is holding something. I cannot see what it is, but it must be small.* The Dwarf examined it and then called something in a language she could not hear at that distance. *It does sound like what little I know of Khitan.* All the brigands stopped searching and began grabbing what they could stuff in saddlebags or carry. The women's sobs continued a little longer and then terminated in two short gurgling screams as men stooped above them. *They take their virtue and then their lives. The tribesmen among the attackers are rounding up as many of the caravan's horses they can as most of the group mount and ride away.*

Bianca could hear raised voices and there was a lot of waving of arms and pointing. After a few minutes Mongtu shrugged and helped the Dwarf mount a horse, before mounting one himself. Both of them then galloped after the others.

Our caravan did well against such a force. It appears to me that there are empty saddles—ten at least—with bodies slung over them as well as horses from our caravan. This still leaves over thirty riders.

With a couple of horsemen moving to each flank, most galloped off to the northeast, keeping to the low ground between the rises in the plains. *Two riders are headed off the opposite way, roughly in the direction that we came from—I think.*

Even with the raiders riding away, Bianca didn't dare move from where she was hiding. She lay face down and sobbed into the grass, its strands coarse against her cheek. *I still am not safe. It is possible that someone, like Mongtu, could circle back and check if I have emerged from hiding. The fate of the women terrifies me.* The light faded around her and the stars became bright, hard points of light in a deep black field. The night began to grow chilly. *I wish that I had a cloak with me.*

As the temperature dropped further, Bianca began to shiver. *I could briefly go down the hill to the remains of my caravan.* She was just about to move when she saw movement among the bodies. *I think that, in between the darker shadows of the night, there may be beasts down there. I cannot be sure.*

I wish that I knew more about the places outside the cities and towns I have grown up in and further abroad than the short trips between them that I have made so far have shown me. I have very little idea what sort of wild beasts live on the plains, beyond what I have heard about in stories. I have heard about giant wolves and cats as well as swift moving two-legged feathered lizards that hunt in packs.

So intent was she on trying to see what was happening that she nearly missed a familiar noise. She heard a whickering sound. *Something is behind me.* She turned quickly around. *Standing below me are two horses.* She began to move down the slope, as quietly as she could to avoid panicking the beasts, but the horses snorted. *It is obvious that they know I am here.* She drew closer. *They appeared to be saddled—they look like the mounts of Paulo and Antonio, two of our guards.* Bianca felt a little nervous. *Both are trained warhorses— each of them far more dangerous than I am in a fight.* Coming closer she saw a pale blaze on the head of the darker horse and knew that this was Sirocco, Paulo's horse. *If the other has white socks it will be Firestar, Antonio's mount.*

Making reassuring sounds she moved closer. They eventually moved towards her outstretched hand and soon the dampness of a nose met her hand. *Luckily these animals have always seemed to like me and, when their owners were busy with other duties, I was introduced to the horses and I am the only one of the handlers who has been allowed to feed and groom them without being bitten or trodden on.*

The other horse is Firestar. "Sirocco—Firestar." *Their ears flick and they seem to recognise me.* She moved along Sirocco's flank, her hand sliding along his warm hide as she moved. Nervously checking the saddlebags she found some apples, which she shared with the horses. Next, she found hobbles and the horses, after eating the apples, let her put them on their feet. *It is clear they are more used to some other form of control.*

Bianca kept searching Paulo's bags. *His spare clothes—including a cloak.* She draped it around her, its hem spilling over the ground. *I dare not take the saddles off the horses, in case we have to move quickly.* Now much warmer, and with the bulk of the horses towering above her, Bianca curled up on the ground and drifted off towards sleep.

It was not a restful sleep, being filled with disturbing dreams. She dreamt of Mongtu and Giacomo alternately searching for her and chasing her. After much tossing and turning Bianca dreamt that she was in a warm but stormy sea trying to escape the two and woke up. *Sirocco is nuzzling me.* Both horses still stood over her. She disentangled herself from the cloak. *It is full daylight.* After taking the hobbles off the horses, Bianca gave them each another apple and checked them over. *Both have small wounds and cuts—they must have been in combat and only moved away once their riders died.* She cleaned these cuts with water and then gingerly mounted Sirocco, slightly the smaller of the two, taking Firestar's reins in hand. *With the horses, I feel more secure about investigating the caravan.* She moved cautiously around the rise, checking first to see if anyone was approaching.

Bianca was horrified at the scene that greeted her. *The bodies of my companions are the roost of scavenger birds, arguing over the spoils.* Suddenly forgetful of being heard she began yelling loudly and charged the birds, driving them off the bodies. Upon seeing the bodies close up she was very nearly ill. *Apart from the damage of battle, I can see that larger scavengers than the birds have been worrying the corpses overnight. Some of my companions can only be recognised by what remains of their clothes.*

I cannot leave them like this. Bianca gathered the carts together and began pulling the bodies under them. *I must steel myself and search each body, each pouch and anything else that may hold anything of use to me.*

She then found her small bedroll containing her flute, and then began assembling a small pile of cooking gear, weapons, food, money, herbs and unguents, even some extra clothes that would fit her. Much to her surprise she was starting to get used to the work until she turned to her seventh body and discovered that it was Rosa, another animal handler, a pretty and happy girl not much older than herself.

Saint Ursula comfort her. Rosa is one of the rape victims. Her head was nearly severed as she was executed. She lay face down with blood pooled under her neck and around her groin. Bianca turned her over to find that her body was covered in cuts and bruises and one breast had been bitten severely by Human teeth. *I can take no more.* She knelt beside the body, crying and vomiting. After some time, and still crying, she resumed her task, starting to recite the prayers for the dead over and over as a shield against the horror she felt.

Why have I been left alive when Rosa died so brutally? Pausing only to occasionally look around and to ensure the horses were watered and fed, she eventually finished her task. Having gathered the bodies, she now had to sort out the goods. Bianca heard a sound and looked up. *There are now three horses.* The two battle steeds had been joined by another; a packhorse with a broken halter.

Bianca caught the third horse and saddled it with a pack frame and added two of the intact horse packs. Adding what she had found less than half-filled them. She hung water and wine skins from the frame and, with difficulty added the only whole sack of feed grain to the top, lashing it between the packs. *Most of the daggers I will add to my body, although I am not used to wearing so many. Most are in sheaths for arm or leg. The ones strapped to my torso and between her shoulders are particularly uncomfortable.*

Sometimes she substituted leather strips for proper harness and took more used tack to make more harness later. She also had three pouches of sling bullets hanging from her saddle, the larger one of plain lead bullets, a smaller one had two hands of silver lead ones and the third were also of lead, but each bullet in that bag had markings of some sort. *I hope that this means they are magical and not maker's marks.*

I am finished, but the day lacks but an hour or so until darkness. I don't want to stay here another night. She said some final prayers, mounted Sirocco, and moved off leading the other two horses. She decided to return to Freehold. *Hopefully I am following the path that the caravan took to reach this point. I need to keep watch in case anyone approaches me.* When she brought herself to gaze back, she saw that carrion birds circled the site of the caravan. *That must mark my position to anyone who is interested.* She urged Sirocco to greater speed, the other two following behind. After a while she brought the speed down to a walk when the packhorse started to lag and pull on the lead rein.

After riding for an hour she rode to the top of a tall rise nearby and carefully checked the horizon. Seeing nothing Bianca rode down into the hollow below and made a camp while it was still light. She stripped the saddles and packs off the horses and carefully groomed them and rubbed them down. At every noise, she nervously spun around. When she had finished, she gave water and a small amount of grain to the horses before preparing herself a cold meal. *The light is fading now, but I need to teach myself how to throw some of my new knives in their hidden sheaths—weapons that are meant for this purpose.*

She practiced until it was dark. *The blades might have been meant for the purpose, but I am not sure that I am. I have seen people do this before and it looked easy, but at present the safest place for a person to be is as my target. I hit the tree I aim at sometimes, but more often with the butt of the knife or the flat rather than the blade. Those knives that somehow land point first sometimes don't even stick in the wood, but just hold for an instant before falling to the ground. I will have to do this every day and not let my disastrous start put me off. My weapon skills are poor. Until I find some suitably shaped and sized rocks, I cannot practice with my sling without perhaps losing some of my precious bullets.*

I really should have brought some of the bags of sling stones that I found back at the caravan, but I was so pleased with the bullets that I didn't bother. I even emptied my own bag of rocks to take lead bullets.

Tonight, I will not hobble the horses, but will let them graze free. They sought me out before and hopefully they will stay with me overnight. I am too exhausted, both physically and in my head, to care too much. Making a bed out of the saddles, spare blankets and her bedroll, Bianca said her prayers, asking again after the souls of her companions, and then lay down. Once she had finished being active, she started to sob uncontrollably and, despite her exhaustion, it was some time before she went to sleep curled up in a tight and miserable ball.

In the morning, the horses were all standing nearby. Bianca woke from a restless sleep populated by people who wanted to kill her. After saying prayers, she again gave each of the horses a few handfuls of grain and some water before she prepared them and herself, for the trail. After having saddled the warhorses Bianca put the pack-frame on the third horse.

"You slowed us down yesterday," she said. "I cannot remember what you were called, but I am going to call you Sluggard." The subject of this conversation snorted. He is a large and ungainly looking animal, bigger than the other two and built more for hard work than for speed. *In reality he did well, given that he had been carrying considerably more weight than the other two horses, both of which normally carry an armed and armoured guard.*

Perhaps I should even up the loads. Having done this, she set off in, what she hoped, was the correct direction. *At least the wind seems steady and, if I keep it in my face, I will not begin to circle round, but will keep to a straight path.* Pulling her flute from her bedroll she began playing a soft tune to accompany their travel. *At least the horses seem to like this and it makes me feel a little better.*

I need to look ahead carefully. She grew used to dismounting short of each low ridge, sometimes every couple of hundred paces, crawling to the top and looking around her—ahead and behind—before calling the horses up and riding on. This caution slowed her progress, but she was eventually rewarded by seeing two riders on top of a ridge to her right and front and at least two hands of hundreds, twelve hundred, paces away—in what she hoped was the north-west. *If I am right, then they might be the ones who split off from the bandits.*

If they are, then they still seem to be looking for something as they sit on their mounts scanning the horizon. When they had moved away from her, Bianca waited for a count of two hands of one hundred. On reaching twelve hundred she again called up the horses and moved on. *With the rises and falls of the plains I can never be really sure if anyone is even one hundred hands of paces away from me.*

Two shallow valleys later, Bianca found a patch of bushes and small trees along with a stream with a small pool that looked as if was sometimes used as a campsite. *It is still daylight, but I will stop now and set up for the night. Hopefully this will allow the pair of riders to move further away and give my horses a chance to graze. She looked after them, fed herself and set up camp before moving to a small shrubby bush near the crest above her camp.*

She practiced her knife throwing and even her ability to draw them out from their various scabbards around her body. By the time she decided to go down the hill to sleep, she had reached the stage where the blades usually landed with the points towards the salvaged shield she was using as a target, even if they only sometimes hit it. *They also land without much force, but I am getting better at that part as well. I hope that I will not have to defend myself by throwing knives, but when I have as few weapons as I do, it seems to be the only thing that I can teach myself and practice on my own.*

The next day went the same as the last, with the horses responding better and better to Bianca's voice. *I wonder if the pair of warhorses are prompting Sluggard or if he is far brighter than the usual packhorse.* She was now proceeding with no lead reins, changing her riding horse, and getting the other two to follow on voice alone. Towards the end of the day, but still with plenty of daylight ahead, she spied a clump of trees on a ridge ahead, in this land almost a forest, with a small heap of stones beside it. *I think that will be where we spend the night.*

She reached the trees only to find out that they continued down the slope ahead to a pool and a small creek. *The rocks have several blue objects tied to them or even buried in among them. I wonder why.* Bringing the horses inside the grove she discovered, in a sheltered dell, a small spring that bubbled away down slope and was joined by a stream about fifty paces below that ran through the small valley. Looking around, she saw a fire pit and a pile of wood. *This must be a fairly frequent stopping place. I will need to be a lot more cautious about setting up camp than I was before. I think that Saint Christopher can only protect me properly if I help him out.* Without unsaddling the horses she loose-looped their reins to convenient small branches and climbed a tree, not without some difficulty. *I can climb walls and all over a loaded wain, but town dwellers don't get much practice on trees.*

Through the smell of bruised leaves and the snap of small broken branches she did eventually get a much better vantage point. On reaching a clear spot she immediately saw a single rider come into view left of the path she had been taking, coming roughly from the direction that the stream was taking. *He is mounted and stationary on a rise looking to my right.* Turning around Bianca saw two more riders. *They may, or, may not, be the brigands. If it is them then they have curved back from the path I last saw them take. It is obvious that each has seen the other and that they are all now heading towards my trees.*

Bianca weighed up her options. *I will stay hidden but be prepared to run, talk or fight.* She moved the horses to the centre of the dell with the spring, putting Sluggard between the other two and looping their reins to their saddles. "Hold". *I think that is the order given to warhorses to put them on guard. At any rate both Sirocco and Firestar have pricked up their ears in response and are looking at me in a way that horses normally don't.*

Taking the bag of, hopefully, magical sling bullets and slinging the bag of normal lead bullets from her belt as well, she sat down behind scrub where she could see the area near the fire pit. *With a little bit of luck, I may be concealed from all of those who are approaching.*

I will work on the idea that if I cannot see the people as they come close, maybe they will not see me. She examined her conscience and said a prayer to Saint Ursula. *I hope that will cover me if it comes to a fight—at least I asked her for the wisdom to choose the right side—if there is a choice—if there is a fight.* Once this was done she settled down and began sharpening her blades on her whetstone. She paid particular attention to the points of the throwing blades that she had been practicing with. The soft sound of steel on fine stone helped calm her a little.

Eventually the single rider came into view, moving up the creek. *He is moving rapidly now and seems to want to reach the campsite first.* Bianca returned the whetstone to its pouch and put her blades back in their scabbards, checking that all were secure and where she could reach them. *This is a sign of nervousness. I need to settle down quietly and stopped fidgeting. The rider below looks quite young, not much older than me. He is checking around as he rides.*

She stilled further. *I am glad of my small size and slight build. Now think of invisibility—it must be working—his gaze has missed my hiding place.* He dismounted and checked the ground. *He is unloading his horse while still keeping it ready to ride off. It may have worked with some but, I am an animal and baggage handler. It is obvious that he does not trust the other two riders. That would be normal though. The pagan Khitan, being without the benefit of God's forgiveness, are always fighting among themselves.*

Soon the other two appeared, five hands of paces from where she was concealed and rode slowly down into the hollow. *If they had seriously looked around I would have been seen but their gaze is intent on the man below. Please horses—stay silent and unseen.* She cast her memory back. *I think the two look like the ones who were a part of the attack on my caravan. Unlike the young Khitan below, but like the bandits, they look unkempt.*

They had to pass very near her hiding place to get to where the single man was. *They are at their closest to me, only a few paces away, and I am getting that strange feeling again—the same I felt about Mongtu and Giacomo. It could not be a feeling about a person being bad or a law-breaker. Working in taverns I have met plenty of criminals and only a few have ever given me this feeling. No, it is something else. Maybe I get a feeling for when people are planning on doing something nasty to others. I don't know, but at any rate, I know now that I will take the side of the young Khitan; if it comes to taking sides.*

When the pair reached the young man, they stayed in their saddles and had an exchange of words. *From my very limited knowledge of the language it sounds like they are exchanging formal greetings. It is evident that they do not know each other. I am feeling more and more tense. Something is going to happen.* The two dismounted and all three men began to unload their horses. Bianca kept a close watch. *There are some odd looks passing between the two possible bandits.*

She eased open the bag of marked bullets and withdrew three that had more markings on them than some of the others. *Hopefully this makes them more magical.* She placed one in the pouch of her sling and held the others in her left hand.

Bianca settled back down. *The younger of the two bandits is stealthily drawing his sword—what do I do?* Just in time, the young Khitan noticed and hurriedly stopped a slash at his neck. A wild fight broke out. *Any one of the three far outclasses me in combat.*

Despite the risk of slinging into a melee, she stood up and moved clear of the bush to cast if the opportunity arose. *The two attackers themselves give me the chance. So intent are they on getting the young man between them, that they stay their distance from him.* Whirling her sling around, Bianca sent her bullet towards the older one, who was the one who was most behind and to the right of their victim. She had been aiming at his chest but in the course of the fight he ducked slightly and the bullet struck him fair on the temple.

At that range the bullet smashed through the skull and into his head and he dropped instantly to the ground in a spasm and lay there twitching briefly as he died. Without pausing Bianca prepared to cast again but the unexpected sight of his companion's fate had caused the younger attacker to pause and look down. This was all it took to allow the young Khitan to quickly strike a blow to the bandit's hip, eliciting a scream which told of broken bones, and which he followed up with a rebounding strike to the top of his opponent's shoulder. The bandit instantly dropped his weapon and shield and fell screaming in pain to the ground.

Only then did the young Khitan look around warily to see who had dispatched the other attacker. *I think that the threat is over. It is time to see if I was right.* Bianca stopped twirling her sling and moved clear and down the slope.

As she moved Bianca called out, "Come Sirocco, come Firestar, come Sluggard," and, without looking back, she headed down the slope soon to be followed as she went by three horses. She moved down through the grass, the air around her full of silence.

Chapter XII

Hulagu

"I thank you, umm, I mean I offer you the gift of hearth and water...no... Who are you? Are you a friend?" *I am babbling, unsure of what to say and surprised both that I am alive and at my saviour; a girl of the cities on her own in the grasslands with horses and very little in the way of weapons.*

She spoke, "Me say small Khitan." *Her Khitan is so bad and heavily accented that it makes it more than clear that she is one of the walled ones.*

"Slow please. Speak Latin?" *Her language. I am as bad in that as she is in mine.*

"Few word, not word I want."

"Me name Bianca. These bad men." *Bad Khitan again.* She must have lacked the next words as she switched to Latin. "They kill me friends."

'Kill' and 'friends' I understand. He nodded.

The girl continued in Khitan pointing at the man writhing on the ground, "Need ask why. You ask?"

I wonder if she knows what she is asking. With the man having broken hospitality, then any measure I chose to employ can be used to make Koyunlu, if that is really his name, talk. Can she, a city girl, watch what may be needed to be done to get the information that she wants?

He nodded. "I do. I ask for me well." *We have quickly fallen to each speaking in the other's tongue and it is obvious that each of us has only a small number of words and little knowledge of how to use them—my manners—she saved my life.* He slipped back into Khitan.

"I offer you the gift of hearth and water and may your sleep be safe and restful here. I am Hulagu of the Dire Wolves and I am on my wanderjahr."

The girl is looking very puzzled. "You me welcome? You name Hulagu?" she said.

She has that bit right. Hulagu nodded. "Family are dogs where?" She mimed looking around and sniffing like a dog.

Not that bit though. Despite the tension Hulagu laughed and shook his head as he pointed in the direction he had come from. "Two days, not dogs—you?"

"No family," she replied. "Friends dead." Suddenly she stopped talking and moved to the injured man. *I didn't notice. He has a dagger near drawn, but the girl kicks it away and then continues with a hard kick on his injured hip that leaves him gasping in pain and clutching it.* She pointed down at him and continued, "He do it and many others." With this she opened and closed her hands four times.

I supposed she means that there are forty-eight bandits. She now held out her open hands palm forward. "Now this many dead. Friends kill. Me hide. Me Bianca. Me no good in fight."

Hulagu took a good look at the girl in front of him. *She is dressed in riding leathers and looks more like a Khitan than the town dwellers that I have seen or imagined. At her throat is a poorly carved wooden cross on a piece of string. It is her only jewellery. She is small and slender, except around her chest. In truth, her face is fairly average in appearance, with two braids of unaccustomed blonde hair curled against her head and pale blue eyes.*

She seems to be covered in knives, although she is uncomfortable with them. Perhaps she has just started wearing them. She still has the cords of a sling between her fingers with a lead bullet, not a rock in it. Another bullet is clutched in her left hand. Near each of her shoulders stands a saddled horse, its reins looped up to its saddle. Each is looking at me as if sizing me up as a target. Each is obviously battle trained, yet obeying this slip of a girl who says she cannot fight, but has just killed one man. Behind them stands a large packhorse, laden but noticeably easy with his load. Its rein is also looped back and tied to the pack frame and it is also obeying on voice alone. Except for the man on the ground, silence has fallen and, just as I am examining her, she is examining me.

She seems to realise this and, as if to break the tension, she again kicks the live bandit in the hip to leave him screaming before she turns to the dead bandit on the ground, draws a dagger and nonchalantly digs her sling bullet out of his head. She cleans it and her dagger on his clothes before examining the bullet and placing it, and the two others she has, back in their pouch and her dagger in its sheath.

Perhaps she might not be the delicate creature that city girls are supposed to be. She then surprised him even more by kneeling and closing the eyes of the man she had killed, using her thumb to force one eye back into its socket in order to do so, then lifting the cross around her neck to her lips in a bloody hand and kissing it before closing her eyes and obviously praying for a man of a different land and faith who may have killed her friends. She changed again by making a cross movement with her hand and again kissing the cross before looking up at Hulagu.

"We talk this now?" She stood and nudged Koyunlu ungently with her foot.

"What need to ask?"

"He attack we? Why? He..." *She is making a circle with her thumb and forefinger while making the forefinger of the other hand go in and out of the circle—that would mean fuck—probably rape.* "Friends? Where others? He follow me?" *That would explain why she does not like Koyunlu then.*

Hulagu held up both hands to stop the broken flow of questions, squatted beside Koyunlu and drew his knife. "You heard her. You can just start talking and I will tell you if I have heard enough."

Through teeth gritted with pain Koyunlu said, "No, I cannot."

"Cannot? I am going to kill you. You can die fast or you can die very slow and painful. How much worse can it get?"

"Much worse. You cannot create pain for me forever. Yeah, we attacked a caravan a few days ago and had some fun with the girls. We knew there was a survivor and Kitzez and I were sent out to find her and that is all I can say. Now do your worst. Once I am dead, I can rest in the afterlife. I am not going to last long anyway."

Hulagu looked at Bianca

"He Koyunlu. He kill friends." He made the finger sign *I have to use Khitan* "and raped the girls," then switching back to Latin, "Not say why."

"Not?" Bianca smiled, a cold, hard smile. "Not?" she said again, this time with a rising inflection and increased volume as she looked at Koyunlu.

"Not," said Koyunlu. *He is trying to look determined through his pain. It is evident that the tone in the girl's voice worries him.*

Bianca drew a knife from her belt. *She is muttering something I cannot understand—that may be 'forgive'. She has kicked Koyunlu on his hip again—hard. His scream is real. She really does not like him.*

"Hold him." She knelt daintily down beside Koyunlu and cut away his leather trousers from his groin with her knife, careless of how deep she cut and leaving his genitals exposed. "Him not need this," and she grabbed Koyunlu's penis in her left hand, holding it tight as she began to draw her blade along its length. *My face must be showing my horror and Koyunlu, with his eyes wide, has begun a new and desperate screaming although he is trying to lie still under her blade.*

"Not," he said, "I cannot tell."

The girl drew another line with her blade, this time breaking the skin, missing vital blood vessels but leaving a trail of slow oozing blood behind.

"Not?" she asked sweetly and smiled again looking at her victim. "Cut off, leave for dogs. String?" she asked Hulagu innocently.

I don't know what to do. It is accepted to cause pain to ask questions of a man. It is another to maim them and make them no longer a man. For us Khitan it is almost the ultimate indignity and by the look of terror on Koyunlu's face as his mouth works and his eyes bulge with terror, it might even work.

Bianca suddenly dropped the penis and reached lower, giving a squeeze to his sack and causing another scream of mixed pain and terror. "Rule head. Cut off...hear good to eat. Rosa pleased." She looked thoughtful again, gave another squeeze, and smiled again. "String? Fire?" While she was speaking, Bianca was moving her knife point to rest on one threatened part after another as if in some bizarre choosing game. "Cut, eat, heal." She brought the knife to rest with the blade at the base of his penis, "then let live."

She is smiling happily as if she has solved a problem. I think that she may be unwell in her head. Through his pain Koyunlu's look of absolute horror is apparent. He has flinched back within himself and begun to just mutter 'no' over and over.

I do not know how Bianca has hit on what may be the ultimate torture, and one no Khitan would do to another. It is forbidden to kill yourself, and no one does, although they may start fighting something that they know will kill them. It is ingrained in our mind that killing yourself will cause the ultimate pain and suffering for the soul. His manhood taken away and deliberately maimed, with it done on the plains and by a girl of the towns that he has been hunting, Koyunlu will be continually shamed in any group, even when he is among the dead and the damned.

I will do as she asks. Hulagu started moving towards his horse to get some cord. "Many cuts or one?" *She has grabbed his penis, smiled sweetly, and asked as if she were a wife asking a husband how he wants his meat cooked.*

It is too much for Koyunlu. Once he broke the words came tumbling out. "We were gathered by a Dwarf who called himself Dharmal. He had instructions and money and used to lead us to do things. We raided places and caravans. Sometimes we killed people and sometimes we got to keep them. Only some of us would go to towns to sell things we had taken and to buy supplies. We have our own village in the southern mountains and the slaves we take work the land for us. We have women if we want them. I don't know who we work for."

He looks at the girl—so do I. In return she smiles at him like a mother pleased with her child. She changes her grip into a firmer hold and her knife point is still playing with Koyunlu's genitals carelessly and the blood is dripping around. He winces with pain at each casual cut.

Koyunlu swallowed and began again, "I didn't care who we worked for. Dharmal got instructions in a mineshaft that we could not enter. He was always gone for at least a day. For us life was good. Dharmal had many magic items. One could hide us if we stayed together and travelled slow. This time we had to find something in the caravan and make sure all the women were dead. Friends in town poisoned guards for the caravan and two of us took their place. We were also told a young wolf might be around, just starting his wanderjahr. If he was and we found him, we were to kill him; otherwise others would meet and kill him later. You were not to meet the caravan. That is all I know." He stopped talking and looked at Hulagu. "Please kill me now—intact. Please. Don't let this demon woman do this to me. I will suffer forever now, but I will suffer as a man."

Bianca looked at Hulagu without changing her grip, "Say more?"

Hulagu shook his head, "No, think tell all."

"Cut now?" *Bianca is pushing a little with her knife through the hair into the mound of flesh around the base of his penis.*

Koyunlu shrank and screamed in Khitan, "There is no more to tell. I have no more. Kill me now." *He has switched to Dwarven.* "I have no more. I have no more. Kill me now." *She shows no reaction at all. He changes to Hindi,* "No more, I have no more. Kill me. Kill me."

Bianca cocks her head slightly to the side before replying in the same tongue, "Do you have prayers for the forgiveness of your sins? I will give you a few minutes." She withdrew her bloody hand and knife from his groin and contemplated them without moving away.

"You speak the trade tongue?" *She still has a marked accent, but it is far better than her attempt at Khitan.*

"Of course, I was learning to be a trader," she said dismissively without looking up. "What I am now I do not know. I am soon to be an executioner." She smiled coyly at Koyunlu. "Have you finished?" He swallowed and nodded. Bianca closed her eyes and said in Hindi, "Our Father, please accept this sinner who has not been able to know you but surely craves forgiveness and repents of all his many sins." She opened her eyes and looked meaningfully down at Koyunlu. "You do ask forgiveness and repent of all your sins don't you?" she asked sweetly.

Koyunlu looked back at her in horror as if she were a stick that had suddenly turned into a deadly snake while he held it in his hand. *I don't think that either of us knows what she is babbling about, but I think that he fears that she is about to change her mind and unman him after all unless he agrees.* "I do. I have done wrong all of my life and I am sorry," he stammered, "very sorry."

"See Lord, he does repent. Please have mercy on his soul. Amen." Having said that she leant forward and grabbed Koyunlu's hair and held his head back. *She has quickly thrust under his chin and into his skull as he just stares at her, his face frozen in shock as the realisation of his death comes to him.* He shuddered as his brain stem was severed and the smell of his body letting go suddenly filled the air. *As that happens she finally reacts. She has given a start, as if she is quickly waking up from a trance.* Quickly she rose and ran to the bushes as a reaction to what she had just done set in and she suddenly began weeping and vomiting. *She is Human after all.*

It falls to me to clean up. Although they were very skittish he caught and tethered the bandit's horses and began stripping the men's bodies of valuables. He was going to drag the remains clear with Bianca's packhorse. *It and her other two are making sure that I cannot approach it. The two warhorses are moving their bodies to interpose them and showing their teeth at me. Not a good idea to persist. I will use my own horse.* He looped a rope around the dead men's ankles and fastened the other end to Kurghiz's saddle and dragged them over the ridge they had come from. *Scavengers will soon take care of their bodies and I am not wasting wood on a proper funeral for them. They don't deserve it.* He left them there in the growing gloom, taking a look around the horizon and seeing nothing before turning around to tend to the other men's horses.

As Hulagu returned he saw the girl standing in her trousers with only a wet gauze undershirt on top emphasising her breasts rather than concealing them. *She may have killed for me but she obviously doesn't fully trust me either. She sees me standing here and she pats at blades to make sure they are there before wringing out her jacket and draping it over a bush to dry a bit.*

Bianca then began unloading horses and setting up camp as if nothing had happened. *I am still staring at her as if she might explode like a wizard's spell. I should try to act normally as well.* He went to join her.

"I am not sure what came over me," she said in Hindi. "I have never killed anyone before, let alone…" a haunted look appeared on her face as she waved a hand towards the patch of bloody earth where Koyunlu had lain.

"You did what you had to do and now I know that I was destined to meet you."

She is looking puzzled. As they set up camp Hulagu told her of his grandfather's visions and tried to explain how she was a part of his destiny. As a fire was lit and Bianca cooked some food, Hulagu tried to explain the signs to her. *She looks doubtful.* As they began to tend to the handful of horses they now had Bianca was still stressing that she needed to return home. After caring for the horses, they ate. *The girl looks oddly at me as I do the normal rituals of eating.* He poured a little drink on the ground and flicked some in four directions. He also threw some food into the air after rubbing it against the fetish that he carried in a bag around his neck to feed it before replacing it. *I wonder if the cross is her fetish. She is going through a series of motions as she did earlier, kissing it, muttering to herself in Latin with her eyes closed for some time then moving her fingers through the air and kissing the wooden cross again.*

After eating they searched the saddlebags of the bandits. They found clothes, which they discarded except for the fur cloaks and gloves, some berries, *probably Betterberries*, money and some books, which Bianca told him was a part of the cargo of one of the merchants, Francesco. They were being taken to Haven and were supposedly a part of a newly discovered library. A look of recognition came over her face.

"Koyunlu held something back after all. He must have known what they were searching for. It was a book; larger and flatter than these."

Among the books, she found one that she said was a holy book that had belonged to the merchant. Not one for sale, but one he carried with him for his own use. *She has grabbed hold of it, clutching it as if it were made of gold.* Bianca seemed to think for a little while and then declared, "You have your signs and portents and I have mine. I will ask the Holy Word for advice as the priests do and I will take what it tells me to do." She kissed her cross and muttered in Latin again before closing her eyes, opening the book at random and placing a finger on the page. *As she reads the words, she is translating it into Hindi so that I can understand. It seems to me that she is relying on memory as much as reading the words. I don't think that she can read her own language very well.*

"To everything there is a season and a time to every purpose under heaven," she read out. "A time to be born and a time to die; a time to plant and a time to pluck up that which is planted; a time to kill and a time to heal; a time to break down and a time to build up; a time to weep and a time to laugh; a time to mourn and a time to dance; a time to cast away stones and a time to gather stones together; a time to embrace and a time to refrain from embracing; a time to get and a time to lose; a time to keep and a time to cast away; a time to rend and a time to sew; a time to keep silence and a time to speak; a time to love and a time to hate; a time of war and a time of peace."

I am astounded. Just as when my grandfather spoke, I am feeling more than a touch of awe and it probably shows on my face. The words seem to speak to us. Bianca has killed and, it seems, has been born to a new life. There is a purpose to it all and it looks as if there might be a war in the offing. Maybe this girl of the walled towns is a seer as well as having her other abilities.

She is muttering to herself again in Latin. I supposed they are prayers thanking her Gods for what she had found. She is once more kissing her cross. She is turning to me.

"It seems that you are right. I will come with you. For the first time in my life I have a purpose." She smiled. *It is a happier smile than she has displayed before. It seems that the words that she has just read go a little way to erase some of the horror of what she has done. She no longer looks quite as sick or haunted.*

I am amazed again. Bianca is a girl of the towns—a Latin of Freehold, but in so many ways she is just like a Khitan. He looked at her again as she worked. *It is easy to see that she has a very nice body, despite her overly plain face. She can cook, train animals and fight. If she can ride, I can see my mother liking her straight away as my partner—but I feel instantly that this is not going to be. I will treat her as if she is my sister, except that I don't want to play a joke on her or tease her. That might be dangerous.*

Now is a time to refrain from embracing. It might even be a time for me to laugh. Bianca had begun her daily throwing practice. *She is so serious about it that I should not.* As she progressed he noticed that even in the one session she showed a marked improvement in her skills as her dexterity and dogged determination to reach goals showed fruit. Already she could throw a blade and have some chance of hitting her target—*something I cannot do. It may not do much to hurt the person she hits, but it will probably hit them.*

I will bet that soon she will be as capable as anyone. It is just as well given the number of blades she has, and with her jacket off, I can see she has others that I did not see before. Part of her practice is to draw and throw from all of her sheaths—those on her legs and arms, those behind her neck and those tucked below her breasts as well as the others on her belt. These hidden blades explain why she wore her jacket so loose. I notice that the heavier fighting blade she used to cut Koyunlu has not been discarded, but has been cleaned and returned to her belt where she can easily draw it if needed.

Eventually, their tasks done, Hulagu set a second small fire near the first and asked Bianca to stand between the two. She did this. *I can see that she is puzzled and that the smoke is stinging her eyes. Her nose is twitching as if she is about to start sneezing, as I begin to ask the sky spirits to take away the*

demons that hang around all of the walled ones and make it hard to associate with them.

When that was done Hulagu took his turn and stood between the two fires and asked the same for any that had passed from her to him, before the fires were lit. *I can see that she is curious but, until she asks, I really cannot say anything to her. Although she seems to be bursting with curiosity, Bianca does not give vent to her questions, instead just putting on her drying jacket, but not lacing it, unconsciously she is behaving more as if she were a woman of the tribes away on an expedition with male relatives.*

I have my horses hobbled, but Bianca is still letting hers roam free. There is an irony to the tribesman having to hobble horses, while the city girl feels comfortable that hers will stay close. He finally removed his armour and they then both sat near the embers of the fire and agreed to tell each other about themselves. As the smoke of the dying fire eddied around them, tickling the nose, they began to talk in Hindi. Bianca occasionally played her flute softly as she listened to Hulagu.

"I am Hulagu, seventh son of Togatak, who is the seventh son of Nokaj of the Dire Wolves—"

"But you are a Khitan," interrupted Bianca.

"Yes, but I will explain us to you. I am of the Kara-Khitan—the people of the plains. But we call ourselves after our clan spirit animal. My clan is the Dire Wolf. As well as my clan, whose Tar-khan, or clan head, is Toluy, there are those of the Thunder Lizard, which is the clan of our ruler, the Kha-Khan, Chinggiz Arghun, as well as those of the Snake, the Lion, the Elephant, the Eagle, the Cow Lizard, the Pack-hunter, the Axebeak and the Bison.

"If I marry a woman of the tribes I may only marry a girl from the Elephant, Eagle or Lion clans or, of course, of the Thunder Lizards and I must kill an enemy in battle before I may marry. I may, with the permission of my wife, marry more than one woman and one of my wives may, with my permission, also marry another man. Sometimes a man will marry women who are sisters to each other or a woman will marry men who are brothers to each other. Some clans we are friends with and others we fight.

"This is one of the reasons that I was wary of Koyunlu and Kitzez—the one you killed with your sling. Koyunlu said that he was a Wolf, the same clan as I am, but I have only ever heard that name used by a much older man— and we have less than three thousand adult males in each clan. I should have at least heard mention of him if he were not outlaw and so no longer talked about. Which means Koyunlu lied about his name or is outlaw. Kitzez said that he was a Bison. We have had a dispute running with the Bison clan over some herds for very many years. A Wolf and a Bison might travel together, but it is very unlikely."

"We all believe in the power of spirits and that everything has its own spirit. Some of these are strong and some are weak. Some will always help us and some will act against us when they can. When we become an adult, at the age of thirteen, we make a spirit store and place a part of our spirit in it." He realised that he was touching his as he spoke. "We care for this and feed it—you may have seen me caring for mine when we ate. We always give offerings of food and drink to the land and the sky as these have two of the more powerful spirits. While the land gave birth to us, it was the sky spirits who made it so. Because we understand and work with the spirit world we usually avoid those who do not understand it and have little to do with them as they pick up bad spirits because they do not know how to avoid them. Luckily the bad spirits do not like fire and heat so, when I had you stand near the fires I asked the sky spirits to rid you of these bad spirits that were hanging on to you.

"It is now my job to make sure that we keep you free of them. Once I had rid you of the bad spirits that were hanging on to you I then had to do the same to get free myself of any spirits that had come from you to me."

Bianca is not good at dissembling on matters of the spirit. Her face shows that she does not believe in what I say, even while she is still considering my words. Eventually she just nods as if accepting what I say, even though her face says otherwise.

"All of the clans raise horses, goats, sheep and usually cattle and, as well they will each raise their totem animal. We care for the giant dire wolves. They are adopted into our families as brothers and sisters and live among us freely. The Cow Lizard tribe raise those giant beasts. They sometimes eat them and use their leather, but they also ride them into battle and a charge of the giant beasts with their two long horns and the small third often plated in metal is slow and ponderous, but hard to resist. The Kha-Khan's clan breed and revere and sometimes ride the thunder lizards. They are hard to control, but they can swallow a whole man, even their tail will sweep aside their enemies and their roar will terrify any horses that face them that are not raised near them."

"That is about your tribes. What about you?" asked Bianca.

"I was born a Wolf. My father, Togotak, is shaman to our tuman, our tribe within the clan. His father, Nokaj, is chief shaman of our whole clan and is very powerful in the spirit world. My mother, Sparetha, is a master horsewoman and horse trainer. You would like her. She is also a fletcher and a very skilled archer. Her mother was captured from the west and was a köle, a thrall—a gulama. I grew up just like all the other Kara-Khitan: riding, playing, hunting, and looking after the flocks. I had little interest in being a shaman and mostly hunted and chased away the animals that would eat our flocks and learned to heal sick animals. When I turned thirteen I passed my initiation into the Kara-Khitan, I cannot say to you what this involves, but if you do not pass, you do not survive. For the next four years, I have worked on the skills that an adult of the tribes need to have. We still guard the herds at this age, but the young adults guard at night and the hunters we look for, instead of being animals, may be from another clan. A few nights ago, it was the celebration of my natal night. It was the start of my wanderjahr and I received prophesy from my grandfather and now you see me here. It was not an exciting life that I lived until now."

"What is a vonder jar?" asked Bianca.

Despite himself, Hulagu laughed at her accent. "Wanderjahr—it is one of our words not Hindi. It is the custom of the Kara-Khitan when they turn eighteen to spend a year travelling to find themselves before they settle down. Usually they just travel within the tents and no one will attack them if they bear the right signs," he showed Bianca the ones he bore. "But, you can go wherever you want. One of my uncles went as far as to sail on the northern seas and he saw ice floating on the water and giant white bears. Surely though you have had a more exciting life. You have seen cities. Tell me about your family."

"I don't have one," said Bianca. *Her voice is sad.* "—and cities are over-rated. You can make money in them, but they stink and people look down on you if you are poor and they take advantage of you. I don't know where or when I was born or even who my parents are or where they are from. I was found on the porch of a nunnery in Ashvaria, the capital of Freehold, when I was about a year old. I had my name written on a scrap of paper stuffed in my clothes and a little purse with a few coins."

"The nuns, who were mainly retired from active service in the Order of Saint Ursula, looked after me until I was thought to be five years old and then they decided that I should learn skills suitable for my station. They put me with a series of different tavern-keepers for a time. So I learnt to cook and look after animals and even to entertain by singing and playing the flute. Every now and then the nuns would look in on me and, if they didn't like my arrangements, they would take me back to the nunnery until they found me a new place. I think they sort of thought of me as a daughter, and they did try and do the best for me. I would have been glad to stay with them, but you must have a dowry and be an adult of respectable family to enter the Order—and I didn't have the first and certainly wasn't the second."

"What is a nun?"

"Religious woman," answered Bianca. "They marry God and most of them live away from the world and work and pray, but the Ursulines are different. They are often out in the world as warrior-priestesses and only retire to the cloister when they are older."

"Your God is a man with many wives?"

"No, He is a spirit. Well his son was a man, until he died, but to marry God means that they are chaste and give up men to concentrate on spiritual things. They are very holy."

I am feeling very confused. It makes no sense at all. "So you were the child they could not have?"

"No, some had children before they became nuns. Sometimes, when their husbands die, women become nuns."

"So their families did not want them and would not care for them?"

"Their families were very proud of them as holy women and would come and visit them and bring presents for the nunnery. None of our priests or monks or nuns are married. The Pope says that this is not right and he speaks for God. It seems your shamen are married."

"My grandfather speaks to the spirits as well, but so do many others. No one person has a monopoly on entering the spirit world and speaking to the spirits and sometimes there are many opinions on what the spirits want us to do." *Bianca is looking a little upset at this. I think that it is time to change the subject.* "How did you come to be out here then? I thought that you would continue to work in taverns until the…nuns found a husband for you."

"I was in a tavern tending animals for them when a trader's groom quit and he asked me if I wanted the job. I wanted to see more than Ashvaria so I asked the nuns if I could go. They thought about it and talked to the trader and finally said that I would be a good girl wherever I went and so I started working with traders working around Freehold. I visit the nuns whenever I can."

"This was my first job out into the wider world. I think Francesco was thinking of taking me on permanently as an apprentice trader. I have worked for him a few times before around Freehold. I am a bit old for an apprentice, but I work hard and have some skills. We were travelling to Evilhalt with a small caravan when we were attacked. We had valuable goods on board and were well guarded, but two of our guards were really bandits in disguise and they betrayed us. As I said, I think that they wanted one of Francesco's books. It was larger than the ones that we just found but much thinner. I don't know why a book would be so important that we all had to die."

They continued talking for some time, until it was dark, during which time they decided to divide the watch up with Hulagu going first. He pointed at the stars and showed Bianca how he would tell the time to wake her up. After this Bianca called to her horses and said goodnight to them before saying her prayers. *They take a long time. It seems that she has a lot to talk to her God about.* Finally, she curls up in her bedroll and goes to sleep.

Around the middle of the night Hulagu awoke her to the sound of scavengers arguing gently over the remains they had left over the ridge.

"As long as the noise keeps sounding like that, you need not worry too much. If it sounds like they are being chased away, or if it goes silent, then you must wake me immediately."

Bianca

I did not pay attention to the night when I was with the caravan. Perhaps I should have. I jump at noises in the trees and the rustling in the grass that the horses are all ignoring. At least if I keep walking around I will stay warm until I must wake Hulagu.

There is a different look to a sunrise in a city. I will wait until the sun is up. Eventually she went to wake the Khitan. They ate and began to prepare for the day ahead. They refilled their water bags. *Hulagu insists that he has to ride up the adjacent hill and circle the pile of rocks with blue things that is on top before we head off. We are apparently moving more or less north and east. I still do not know my directions here, but the sun is in a different place to where I thought it would be.*

We are following my strategy of early halts at night so that we have plenty of time to see anyone still moving around while we are concealed. We have agreed that the slower progress from this and checking at each ridgeline is justified, seeing that someone seems to want us dead.

"After all, Koyunlu said that there would be someone else for you if they didn't meet you and they already suspect that I escaped their slaughter."

Hulagu

A s they rode across the seemingly endless grass Hulagu tried to point out to Bianca all the things that he thought she should know about what was around them. What the grasses and birds were, the tracks of animals and the sign of where people had passed by in the past.

"You will not make me a bushman in one day," she laughed.

I am bursting with questions but it is rude to ask too much that is personal. She seems to be able to make her warhorses do almost anything she wants, almost just by asking, yet she is only a bit better than average as a rider and not as good as any Khitan except the very young. Why? She treats them and they treat her, with easy familiarity. Given her history, how did she get them? She doesn't even use a lead-rope for her packhorse. It just seems to follow the other two.

They camped for the night and Bianca prepared food for them. *She took one look at my attempts in this regard and sent me to stand watch on the ridge above the camp to see if there is any movement around us while she proceeds to set up the camp and look after the horses. Eventually my watch is rewarded.*

"Quick, Bianca, come up here." He stood and waved for her to come up. *She is putting the food to the side where it will stay warm before she runs up the slope—followed by a horse.*

When she had arrived, he pointed. *Some distance away to the south, a large number of horsemen are crossing our path. As well as many extra horses, running among them are the Dire Wolves of my Clan.*

"See—my clan rides to battle."

"How do you know?" asked Bianca.

"That they are of the Kara-Khitan is clear, even at this distance, and see the wolves running with them?"

"How do you know they are off to combat? They cannot be wolves; they can only be small horses. They are too big!" objected Bianca.

"They are dire wolves, the totem of my clan and yes, they are that large. Small children sometimes cling to their back and ride them, if the wolf is agreeable. We often regard this as a mark of a future shaman. As to how I know that they ride to combat, well they look to all be warriors, they ride fast, they have many spare horses and they show no sign of stopping for the night. Lastly, we only take the wolves with us to war and the hunt. That is no hunt. As well, no one has turned aside to us and we are clearly visible in clan lands. There is more than a tuman there, but not quite two. My grandfather, as I was leaving, was talking of rousing the clan to deal with an evil. So they may be chasing the bandits who attacked your caravan."

"I hope not. I swore an oath to Saint Ursula that I would avenge the women. It is my geas to bring them to justice or to kill them," said Bianca.

"But since the crimes were committed on our land, they are also a crime against our clan. We keep the peace. On this part of the plains, we are justice."

Bianca nods at that, as if reluctantly accepting my logic. They watched the war band ride on for a while before Bianca demanded that they eat before the food was completely spoiled. Food, practice, horses, talk and prayers; we have quickly settled into a pattern. *It seems to me that Bianca's prayers are longer and more elaborate today.* When he mentioned this, she explained that Krondag, the sixth and last day of the week was her holy day. Now each talked in the other's tongue as much as possible in the evening and only used Hindi when they needed to explain something complex. They set their watch on top of the small rise and, without a good supply of permanent water and cover nearby; this night was much quieter than the last had been.

The next day, after noon, Bianca began to look around as they rode. *She is growing nervous.* It was not until she peered over the next rise that he realised why.

"This is where we were attacked," she said.

That would have been apparent, even if she had said nothing. Below are the remains of the caravan, the bodies now torn by scavengers and everything else scattered around.

"We should do something," she said.

After a long look around, they rode down the slope together. Hulagu glanced sidewise. *I am hearing her mutter quietly in prayer again. Tears are coming back to her eyes. Our arrival has disturbed several birds, which were picking over the remains.* They flew off to circle overhead, waiting to return.

Hulagu looked around at what was left of the caravan. *The raiders have left items of low value and high bulk, or that they have no use for. There are some pack frames. We can change the two spare horses to being pack animals.*

Bianca is confused. She heads towards someone or something and then stops and stands before moving off again towards something else. Her horses seemed to follow a few paces behind.

"I know this is painful, but if we take all that we can salvage, I will then pull the carts together and put the bodies on them and set the carts alight. That way, even if we cannot bury them all, we can protect them from the scavengers. See if you can find more food that is unspoilt and get together what you can of the feed grain."

Hulagu stripped the carts of anything useful, cutting some apart with an axe to see if there were hidden panels and to help them burn better. He pulled them into a pile as well. *At least there is something hidden on one cart—a concealed compartment above the wheel has given us a largish store of money of various sizes and metals and gems from different lands.* He began moving the remains to the carts, checking if anything had been left on the bodies. *The attention of the scavengers and several days of exposure to the sun have left only grisly remnants, which should be consumed with the carts.* Once the task was done they had two bags of grain, some veterinary gear, some cooking equipment and oil, some food, and several sheaves of arrows. *Unfortunately, these are all fletched with three feathers and so useless to me. Still, they can be sold.*

He also found a bow. *It may be light enough to start in teaching Bianca, although it is a short town bow. It is a pitiful remnant of what had once been a prosperous caravan.* The horses are loaded, with their saddles sitting on top of their loads. "Do you want to say anything?"

Bianca prayed again. *She has tears rolling down her cheeks.* "…Ashes to ashes, dust to dust, in true and certain knowledge of the resurrection of the body. In the Name of the Father, and of the Son and of the Holy Ghost. Amen."

By now I have often heard her pray and they all end the same way, so I guess that I should say 'amen' as well. Bianca turned to him. "This is not the way it should be done. They should be buried with their heads to the east, where Jerusalem is, but it is better than leaving them as they were. Do what you should."

Hulagu had already set some tinder alight in a fire pot and now he spilled it out onto some oil he had put on a cart. As the flames grew he tugged Bianca's sleeve to move her away from the flames and to get her moving. Gently pushing and pulling he got her mounted and they rode away from the growing flame. Behind them a column of smoke rose skyward as frustrated scavengers rode it, spiralling upwards. *The smoke reveals to the world that something happened here. The birds say that it involves death.* They moved on for another two hours, with less caution than usual and, while Bianca set up the camp, Hulagu kept a very close watch for anything that may have been attracted by the smoke. Nothing appeared that looked worrying and they soon settled into their developing routine for the night.

Chapter XIII

Bianca

On the third day, as they were setting up camp at a permanent spring outside what Hulagu had called his clan's lands *I can see no difference between the rise and fall of the plains in one part and in another*, Hulagu called down from where he was on watch and said that three people were approaching. *He does not seem concerned, so I will just continue to set up camp.* He came down from the ridge just before they arrived and just before dark. She looked the new people over. *They all wear clothes much like mine, not leather lamellar armour like Hulagu. I can see that they all wear a stylised two legged lizard motif somewhere on their clothes. They are armed like hunters and the very full packs on their horses have pelts hanging off them. They show no surprise at Hulagu's presence, but they are all looking closely at me.*

Hulagu is giving the greeting that I heard before but he has added to it. "And this is Bianca of the Horse. She is from among the Latins but she travels under my guarantee and that of my clan. I speak for her deeds and she may be spoken to."

They are surprised, so am I actually. It seems to be something that they have heard, but not very often. They heard the mention of a horse and they look at mine, which are looking back at them. I believe that they think I have a totem. Not one of theirs, but you could see from their nods that they regard it as obviously a totem animal of power.

"I am Malik of the Pack-hunters, and these are Tzachaz and Uzun, also of my clan. We accept your hospitality and thank you for it. May prosperity attend upon you and yours." *Looking at the men I feel none of that strange sensation I felt with Kitzez and Koyunlu. After introductions, they show that they are cheerful and happy, particularly once it becomes apparent that they are as useless as Hulagu in preparing food. I have to expand my plans for the meal.*

They contributed fresh meat and some herbs and explained that they were on the way back to their tribe and showed off the plants and pelts that they had collected. *They show a fondness for such small practical jokes that are often shared by those who live together for long times and are greatly amused by my use of Khitan. They are not worried in showing it. I notice that they steer clear of my horses however.*

Malik said he was surprised that they would bother with watches. *It was nice of Hulagu to check with me that the tale can be told. He explained why we took this caution and they seem happy to take part. They are even happier to hear the full tale when I tell it in my halting Khitan and more fluent Hindi and happier still to hear me sing and practice my flute.*

She was glad when they began humming some of their clan songs so that she might learn them. *Hulagu cannot hold a note and so has been unable to help me. Malik and Tzachaz will take the first watch, Hulagu will be alone on the second and Uzun, who speaks some Latin and so can talk with me, will join me on the third.*

Hulagu

W*e keep our watch on the crest above the camp and it is well that we can see further.* Towards the middle of the night Hulagu heard two faint popping noises in the distance. As luck would have it, he was looking in that direction. *Although the light is only half that of mid-month the sky is clear. That is enough for me to see two shapes suddenly appear a bit over two hundred paces away. For a brief while they hover in the air. That is not good. They turn directly towards where I lie and start flying in my direction. They don't look friendly. I will loose a shot at them, before running down to wake the others.* He stood. *Night shooting is tricky, even on a clear night. I need to aim carefully before firing as they enter my middle range.*

He was rewarded with a squawk—*as if I have hit some sort of giant malignant bird*—but it did not stop them. *They both keep coming—at least I know they can be hurt.* Hulagu turned and ran down the short slope, shouting of danger and hoping to wake the others. *Now I have the undivided attention of the two warhorses. They stand over Bianca, who is pulling on her jacket without lacing it. She must sleep in her knives, even when she takes her clothes off. I hadn't noticed that before. That would be uncomfortable. The others are stirring and prodding each other and should soon be on their feet.*

"Two monsters are coming. They must be nearly here. They are flying, but my arrows can hurt them. We should get two clear shots as they come over the ridge before they close."

Bianca

Monsters—I need my pouch of magic bullets—one with many markings. This one has different markings to the last one I used. It has just as many, but they are different. No one attempted mounting their horses, instead standing well forward and clear of them. "Why not mount?"

"Without a saddle to give you a firm base," said Hulagu, "we are best fighting a flying creature from the ground. We have no time to saddle up."

Nodding in understanding Bianca then turned to Sirocco and Firestar standing behind her. *I need to move them, so that I can still use my sling—* "Hold." *Again, their ears prick up.*

The Khitan are all checking their martobulli in their belt quivers and strapping on shields. The heavy throwing darts do more damage when closing and are quicker than a bow and Hulagu said his people favour them at close range and when one arm has a shield on it. The four tribesmen stood in a line with Hulagu on the right. *My horses and I stand further to the right and back a bit.*

We are set—that is three of the creatures coming over the rise. They have long leathery wings around four paces across, a bird-like head with a sharp, but toothed, beak and four clawed limbs. The upper limbs are tipped with fingers with sharp claws instead of nails, the lower ones with bird-like talons instead of feet. What are they?

"Bird demons," said Malik, "they can bring others of their ilk in from somewhere."

The tribesmen's arms moved almost in unison and four darts flew through the air. Three struck home, but the fourth stopped in the air and just fell to the ground. *The three hit chests—one in the left-hand beast and two in the centre one. This does not seem to slow them much. My sling bullet is a heartbeat slower, but more devastating. I aimed at the right-hand beast and hit it in the head.* The demon made a short bleating noise and tumbled out of the air in an ungainly heap.

Globes of darkness started to coalesce around and surround the survivors as they continued down the slope. *Four more darts and a bullet have gone into the globes, who knows—they still move. At least with the clear cloudless night the globes, being about the same size as the demon's wingspan, seem to make little difference to hitting them as they fly. We just aim at the centre.*

The four Khitan now pull out their sabres and horse maces and split up two and two. While they were doing that, another demon has appeared on the rise.

"Becursed," said Uzun, "more!" At that the two globes of dark struck the pairs of men. *With just my daggers I can do little. To hit the demons with hand weapons the men have to step into the dark. Each man is trying to stay opposite their partner. The demons in the globes have no such restrictions. The beasts seem to be able to see through the dark and the claws and beaks are starting to inflict wounds, although most blows are stopped by the padding and leather that is often slept in for the warmth—luckily in this case. The shields seem almost useless as an active defence. The men are just waving them around in the hope of feeling a target.*

Bianca was casting at the new demon. One stone fell out of the air, but the next hit it in a wing, causing it to tumble to the ground. It is soon up and running, but with a wing dragging along the ground behind it. *This gives me another shot. I hit its chest. It seems to have partly caved it in. It doesn't slow, but still keeps running down, not aiming for me, but seems fixed on Hulagu. His back has turned up slope during the fight.*

Bianca surprised herself by running up to leap in the way unconsciously yelling 'Kill!' as she did so. She got in a couple of quick cuts with her daggers, one of which struck home in the demon's other wing, slashing the membrane in two. *Sirocco has just shouldered me aside.* In a moment, the demon only had attention for defence, as it belatedly attempted to put its shell of darkness around it before it was driven into the ground. *The darkness has gone up, but my horses continue to take turns attacking the centre and recovering, attacking and recovering. They are taking some small cuts in the process, but from where their hooves stop and the noise that is made, they are pummelling the demon into paste.*

Bianca was left to look at the other combats. *The men seem to have a harder task. Saint George, please protect them. They have no idea how effective their blows are or what weaknesses they can exploit, even with my inexperience I can see that they are blindly striking out and only connecting by luck. In the meantime, when they come out of the dark I can see that the cuts on their bodies, limbs and, more worryingly, heads are becoming more numerous and they are starting to run with blood.*

All at once Hulagu swung his mace in an upper cut through the blackness. *It seems to intersect with something.* A high-pitched scream erupted and the darkness vanished. The demon lies stunned on the ground in front of Hulagu and Uzun. *They quickly dispatch it.*

Just as they were turning to the other two Malik slashed at head height through the dark sphere. *He is rewarded by seeing the darkness around the demon vanish. Its head is flying away—the body falling to the ground. All four turn to me. I get to just stand and watch for more demons. Firestar is still pounding an obviously dead demon with his hooves, minor cuts streaming. Sirocco stands aside with blood running from a fairly deep wound on his shoulder. It seems that the attack is over.*

Hulagu ran back up the ridge and scanned around the area. *Everyone tries to stay still as he listens for more ominous popping sounds.* "Clear" he calls. Tzachaz gave a sigh and fell to the ground, bleeding from a cut to the head. Malik began stemming the flow of blood as Uzun rummaged for bandages. Tzachaz was bleeding from many wounds but the one to the head looked serious. Bianca ran to the horse packs and pulled out the bandages and compresses and began attending to the horses' wounds, in particular, Sirocco's shoulder while the others tended to the man.

Once the bleeding was stemmed on people and horses, Bianca dug out of the packs the small bag of what they hoped were Betterberries. Uzun volunteered to try them and ate three. *It looks like some of his wounds are closing slightly. The bleeding has certainly stopped.* By that time Tzachaz was almost unconscious as the exhilaration of combat was replaced by pain and the loss of blood. Before he could no longer swallow they made him eat half of the berries while Hulagu and Malik had three each. Tzachaz continued to lie down, waiting for the berries to work their magic.

Hulagu went back to the top of the rise to resume his watch, while Malik and Uzun began dragging the demon's bodies clear. *These stink already. It seems that they rot quickly. It is time to give a prayer of thanks before trying to go back to sleep.*

In the morning, Malik spoke up, "Those things are not supposed to roam around. They are either left in a place or are summoned or sent. I suggest that we look carefully around as we try and find our darts."

Several of these, and most of my bullets, are in what remains of the bodies, but the others need looking for in the long grass. It didn't take long to get a result. Near the place where Bianca had brought down the first demon, Malik found a small oaken rod. He picked it up and turned around, immediately dropping it with an expression of surprise on his face.

"It went 'beep'," he said.

He sounds embarrassed.

"What do you mean?" asked Hulagu.

"I picked it up and was turning around when it made a soft 'beep' noise. I was surprised and dropped it," replied Malik.

Uzun picked it up. "No noise," he said and waved it around.

'Beep', went the rod. They all crowded around and looked at the rod closely and saw that there was an arrow engraved into the wood. Uzun tried to point it at things to no effect. *He points it at people. Nothing happens until he points it at Hulagu.* It went 'beep' again. We get to pass it around. It only makes noise when it is pointing at Hulagu. *It does not matter who holds it, but it has to be held.*

"We have a wand of detecting Hulagu." She turned to Hulagu. "Remember that Koyunlu said that you would be taken care of. It looks like these were what had been sent to do that. They would have succeeded if you had been on your own or just with me." *The Pack-hunters look impressed. I guess that they have never known anyone before that has had demons sent after him, and especially seeing that the demons were given some magic to help them find him as well.*

Hulagu nodded in agreement. "The more we see, the more grandfather Nokaj's prophecy is confirmed. We must be off." He looked at the Pack-hunters. "We thank you for your aid. It helped to save our lives. Now Bianca and I must be on our way as quickly as we can."

"No!" said Malik, glancing at the other two of his kin. "Your story was glamorous, but it was just a story until now. The attack and this rod confirm that it is a real and important story. You are on the land of our clan and we must, in honour, make sure that you are safely escorted through it to your destination. We will escort you towards Evilhalt. The honour of our totem is at stake here and, perhaps, even more." *He looks at the other two. They both nod back.*

"Again, I thank you, and gratefully I accept your offer. Still, if we have recovered our weapons, we must now be off," said Hulagu.

Quick preparations and checks followed as they mounted and rode off. Bianca mounted Firestar and let Sirocco move unencumbered, his saddle on top of Sluggard's packs.

"Hulagu is right," Malik said to her as they rode off. "Your totem is indeed the Horse. I have seen many of these Latin fighting horses, but few that are eager to fight when their rider is off them, except to defend themselves or their rider. I have never seen them following like a puppy and coming when they are called as yours do."

The day passed uneventfully with grass and wind until they reached the Baerami River. Here they had to move along it until Malik showed them a ford so that they could cross without getting the horse packs wet. Bianca was shown the mouth of the Aissa Flow where it met the Baerami as they moved east. Malik showed her the great crocodiles of the river, which can take a horse and man easily. They saw several sunning themselves on the opposite bank and even some below them on their side. While crossing, they were even more vigilant and the men all had their bows or heavy spears ready the whole time.

Once across they moved a short distance to where Malik showed them a spring that led to a small trickle of water running to the river. It was now late in the day so they decided to set up camp here. Bianca started cooking, and Hulagu took up station on a rise while the Pack-hunters made a thorough sweep of the area. They reported no sign of anything suspicious.

Everyone went through their evening preparations and, in Bianca's case, prayer. *Already I feel that I am getting more of a handle on my knife throwing and am becoming more confident in it. I am no expert, but at least I feel like I am throwing harder and the knives stick into the shield better. Perhaps now they will cause some damage, as long as the target has no armour to protect them.*

Before the watches were set and they went to sleep, they all made their final prayers or rituals for the night. *It seems that it is not just me that is a little worried, each of them seems aware of how close we came to dying last night, even if the men do make light of it.*

At least this night proves to be quiet and uneventful, even if I toss and turn as I do every night with dreams of rape and torture and now fell beasts — not pleasant ones at all. I am glad to wake up slightly damp with sweat and with a pounding heart, but with no actual threats present.

I have to admit to enjoying the next four days and nights that followed. We moved north with the Aissa Flow somewhere to our left, passing herds of eland, zebra, wildebeest, and the occasional mob of hoppers. Now, midway through our fifth day, a line of trees is visible on the horizon to the northeast.

"We will reach the tree line within a few hours," said Malik. "Do you want to camp before we reach the edge of the trees, or at their edge, or do we keep going and look for a clearing within the trees? We still have several day's travel within the trees before we reach Evilhalt and I would prefer to spend the time in the clear on the free plains, rather than confined."

"I agree," said Hulagu. *He is looking at me for my opinion.*

"Why are you looking at me? I was raised in cities. I know nothing at all of the land outside. I do, however, expect you to listen to me when we get to towns."

I was getting used to the noises of the grasslands, even if I am not sure what made them. Now unfamiliar noises come from the thick woods beyond the edge. At least, the night is passing uneventfully.

The next day Malik led them further north. *We are staying well out of bowshot of the trees. I think that I recognise many of them from around Freehold, but here they grow in untidy profusion, unlike the few coppiced and tended forests that I have seen before.*

Just before noon we come upon a track from the west, although track is probably too generous a term for it. I can see that there is a lot of traffic along it, but each set of travellers seems to make their own choice as to which way is the best to follow through the grass and low scrub. The result is a braiding of wheel ruts and hoof prints. It is obvious even to me that we are following another of these threads that moves beside the trees, one that is less travelled than the other. All of these paths, wherever they come from, have a common destination. In the wall of trees there is but one large gap and all of the tracks lead there.

As they turned and entered the forest, the winter sun was cut off. *We are in a dappled world. The clarity of light on the plains is replaced by the muted sounds, soft chirrups of birds and occasional patches of sunlight that work their way through bare branches to fall stippled on a litter of leaves. Overhead are large and old trees, mainly with spreading branches. Underfoot, at the sides of the path, are short, well-eaten grasses, small herbs and patches of bracken and brambles. Every now and then a small clump of rocks can be seen. It is much cooler here in the forest and I am not the first to reach for the cloaks that we needed only at night on the plains. Soon we are all wearing them.*

This was a very different part of the trip to Bianca. *The path we are following tends unmistakeably east, but in doing so it meanders around trees and rocks, over small rills and sometimes through open glades of different sizes. I can usually see quite a distance through the open spaces under bare branches, but sometimes the sight of cattle or deer at close range surprises us. Once we even rounded a clump of evergreens to see, two hundred paces away, a small herd of cow lizards moving away from us in an unhurried fashion.*

They set up camp that night in what was obviously a well-used campsite in a clearing. There was even a rudimentary enclosure for animals and a low wall between the campsite and the forest itself. Malik led the way and explained that the enclosure and the wall are being built by the persons who use them. He looked around on the ground outside the wall until he found a few rocks. *They may have once already belonged to a structure of some sort as they look shaped.* He brought these and added them to the wall where it looked like they would fit best. *The others follow suit and bring in wood for my fire while I, as usual, end up cooking.*

All of the horses, except mine, which are left to roam free, are put inside the enclosure for the night and a pole, sitting there waiting on top of the wall, is put across the opening. Hulagu, who declared himself skilled at animal physicking inspected Bianca's dressing of Sirocco's wound, although he was only allowed close once Bianca had hugged the horses and instructed them to allow him. He replaced the poultice and inspected and approved her stitching. Sirocco had moved slowly that day, but without much of a problem. Bianca softly accused him of trying for sympathy as she rubbed him down. He snorted.

After checking the surrounds, the men took turns keeping watch and fetching water from the stream for the horses and for Bianca, while she kept cooking. *A closer view is forced on us by the trees and I even have to adjust to having less light here in the forests.* She checked the sky. *Although Terror is now waxing in the sky and the smaller Panic is getting near its maximum the leaves cut out so much light that they make it harder for me to see.*

To add to her discomfort, the next day it started to rain, not heavily, but in a continuous light drizzle. *It is enough to make everything damp and to slowly soak through cloaks, wetting any bowstring. The Khitan have unstrung their bows in disgust.*

They were to stay unstrung for the next two days as they squelched along the sodden path. *I noticed that the men, more used to the outdoor life, had already put tinder and wood in one of the horse packs to keep them dry when we entered the forest. That, at least, lets me light a fire, but once we add damp wood to the flames, columns of smoke announce our presence. This forces us to only light a fire late in the day when it is unlikely to be noticed. I would not have thought of that. Apparently, it is important and the men take turns climbing trees when we stop to see if they can see smoke from anyone else.*

On the third wet night, they shared their campsite with a large and well-armed group of Havenite traders headed west. *They have an escort of seven well-disciplined Freehold mercenaries. They look down their noses at the scruffy looking and damp Khitan. From the way they act, I think that they assume I am one as well.* While she was unloading the horses Malik and Hulagu tried to find out more from them. *They do not even try and be polite to the Khitan and speak only in Latin. Luckily Malik has more of that than Hulagu did when I met him.*

They say they are carrying spices, cloth and 'other goods' and do not want to be more forthcoming with the Khitan. Later Hulagu explained that the traders feared the party might turn around and announce what they carry in their cargo to raiders on the plains. *The Khitan seem amused by this, but I find, to my surprise, I am offended at the succession of slights being offered to my friends. The merchants only grudgingly let the two know that we will see Evilhalt the next day.*

Hulagu suggested they set their sleep a small distance from the others. *None of the four offered any formal greetings to the merchants.* Once they started to set up their camp Bianca shed her jacket and started working, like a Khitan girl would, in her damp gauze undershirt. *I seem to be distracting the guards. I am ashamed of the rudeness of the people from my land. It is so unlike the hospitality I have been shown by the Khitan.* Without really thinking about it, she started to distract the caravan even more.

Once they had completed their routines, she stood where the fire lit her up from behind and sang, in Latin, the bawdiest tavern songs she knew from her life of working in taverns which were frequented by traders and their guards. *The Khitan seem to realise what I am doing and laughingly accompany me by beating time on anything that resonates.* She glanced over. *The guards seem to be paying little attention to anything except our side of their camp, to the annoyance of their employers. Saint Ursula, I pray to be forgiven for such lewd behaviour, but I am pleased with their reaction although, at the same time, I am somewhat surprised with myself for doing it. I am changing.*

During the night, the rain stopped and it dawned bright and fair. As they were packing and setting out they were all jacketless and again Bianca provided an overwhelming distraction to the guards. *The Khitan are behaving as brothers and ignoring me.* The display of her small but generously endowed frame, easily seen in the morning light, meant the caravan workers had to be often crossly reminded to keep at their jobs.

Soon after they headed off, and Bianca had put her jacket on, they started to see small assarts in the forest and people working them. *All of the assarts have roses growing in dense hedges around their tall fences and walls. It seemed these are one of the first things the locals plant when they move to an area.*

Occasionally they shared the track with a person or two. *Unlike the traders these people are reserved, but polite. They seem to have no fear of our little group.* Near midday they reached a small and new looking hamlet of half a hand of buildings, with another larger structure being built. Malik asked where they were and were told proudly this new building was to be the tavern of the new village of Westway.

Eventually, the five reached cultivated land and only a couple of clumps of trees and fields, either meadow, fallow or planted with roses, stood between them and the town of Evilhalt, whose walls they could clearly see. *Beside us, and set apart from the forest, there is a large open hut beside a stone circle, which can be barely seen through a grove of ancient looking and giant trees. A group of people some horsed and some on foot are in a nearby field. None look like farmers.*

"We go no further," Malik said. "We have seen you safe off our clan lands and to this destination. We were due back to our clan some time ago and all of us have wives who will want a very good explanation for our continued absence. We will tell the tale of your adventure and of your quest and make sure that the story spreads and we will send a messenger to tell your family we have brought you safe to this point."

"Again, we thank you," said Hulagu, obviously speaking a fixed set of words. "May the plains ever be flat beneath your feet, may your herds prosper and may you die content in front of your children after a long life."

Without thinking Bianca went up to all three of the men and, while all were still mounted, kissed them on both cheeks. *I guess that this is what one does to a brother. This is all unknown territory for me. From the reaction of the Pack-hunters I have done more or less the right thing.*

Malik replied in a similar formal tone for the three, "We thank you for these wishes. We wish you the same and, above all, we hope your quest is a success."

With this the Pack-hunters turned their horses and both groups went on their paths without looking back at each other. *Hulagu had quietly explained to me last night that this is how we would part. This is normally how it is done on the plains.*

Chapter XIV

Christopher

Brother Christopher, I believe it is time for you to make a decision about your future," said Abbott Theophilus.

I am a novice standing in front of the Abbott. I feel nervous. "I wish—"

"I know very well what you think you wish," the Abbott interjected. "You think you want the life of a monk and a teacher—perhaps even that of a solitary. However, I am far from convinced. I think you should marry and take a church and a village to tend. I have watched you since you were young and know the things that have sent you to us to be raised. I have even discussed you with the Metropolitan and we have both had occasion to include you in our prayers. We have decided to ordain you and send you into the world for a few years to find out which of us, you or I, is correct."

"But—"

"There will be no buts." *There is just a brief smile flickering over his face.* "Such would be disobedience and that is obviously the wrong thing for a monk to display. You will head out. You may be the missionary who will return the errant to us. You may find a wife and return to care for a flock or you may not survive. However, all of our prayer and our observation of the signs and portents tell us you have a destiny that would be wasted in a life of contemplation and that you need to leave now. Your way lies south."

"But Abbot, I know so little of the outside world. I have been here since I was a small child and barely remember else." He looked around him, bewildered, at the familiar walls, at the crucifix and icons on them and at the Abbott's desk with papers on it. "This is my world."

"We know this and count it another reason for you to go. Most of us within these walls came to the monastery after a full life outside. Even Brother Petrus, who is only just counted as adult, has been raised as a part of a large family and, for him they all agreed that his choice and vocation was clear for over ten years. Why, Brother Theodule was a grandfather of forty summers and a priest for many years before that, when his wife died and he decided to join us. If you became a monk straight away, you might come to regret never having been a part of the world."

He held a hand up to forestall any comment. "A poor show of the obedience a monk requires it would be if you were to refuse. The Metropolitan and I have decided that you must spend a minimum of two years outside, and away from Greensin, before we accept your decision to renounce the world, if that is the way you finally decide. In the meantime, we are very happy for you to make yourself useful. The copy of the Gospels that is held at Evilhalt has grown old from use. As you know we have just completed a new copy and it has just now finished being checked for errors. You are to deliver it. After you have done this you may travel the world as you wish. We simply ask that you call into any church that you are near and help them for as long as you may before moving on—but do not outlast your usefulness nor stay in just one place unless they lack a priest. On your return, or if you can send a message before that, you are to tell us if any have needs or problems that they have not mentioned."

Christopher sighed. *It seems that I must accept my fate.*

The Abbott continued, "Being ordained, you are also to minister to any of the flock that you may encounter. There are believers all over the Land. Some may not have seen a priest for quite a while. As well, we charge you to not hesitate to bring back to the True Faith any schismatics that you may meet in your travels."

Christopher again nodded his assent. *I do not feel convinced. I want to stay here.*

"Now go see Brother Porter. He will equip you. Once that is done, spend the night in contemplation. You will be ordained in the morning and on the next morn you are to set out."

"As you wish, Abbot." He suppressed a deep sigh. Again he looked at the comforting sights around him in the office. *This might be the last time I see it. I have just lost the security that I have felt for most of my life. I might never feel that comfort again.*

That night, which he spent entirely in the basilica itself, was the longest of Christopher's life so far. He sat there in his coarse habit, in the chill of the empty basilica until he was interrupted by the midnight service. He prayed for guidance, for help and, belatedly, in thanks. He wandered around and viewed the mosaic icons on the walls and roof, from where they were meant to be seen, contemplating the mysteries and miracles they portrayed. He lit candles and prayed to the saints depicted in other mosaics and on the smaller painted icons. *I am going out into the world. I have little skill at arms or indeed at anything worldly. I can only just use the sling and staff that Brother Porter has given to me. At least the latter has been prayed over to enhance the damage that it does to evil and its creatures.*

I have been given an icon—it is a small icon of my namesake, the patron of travellers. I have a pen-case and ink, a small prayer book, a book of services, and my notes on the miracles that I am able to use, or might have to use, all held in a scrip. I have a rosary at my waist, a cross around my neck, with holy water and an asperser in my pack. I suspect that these last few items may be of more use to me than any weapons. I have my medical kit. I have a supply of dried and smoked food that seems large to me, but probably will not prove to be. I will soon be relying on the help of other members of the ecumen to survive. I even have been given some money in a little purse tucked away in a scrip hanging at my belt. I am not used to having money.

In the morning, his ordination was presided over by the Metropolitan. In a cloud of burning incense and before the other monks it all went smoothly. *Once it is done I feel a sense of—completeness—that worries me somewhat.* Father Christopher then spent the remainder of the morning being congratulated by those he was leaving behind. *The ordination of a new priest is a rare enough occurrence and it is just cause for a day of ease to be given to everyone.*

The next day, after saying his first service of Orthros, Father Christopher was seen off by the entire monastery. *Normally a messenger, such as me, will be sent off with merchants, but none are expected to pass through in the right direction for quite some time. In such cases the decision is usually to trust in God and His protection.* Christopher set off joyously into the world. *I also feel more than a measure of trepidation. Except when gathering herbs and timber from the woods with other monks, or tending to some of the nearby sick, I have never really been outside the monastery. If I am truly honest with myself, and I may as well be so, I have to admit that I am rather unworldly. All my life that I can remember, I have always counted that as a virtue.*

Leaves of green were turning rust with autumn, but still there was some warmth in the air that was around him. Christopher had been given his directions and so, waving at those behind for the last time he left the town of Greensin behind him.

Once he had left the hamlets and assarts that surrounded the houses behind, the smells of wood smoke and fields gave way to the smells of the wild—or forest and wilderness. As he walked he prayed about his destiny. So lost in his personal contemplation was he, that he wandered along the road without paying total attention to exactly where he was headed. *Still, I seem to be making good progress as I travel through the day down a road that is bright with birdsong.* Christopher rambled along happily. *I feel, at last, a part of the entirety of God's creation.*

As the day moved towards dusk Christopher began to hear the sound of axes and he moved towards it a trifle quicker. After an hour, a clearing appeared to the right of the path. In it eight men had felled a forest giant, some sort of gum, and were trimming it. *To one side a group of bullocks are roughly fenced off with rope and some trimmed branches. The men are there to haul the timber off. Two pairs of giant wheels lean against a nearby tree. They are ready to be attached to the trimmed trunk of the fallen giant.*

"The Peace of Christ on you and blessings be upon your labour."

They all stopped and looked at him. "Hail Father and thank you. Where are you off to alone?" said one of the men, a bearded giant with a bare torso, a man who hefted a gigantic axe as if it were a willow wand.

"I am Father Christopher and I am off to Evilhalt."

"Evilhalt? Then you are on the wrong road," said the giant of a man. "This is the road to Wolfneck. You must have turned left instead of right after you left Greensin."

"Did I? I cannot get to Evilhalt this way?" *I am bewildered. There was a turn off? I wonder if I inadvertently took the wrong exit from the clearing. It is quite possible.*

"No Father. You will either have to retrace your steps for over half a day or else go across country. That will be shorter, but you may get lost in even a worse fashion."

"I thank you. I must be off." He stepped off to the right of the path.

The large man spoke again, "Wait Father, it is best if you stay with us for the night and start fresh in the morning. These woods are not always safe at night."

I have never been in danger before. "I thank you. Yes, I will stay."

Introductions were made and the men turned to finish their work for the day. Christopher looked around. *There is not much I can do.* Using the one thing he had experience with, he set himself to gather firewood, carrying and dragging it to near where the men had set up a camp. *I feel my contribution to be meagre.*

The men finished their work and started to get food ready. *Some of them are looking at me expectantly. I am unsure what they want.* He started on his evening prayers. *This is what they were waiting for.* He ended up the day conducting his second service of Hesperinos. *This time it is done in the forest while a meal is being prepared, with the men alternately cooking and helping then sitting on the ground before him.*

He contrasted this to his first service. *The painted and mosaic covered walls of the basilica are transformed into leaves and branches in the deepening dark of the wild forest. The chanting of monks is translated to the lowing of bullocks and the black-clad monks in robes changed to semi-naked, work-stained and sweaty foresters. As I pray and speak I wonder if maybe God is speaking to me and telling me that I have now decisively moved from the spiritual into the temporal world and am now firmly a part of it.*

The next morning, after morning prayers were said, Father Christopher set out, full of instructions from the men as they began to finish trimming the tree. *I have decided to cut across country. The timber cutters think that it will be much quicker. They have showed me how to find south by looking at the moss on the tree trunks.* As he went, he smiled. *I can find north easily. All I have to do is keep the sound of their axes, echoing through the previously untouched forest as they clear a tiny bit of it at my back—again perhaps a metaphor for me putting civilisation behind me. Gradually the sound fades, but the woods are so quiet that I have reached what I hope is the right path and have turned towards the east, that is towards my left hand, before I can no longer hear them faintly behind me.*

For Christopher, the next few days were uneventful and joyful. *I find myself ambling down the path marvelling at the beauty of God's creation that I see around me. I spend hours contemplating the Great Chain of Being and man's place in it.* He did see many small animals and they seemed to have no fear of him. His thoughts turned to Saint Francis and Christopher specially addressed him in his prayers. *Whether the Saint aids me I will never know, but I have only seen one predator and that is a large cat that lay asleep in the sun on the branch of a tree as I passed by.*

He ate of his dried food and pickles—*ample food for one accustomed to monastic fare*—and drank from his water skin, refilling it at small streams and only taking from swift running water. *I cannot remember why the men insisted on me doing that, but they did, so I do.* At night, again as he had been firmly instructed, he climbed into a tree and slept there, hoping to avoid most of the predators of the forest. *I am not very good at climbing. I did not have a normal childhood, but at least I collect fewer scratches as the days wear on.*

He did discover his rough cassock and sandals, really the only clothes he knew, were not well suited to the outdoor life and he soon learnt to remove his sandals to climb. *I should not have rejected Brother Porter's offer of more normal clothes.* Despite his continued concern at falling out, the broad tree limbs were nearly as comfortable as his customary cot and the unfamiliar exercise of walking so far led him to sleep both quickly and soundly. *Each day I wear the soreness in my muscles proudly and each day I am sure that the soreness grows less and I walk further and further.*

One day Christopher heard what he thought was most likely a wolf howling to the east. It sounded to be to the south of the road. Christopher thought little of this and continued on. *That is a second wolf howling—this time north of the road. I don't know if wolves really attack people, or if it is just that way in stories, but I do not want to find out.* He started to look for a tree that he could quickly climb, but climbable trees seemed to be scarce here. The first wolf howled again, this time more closely followed by the cry of the second. *They seem to be much closer now and they are joined by a third. This one seems to be straight ahead of me.*

Christopher hastened his pace. *What miracles can I summon that might prove to be useful. Are wolves evil? I do not know, but a miracle of protection from evil creatures might help. I do know how to compel sleep. That miracle is meant for a person, to aid a sick patient, but if I change the words there—how many should I allow for? I have only heard three, but there could be twice that many—better allow for eight.*

If I need to cast my protection, then the miracle cannot last for long, and I will have to change it from a compulsion to just inducing, but it should work. I cannot make it specific to wolves, although that would save a bit of mana, just to canines. They sound like dogs of some sort, but they might not be wolves. Oh—the incantation is meant to be on touch. I need to add some range. Twenty paces will have to do. Now I feel as prepared as I can be.

I will cast the sleep first and wait and see if I need the protection, or even another sleep. As he walked he practiced each line separately. *It is always better to be prepared.* The wolves howled again. *I think that they are quite close now. I wish that I had the strength to radiate a circle of complete protection. If I worked out how, perhaps I could do so in a dire emergency. I will have a high risk of failure and will be drained for days, but I may need it one day—later—I will work on this later. No, now it will be best to stick to my plan.*

He saw the wolves and a suitable tree to climb at the same time. *The tree is much closer, but they can move much faster than I can. I keep moving but the jet-black beasts stop on seeing me. They seem to briefly look at each other before they resume moving. I need to keep walking, clutching my staff. My hand on it is suddenly moist with sweat. There are six of these dark-looking wolves, running as a tight group.* Quickly he started to say the words of his chant, almost fumbling them out of nervousness. *Timing is everything.* As the wolves passed the tree he slowed his speech—*almost there.* The closest wolf was at the very most ten paces away when he finished.

They have all stopped, obviously fighting God's will as expressed through my words. Christopher felt a wave of relief as they failed in this. *For a moment, I am tempted to kill them as they sleep, but I think of Saint Francis and of mercy and cannot bring myself to do so. Perhaps they are innocent creatures and, when they awake and find that they cannot have me, they will just leave on their own and let me continue.*

He walked through the sleeping group and reached the tree and climbed it quickly, scraping his hands and knees on the bark as he did so. *I am up in its branches only just in time.* He looked down. *The wolves are already starting to wake up. They are yawning and shaking their heads, getting up and stretching, sniffing the air and the ground. It did not take them long to find out where I am. I was wrong about them leaving me alone. They have taken up station under my tree. Every now and then one howls.*

Christopher waited, considering if he had any options. *My staff is still leaning against the tree where I put it to allow me to climb. I am not even sure that I can get down far enough to gain hold of it without risking falling out. Under me the wolves wait, seemingly listening for something. Another one howls. They are keeping this up.* Eventually, in the distance, could faintly be heard an answer. *It seems that there are more of them around than the pack that I have here. I wonder what I should do—what I can do.*

The wolves looked at each other. Another howled. *That cry ended in a strange noise.* He looked down. *One wolf lies dead underneath me, its head transfixed by an arrow. The others have leapt to their feet and are looking to the north. Another wolf is hit and they have broken into a sudden run. I can see that it is a race, arrow after arrow bringing down wolf after wolf as they close on their attacker.* In his efforts to see who was helping him, Father Christopher nearly did fall out of his tree. *I cannot stay here while someone is acting for me, doing what I should have done for myself. They might need help.* With some difficulty, he started to slowly climb down from his safe perch to the ground. He ignored the scrapes leaving him scratched and bleeding and tugged his robe free of an obstacle, tearing it as he did so.

Chapter XV

Astrid

I know that I am more than just good-looking, if I don't smile too broadly. Not just by the standards of Wolfneck but also from the reaction to my appearance from outsiders I have met during trade. Wolfneck people tend to be at least plain. All I have to show for my part Kharl heritage is a strong jaw, a more than slightly cat-like appearance and long tongue, and the long and strong incisors of a large hunting cat. Otherwise I am tall and athletically slender and strong with breasts large enough to sometimes be a nuisance when firing my bow and with very pale blonde hair. Usually my hair is in braids that I curl up against my head, but when it is loose it hangs down near to my waist. I am equally at home hunting in the forests and snows of my land, or on my father's ship, seeking fish or whales.

Unfortunately, my appearance and skill are also my curse. If I was more Kharlish in appearance like Helga, or with faint greenish skin, like Gudrid, then perhaps Svein would be less interested in me. It is a marriage alliance that will at least heal years of bad feeling between two of the village ships. I would have been able to handle his appearance if he had been pleasant. I am sure that I could have coped with him being a childless widower and near as old as my father if he were gentle. Instead, when he is on shore he is an ugly, violent, lecherous, loud-mouthed drunkard. When he is at sea he is supposed to be just bad tempered, even if still ugly—a true throwback to the past. The Darkspeech that is used in Wolfneck is well suited to invective and most of it is used by, or can be used about, him.

I keep telling myself that my widowed father is not a cruel man, but his main concern is with his several sons, who will take over his ship, not with his single daughter. As far as he is concerned, the lack of unrelated men in town, as well as the high bride price I command, restricts the field of eligible partners to just one—Svein. While I don't care about the bride price, none of the available men with fewer resources interest me either. The men who are free are either dull, ugly, or nekulturny or, even worse, are some combination of these three. Is it too much to ask for, to be happy with the choice that is offered to me?

Last night in the tavern was probably the trigger. My father is at sea with my brothers and Svein started by doing what he has so many times before, making lewd remarks about my figure and what he will do to me once we are married. Last night he had made those comments publicly and loudly, boasting about his prowess, experience and size and comparing them to my virginity and lack of experience. He boasted how he would make me beg for him to take me every way—and he was explicit in this, even promising to make me ask to be shared with his friends like a jug of ale. The shame of his words still burns on my cheeks and his promises of undoubtedly rough sex in no way interest me. He has never been this blatant with his behaviour before.

This morning she had gone hunting to clear her head and to get out of town for a while. *The quiet of the northern forest has been ideal for my mood, but my mind is just not with the hunting.* Even though, out of habit she moved with all her customary stealth and skill, all she had really done was to move around the forest in a mental fog. *I am sure that I have ignored animals I could have taken.*

I have realised I really cannot put up with a beast like that as a husband. I have to do something. I could marry him and then kill him on the wedding night, but that will mean I will have to put up with his touch until he dies and will face trial and, at least, outlawry. Why not run away? My father will scarce notice that I am gone. Svein will find solace with a jug of spirits and a sheep or something else of his level. There has to be someone out there who will respect me and care for me.

I will go—now. My father took the boat out yesterday morning and my brothers are all with him. I am alone in the house for a while. Now is the best time. Even if he decides to bring me back then I will still have a few day's head start and should be able to evade him.

Astrid turned her feet towards home. She might have been wandering around without thinking, but in this forest, that would look the same everywhere to an outsider, once she concentrated on the details around her, it took but one glance at the trees, the infrequent rocks, standing water and the slope of the land to tell her where to head.

I am beginning to have second thoughts. This is, after all, the only home that I know. Here is where my friends are. I know my mind is going backwards and forwards. Arriving back in Wolfneck and walking to her house, Svein saw her some way off. He outlined her shape with his hands, made a lewd gesture and loudly suggested that they start on their marriage celebrations while her father was away and formalise it later in the old custom. She shuddered and shook her head.

For the first time in my life I feel a degree of gratitude to Svein. She went so far as to briefly thank him in her thoughts for helping her to make up her mind. *Yes, I am definitely leaving him behind and going now to a new life— whatever it turns out to be.*

She hurried home and prepared a well-used backpack, grabbed the jewellery that her mother had left her, some money, food, a big bag of salt, spare clothes, hunting gear and her weapons. *It is too early for serious snow and I am going to head south, so I will leave behind my skis and snowshoes. I will take my glare-wraps for bright light.* She looked around and drew a deep breath. *These are the sights and smells of home and this is the last I will know of them.* She had just cooked. *The biscuits from the griddle are coming with me and so are the griddle and some cooking gear. Everything of my life so far will now be behind me. Thank goodness.* She only just remembered to leave a brief note to say that she was leaving. She pinned it in place on a cutting board with an old gutting knife. *I am not saying why I am going or where. It would make a bad situation worse in such a small town.* Peering cautiously out of the house, Astrid waited until no one was in sight to see her laden down before heading out of the town and out of her old life.

She started by using the trail south. *There are always so many people using it that it is covered in tracks—I used it when going out hunting earlier If they start right behind me, only the best local trackers will be able to make out which tracks are from my earlier trip and which are from now. Even if my father caught a whale straight away, which is unlikely at this time of year, I won't be missed for at least four days. If I am not seen then, after what had happened in the tavern last night, the whole village will easily believe that I am staying in the house and hiding away from Svein. The extra time will lay down even more tracks over mine. It will not take much luck for it to rain or even to snow and that will wipe out the evidence of my passage almost completely.*

L ate in the afternoon Astrid took advantage of one of several rocky outcrops that crossed the path, but not the first, to move off to the right of the trail. Once she left the outcrop she used her skills as a tracker to hide the evidence of her passage for some way. It was slow, but she was confident that she had done a good job. By the time she was happy to move quickly again, it was almost time to sleep for the night.

Travelling alone in the north, where the giant and ancient conifers are hard to climb and there are few settlements, there is very little choice as to what to do at night. All that is possible for me is to go to sleep and hope. She was pleased to have the good fortune to find a tangle of fallen trees and was able to make a passage into them. After eating she crawled in to a small and fairly open cave of logs floored with pine needles, and pulled some branches after her. *Snakes are very rare this far north and, hopefully, if anything large tries to come after me I can use my spear, lying back along my entryway, to repel it.* However, her precautions were unneeded. She slept undisturbed.

Day after day she followed a routine of travel and sleep. Sometimes she laid snares at night and once she shot a small hopper with her longbow. That night, having eaten some of its meat and more out of habit than anything else, she used her skinning knife to scrape and rub its skin clean and then rubbed some salt into it before rolling it up. *As I move further and further south, a feeling of lightness is filling me. I am free at last from having to care for a father and brothers who only notice me if something isn't done around the house. I am free from a marriage that I dread and I am free to choose my own path and destiny.*

Astrid had originally thought to stay in the north and headed roughly for Greensin. *To be truly free, I will at least have to go to some place that is truly different. Too many from Wolfneck will see me in Greensin. I am not an outlaw and I might decide to return to the north someday, but I will have to start by going outside it. I will go to Evilhalt, at the centre of The Land and, from there, why, I will just see what happens. I will just waft as I feel the urge and let the winds blow me. This is freedom. This is what choice is about.*

She changed her direction of travel towards her left hand and, over the next several days, she drifted slowly south through untracked forest. Once she was laid up for a whole day in a providential cave when the first snows of the season came in. *They are only light and I could have easily travelled through them, but I am in no hurry to get anywhere.* She spent the day lazing over a fire, repairing the small rips and tears in her clothes that came from travelling off road in the wild. She found this relaxing. The snow was still on the ground when Astrid set out refreshed the next day. *It could possibly stay there now until spring, getting slowly deeper and deeper. Gradually the pines of the north around me are beginning to be replaced by other trees, some green, some already bare, others with leaves turning red or brown. I can hear birdcalls I don't know and even some of the animals that I am seeing are different.*

It is not just the sights. The smell of the forest has changed completely. My nostrils tease out the new scents as I try to work out what they mean.

A few days later her easy routine was interrupted. She had wandered west, away from the mountains and the Methul River and was probably only a few days south and east of Greensin, probably nearing the track from there to the east when she heard the baying of wolves break out. *It sounds like a pack.* She kept going. *Wolves rarely bother Humans, particularly armed ones, unless they are very hungry. That is unlikely when there is so much game around that has the fatness of the end of summer on their bodies.*

Eventually it became apparent the wolves were not moving. *The baying is less frequent now, but it is all coming from the same place. This time there is an answer in the distance. If the wolves are not moving it usually means they have their quarry cornered and cannot get at it.* She looked around. *There are no rocky outcrops in the area, so the prey has to be in a tree. In this area that means that their prey has to be Human and, if they are persisting, then the person cannot harm them.*

Astrid sighed. *I suppose that I should do something.* She checked the wind. *It is coming from the southwest. Good, they will not smell me and I will have some cover for the sound of my approach.* Moving with increased caution she proceeded, looking ahead for sounds of life, but checking her sides and rear to make sure that there was nothing stalking her in turn.

A wolf became visible about three hundred paces away, just glimpsed through the trees. *It is as black as night. That explains it. Of all the wolves, only the large black ones attack Humans on sight and they regard people as their favourite food. Many hunters have been lost to a pack of them. They are not the same as normal wolves and it is said that they will even take many losses from their pack in order to kill a person.*

Astrid kept going, moving from tree to tree and trying to see more of what was happening. Eventually she was rewarded. *Around a hundred paces away four wolves sit or lie under a tree and two are pacing around it, all watching the tree. There is someone in it.*

Astrid propped her spear against a tree before taking off her pack. Next, she took off her quiver and placed eight arrows point down in the ground in front of her. Looking up she saw that the wolves still had not noticed her. *Good.*

Astrid took another arrow from her quiver and put it in her longbow, a stave her own height, a full fathom long. One of the sitting wolves bayed. She drew back her bow, took aim, and fired. It struck the wolf, the one that had just bayed, in the head and it fell dead. As one the wolves looked in her direction. She fired again. This time she was not so lucky. It struck a wolf, but only wounded it. She fired a third shaft as they bounded towards her. This time she killed a beast, striking it full in the chest, the shaft buried up to the flight feathers in its flesh.

Arrows four and five killed a third wolf, the next nearest. Six and seven dispatched the next. Arrow number eight hit the fifth in the leg, slowing it. *There will be no time for the last arrow.* Astrid dropped her bow and grabbed her spear. She just had time to prepare, grounding the butt and dropping to one knee as the wolf leapt. *I have just one chance.* The wolf flew, jaws agape, attacking the figure crouching before it. Astrid raised her spear and the wolf struck its point. The long wide blade entered the wolf's chest and it ended its leap and its life, slumped against the crosspiece immediately behind the blade.

Astrid rose and struggled to clear her blade for the last, wounded wolf that was approaching. She was able to get it clear but was unable to bring the point to bear. She had to desperately fend off the attack with the spear clutched in both hands as a staff. The wolf's fangs brushed her shoulder as it went past and there was a small stab of pain. The wolf landed clumsily as Astrid took a better grasp on her spear. Both recovered and faced each other, each trying to stare the other down. The wolf raised its muzzle and howled.

Distant howls answered it. Astrid desperately lunged at the wolf's extended throat and was rewarded. She met the resistance of flesh, but it did not go far enough in. *The wolf is moving back.* It moved sideways and feinted forward. Astrid just tracked it with her blade. It moved the other way and repeated the move. Again, Astrid showed no reaction. It moved sideways and looked to be doing the same, but this time the attack was real. Astrid reacted a little slowly, a step back caused the wolf to pass to her right, but she did not have time to bring the point of her spear to bear.

Instead of impaling the wolf, she had managed to bring the blade against the wolf's side and as the keen blade knocked it further aside it opened up the wolf from shoulder to flank. As she turned to her right she saw the wolf lying on the ground, its guts spilling out onto the ground but still trying to rise. She drove the butt spike down into its ribs, shattering them. It shuddered and died. Looking up she saw the wolves intended victim awkwardly getting out of his tree onto the ground, almost falling flat as he did so, unbalanced by a large pack on his back and made even clumsier by the cassock and sandals of a cloistered monk that he wore as his garb. *I have to move quickly. By the sound of it the others will be here soon.*

Chapter XVI

Christopher

Father Christopher stood on the ground near the body of the first wolf to die. *Approaching me is a beautiful young girl. She is dressed in a man's clothes but, from the way the low-laced neck opening is filled, is very obviously female. She is a pale ash-blonde and wears her hair in braids rolled up near her ears. Her eyes are dark-green. Her clothing is a jerkin in dark-green with trews and shirt in brown. In her left hand she holds a long hunting spear, its large blade bloody. Over her shoulder is slung a long bow—very long—and she looks to be a bit taller even than I am. With her right hand, she is pulling arrows from dead wolves as she walks. She stops to check that each one is truly dead.*

Nervously he made ready to greet her. *I do not have much experience with women, and what is more, most of those I do know are either elderly or sick or both. Now I have to greet an attractive woman who has probably saved my life—in the wild and with no chaperone.* He muttered a few words of prayer and asked himself if he was safe.

As she came closer she smiled and Christopher found himself nearly panicking.

Dear God, she has fangs like a beast! Has she saved me from those beasts only to eat me herself? No, that is unworthy. Something connected—*animal teeth and blonde, braided hair—she must be from Wolfneck. The people there are even Orthodox in belief. I will test this by trying out my Darkspeech on her.*

"May the blessings of God be unto you, young lady, and my personal thanks to you as well. I am Father Christopher from Greensin. I was able to make the wolves sleep but could not bring myself to kill God's creatures." He looked around at the bodies. "This may have been an error. I was not sure what to do next. I thought that they would leave if they could not have me."

Astrid

*H*e is not unhandsome, a bit shorter than me with a brown beard and hair and soft brown eyes. He has an unworldly, or is it just confused, expression on his face. He must be either a priest or a monk. His cassock shows signs of travel with stains and many small tears and one big one. She moved closer. He has a tonsure growing out—a new priest then. He has a very large backpack, obviously with something bulky in it. Around his neck hangs a crucifix of silver and a flat rectangular wooden object—the sort that usually opens to reveal an icon. His sole weapon seemed to be his staff.

My God, how has he survived this long to be this far from a village? Despite his beard, he is only young, older than me by only a few years at most. It looks like my freedom is about to be quickly curtailed. Someone has to look after him. He looks like he belongs in a monastery and knows nothing of the world. Oh well, at least, if he is still thinking like a monk then he won't be interested in me as a woman. Travelling with him should keep most men at bay, or at least get them to be of good behaviour in front of him. She prepared to greet him and put on her friendliest smile. Not too far in the distance wolves howled.

"Greetings, Father." *I was going to give a different origin, but my speech and teeth betray me and besides, it is probably a sin to lie to a priest.* "I am Astrid, of Wolfneck, and I doubt much that these are the creatures of God, more the creatures of the Adversary. Now we should put off any more theological discussion about them until we deal with the rest of the pack." She waved her spear in the general direction of the approaching howls. "These are black wolves. They delight in killing people and even other wolves. They are evil creatures, not really natural at all. My people kill all of them we find. Now, do you have any way to defend yourself?"

The priest sounds eager when he replies, sort of like a retriever dog in willingness to help. "If they are truly evil, then I can ask God for some protection for us," He continued, sounding happy as he did. "But apart from that, although I have never used them in anger, I have a little skill with both a sling and my staff."

"Unless there are more of them than there seem to be, that should be enough. From their noise, they are at least ten minutes away. Please make any preparations that you may need—but make them quickly."

Christopher nodded and, moving to a clear patch of bare dirt, began to make marks on the ground with the end of his staff. Astrid cleaned the arrows she had used and began to check that they were all still suitable to use again, placing them point first into the ground once she was done. *This Father Christopher made only a simple circle with a few lines in it and then he has spent most of the time praying before motioning me over to stand inside the circle with him.* She quickly did that and he took her hand. *With his other hand, he has taken a small book out of a pouch and opened it and, still holding my hand, he recites what I presume is a prayer. My Latin is very poor, but I think he said something about evil—but is malus 'evil' or 'apple'—it couldn't be apple.*

After he had finished, the priest nodded at her, Astrid also said amen and he motioned her to move out of the circle. *The howls are closing on us.* Astrid moved over to near a tree where she had her arrows. *The priest is following my lead.* When she leant her spear against the tree and nocked her bow, he did the same with his staff and readied a sling.

"Stand a bit behind me please Father." *At least the priest obeys me.*

Presently the pack came in sight. *This time the pack is much larger. Perhaps two smaller groups have joined. We have two hands of black wolves loping towards us.* Astrid began to fire and she heard the sling whirling soon after. *Wolves are beginning to fall, mostly from my arrows, but sometimes it must be from the priest. The wolves keep closing—I wondered if something is pressing them on. Surely they wouldn't normally keep on coming like this. If am lucky we will kill them all—and if they stop dodging behind bushes and trees when they can.*

Three are left. It is too close for a last shot. She dropped her bow to the side and behind her and leapt for her spear. "Take your staff. Keep behind me." She impaled the first wolf as it leapt towards her, at the same time trying to sidestep another. *It shouldn't have missed me, but it did. The protection must be helping.* At the same time, she heard a thunk. *Christopher's staff has hit the third wolf. Unless he hits something vital, that will not stop it.*

The next few seconds were filled with snapping jaws and two quickly moving weapons. Astrid dispatched the second wolf, but not before it had briefly latched onto her leg in a painful bite. *'sblood. That hurts.* She turned. *The Father has his back to the tree and is simply using his staff to fend off the animal, focussing only on defence. It is intent on getting to him but, between the protection and the staff, has not yet succeeded.* It didn't even notice as Astrid placed herself behind it and slew it with a thrust into its spine that first made it drop to its haunches as it lost the ability to stand and then followed up with a thrust into its body that made it scream in an almost Human fashion as it died. Christopher went to say something, but Astrid held up her hand, listening. *Good. No more howls are audible and there is no sound of rushing animals. There is an almost complete silence around them. Even the other animals of the area have gone quiet.*

"Now we recover our missiles." Taking her spear in hand and regaining her bow and putting it over her shoulder Astrid started to move towards the first dead wolf. "It is one of yours. Are you using bullets or stones?"

"Lead bullets. Why?" asked Christopher.

"Because if they are bullets you will need to dig them out in order to reuse them."

"Dig them out?" said Christopher. *Oh Lord—he is bemused as to why.*

"Yes. It is hard to replace them in the forest and you will need to glean them. We even need to look and try and find those that missed. Any that you lose now may be needed later. You never know what may happen out here."

Christopher approached the dead wolf. *He is obviously at a complete loss as to where to start. He is looking up at me with an expression on his face that says 'What next?'*

"Here, let me." Astrid sighed before producing a skinning knife and digging out the bullet. She paused briefly and then she started to skin the wolf.

"Why are you doing that? Is it a shape shifter? Will it rise again with its skin on?" Christopher asked.

Does he always sound bewildered about such simple things? "I do it because the pelts are valuable and, even if you don't, I need the money. I have to support myself. Now, please stand watch while I do this." Astrid felt quite happy. *Not only have I gotten rid of the wolves, and while the skins are heavy and will slow us down a lot, even with the holes they have, they will sell for a goodly sum in most towns.*

"You are limping." He grabbed her hand and led her over to the circle he had drawn. He looked at it briefly before putting them both inside and praying again.

When he had finished, Astrid gave a slight start and looked down at her leg. *My pants are still torn above her boot, but the bleeding has stopped and my flesh, although still sore and red, seems whole again and I feel a little better, more whole, although a little more weak and tired.* She gingerly felt the wound with her fingers. *The skin is unmarked and smooth. I have never been healed this way before.* Thanking Christopher, she resumed her tasks.

As she worked she noticed the priest looking all around and almost jumping at each bird song. *I hope that he has the sense to call me if something real appears.* Astrid checked each arrow as she removed it. *I only missed once, but I found that one as well. It turns out that the priest missed four times, but I have even found two of them, so he has lost two bullets.* Eventually she finished and had a pile of bloody skins and bloodstained hands and a knife.

Astrid removed leather string from a pouch on her belt and quickly bundled the skins, fur on the outside and, with Christopher's aid, hoisted it onto her back on top of her pack. He strained at this. *He may be a man, but it looks like I am far stronger than he is.*

Astrid next led them east in search of water. "We need to get the smell of blood off everything and be as far away from the carcases as we can be before the light goes."

They travelled for around half an hour before coming to a small stream. Astrid dumped her bundle and started cleaning herself and everything with blood on it, even washing the pelts. "Can you cook?" Christopher shook his head. "Then how have you been feeding yourself?"

"I have lots of preserved food: hard bread, cheese, olives, pickles, some smoked and dried fish and salami. It is more than enough when you are used to the normal fare of a monastery."

"Get me some firewood please. It is a bit late to light a fire and cook properly, but at least we can make ourselves something warm to drink." Astrid busied herself gathering some kindling and starting a fire. By the time she looked up, Christopher had gathered enough for a small bonfire. She laughed. "Father, that is far too much. We only want to heat some water."

"Won't we leave it alight? The woodsmen I was with briefly did so. There are two of us and one can sleep and the other can stand watch. That way we can sleep on the ground." *It seems to me that he is quite eager for this to happen.*

"No Father, listen."

He cocked his head.

In the direction that we came from I can hear some low growls and other noises. From the expression on his face he has now heard them as well. "The wind will carry the smell of the bodies past us. Scavengers will come through here to feed during the night — and perhaps other things as well. We will climb high tonight and sleep in the trees. We will still keep watch. We are far enough south now. Perhaps one of the many giant killer lizards will come and we cannot fight off one of them with just the two of us." Astrid boiled some water and, getting his wooden goblet from the priest, added a dark powder with lumps from another pouch to it, giving half to Christopher. *He sniffs at the liquid, as if unsure what it is. It smells good. He may have salami, but a lot of my trail food is this — beef soup with lumps of cooked and dried peas and carrot.*

They finished their meal and, putting the fire out as the light went, climbed high into a large tree. Astrid helped the priest climb. *I have to get him to go higher than he wants to.* When she allowed them to stop, they each found a place to perch; she settled Christopher nestled into the junction of tree and branch, while she went further out. Astrid spent her watch scraping the skins clean in the moonlight with a sharp knife. *I regret that I am leaving small bloody scraps under the tree, but it will reduce the weight of the pelts and make it easier to preserve the skins and stop them going off.*

Christopher woke her as a booming growl came from below. *Below me I can see a large bipedal shape—one of the giant killer lizards. Its body is held nearly parallel to the ground and its head moves from side to side. I can see the huge eyes of this night-hunting species peering all around. It stops to sniff at the remains of our fire, giving a surprisingly small sneeze as some ash goes into its nose. It moves to beneath our tree and stops; it seems puzzled. It sniffs the ground—the scrapings—it peers around for a bit and then, finding nothing substantial, moves off to the west.* As it left she heard a sigh from the priest. *He must have been holding his breath. I guess that he has realised that, if we had stayed on the ground we would now be dead.* Astrid started to go back to sleep. *As Christopher returns to keeping watch, he is silently telling his rosary and looking nervously about.*

The next morning, after prayers and a cold meal they set off to the east. *We are travelling by day and roosting in trees at night like birds.* After another night in a tree Christopher complained mildly to Astrid that he was starting to long for the hard bed in his cell. "At least it is flat." Astrid grinned and explained that the hunters of her village often sleep in trees.

As they went they swapped their stories and Astrid, the younger only in calendar years, began to teach Christopher about The Land—or at least as much as she knew. *I am glad that we are not on a fixed timetable. Christopher insists that we stop and pray every few hours and that he has to hold his daily services. I suppose he is still tied to the monastery times. A real person could get nothing done if they had to go through this continual round of prayers every day. I am getting exposed to more religion than I am used to. I even get to hear about several saints and why they have that status. Old Father Simon, our chief village priest, is not quite as rigorous in his habits as my new companion. I don't dare criticise my old priest to this new one, but—*she grinned to herself—*maybe Father Simon has just learnt to fit in with the, not very devout, lifestyle of the parish he is condemned to in the frozen north and, as a practical man gives us only as much religion as we will accept rather than alienate us from him. As well, I have to admit, I may be paying more* *attention to my companion than I normally do even when I go to church—which is normally not quite every week.*

As they travelled Astrid used the stops to repair the rips in their clothes. Once she even had to leave the priest sitting forlorn and embarrassed in his loincloth as she repaired his cassock. *As if that were not bad enough for him, he is soon even more embarrassed when I strip off to repair clothes or to wash. Caring for Father Christopher is almost as bad as looking after my brothers. Still, at least he doesn't get drunk every day and a rain of near constant prayer is far better than near constant swearing.*

Two more days found them on a track. *I am sure that it is the road south from Wolfneck. I can feel the chill of approaching winter on our heels as we head south. Around us the leaves are falling from those parts of the forest that shed them, blanketing the ground in a brown and orange carpet. It contrasts with the stands of evergreens, either conifers, different to those of the north, or else gums.*

After a couple more days, a river appeared to their right. *I don't know its name and, of course, neither does the priest. We may even have crossed it earlier when there was a section of braided streams where we crossed one middling watercourse after another. From the direction that it flows it could even be the Methul that ends at my home.* Astrid realised two things. *Firstly, I am well outside the boreal forests I know so well, and secondly, Christopher has only a vague idea of anything. He knows the names of the main Orthodox villages in the north and has an idea of their direction from Greensin and that is about all.*

Eventually, however, they started to come upon isolated assarts, small clearings for crops or pasture, each with a house for a family. *Unlike those around my home village, all of them are palisaded. It looks to me as if these people fear their forests. In all cases the fences are more substantial than the houses they protect and in two cases they have been built before the still incomplete house as the people there still have tarpaulins rigged as tents. Outside each palisade there are rows of roses planted. One place is obviously based on an earlier settlement as two legs of the fence are on top of a large earthen wall. It seems that the people are glad to see a priest and our journey slows even more as we are fed well, performing services as we go.*

Father Christopher even baptised a newborn child a couple of weeks old. At our first stop, at an incomplete house, he had to perform a marriage—the bride already well pregnant. He had to read these services from his book. He has never done them before. I held the book up for him to read. I am an unlikely altar boy. Astrid rarely smiled now and tried to hide her eating. *It is hard to get used to the reaction these people have to my teeth. Anyone would think that I am a full Kharl. It is countless generations since my people had purebred Kharl living among us, but for these people it may as well have been yesterday. If it was not for the company that I am in I might not have been very welcome here among these country folk. The people warm to me—but I wouldn't have gotten the chance on my own. I am too strange for them.*

Four days of slow travel saw them standing on a riverbank staring over a ford at the stone walls of Evilhalt. *It is the most impressive town that I have seen. The fields around it are huge. We will arrive wet.*

"Oh well—it has to be done. At least this water is warm. Come on Father."

They emerged from the water soaked near to the waist. *Christopher's cassock, despite him girding it up, is sodden and insists on trying to trip him up. I am sure that he is more interested in making sure that his backpack stays dryer than that he does.* On reaching the gatehouse Father Christopher was directed to the church by the well-armed and alert guards. Astrid asked for a furrier and was given a small boy to lead her there. *We go through streets filled with houses that are very different to those I am used to. Most have stone first floors and timber and plastered uppers and there is no space between them. None have the homely look of being a part of the earth that many houses in my home had, none have the upturned eaves and stacked logs and, more importantly the streets are paved and not just dirt or mud.*

She arrived at the furrier's shop. *I wish I was more skilled at selling. My father taught me some bargaining skill—often unconsciously as I sat silent near him—but the furrier is far better at it than I am. At least I know that my pelts, although now drying out and not in the best condition, are rare and the furrier will want them. As well I salted them, although I will need more salt before I head out again.* Eventually they arrived at a price. *It is one which is a lot higher than I expected and so is probably far lower than the furrier would have paid. At least I now have a fair amount of cash and can better pay for my stay here—if I am going to do that for long. I do not want to settle down so soon and still so close to Wolfneck.*

Having made her sale, Astrid next went in search of Father Christopher. *The church is not hard to find. It is squarish and built of stone, unlike the tall and flowing timber church at home with its carved roof and wooden shingles. It looks both more solid and yet less graceful. The slate roof does not match the beauty of the whimsical wooden carvings on the eaves and roof that I am used to.* Propping her spear and bow in the entrance she entered. *Inside Father*

Christopher is huddled with two other priests at the altar. They are so excited that they don't even see or hear me approach. They are clustered around something. It must be the Bible that Father Christopher said that he has been carrying, carefully wrapped up and sealed in oilskins. It is the most beautiful thing that I have ever seen. Its pages fairly glow with colour. Eventually the three noticed her presence behind them.

"This'll be t'young lady who saved you from wolves," said the eldest priest in Greek with a heavy accent of his own. "Our t'anks be to you an'may blessings come to you from God. By your deeds in savin' Father Christopher an'enablin' this to be delivered you be aided His work in no small way. Would you be likin' to see what he 'n' you hast brought us?"

Astrid nodded and was admitted to the admiring circle. The priests were introduced as Father Anastasias, who was the elder, and Father Giorgio. *Although I can speak and understand some Latin and Greek from church, enough for simple talk, I cannot read either, but I don't need to be able to read it to admire the beauty of the book.*

When everyone had looked their fill, Astrid spoke up in Darkspeech, holding out a purse. "Father, this is half the money from the sale of the pelts. It is yours."

"I could not take that," said Christopher. "You killed more than half of them and did all the work of skinning and carrying. It would not be right."

"Father" *I need Greek I think.* She looked at Father Anastasias for support. "I think that wandering priests are supposed to either support themselves or that they have to live on charity. You must take it. You are going to be out in the world for some time. You may not be in a Christian area all of the time and may be unable to claim charity. If you do not think that you have earned it, then let it be my gift for the support of the Church."

Father Christopher is looking dubious and Father Anastasias is nodding. "T'Church be always in need of support an' Father Christopher he be glad to accept your generosity."

He gave a meaningful look at Christopher as he said this. Now he turns to me. "However, t'Father he be out of the world all of his life an'do not realise how hard it will be for him to make his way. You be a good daughter of the Church."

He speaks with assurance but I am dubious as to whether anyone has previously ever called me a good daughter—of any sort.

"Will you be a continuin' with t' Father in his travels? He be needin' someone to show him t'world."

To my ears the studied innocence with which he asked that question shows that he, at least, is well aware of the world. It seems my freedom is over then.

"I have no plans, beyond staying away from Wolfneck, and would prefer to travel with someone. So, if the Father wants me to do so, I can be his travel companion as long as he wants one."

"Then, seeing t'at you be t'more practical an'experienced with t'world, why don't you be holdin' t'money for your companion?"

Father Christopher interrupted then, he sounded a trifle annoyed. "Am I not to be consulted? Don't my wishes count? I admit that I cannot bargain and have little experience to draw on outside the monastery, but how hard can it be?"

My broad smile is matched by the two other priests and that is the answer—I should perhaps be more diplomatic than that. "Father, if you do not want me to travel with you, then I will not. However, I have no plans in my head beyond simply fleeing a poor arranged marriage. I would feel far safer if I were travelling with a priest so that no man would dare misunderstand me. I am happy to go where you will. I can hunt and cook and look after you. You must admit that you need that—at least I have been helpful so far. Two are far better for travelling than one. Indeed, if you have no true plans, then we might best be finding others to travel with. The giant lizard we saw is not the worst threat that is in the wilds."

"T'at be true," said Father Anastasias, "an't'is be a good place to be findin' others. We be at crossroads o'travel between t'different parts of T'Land."

"Perhaps you are right," *Christopher now sounds resigned.* "I also admit that, having delivered this copy of the Holy Writ, I have no plans for the future. I suppose that I must trust to God to set my feet upon the right path."

I am sure he was going to add to that, but Father Anastasias is quick. "Good. T'en it be a settled. Father Christopher will stay at my house an'we will get him proper dressed 'n' equipped. Young lady, Father Giorgio be a takin' you to t'inn an'arrange room t'ere for you. You be a lookin' for some people to travel with. Perhaps t'ey be merchants or perhaps be other wanderers such as yourselves. As we recover from t'plagues an' Darkreach opens t'en t'ere be many more a wanderin' nowadays. Do not worry whether t'ey be Christian, just see if you t'ink that t'ey be good people, but do you be makin'no offers to t'em until I be met of t'em."

"Yes Father," *I am surprised in myself to note that I said it meekly and I meant it. I would not have taken such an instruction from my own father near as well as I have taken it from this stranger priest.*

"T'en off you be goin'. You can tell me who you find after even service each night."

Evening service? Each night? I have never seen so much religion in all of my life. I usually go to the Krondag service—unless I am at sea or in the forest or busy with cooking, but daily? I suppose that if we are travelling in dangerous places, then it might be a good idea to have my soul in good condition. "Of course, Father."

Astrid was led to a building with two stories of stone and a third one of timber that overhung the street. It had a sign proclaiming it to be 'The Slain Enemy.' *I note that the sign has recently been painted and it is impossible even to tell the race of the body on it. I am willing to bet that it used to be a Kharl. I wonder how well my teeth will be accepted. At least the innkeeper will know that the Church brought me here.*

Father Giorgio had a short and rapid conversation with the innkeeper in a low voice that she gave up on following before she was handed over to a servant girl who led her upstairs to the third floor. *No one has asked for any money, so I must even be here as a guest of the Church.* She was shown a small room—*so small that there is only room in it for a bed. There are pegs and shelves on the wall and I have to put my spear diagonally across the wall behind the bed to fit it in. Still, it is snug and comfortable and it feels warm.*

"Do you be havin' any spare clothes?" asked the servant girl in Dwarven. *Here it is lucky I speak a little of that.* "We could wash t'ose you be in while you have bath an' t'en you could be getting' into somethin' clean. T'ey be dry in a day."

Astrid looked down. *What I am wearing certainly does show signs of being a few weeks on the road, sleeping in trees and, now that my attention has been drawn to it, so do my hair and general aroma.* "Yes, thank you. You are right—I smell." She smiled ruefully.

The girl barely jumped, but my reputation will soon be spreading. Taking off her quiver and bow, hanging them from more hooks, and unpacking and carrying her spare clothes and a hair brush she allowed the girl to lead her downstairs. She left behind her weapons. *I have to assume that, being under the protection of the Church, I will be safe here.*

Chapter XVII

Rani

Asking the cards to tell you about the broad sweep of your future does not normally give you a very precise answer. It is not meant to do that. However, when your own reading of the cards sends you to ask the same questions of your grandmother and the professional seers in the Temple of Ganesh as well as getting a similar and long recorded result from the sages at the university, and they all agree as to the main thrust of the answers, then you have little choice but to act. You just don't have to be pleased about it.

I know that I am unhappy with my life at the University of Pavitra Phāṭaka, the city known as Sacred Gate to the outsiders, but I do not know why. I know that I have great talent as a mage. Being born on the ninth hour of the fourth day of the fourth week of the moon of the Dragon, and in the Year of the Fire Dragon is all very auspicious. My hold on mana is strong and my spells are well constructed, efficient and destructive. I am bright and learn quickly and from what I hear, most think that I teach well. Although I still have much to learn and feel that I have much more power to gain, I may potentially be the most potent battle mage Haven has seen for at least a century.

However, after eight years of study as a Master of Magic, the only classes I am allowed to teach are for the daughters of Brahmins, none of whom will ever get much further than lighting fires, warming an infusion or other minor glamours. Other mages my age are given far more responsibility—but they are all men, to make it worse some are really only boys. I have not even spent as much time with the army in the field as I would like to; and that holds me back as well. At least as a Kshatya of a long line of seers and mages I am respected and have a secure place to sit down and study and to prepare my battle magic and I am expected to do this.

Haven has not had a war for some time, but I can at least hope. If the savages of the swamps keep stealing cattle and openly sacrificing them then perhaps I will get my chance. Other than a war, all I want is more responsibility as a teacher, better students—perhaps ones who have returned to do more study and want to add skills to those that they already have. All that the people around me at the university seem to want from me are for me to keep on making magical items until I marry so that I can produce acceptably male mages.

I am not totally averse to this idea and, at thirty it is odd to still be unmarried, but I have not met anyone I want and, more importantly, my parents have found no one that is suitable for me. Even in the largest city of Haven the number of eligible partners who are of the correct caste, age and ability is very small. In fact, unless someone's wife dies, at the moment for me the number of suitable partners is, in fact, zero.

In an almost bored fashion Rani decided to resolve her problems by asking for advice from her cards. *Like most seers, I am reluctant and, to be honest, too scared to ask too closely about my own future, and thus the question must be broadly framed. Any time I ask about myself I am reminded of the continuing story of a mage who carefully constructed and prepared a spell that would let him know exactly when he would die.*

The story goes that all the witnesses to his casting swore that they heard the word 'now' as he fell to the floor dead. Senior mages all say that this never happened, but the story will not go away and actual spells of personal prophecy are completely unheard of. Still, I have consulted my cards to some degree about myself and the answer has come back.

'Unless you journey north and find the one from the East then personal and general disaster will fall.'

After getting this, I tried asking the same question in different ways, but the answer always comes back more or less the same. The only difference is that in the more detailed readings the feelings of great evil and potential doom are emphasised.

After spending the night thinking about the answers that she had received, she returned to her home on another island to consult someone she trusted. "Grandmother, I need your help. You are by far the best seer in our family. I have looked at my own future and I am unsure what I should do next."

Usha, her grandmother, was old and had shrunken a little with age, but she was still sprightly and sound of mind. *I can see her eyes twinkle at my discomfiture.*

"You have to come to cast some doubt on your own abilities and your skills? I am glad to hear that, for that in itself is a hopeful first. Now, what would you have me do about it?"

"I want you to look into my future. I foolishly asked what I should do with my future and the answer troubles me."

My grandmother is giving me a long look before she replies. "Come here and sit down. Concentrate on your question while I prepare."

Rani sat quietly while her grandmother went through her familiar and comforting preparations. *Black silk, embroidered with designs of significance, is spread over a table in front of me. A stand is brought out and placed in the centre. From its box of inlaid and polished timber an unblemished crystal sphere over a hand-span across was floated out and placed on it, without being touched by a naked hand. Cones of incense are placed on small plates, lit and placed on the corners of the design, and finally my grandmother sits and stares at the ball. The smell of potent incense begins to tickle the nose. So many cones have been lit that I have to try hard not to sneeze as they all hit my senses at once.*

My grandmother is looking sternly at me. "Concentrate on your question and cast your mind's eye into the ball," she said. They sat before the ball for some time. *The glass has gone opaque and that is all. Grandmother peers at things in it, her face is frowning in concentration.*

It was some time before her grandmother, with a concerned expression on her face, said worriedly, "There is something that is fighting my gaze. It is something that I have not met or heard of before. I had many glimpses of things, of people, and of places, but I am not sure if all of them were real. All I can be positive about is that your life, love, and future are bound to the golden eyes. That much is clear to me. As well I know that you will find them to the north. I also have a vague feeling of great evil that you must fight. As a prediction, I know that this is not very precise. Indeed, it is almost as bad as you would get on the streets, but does it tally with what you found?"

"Yes, grandmother, it is similar enough."

"In that case I am sending you to the Temple of Ganesh. I wish them to try and see something. Perhaps they can lift the fog from your path, as they will look differently forward to the way I do. I want you to give them a note from me. Do not read it."

"Of course not, grandmother," *Grand-mother is sending me to the Temple? Usually she is scathing about the men who work there on behalf of the God. She must be worried.*

Her grandmother got out paper and a pen-case and, after sharpening a bamboo pen, began writing, pausing to think on what to say. Eventually, after waving it in the air to dry the ink, she folded the paper and gave it to Rani.

"Go now child. I will tell your parents that you will be leaving us. My son may raise objections, but he will listen to me far better than he will listen to you."

Rani put on a formal sari, chains and decoration and renewed her makeup, outlining her eyes, and making herself more formally presentable. She gathered some flowers from the garden and took some money to put with them as offerings and placed them in a basket with the letter and set out for the temple. *I would normally just hail a passing waterman and his boat but, with my letter to the priests, my grandmother has made this occasion more important.* She roused her father's watermen to get the small boat ready. With a boatman sculling at the stern and a servant sitting behind her with an umbrella of rank, she sat under the shade as she was propelled through the waterways and canals of Pavitra Phāṭaka, over the channels of the Rhastaputra River from her parent's home on Hāthī Dvīpa or Elephant Island to the Temple of Ganesh on Mandira Dvīpa, or Temple Island.

Rani had the boat wait. The servant with his umbrella took his place and, with this mark of status over her head and the servant carrying the basket, she strode into the temple. She looked around. *There is a full courtyard waiting. The air is redolent with incense, noisy with the rattle of cast sticks and dice and other tokens.* She sailed in past the other waiting supplicants, avoiding passing near those of too low a caste. She ignored the minor priests seated in a row behind tables covered in the apparatus of their preferred method of divination, each with a client in front of them already. She went straight to the highest ranked priest that she could see, one who was standing aside and alone, watching over the activities of the others. Without a word, she nodded to the servant who offered the basket to the priest and handed him the letter.

The priest takes the note with quite some reluctance. He is obviously not used to such a direct approach to the priests of knowledge and wisdom. He is reading the words and glancing up a few times at me.

"Do you know what is in this?" he asked.

"I know what it concerns, but my grandmother," and she stressed this word, "did not tell me the details of what she wrote."

The priest waved and summoned a junior over to him. "Take this lady to the temple garden," he said, "and make sure that she is comfortable and looked after. I must see the Chief Priest."

As Rani left she could hear him reorganising what was happening, calling another priest over and designating him to take his place in charge overseeing the appointments with the more normal querents before he hurried off.

Rani was taken to an enclosed square with shade trees keeping the heat of the day out of it. In the centre was a rectangular pergola made of ash and carved with a mural that featured horses dancing around images of Ganesh as he rode his mount, a mouse. She was offered a seat under a tree and a servant soon appeared to offer her a chilled mango sherbet. She graciously accepted this and sat patiently to wait and see what would happen next.

Eventually the Chief Priest approached her. *His long mundu of orange hempen cloth, its end brought over his shoulder and down again, seems hardly able to contain his girth, an attribute which is unusual in a priest, but he has the benevolent and gentle smile of a man who is happy in his choices and with his fate.*

"Welcome to our temple," he said jovially. "It is very unusual to see one of your family come here to ask a question. We have the greatest respect for your grandmother's skill and find what she says profoundly disturbing. Come with me child." The priest pointed for her servant to wait there while he took Rani to the pergola where they sat upon cushions in the meditation position. The priest took some berries—*I presume they are Spearleaf*—and sat for some time, going into a trance. *I am used to this. I can use the time to reflect upon what I have learnt so far.* She waited in a breeze made fragrant by the profusion of flowers in the garden around her. *It looks as if I might see battles after all, but not in the way I expected. I wonder what I should take and how I should travel—and what my destination will be.*

The priest is returning to his body. His face looks more worried than grandmother's did. He speaks in an oracular tone and the pupils of his eyes take up most of his iris. The drug is not fully out of his body.

"Your future lies to the North and it is possible that you may never see your home again once you leave here. You will find unexpected completion with another. I can also tell you that you are crucial to something of great importance to us in Haven. It is vital to everyone and there is a great threat that hangs over us all somehow, but I know little else."

His voice changes and he now looks more at me instead of through me. "Your grandmother is right about the fog and imprecision and this is a worry to us. Our work concerns futures and knowledge and anything that interferes with our work is a problem. I have not encountered it's like before.

"Now you must leave without delay. I have a feeling of urgency. I know that you must be in place somewhere and that the time for this is very, very, short. You will be just in time for it if you leave now, right now." *I am surprised at the urgency in his voice. It is rare to see that level of emotion in a person just coming out of the effects of a drug of prophecy.*

R ani thanked the High Priest respectfully and, gathering her servant, returned to her boat. *There are things that I will need at my rooms at the University.* Instead of going home she directed the boat to land on Vidvānōm Dvīpa or the Scholar's Isle. Along the way, the significance of what had been said sank home for her. *My casual enquiry somehow has great significance for Haven? I might never see my home again? In that case I must send my things home from the university as well, and tell them that I am going. At least it is midyear and there are none of my trivial classes to cancel.*

Upon docking at Scholar's Isle, she told the boatman to return home and bring the larger and less formal boat, and many boxes and chests and more servants, and went to her rooms. She found all of the wands and other items that she wished to take with her and put them aside. In particular, she made sure that she had all the items she used to aid her in her casting, especially the rolled-up canvas with the embroidered pentagram.

"The rest must be packed up and taken home," she told the servant. "I will return here later to see how work progresses." She then went to see the Recorder, who was in charge of all the staff and students at the University.

I must look very determined or something. I have hardly told the babu that I need to see the Recorder when I am ushered into his presence. He is not even waiting for me to speak before he starts.

"We have received word that you have just hurried here from the Temple of Ganesh and have started packing as if going away. Is this true? Are you going away?" he asked with a note of concern.

"Yes, Your Eminence."

That is puzzling. How did he know? Does the University have me watched? Why? Has the Priest sent word? Is my destiny that important?

"We have waited for this time since you started with us," the Recorder continued. *He sounds both nervous and concerned.* "You have probably wondered why we did not give you more responsibility within the University. You probably felt that you were wasting your time here."

It is hard to stop nodding agreement. He waved her to a seat.

"It is because we knew you would be leaving us at some time and quickly. We just did not know when. It took far longer than we expected, but obviously, the time is now. I must tell you that, since you have been here any suitors for you in marriage have also been discouraged. We knew that you had to have no fixed ties."

They played with my life this much?

As he talked he withdrew a small key from his pouch and opened a little inlaid box on his desk. From this he removed another, larger, key and went to a cupboard on the wall, a pace high and wide. *I have never noticed that before. I have not even felt something there. It must have a very competent spell of misdirection on it. It is obvious that it is also lined with a metal to make it harder to physically break into. Inside are a large number of small books.* The Recorder carefully selected and removed one, relocking the cupboard and replacing the keys.

He then turned to Rani and started talking. *He is hardly glancing at the book open before him.* "As a matter of course, all staff at the university have a complete and detailed horoscope cast for them when they are about to start with us. It is a system that has proven itself useful in the past. I can tell you now some of your prediction. The rest you are best to discover for yourself. We have long known that you have a destiny to the north. You must go there and gather together a group of strangers. Some might already know of this destiny. Others do not. You will meet several trials that will prepare you for your life's task. This will be to fight a great threat. The nature of this is not explicit to us but will gradually become clear to you. I can tell you that along the way you will find love and many surprises. We cannot tell you any more at this time, as it may influence you wrongly, but when you leave here you will have as much assistance as we, that is the Kingdom of Haven, can give you." He felt inside the cover of the book and removed a small sheet of vellum from a pocket. "Take this and use it wisely as you need."

He handed the sheet to Rani and she unfolded it and looked at it curiously. *It is dated eight years previously, when I just started teaching at the University. After a preamble it states, 'The bearer of this note, Rani Rai, acts on my behalf. Whatever she asks, she asks for me. All Havenites shall take her words as direct orders from me. I will reimburse any money or goods she asks for. Through my servants, my eye is on her. Hinder her at your peril'. It is signed 'His Most Illustrious Highness Shri Sudacanth Rajnavamurthi, Maharajah'.*

Rani nearly fainted. *My shock and curiosity must register on my face.* She looked up at the Recorder. *He is waiting.*

"You are a battle mage of Haven. You are to report to the Royal Armouries to be equipped as you choose. You will leave tomorrow at dawn from the messenger station. You will travel by chariot to Garthang Keep and from there be escorted to Evilhalt. We have thought long about this and believe that this is where you will be needed to start what you must do. I will send off now to make the arrangements for that. Unfortunately, we know that we cannot send anyone with you all of the way beyond there, but His Highness believes that the note he has given you may be of some use. You must use whom you find or who finds you and no, I cannot tell you anymore.

"This is important and, if I say too much, it might well interfere with the workings of fate. Go now and may the Lord Krishna smile upon you and favour you with his blessing."

Upon leaving the Recorder's office, still stunned, Rani returned to her rooms. A University porter followed behind her. When she indicated what she wished brought along, he put it in a basket. When she was finished, she found herself led to the University docks. A University boat waited to take her to the dock of the main armoury on the north end of Hāthī Dvīpa. *My family craft can organise the transfer of my property.*

*T*his is where the main military bases are located, as well as the home of many of the senior Kshatya on its downstream end. Someone must be sending messages ahead of me as people are waiting when I arrive.* She was led into a special section of the armoury, a cross between a museum and a weapons store, by a senior officer whom she vaguely knew. He led her through a selection of weapons, armour and other items that might suit her. *It seems that I have a completely open choice. No one forces any selection on me and I have to choose items as I feel fit. No one says no to anything I ask to look at. Although I already have some magical weaponry of my own, what I am shown is of so much higher workmanship that I cannot resist. In particular, a wootz broadsword and a near matching main-gauche catch my eye.*

I regard most mages' refusal to learn how to use a sword as both stupid and overconfident. In a real battle you eventually run out of mana and devices and you may still have enemies to fight. A mage who cannot defend themselves physically is a dead mage. I may not have the best sword arm in the army, but at least I can use a sword. I have never learnt how to use a shield. They get in my way as a mage, but I have made sure that I learn how to use a parrying weapon.

The pair seems to suit me. She picked them up and went through some moves. It was only after she had decided on them that she asked about any magic attached to them. *I can feel it there, but of course do not know what it is. It seems that they are equally enhanced to help them both hit a target and to hurt it more. In addition, the main-gauche is charmed to protect its user. These are expensive weapons, as a matched pair worth well beyond what even my family can casually afford.* She also selected a new long bow of minor virtue, but good quality, and two quivers of highly enchanted explosive arrows to go with it as well as some plain ones. *I can make more explosive ones myself later when I need to, but I have none at hand.* She looked at the available belt daggers. *I will keep my own.*

Rani looked at the room full of armour. *Something is telling me to look in that large cupboard at the side.* Opening it, the smell of camphor was released into the room and revealed a selection of tailored padded female garments — all done in silk. After chasing away the men she tried on several, most being too short for her frame, or designed for more muscular women. However, a dark green pair of loose trousers and a matching knee length coat fitted her perfectly. *Their cut is old, but they are well tailored and suit me well.* She felt the material. *It is still smooth and beautiful to the eye.*

Whoever the woman was that they were made for, she had the same tall and shapely figure that I do. The coat even has four long pockets for individual wands sewn into it. I can sense the magic sewn into the garment, but have no idea what it is, nor is there anything in the way of an explanation in the box. She was putting the other garments back when a green padded cap fell out. *It seems to match what I have chosen and am wearing. I will take that as well.*

Choosing the cap puts me in mind of a light helm, with a mail drape that can be let down if needed. I remember seeing a set of mail armour outside. It belonged to some ancient female ruler of Haven, one whose name has been lost in The Burnings of the plague. It is made of star metal. When she tried on the helm it fitted her perfectly. As she held up the helm, she again had the feeling that it was magical in some way. *It is all I will take of the armour—the rest will weigh me down too much.*

I am equipped in a fashion that would provide the money for a mercenary company of high repute for a year. I may have reached the limits of what I can expect to take, even with her letter. She bowed with her hands in a respectful position and thanked the officer and the other people who had been helping her and, still wearing her new padded armour she gathered up the porter, who now had added her clothes to his basket and set out again for her family home.

I wish that I had time to seek an information mage to find out what the magic is that hangs on my armour and helm. I am a battle mage. I kill people. It seems that I will have to find out what the magic on them is the hard way. Information mages specialise in knowledge. They are thorough, but they are also very fussy and take a long time to get their spells set to their satisfaction. In particular, they are notorious for their lack of any sense of urgency. The afternoon is drawing on and I still have to select what else to take and to face my parents. Despite Usha's assurance, I am not sure how they are about to react.

When she returned home she found that the answer was—badly. *My father is ready to rush out and ask an elderly widower friend of his to marry me to prevent me leaving. I know him. He is an ancient man, but he is of the right caste. My mother has burst into tears. She fought against the tradition of me becoming a fulltime mage. She wants more grandchildren and believes this is what I should do to the exclusion of all else.* It took the use of the Maharajah's note waved under her nose to restore some semblance of order, and even then, her mother tried to tear it up—*luckily it is written on vellum. It is well past dark before I can get away and pack—and I left grandmother still arguing my case.*

Luckily, I cannot take much, my magical equipment, a couple of changes of clothes, money, toiletries, a little food to still urgent hunger and sleeping gear. I will get a horse to ride and a packhorse at Garthang Keep. After packing two saddlebags, she included enough other things to half fill two horse packs. *I will add other things later as I need them. I hope that I can get a servant later. While I can brew powerful magic, I know that I am a total loss at cooking or caring for animals—and it would be wrong for me to even try these things. As a Kshatya someone has always done these things for me and so it should be. At least I will not have to worry about such minor matters for a week or so.*

Having finished packing Rani went to sit on a stone seat in the family garden for a while to smell the jungle and ocean scents that meant home to her. *The rock under me is familiar to sit on and to my hands as they lie on it. Generations of my family have sat on this worn seat in the warm winter evenings listening to the rustle of the bamboo in the slight breezes and hearing the songbirds concealed in the bushes—kept in cages there by a succession of special gardeners just for this purpose. I may never do so again. Now as I am going away I am starting to have regrets—but it is now too late.*

Around midnight, having left instructions for the morning, she went to bed to be woken only a few short hours later. Having eaten and dressed in travel clothes she put on her weapons belt and strapped a wand to each arm in a small sheath made for the purpose. Going downstairs she found her whole family there to see her off and escort her to the dock. Grandmother, parents, brothers and sisters, their partners, even her nieces and nephews were there. *My parents are barely reconciled to what is happening. Goodbyes take longer than I have allowed for and the boatmen work hard to get me to the military station at the southern end of the road to Shelike and the north on time. A royal courier chariot is already waiting for me there with a cavalry escort.*

From the curious looks I am receiving, the troops have been given instructions, but no explanation for this mysterious trip. Her baggage was transferred and strapped in place. She took a seat under the umbrella on a wide leather seat hanging from side to side across the chariot—*a seat I know from experience will soon get very uncomfortable for me, despite being the best that the chariot can do.* The chariot started across the cobbles on its journey. *I feel the jolts as a continual series of short shocks.* She hung on to the grips that were there for the purpose. *Even as I take hold of the soft leather covering the grips, I know that I will soon grow to hate them and indeed the whole conveyance.*

Dawn was just breaking to the east over the paddies and distant jungle as she emerged from the last buildings of Pavitra Phāṭaka on Pūrvī Taṭa, the eastern shore of the Rhastaputra, and the end of the cobbled road of the city onto the hard-packed earthen road to Garthang Keep well to the north. The chariot sped north against a constant stream of farmers bringing produce into the market and once it had to swerve quickly to avoid a cow that wandered out into the roadway and sat down.

It took two and a half days to reach the keep through the dense wet jungle of Haven and past the towns of Shelike, Vinice and Peelfall and their many lesser villages and extensive farmlands. *It is two and a half days that I will forever try and forget, when the horses and escort are changed every two hours, drivers every four hours and, in Peelfall, even the chariot is changed when the last driver decided he didn't like one of the wheels. The only thing that does not change is the passenger.*

Despite a short hammock strung across the rear of the chariot, one far too short for her to do more than miserably curl up in, Rani had only been able to get short snatches of sleep—usually when the chariot was stationary for a few minutes for a change of some sort. *The changes do not take long. A series of even faster riders have preceded me announcing my coming. A trip that takes weeks at a normal pace is over very soon.*

She arrived at Garthang Keep having crossed a river on a ferry exhausted, sweaty, and irritable, sweeping through the outer gate and then around the waterfront that curled around the fortress itself. Seeing the layers of ancient walls—so different from what her people built now that many thought another long-vanished people had built it. *This is the first real touch of the alien for me. It drives home that I really am leaving behind the familiar.* The chariot took her through the outer gatehouse at the end of a spit of land and then took a hard left turn over a drawbridge, one not much wider than the chariot team, and into the drawbridge gate. *Waiting inside, in front of the gate to the central keep, are the governor of the keep and some of his officers.*

After a brief formal exchange of greetings he said, "I have only recently received instructions to expedite your trip to Evilhalt, but I have been given no explanation as to why." *His face and voice both clearly show his displeasure at being ordered around like a servant without explanation.*

"I am not sure that I can tell you. I only know part of the reasons myself— *those that relate directly to me*—and have not found out why the Kingdom is so keen to get me there when it now seems they have known of the reasons for my leaving for a very long time. It seems that the good grace of the Maharajah has placed many things at my disposal, but I have been told little in the way of explanation."

"I did not think I would find out," said the governor sorrowfully. "I set my seers to seek more knowledge and all they told me were 'difficulties' or 'a fog clouding the future'. Why are they always useless when you need them most?" he added ruefully.

He may not like his orders but is carrying them out.

"I have two ways for you to proceed from here to Evilhalt. The first is by a River Patrol proa. As you can see," he indicated to his left where two large canoes were docked, "these are large and they are fast but, while the people of Erave Town are happy for us to travel as far as their town, they do not like us to cross the lake to Evilhalt in our own military boats. The other is to send you with a patrol of cavalry up the river and to the east of Lake Erave, crossing the river at Evilhalt, which is the first ford on the Rhastaputra since the sea. This will be slower, but less likely to cause us problems in the long run. The choice is up to you."

Rani thought for a moment. "I would like to obtain a pair of good horses, one for riding and one a pack animal. I can ride, but I am not an expert in buying horses, and I assumed that someone here would be. I would also prefer to get good ones here where I can trust the seller. I think that I can assume that the River Patrol would not like to carry them in their boats, so I suppose I must travel by land."

The relief on the face of one woman officer is quite evident. "Before I sleep, I wonder if some things could be arranged."

The Governor nodded.

"Firstly, I am in need of cleaning and, before I leave civilisation, depilation. Please arrange for a bath and a supply of Tahlin unguent."

The governor claps his hands and a servant runs off.

"Next, these clothes will need to be cleaned and ready for me to take tomorrow and I would like to wear something tonight that I do not have to pack for the journey."

Again, the governor claps his hands and another servant runs off.

"After I have bathed, I would like to see a couple of horses for me to take." *This time the Governor nods in the direction of an officer who nods back and quickly moves off.* "Lastly, if it is possible, I would like to hear from your patrols and officers of anything that seems strange, or unusual, that they have seen or heard of over the last month or so. I am not sure what I am looking for; it could be anything. We could do this over our evening meal or after, at your convenience."

A battle mage is automatically an officer of Haven's army, but I have rarely felt comfortable giving orders as a right. For once it seems right to do so, even to the governor of a major fortress town. What is more he seems more than happy to accede to someone who seems to know what is happening.

"Over dinner is fine," he said, "until then—" he waved for a servant to escort Rani away before turning to confer with his officers and the senior servants.

After a proper massage, and luxuriating in this final touch of pampering she was leaving behind, Rani emerged from her bath clean and smooth skinned, smelling faintly of roses and cinnamon. She was dried and assisted into a clean silk sari by a pair of servant girls. *After the trip north, it feels wonderful against my skin.* She strapped two wands onto her forearms—*a touch slightly at variance with the setting and the clothes, but I am entering a realm where anything can happen. I will not wear any other weapons to dinner. It could diminish the reputation of the mage caste to be seen as unable to cope with anything that may happen here in a fortress with just her magic. While I am doing this one of the girls is running ahead to acquaint everyone with my movements.*

The second girl showed her down to where a cavalry officer waited with two grooms, each of whom held a horse by a lead.

"Shri Rani," he said respectfully, "I believe these horses may be what you need." He indicated a large black mare on his left. "This is Lakshmi, she has been in many combats, but is not a warhorse. We traded for her with the Khitan and under them she became inured to the larger reptiles. Under us she has grown used to working with elephants. I understand that you are only a fair rider."

He pauses until I reluctantly acknowledge that.

"She is both surefooted and intelligent and has good stamina." Rani looked at Lakshmi. *I am unsure if checking too closely will be seen as an insult—it probably will, so I will just nod.* The officer then turned to the other horse. *It is a huge grey animal of a breed I have not seen before. It seems closer to an elephant in size rather than any horse I have ever seen and it towers over me.*

He continued, "This is Juggernaut. He is a horse of the Latins of Freehold and they rarely allow his kind out of their land. We also obtained him from the Khitan and they may have stolen him. The Freeholders use his breed to pull their large ploughs and for heavy hauling—as we would use elephants."

Rani looked from the hooves up at the head of the horse towering over her. *Its hooves and lower legs are covered in hair and such a huge animal will be able to carry anything that I want.*

"Do they meet with your approval?"

"They appear to be suitable for me, and since you are the expert I defer to your far superior judgement in this case." She moved up to each of the horses. *They snuffle at me and do not seem to object to my smell. Both seem to be of a gentle nature—at least in this circumstance.* With a nod from the officer the grooms were dismissed to take the horses back to the stable and the man indicated that Rani should walk beside him.

"I am Subadar Sanjeev Dahl," he said, "and I will be in charge of your escort to Evilhalt. You said to the governor that there is much that you cannot say. Is there anything that you can say to me less publicly, that I might need to know to get you to your destination safely?"

"No, not really. On my part I know only that I have to go north. Some people think that this may be to Evilhalt and once I arrive there, then I will work out where to go from that point. It is fair to say that there may be at least one attempt made to stop me going. There may be more. I do not know this as being definite, but it does seem reasonable. Now, as to why the Maharajah, may Lord Krishna smile upon him, should act as he has I do not know. He seems to think that I am so important—or dangerous—that I must be hurried from Haven as soon as I found out I had a destiny."

She took a cylinder from a small pouch that she had concealed in the folds of the sari—*I am not letting this out of my reach.* From the cylinder, Rani removed the now rolled up note and showed the roll to the Subadar. "Seeing that you are in charge of my escort, I must trust you. Do not mention this to anyone. It may either make things clearer, or else it will completely confuse them." She handed the note over.

Sanjeev read the short note and handed it back. "It is dated a long time ago and yet they only just gave it to you and hurried you here. Even for the army this is very odd. We can only assume that the Maharajah, may Lord Krishna illume him, and his advisors know what they are doing. However, it does make my orders clearer and more serious. I thought, and please forgive me for this, that you, as a mage, had decided to just travel for some strange reason— to gather herbs or something and we were being detailed to care for you as one would care for a small child for their parents. We plain soldiers do not always understand the ways and motives of mages—even of battle mages." He smiled to show he meant no malice with his words.

The pair arrived at the dinner room deep in conversation. They entered a room with a large table taking up most of the space as a hollow square with a gap near an entrance. The governor sat opposite the gap. He beckoned them over and seated them. Musicians played softly in another room as the governor introduced Rani to the officers of the garrison. *As is usual in such cases I promptly forget all of their names and remember them by their jobs: senior*

*battle mage, River Patrol commander, elephant Subadar, garrison infantry and
so on.*

*I am not the only woman present. There is the river patrol officer I noted
before, as well the elephant Subadar is an older, small and wiry woman
with grey hair and a placid smile and one of the infantry commanders looks
incongruous and uncomfortable in a sari. She is taller and weighs more than
most of the men present but she is not fat. She would obviously feel more at
home if she was dressed in some form of armour and ready for a battle.*

*The meal is typical Haven fare, although better cooked than I thought it
would be away from Pavitra Phāṭaka. It is made up of rice, some flavoured
and coloured with saffron, hot dishes of goat, different types of giant lizard
and chicken, often hard to tell apart in flavour, naan bread, chapattis and
various chutneys, yoghurts and so on.* Chilled wines and cordials were served
with the meal. Musicians played softly behind a screen. As a dinner party it
was a huge success and Rani enjoyed it, complete with the inevitable shoptalk,
immensely. Once the meal was finished and cleared away, glasses were refilled
and cool ices were brought. The governor clapped his hands and nodded to the
senior servant who dismissed the musicians and moved all the servants away,
closing the doors to the room behind him as he left.

"Except for those on duty," said the governor to Rani, "this is the entire
command of the garrison." He turned and looked around his officers. "As you
know, Shri Rani is on a mission, sent by the Maharajah, may Lord Krishna
bless him. She wishes to know if there is anything, no matter how minor,
that you have noticed that is strange lately in your duties or otherwise. Please
start," and he indicated an officer on one side of the gap.

Starting with him, officers gave a report as to what was happening in their
area of operation. *It can all be summed up as 'nothing much' or 'all is quiet'.*
This continued until half way down the second side, where the female infantry
officer was seated.

"I don't know if this is important," she said in a surprisingly soprano
voice, "but several trade caravans are very late and well past their expected
return date. Not one caravan has come in to the keep for over four weeks that
was supposed to come across the plains by the northern route or from the far
north."

"None?" asked the governor.

"None," she replied. "I suppose that no one has thought it important
because there have been plenty of caravans from other areas and caravans are
often delayed due to weather or other difficulties. It is only minor, but this is
the only thing that I have noticed."

"Has there been any indication that the tribes have been making more of a
nuisance of themselves than usual?" asked the governor.

"No, the opposite," said the senior battle mage. "We are coming up to their Festival of the Dragon, although why they hold it at the end of the sign of the Butterfly—over four months late—no one knows. In the lead up to the festival, they usually do not even fight one another. This is always the best time to cross the plains. Many merchants will sell everything they carry to the Khitan before they make it all the way across. They then get to return early either here or to Freehold back to their homes. Some may even manage to fit in a second trip into the season. We have not seen any of those for a while either, now that I think of it."

The discussion continued for a while, but nothing important was added. Eventually, as the night grew late, Rani stood and thanked the Governor and the others for their hospitality and retired.

Chapter XVIII

Rani

Rani woke up in a guest house at Garthang to find that a breakfast of cool juices and fruit, naan bread and yoghurt was laid out on the veranda outside her room, overlooking the river. Her travel clothes, those that she had arrived in the day before, were laid out dry upon her bed when she returned inside. Rani looked at the clothes. *In light of the attention that I am receiving and in particular what Sanjeev said about what he thought I am about, I should go dressed as a soldier, not a dilettante lady on a holiday jaunt.* She packed away the riding clothes and donned the padded armour, strapping on weapons and a wand pouch, and slipped four extra wands into the long pockets on the jacket.

The pouch with the Maharajah's note in it goes onto my weapons belt. Rani hesitated over wearing the helm. *My equipment is incomplete without it. However, until it is needed, I will keep the mail drape of the camail up off my face.* After letting the servants in to take her baggage she proceeded down the stairs to find most of last night's party assembled to see her off. *They all wear their armour and look ready for battle. I am glad that I decided to take this course for myself.*

Rani greeted Sanjeev. The Subadar had a patrol of two hands of cavalry and a junior battle mage standing there in front of their mounts. Two grooms held her horses. Sanjeev introduced her to the other mage, Amin Ramanujan. *He seems a little nervous. Perhaps his patrol leader has told him of the note.* Rani thanked the governor for his hospitality and then turned to the Subadar.

"Shall we be gone then?"

He nodded. "Mount." he called. When all had done so and the packhorses were collected he added, "Danger trail formation, ride out."

One rider went out fifty paces before the next moved. When he had moved thirty paces two more started out, riding abreast. When they had moved ten paces Sanjeev turned to Rani. "We ride," he said, and they set off, followed by Amin Ramanujan.

Looking back Rani could see that next in line came a pair of riders leading the packhorses, including Juggernaut, who dwarfed the other animals and finally there rode the last hand of cavalry, moving in pairs knee to knee. They all were clad in fine mail and, except for the first two scouts, wore their camails down over the face. Green cotton was wrapped around the helms and a gold-plated unit badge held it in place at the front. They all carried a round shield on their left arms and held long stout bamboo lances, each of which had a small green pennon edged with gold near the head. All of the lances were held at exactly the same angle as they rode out.

I have been to Garthang before. The Keep is the very frontier of Haven and it is more a defensible border and trade settlement than a real town and so, while there are farms around it, mainly to the south over the river, they are nowhere near as extensive as they are elsewhere. Around the keep, forming a muddy moat that covers most of the land approach from the north, are rice paddies. The elevated road is three hundred paces long—a very long bowshot and dominated by the ballistae of the keep. After that comes higher ground. It is dotted with orchards of palm and fruit trees, gardens of berries and herbs and even some wheat. Further out is the jungle. It is not as dense this far north as it is around Pavitra Phāṭaka and the firmer ground here makes for a long and wide path that is easier to travel on than the wet-footed jungle, in places marsh, that makes up the Swamp to the east.

The road disappeared ahead into a wall of green. The sun rose, golden and blinding, to the east. Suddenly, when they were almost across, an arrow appeared from the glare, aimed directly at Rani, and from so close that there was little chance to dodge it. Even as she noticed it, the arrow stopped, scant hands from her face, and fell to the ground.

Sanjeev yelled a command, "Forward to the trees," blew a whistle and stood in his stirrups. He turned so the guards in the keep could see what he was doing and waved his arms in battle talk before pointing to roughly where the arrow had emerged.

Rani and the rest of the patrol headed into the forest while this was going on, the soldiers closing around her.

"Get clear. How can I use magic if you crowd me?"

Amin was left holding the packhorses as two sections of a hand of cavalry each formed a line in front and behind Rani, facing forward and back and leaving lines clear along the sides. No more arrows came in, nothing looked suspicious.

By the time Sanjeev had joined them, the duty patrol was galloping from the keep over the raised road and towards the jungle, lances at the ready. *Two files of infantry are running after them, one of spearmen in kilts with wicker shields, their bamboo spears of over five paces length held at the slope and the other of archers with long bows and wicked two-handed swords slung over their backs. At the end of the procession are two mounted mages with wands held ready to be fired at anything that is found. The cavalry is there to flush out any major threat and to allow the others to deal with it, but this didn't stop us.* Sanjeev didn't wait to see the outcome but, once they were past, urged his unit on in a return to their original formation. Rani now held a wand in one hand for offence.

Rani turned to Sanjeev as they moved rapidly along. "At least I now know that something I am wearing stops missiles. I am betting on the helmet."

When they camped that night, at a caravan campsite, she tested this by getting Amin to throw a rock at her in full armour. It stopped just short of her, as the arrow did. Gingerly she removed her helm and placed it to one side and Amin threw again. This time only her nimbleness saved her from being hit, the rock kept coming.

"I think that we can safely conclude that the helm has a virtue of protecting its wearer by stopping at least some missiles. Trial and error testing of magic items—" *I am slipping into the role of a teacher to a student.* "—can be dangerous and should be discouraged generally. In most cases an information mage will give you more detail, more quickly and far more safely. In this case, however, I have no choice. We will test my armour tomorrow."

They would have three watches, each of four soldiers for the night. Rani insisted on being a part of the watch, so Sanjeev took the first watch as the heat of the day faded, then would come Rani, and lastly Amin. Before retiring, Rani looked at her cards to see if they could tell her anything at all about the day that lay ahead. *It is not something I do when I am at home, but it is safer to make this a part of my daily routine now. Apart from a need to cautiously make haste, there is nothing new.* She also laid out her rolled up pentagram and carefully pegged it down so there were no creases. *Add this to the list: another item to do nightly.*

We may as well have all just slept through the night. It all passed uneventfully. Not once did anyone raise a peep on their signal whistles.

*T**he next day's travel is still mainly through jungle, but the occasional cooler weather plant shows that we are moving north.* At lunch, Rani had cut two lengths of paperbark and spent the afternoon's ride peeling, trimming and then smoothing them until she had two rods, each a bit over a pace long and about an inch thick. When they stopped for the night she again asked Amin to help her.

"I notice that you wear a sword. Can you use it?"

"I am no master," he replied.

He is a bit smug implying that he is no novice either.

Rani then handed him a rod and they moved clear of the activity of setting up a camp. *It turns out that Amin is in fact more adept with a blade than I and is able to land blows on me fairly easily—especially since I did not cut myself a parrying weapon.* Amin gave a particularly strong cut. *I am being hit but not feeling anything. It looks like the padding's virtue is to reduce the power of a blow.* To test this Rani forced herself to stand still and had Amin hit her with the stick hard across the stomach. *I know I am being hit, but it has no effect on me, so at least a small amount of harm is being absorbed. I cannot think of a better test than this for my armour without a considerable risk of injury to myself, but this is as much information as I really need at present. I have some protection at least, more than I had looked to have.*

T hree more days saw the jungle plants disappear and the oppressive heat of the south lessen as they moved up the east bank of the river. *On the first day, I saw it close on our left, now sometimes as we move through low hills and across streams that are running down from the last vestiges of the swamp that lies to our east, there is no sign of the major watercourse. Mostly I cannot see the river at all.*

They came upon some small-scale traders returning from Erave Town, but they passed no long-distance caravans coming from further away. They met and overtook one going north and spent the night with them before continuing. Eventually they moved well away from the river and entered the forest itself.

During the trip north, I have become quite familiar with Sanjeev. He is handsome, friendly, intelligent, and witty, and the fact that he has been given the job of escorting me probably means that he is well regarded by his superiors. Even though he is Kshatya, it is a pity he is merely an armsman and not a mage. But that is not insurmountable. I might look for him when I return. Amin is the right caste, but I now remember his face as a student in the last year, although not one of mine, and he is far too junior. I am sure that the alacrity with which he obeys me is partly because he remembers me from the faculty as well.

Still, if I am really not going to return, I might have to send for a husband willing to follow me. I don't feel anything for him at all, but then few have that good fortune to start with. If I have to send for a husband, it may as well be someone that I like as a person and so I might try and make sure my parents knew of Sanjeev.

It took a bit more than a week of travel, but eventually they came across assarts and a hamlet and then, close by, the clearing around Erave Town. Rani looked at it as they finally left the forest behind. *The cleared area is far bigger than that around Garthang Keep. It surrounds a fortified trading town that I have been told has more than three thousand people inside the wall. Also, like Garthang, it sits upon a spit of land. In Erave Town's case I can see the sparkle of water from the lake. I know that the Rhastaputra River leaves the lake here to head to Haven, but I cannot see that from here. I can see boats drawn up upon the sand beach of the lake and have been told that there is a river port as well.*

As they rode upon the road into town, Rani hit upon an idea and turned to Sanjeev. "We are quite obviously a military party. In case someone is searching for me let us take advantage of being seen as merely military and so hide our true purpose. We will tell them that we are enquiring about the missing caravans. Such an issue will justify our presence and will even explain a Haven military party continuing further north. On the way back, you can even say that you left me behind to keep trying to find an answer."

Sanjeev nodded in agreement.

They passed the campsite where trade caravans stayed, intent on being inside the walls. *There is already a group of traders there and it looks like not all of the guards are fully Human. Some are at least partly Kharl and the rest are more than partly so. From their appearance and weapons, it looks like at least two tribes of Kharl are represented. Both of our groups are looking at each other in open curiosity. Neither of us have seen anything quite like the other before.*

They entered the town on a drawbridge, over a ditch that nearly made the town an island, with Sanjeev in charge. He had been here before and he indicated to a guard where they would be staying and asked to see the mayor. *We have been invited to go to see him when we are settled in.* Sanjeev led them down the street. *That unfamiliar, but large building seems to be a temple. I presume that is one of their priests standing outside it. He is a tall, broad-shouldered bearded man dressed all in black and wearing a strange black cylindrical hat. He is watching us go past without comment.* They rounded a corner and she finally saw the docks ahead, just past a building that Sanjeev was turning into.

Rani looked up at a sign with a net and two crossed poles on it. *It has a* name, *'The Fisherman's Arms' written on it, incongruously, in Hindi. There is a ground floor of stone and two upper stories of timber.* Sanjeev left his soldiers with orders to take their gear inside and stable the horses down the road while he gathered up Rani and went across a lane to where the noise of metal beating metal indicated a smithy.

"The mayor is Cynric the Smith," said Sanjeev.

I am aghast. It is all that I can do to prevent my jaw dropping open in astonishment. The ruler of this overgrown village is standing before us engaged in the hard, manual work of a blacksmith. All my life rulers have been Kshatya, while a smith is Sudra. Although she spoke other languages; Darkspeech, Dwarven, and the Faen of the Swamps as well as her own tongue and the High Speech of magic, Rani had never been outside Haven before and so had had limited contact with real outsiders other than sometimes with people studying at the university.

Although, intellectually, I know that foreigners have little notion of propriety and the dire implications that it has for rebirth, this crossing of caste boundaries, and by a ruler, is a shock. I am going to have to get used to such things. I will be in constant contact with these people and will have to worry about getting cleansed at another time if I manage to return to civilisation. In the meantime, I have a prophecy to fulfil and will have to pretend that none of this matters. This is going to be very hard for me. I have, after all, been properly brought up and, although I only go to the temples occasionally, I do know what is correct.

The mayor is a taller man than I am used to seeing and very wide. I have seen tall and large men before, but his most striking features are his hair, the colour of beach sand, and his vivid blue eyes. They contrast with his darker skin that tells of someone from Haven being in his ancestry not too far back. I can see that the mayor is just completing the bit for a horse and it looks to my untrained eye to be very good work.

"So," said Cynric as he began racking up his tools, "what does the army of Haven want from Erave Town? Do we need to man our defences? Isn't it enough that you are running a new route for your caravans and trying to bankrupt us? Do we tax your traders that much?"

"A new route? What do you mean?"

Cynric is looking at me cautiously. "Some of your traders from the west and the far north are avoiding us and have been doing it for more than a month. Are you trying to tell me that this is not deliberate? Where are they going if we are not seeing them?" asked Cynric.

"Actually," said Sanjeev, "that is what we came to ask you. I am a part of the Garthang Keep garrison. We are seeing all of our caravans come in from every route except these two. We wondered if you might know of anything happening that might stop them."

"Damn," Cynric spat out, his brow wrinkled. "It was such a good explanation and simple. Who could target and stop that much trade? It would be much simpler if it were just re-routed. Fetch Leonas and Metropolitan Cosmas to the hall and tell the Metropolitan that we need the map." *This last is addressed to a young man who has the look of an apprentice.* He nodded and hurried off.

Cynic turned back to the Havenites. "Leonas is the Captain of our militia and Cosmas is the Metropolitan of this part of The Land. Let me wash up a bit and I will take you to meet them."

Cynric did that, keeping up a loud commentary on the weather—*warm for late autumn*—and on the possibilities becoming open now with the start of trade with Darkreach—*good. Neither Sanjeev nor I are able to get in more than a word or two and, after exchanging looks, we settle for nodding and making 'yes' or 'no' sounds. This seems to be enough to content the Mayor.*

Eventually he led them down the street that separated his forge from the inn and past the stables, where the horses were being installed, to a large two-storey hall. Cynric ushered them upstairs where two men were waiting. *The first is the man in black that we saw upon entering the town and the second is a grim-looking stocky man, with a much shorter square beard, who is clad in half plate even while inside the town. He indicates the man in black.* "This is Metropolitan Cosmas Camaterus. He is the head of our Church for this area."

The Metropolitan smiled and held out his hand to Sanjeev, who took it in his own and shook it.

"I am Subadar Sanjeev Dahl, and this is Shri Rani Rai."

Rani reluctantly held out a hand towards the Metropolitan. *What do I do?* He grasped it, but instead of shaking it he held it to his lips and lightly kissed the back of her hand before releasing it.

"We are on a mission of importance from the governor of Garthang Keep to see what is happening to our trade caravans," he finished.

"Delighted to meet you," said the Metropolitan. *He has a broad smile that is clearly visible through his expanse of beard and a strong Greek accent to his Hindi.*

"And this is Captain Leonas of Goldentide. He left Freehold behind many years ago and is now our military commander."

The soldier gave a short bow to each of them without speaking. Sanjeev immediately returned the bow, while Rani was a bit slower. *How many different ways can these outsiders find to say hello?*

"Your Reverence, do you have the map?" asked Cynric.

Metropolitan Cosmas indicated a table over by the side and led them over to it. "This is a map of The Land," he said. "It is as accurate as we have been able to piece together from old maps and information we have gleaned since the passing of the Plague. These lines," he indicated on the map, "show what we know of the usual paths that traders follow."

Cynric took over, "We were worried that your people had made a deal with the Khitan and started new routes from Freehold," he waved a hand, "to Haven," and pointed. We control only this area, including the paths through Glengate," he pointed again, "and Evilhalt care for a similar amount. We have hunters and trappers who venture further out than our fields, but we have had no reports of anything amiss. Metropolitan—"

"Our Church is not strong in seers," said Cosmas, "we are good at spells of healing and fertility. There has been something interfering with far-sight, but what we have seen has indicated a major realignment and upheaval. We thought that this referred to the opening up of Darkreach and lately we came to have the opinion that you may have deliberately diverted caravans to attack us financially. We may have been wrong about this prediction." He turned to the captain. "You may have to send patrols across the river on the ferry and out a long way to see what is happening," Cosmas then turned to Cynric, "and this may mean stepping up all of our militia obligations. You will need to discuss this with the town council."

"They won't like it," said Cynric. "Each day a person spends as a soldier means a day less they can spend earning money."

"True," agreed Cosmos, "but if the caravans stop, or we are overrun, then there will be no money coming in to the town at all."

Cynric grunted and nodded unhappily at the logic.

"What are your intentions?" Leonas finally spoke and asked Sanjeev.

He paused and then turned to Rani. "What can we tell them?"

This may lead me to some of those people that I am supposed to gather. "All." Sanjeev turned to the other three.

"Shri Rani is headed north on what we thought was another matter. Be free to talk about our concern over the caravans, but we ask you not to tell anyone of this second matter. It seems now that it may prove to be connected with the problem of the caravans. We only realised that situation a week ago. We decided to use this matter of the caravans as a cover for her real trip and we will continue to Evilhalt where I will find out what I can and where I will leave Shri Rani. Once I have found out what I can I will return home and report. This is a not just a problem for Haven. Trade disappearing concerns us all. If you wish I will share as much as I can with you. I am not sure what will happen when I return, but I am sure that something will." He paused. "Would you like to send someone with us to Evilhalt who can speak for you and your concerns?"

Having spoken as a military man, he suddenly thinks to look at me for confirmation. I nod back. It makes sense to me as well.

The Metropolitan took the lead. "Father George has just arrived back here from the seminary and currently has no other pressing duties. He can ride with you tomorrow. Would you mind bringing him back with you?"

"A priest of yours?" asked Sanjeev. "He will behave with propriety I assume?"

"Don't worry," said the Metropolitan with the smile returning to his face. "I know that your people are a bit isolated away in the south, but since we lost out in the schism and only retain the churches outside Freehold we have become much better at getting on with others—we have had to," he added wryly. "He will not try and convert anyone or offend your beliefs. In much of The Land we are now the mediators. It is just to Freehold, and of course to the Brotherhood, that we cannot go." He turned to Cynric, "Do you want to send anyone?"

"No, Father George was born here and knows our situation well. As long as he is looked after and returns safe, then I am happy." He smiled and turned to the Havenites. "Father George has just married my eldest daughter, Godiva. If any harm at all came to him then it would be visited on my head threefold."

The discussion continued a little longer, but nothing useful was added. Eventually Sanjeev took leave for them both and they returned to the tavern. Being used to Havenite visitors, the cook provided a series of tasty curries for them in a room upstairs. *The military are looking forward to all going to a real bed immediately after eating, but I want to try and find out if anything interesting is being said.* "Sanjeev, are any of your soldiers good at finding out things without being obvious?" He indicated a small and pretty cavalrywoman, Indira, his second in command. Rani gave her a supply of money. "Find out what people are thinking and saying please."

Rani went to her room to take off her padding and put on travelling clothes. She put a wand on each sleeve and went to step downstairs. *I already feel uncomfortable without my weapons.* She put the belt on as well.

Entering the noise and commotion of the common room is a major shock. As a Kshatya and a Master of the University, I am accustomed to a certain deference being paid to me. Here, as she crossed the crowded room towards the bar she felt a sharp tweak and leapt in surprise. *My bottom was pinched. I am not sure who did it.* She glared at the group that the culprit had to belong to and clapped a hand on her sword. *At least that cleared a little space around me, even if there are several suppressed smiles I don't like.*

My beauty is making me the centre of attention for most of the men in the room and perhaps a few of the women. On the other hand, I want to talk to the men I hear talking in Darkspeech, even if I am unsure of their caste and whether even talking to them will pollute me. All of them are apparently at least partly Human. They must have left the fully Kharl outside on watch. Whilst as a battle mage I have, of course, learnt to speak their language fluently, it is only recently that people from that realm have been seen west of the mountains except as invaders and I have never actually talked to anyone from there before now.

It turns out that these men are from a trade caravan, which is hoping to push further than they have previously. All previous trade during the whole year of the open border has been either with the Caliphate, high in the mountains and virtually inaccessible to the rest of the world, or with Evilhalt, for as long as anyone can remember the controller of all forms of access to Darkreach. This group of traders are hoping to trade much further afield. It seems that they are peaceful and interested in real trade. Rani assured them that, although she was not a trader, but a Master of the University, her land is always interested in new trade. *At the news that I am at the University I notice that a reticence appears in my audience and they move a little back from me, although they are eager to keep talking, pumping me for information.*

In my attempts to learn from them, I think that they have the better of the exchange. The only other item I gained from them is that these particular Darkreach citizens are Orthodox—the same as our hosts. Apparently, they do not worship Hrothnog their ruler. I wonder if any do. I also wonder about all of the other stories I have heard of Darkreach and how many are true.

It seems that, although people are happy to talk to me and, in particular, to try and buy me drinks, I am not going to get any useful information from them at all. I will leave the issue to Indira who, without creating as much attention as I have, seems to be circulating through the room, matching the people in it drink for drink and talking to almost everyone there quite happily and inconspicuously. Perhaps I have been of some use tonight after all—as a distraction for the other woman. Rani sighed. *It is time for me to go to bed.*

That night, when she looked at her cards she received a reading that made no sense at all. *It is not the first time this has happened on this trip.*

What am I to make of the way forward when the card bears a couple with hands linked and kissing pictured under a woman driving a chariot pulled by doves, its archer being a chubby child with wings? It is the card of the lovers. I have even seen several times in the position of resolution the ace of talents; the head of a goat-horned man depicted on a large coin and held aloft by a hand. Its meaning, usually, is the element earth but it also means prosperity and a hidden wealth of metals and minerals, security and well-being. What place did that card have in the mystery that I seek to untangle? I am going to become a miner? It seems as if the more complex readings, usually the most reliable, are the worst affected and the least helpful. Until I have a very clear question in my mind, I will not make any more attempts to put together a reading and, when I do it will be only a simple pattern that I use—one that can only have the simplest of interpretations placed upon it.

In the morning, as the horses were brought down the street from the stables, Indira briefed Rani and Sanjeev on what she had found out. *To my disgust the girl shows no effect from her night's drinking. I feel worse myself. The woman seems bright and cheerful.* Indira said that she had found out nothing new in regard to the caravans. The matter is an open question in the town and discussion is heated, but that there is no information to back any of the speculation up. However, she had heard a hunter say that he had called to see a friend who had started a new assart to the far south with his family and had found no trace of either him or his belongings. It had first been supposed that he had moved back to the town, but no one here has seen him either.

They began to mount. *A young bearded man is approaching. He wears lamellar armour like the Khitan wear, but made of bronze, and with a helm that is similar to mine. He is leading a horse. On his left arm is a teardrop shaped shield with a series of straight lines on it. Tucked under his horse's girth is a staff sling and at his side is a horse mace.* He introduced himself in Hindi, but with a local accent, as Father George.

"I have a letter from the Metropolitan and from the Mayor to the Baron of Evilhalt. I believe that both urge cooperation with you and advice, respectively of vigilance and caution."

He took a place with the other riders. Sanjeev had them ride in pairs, placing himself with Father George and Rani with Amin. The cavalry's lances were kept at a uniform level as if on a parade and the packhorses were kept at the rear.

They left the gate to the town and went through the caravan campsite. *The Darkreach traders are preparing to leave. They nod politely to me, but this time the guards are paying more attention to what they now realise is a military group from Haven.* She looked at the group as they passed. *The traders and animal handlers might be partly of Kharl heritage, but the guard itself consists of a hand each of large and of small Kharl who are observing everything they can.*

The larger ones have a lighter skin tone than the smaller ones, but both have facial features that are much more animal than Human. The closest would be to describe them as having flattened pig faces—complete with tusks. They guard a caravan made up of twelve light two-wheeled wagons. It appears that the guards have no mounts, so they either ride on the wagons or walk beside them. The smaller Kharl all have short recurved bows. The larger ones have shields on their backs and swords or axes on their belts. There is also a sheaf of long spears standing upright near one of the wagons that likely belongs to them.

Following the trail out of town, and keeping the lake on their left, Sanjeev had them maintain this formation until they were nearly at the tree line. *Once there we revert to our normal movement formation and enter a forest that is again different to that we came from, even though we have really just crossed a very large clearing. I am not an expert on plants, but to my eyes, although there is still a remnant of southern vegetation to be seen here, the dominant plants are already cooler temperate trees and shrubs.* She was told that they were towering tiny-leaved myrtle-beech, broad-leafed conifers, oak and brambles of all sorts. The air here is even made cooler with a breeze coming off the lake. *I am glad to be wearing the warmth of the padded clothes.*

Sanjeev had let Rani know that four days' travel lay ahead of them, along a well-travelled trade route, patrolled from both ends. *Father George fits in well with the patrol, his quiet regular prayers offend no one and he is jovial and friendly, willing to assist with work around the camp.*

"If I am destined to look after people in a new village, then I must know what everyone does in it." *He takes his watch with Sanjeev but keeps us all awake late by telling us the history of the Lake Erave area: the two towns, the one controlling the lake and the river and the other controlling the ford and through this control being the gatekeepers from Darkreach to the west. He tells us the legends of battles that have survived The Burning of the plague. He tells us of the final battle at Evilhalt where armies bigger than any of today's nations fought for control of the ford and the way south for over a week until the very ground they walked on was made mud with the spilt blood of men and Kharl and of the last of the Elder Races to stay in The Land, and became laden with bones and artefacts. Not many believe all that the good Father says, but he is a good storyteller, so everyone listens eagerly. I am sure that some of these stories I have never heard before.*

They were attacked on the last night of travel before reaching Evilhalt. They had camped at a caravan campsite, one that was much too big for them, beside a small stream but well away from the river. A nearby ruin, probably of some settlement lost in The Burning, had provided a plentiful supply of well-dressed stone that had been used to make a large yard for animals. On one corner of this a raised platform had been built about four paces high and it was the cavalryman on watch here who raised the alarm with a long, shrill blast on his signal whistle and a cry of 'Look' as he pointed to the east. Panic was at its brightest and Terror was at half. In this light Rani and the other three on watch could see a moving wall of beings coming out of the woods towards them. Rani peered intently. *The moving wall is made up of undead— skeletons—perhaps hundreds of them.*

"Quick—Wake the others. Get the priest first, then Amin. Do not get between me and them." She strode over to where she had laid out her pentagram so that she could quickly step into it at need and then drew her wands. *The skeletons are already within my range.* She began firing. *Nine blasts of fire for each wand, each blast removes a skeleton. Even though they move slowly there are more of them coming than I can account for.* Rani was vaguely aware of the rest of the camp slinging on armour as she bought time by removing the closest skeletons. *Still they come closer. I have six wands, two on my arms and four in my coat. I have more in my baggage, but I had not expected to need them. Now they are too deeply buried to get out in time.*

She jumped into her pentagram. *The undead are very close and the soldiers have formed up on either side of me.* Rani took a moment to collect her thoughts. *Amin has joined in, throwing a few smaller bolts, but he has quickly used his entire mana supply in a few spells and it seems that he has no wands with him. Still, each time he hits he eliminates another menace.* Rani finally fanned her hands and cast a spell. Drawing flame from her small fire pot she magnified it and a sheet of flame erupted from her hands and took out twenty of the advancing undead leaving a smell of old burning bones and mildew. She paused to wait for more to come into range. *There are still over sixty left.*

Father George now stood forth from the line. "In the Name of the Father, and of the Son, and of the Holy Ghost I abjure thee to be gone thou creatures without a soul and to return to your graves," he intoned. *He holds up his shield and a cross. The lines on the shield seem to take a new significance. Whatever he does works at least a bit. A hand of the creatures turn and begin to leave, while one just crumbled away to dust. The others pause briefly, but soon resume their slow march forward.*

Again. Rani fanned her hands and drew flame. She had less success this time; *the surviving creatures are more spread out. Those on the wings are already engaging the patrol. I will cast one more spell, intoning the phrases as the undead close on me.* When she let the fan of flame go out the closest skeleton was only a bit over an arm's length from her. *I'll not risk another blast. My mana is near exhausted and to overdraw it, at the same time as most likely being hit while casting gives me too high a chance of a miscast—*

something that is at least painful and possibly even fatal.

Rani leapt out of her pentagram, drawing her sword and main-gauche and looked to join the fray. *To my right Amin stands back to back with Indira over a fallen trooper. To my left Father George stands over two fallen soldiers trying to protect them, his mace striking out as he intones in Latin what sound like prayers, but could be a recipe for soup for all I know. I cannot see Sanjeev and do not have time.* She moved quickly towards the priest. A cut removed the head from one undead trying to attack him from behind, but it kept fighting until she stomped on the skull, shattering it, and struck a blow at its body, scattering ribs around and cleaving its spine. Yells and curses announced success and failure on the part of the soldiers; the skeletons struck and were eliminated silently. *Eventually there are no more to hit. There are eight of our group still on our feet, some just barely, including Sanjeev.*

Father George now began his real work. *Onto his back goes the shield, into the baldric for the mace and out of a horse pack come bandages, ointments, needle and thread.* He scurried around the victims. *One rider is dead and another is close to it.*

"May I pray over her?" he asked Sanjeev. "Your religion is not the same as mine, but I am sure my God will look after anyone who fights evil, regardless of who they pray to, and I am also sure that your gods are not known to be very jealous of the work of others."

"If it will help her live, pray on," said Sanjeev.

Father George stitched and bandaged the rider then, asking for light, which Rani produced, making it as light as if it were day over a small area from an amulet around her neck. Once she had done this he drew a design around the seriously wounded soldier in the dirt. *I have not seen much in the way of clerical miracles close up, but the design looks very similar to some of the magical ones. On top of the woman he lays his shield, he takes a censer from his pack and lights the incense in it. The fragrant smells fill the air.* He asked Rani to stand beside the pentagram and slowly swing the censer around to distribute the fragrance. He then removed an asperser from his pack and filled it with water. Getting Indira to hold a book open so that he could read from it, he began praying and using the asperser to sprinkle drops of water on the scene and all that were in it as he said his prayer, in what those who could speak it said was Latin. When Father George had finished and the rider was brought out of the pentagram her bleeding had stopped and she was at least breathing easier.

"We should not waste the circle," the Father said. "Sanjeev, you are next." *Sanjeev has taken a lot of damage. He seems to have tried to be everywhere protecting his patrol.* He received similar treatment, as did another trooper.

Neither have major effects, but their wounds stop bleeding and they both feel better. Father George is plainly exhausted.

"You idiot. You used up more than your mana, didn't you?"

"Yes," said the Father.

"You put yourself at risk. Only the first was truly essential and, thanks to you, she is now out of danger."

"No," was the reply, "what if there is a second attack? You are out of magic for the night, as is Amin, and we would need to repel them physically. Everyone needs to be as well as they can be."

"True, but you are now weak and, while I have very little left in myself, I still have wands." She went to her pack and removed six more wands, which she replaced in her arm sheaths and in the pockets of her jacket. *That is not enough.* She removed four more and returned to Father George. "You are right though, we do need more firepower. In case you are right about a second attack it is best if you take two of these. Point the end with the arrow carved in it at a target and think of fire. I am a battle mage and I made these wands myself. You will find them easy to use." She then went to Amin and just handed him the other two. *He is only a junior battle mage, but he knows how to use a wand.*

The body of the dead cavalryman was put aside and covered for the next day and those off watch retired to get what sleep they could.

Father George's fears proved groundless and, after eating and packing they headed towards the river and the ford, taking the body with them. Rani commented to Father George on the sheer scale of the magic required to produce such an army of undead.

"As I described in my stories, this area is rich with remains," explained Father George. "Perhaps someone has been creating them slowly and storing them for when they were wanted. They do not need feeding and they could be kept against need in a ruin or a cave. I know that this implies a lot of forethought on someone's part, but they could have made them for another purpose and just used them casually as the weapon that they had ready to hand against us."

"True, but who would do it and why?"

"Perhaps," replied the Father, "the same entity that makes caravans just vanish as if into thin air. You told the Metropolitan that you had another reason to be here. Perhaps that is connected to this as well. Is your reason to be here likely to make powerful enemies for you?"

"Possibly—I just don't know." *I am terrified by that idea.*

Eventually they came out of the forest and could see the river. Sanjeev moved them all to the shore a bit downstream of the ford, and the soldiers began to drop timber they had carried with them and to gather more. A bier was built and the man's body was placed on top. *No Hindu priests are available for the proper prayers to be said*. The patrol stood silent while Rani used some magic to set the bier burning fiercely. Father George said some prayers under his breath as they all stood and watched the body being consumed. Once this was done and the fire reduced to embers the remaining ashes of timber and person were pushed into the sacred river to return downstream to Haven. After this was done, all of the Hindus washed themselves in the stream and, still wet, rode up to the ford to cross into Evilhalt.

Chapter XIX

Stefan

Stefan sat working at his bench in front of his father's shop. *I want more from life than this. I have only recently become a journeyman leatherworker. I am still working under my father and, it seems I will forever! I know that I am a solid and competent worker but my younger brother, younger than me by several years, is already better at the trade than I am and our father will understandably allow him to inherit both the business and the house. The idea of remaining single in the family home and working under the direction of my younger brother does not appeal to me at all. It will mean remaining unmarried, forever the failure of the family, taking part in raising my brother's children as if they are my own. Others do it, but it is not what I want.*

There is the rich smell of leather and oils and the happy sounds of the village around me, but I feel somehow incomplete. He mulled over his options as he worked. *I could always go elsewhere seeking a place that needs my skills as a craftsman. There are many hamlets and assarts, even around Evilhalt, who would love to have me. However, there is also another choice.*

I like it here in my own village and I have always paid more attention to my militia duties than to my craft, perhaps this is the reason I am not better at my trade. Paying attention to the militia is easy to do in Evilhalt, which has always demanded that everyone who is physically capable devote at least one day each week to either training or working as a guard. The district only has a few permanent cadres, but it can field a sizeable and formidable force to protect itself very quickly.

The people of our town have learnt, over the centuries, that this preparedness is a good idea, so good that we have not forgotten it, even during The Burning. We have not been seriously attacked for some time, but we have never relaxed our vigilance. I certainly am not the best soldier in the town, but I am one of the best of my age cohort. I am good at training and teaching and have a grasp of what to do with people in the field. I expect to be made a sergeant soon and to be given a squad of new recruits to train. Wouldn't it be fun if my younger brother were one of them? Amos would not like that a bit. Maybe I should apply to join the cadres and stay here, or I could even become a caravan guard and see home again only when I pass through it on my travels.

He finished up the stitching on the bridle he was working on, ran the smooth leather through his hands and then put it aside with a sigh, neatly racking his tools as he did so. *Oh well, for now another working day is over.*

Stefan went out of the rear of the workshop, past his father still working away, to the kitchen. *Dinner smells good, but it will not be ready for some time. Today is washing day, so everything else is delayed.* He told his mother that he was going to the inn and went down the road. *Let's see if there is anything different, anything to break me out of the trap I am in.*

Stefan entered the cool, dim room. Looking around he saw familiar faces on every side. Seeing some of his watch at a bench near the empty stage he went over and joined them, grabbing a drink on the way. *No, it seems that the evening is going to follow the familiar path of many others.* He was just starting on his second ale when the familiar routine was broken.

A girl has come around the bar and headed to the stage. Behind her is Howard, one of the stable hands. He is carrying a small drum that he sometimes plays at dances. The girl is dressed in—well—not much really. She has loose and translucent baggy trousers that hint at her having shapely legs and, on her top, a small embroidered silk bodice with no shirt under it that does a lot more than hint. I know that she is from the Caliphate from the veil that she wears, although I always thought that their women wore a lot more in the way of clothes. However, I have never seen one of their women before so have nothing to judge by. I wonder if they are all as stunning to look at as this one. Her body is superb and athletic, and what you can see of her face is also beautiful.

She carries a handful of unsheathed knives and, as she walks to the stage, she is juggling them to gain attention—not that she needs to—every eye, at least those of the men, is already upon her. She keeps up the juggling for a while, doing some tricks, as if juggling five sharp blades is not impressive enough. She had Howard throw her apples. She impaled them with knives as they came and keeps juggling, eating bits from them as she went. Eventually she put them all down to the applause of hands and money. She bowed and then started to sing. She sung in Dwarven: songs of mining, of lost Dwarvenholme and of the mountains. She sang in Hindi: songs of jungles and love and travel. She also sung in Khitan and Faen. *I only recognise a few words of those, but*

I can work out that the Khitan ones are of love, the plains and horses, while the Faen are of raiding and adventure and of the great beasts of the Swamp.

Howard kept up a steady rhythm behind her, trying to match his drumming to her singing and the finger she waved in his direction. *Gradually the inn is filling with far more than the usual number of patrons.* She took a break, introducing herself as Ayesha and explaining that she was going to be staying in town for some time. *It seems like everyone wants to buy her a drink.* She declined politely and poured herself some water. Stefan grinned. *She is a smart girl; people have to show their appreciation with money.* Soon it began to tinkle down onto the area in front of her, coins sometimes rolling across the floor to be thrown back by spectators.

After a break, Howard began to play again, a peculiar and insistent rhythm while Ayesha just stood there looking at him and making sure he had it right. Then she turned to the audience and began to move, at first it was just her hips, her belt jingling, then the rest of her body and her arms. *Her body is moving in ways that I didn't know a body could move. Her hips seem to have a life of their own, setting up a rhythm much faster than the rest of her torso and hands. The small metal objects that she holds in her hands, which tinkle loudly like little bells, punctuate the drumming. She undulates her stomach and makes the muscles move in ways that I did not know stomach muscles could move and that, combined with her swaying breasts and rapidly moving hips, have an effect that is decidedly erotic in nature.*

Eventually Stefan ducked home to eat, only to discover, on returning, that he had to work his way back to where he had been and squeeze in as an extra person, to get onto the same bench. The night turned out very different than the way it had started. Stefan went home late. *More than any of the other travellers that have come through town, this girl with her songs and dancing, seems to blow a breeze through my life—a wind of change.*

The next night Stefan went back to the inn. He did the same on the third night as well. That night the girl asked everyone to please go outside to the street. Most people wandered outside, bemused and wondering where she had gone, as she was not with them. Soon Howard started a drumming from above their heads. Stefan looked up. *There is a rope stretched across the intersection of streets that the inn is on.* He pointed it out to the others.

Ayesha appeared at the window that the rope emerged from and, if anyone had not noticed the rope, seemed to stand on the air as if she were a mage. She walked above their heads carrying a pole as calmly as if she were standing on the street. She reached the other side and turned, walking back across. This time she returned the pole into the room, handing it to one of the serving girls through the window, and started out again without it. She moved more slowly now and had her hands held out from her sides. Her eyes were on the rope ahead. When she had reached the centre of the street she stopped and bent backwards. She bent over so far that her hands touched the rope and then grabbed hold of it. Now she slowly unbent, but her feet were in the air, rather than her hands, which instead were held wide apart on the rope.

Once erect, she stayed stationary for a while. Her hands were grasping the rope while her feet pointed to the moons. All of a sudden, her feet started falling and the crowd gasped, but her hands stayed on the rope and she swung around it, letting go of it only on the upswing. The crowd gasped again, but this time she landed with her feet on the rope. It swayed, and so did she, but she kept her feet, waiting and concentrating on balance until the rope stilled. Once it had done so she slowly walked off to the window and acknowledged the crowd's applause from there with a small bow.

Back inside to the gossip. *She has been down at the town's archery butts practising, has she? She uses a bow like those of the Khitan and can shoot as well as anyone there—so she is not just decorative and entertaining. She proves you can be more than one thing. I have to meet her and talk with her. I am comfortable with the way I am, I am just not happy.* He smiled. *I acknowledge that I might need her example of escape from her old life to provide me with the spur to do the same with mine.*

Chapter XX

Ayesha

Within a week, Ayesha found herself settling into a comfortable niche in the town. *Allah, the Kind, is good to me. My entertainment is a huge success and my courtesy and complements to all stand me in good stead. While I have never made as much as I did on those first few nights, I am sure that the town will always like what I do and will provide me with a very good living. Caravans coming through will boost that sometimes. It appears to have been quite a while since the town had a good permanent bard based here and they like having one again. I can even learn new songs from them and from the travellers that passed through.*

She started joining in the activities of the town during the day, often practicing with her bow and sometimes with her mace and parrying dagger. She made sure she was eager to accept. *The black-robed priests will talk to me and the elder man has even read the Qu'ran, and can quote from it in Arabic. This is a surprise to me. I am sure that none of my teachers can do the same from his holy book.* Ayesha was careful to make sure that there was no one that she became close with however. *Without an innocent excuse for such contact they might assume that I have a romantic purpose and that particular entanglement is one I wish to avoid. Even though I cannot guarantee that what I eat is halal, I am at least glad though that the meals are served to each person individually and that the kitchen maids wash their hands. I notice that all of the people here eat with both hands.*

Ayesha started to feel a growing sense of danger. *Perhaps I am getting too comfortable in this alien land. Perhaps I should prepare to leave on a moment's notice.*

She soon had enough, with what she had brought, to buy herself a horse. It came with a saddle and bridle and she was easily able to obtain large enough saddlebags. *However, no one here has the means to attach my bow case and quiver of arrows to the saddle. I am annoyed about that, but in this town, while they are all ready to ride off to battle, when they get there they dismount from their horse to fight. If they have any real skirmishing cavalry, they simply sling a quiver from their belt and use shorter and less powerful bows. You would think that they saw enough Khitan to get the idea.*

I am sure I have seen a leatherworker's shop around a few corners. She was soon able to find it again. Going inside she saw a young man. *He is familiar to me. Mind you, by now I have seen most of the people in the town. Of course—he sits at the front bench on the left almost every night and I am sure that I have seen him at the practice areas.* She smiled. *Not that he can see my mouth, but he can see my eyes. He has leapt to his feet, very nearly dropping what he was working on.* They introduced themselves to each other and then Ayesha explained what she wanted and drew things on his slate.

Stefan looked at the sketch for a little while, his face screwed up in thought.

"I could do t'at," he finally said, "but my father be a much better craftsman t'an I am an' he'd ne'er forgive me for not lettin' 'im learn how t' make somethin' new. I'll be a gettin' him for you."

He left returning shortly dragging an older version of himself and followed by a younger one—*a brother probably.*

"T'is be Ayesha, t' new girl all be talkin 'bout at t' Enemy. Ayesha, do explain to my father what you want."

Ayesha showed the master leatherworker her bow case and quiver and explained how she wanted to be able to attach one of them to each side of her horse harness. The father had her sit on a stool and then nodded and sketched things and then measured things and how far she could reach and then wrote the measures on a slate.

That night, during her breaks, Ayesha sat and chatted with Stefan, to the envy of his friends. She insisted that he introduce her. *Now that I have an excuse and have met some of the locals to talk to in a non-romantic way, I can start to learn more about the town and I can be more certain to hear any rumours about any people passing through. As I surmise, it turns out that they are all soldiers, part-time, but still soldiers and, as a part of their duties they patrol all around the town and the hamlets that surround it. Good. That serves the purpose of my mission well. Now it will be harder for Theodora to pass by unnoticed and thus elude me.*

Ayesha found that it did not take long to settle into a routine. To her delight the inn had a large bathing room and a hot spring that was under the town was tapped into there. This gave the inn copious hot water for bathing, even if it did smell slightly of *al-kīmiyā*. *Sulphur is one of the chemicals. I wouldn't drink the water from it unless I need a medicine. The only drawback of the baths is that the people who use them have to help empty them—but this is only a fairly minor task as most of the work is really done by enchantments. Seeing that there is one room for men and another set aside for women I can even shed my veil when I am inside the room just as if I were bathing at home. It is an unexpected, but welcome, pleasure.*

Late one afternoon, before getting ready for the night, while she was just relaxing in the bath on her own, there being no other female guests and the house girls being busy with preparing for the evening, there was an interruption. A tall girl—*from her blonde hair a northern barbarian and obviously just arrived*—came into the room with Ava, one of the servants. As they entered Ava looked a little nervously at the barbarian girl before addressing Ayesha.

"Astrid," said Ava, "t'is be Ayesha. She be a workin' as entertainer here in tavern. Ayesha, Astrid has just walked here from Wolfneck in t' far north an' has brought us new priest an' grand new Bible." Turning again to Astrid she continued, "Ayesha be a showin' you what to do here." Again, to Ayesha and in a pleading tone, she said, "Can you please? I be a needin' to get her travel clothes clean an' t'en get on with t' servin'." She looked ready to flee as soon as she could, holding out a hand to Astrid and glancing nervously at her.

Wolfneck—that is a long way to walk with just one of their priests for company. I get to practice my Darkspeech.

Astrid started removing garments and Ava collected them, holding each item a little away from her. Ayesha sized the new girl up. *She is a large girl, tall and buxom with the palest hair that I have ever seen. It is obvious that it is naturally that colour. Her skin and nipples are also very pale.* "Climb in, O well-travelled lady of the North."

"You speak my tongue! Are you from Darkreach?" asked the big girl. *She is smiling and revealing her teeth which, if what I have heard is correct, definitely confirm her origin. It is hard not to stare as, when displayed, her teeth make her beautiful face look quite cat-like, still beautiful, but also disturbingly feline. I make sure I show no reaction to the sight.*

"No, the Caliphate, but by the Grace of Allah, the Wise, I have learnt many languages as a part of my training. I am what your people call, I believe, a skald."

"We haven't had a good one in our village for many years. Are you any good?" she asked.

She just asked. She has an almost child-like innocence. She is still talking as she climbs in.

"I am glad this bath is here. It is almost hot enough. At home, we don't have much hot water, but we clean off in a sauna, a steam room. It is far hotter than this. That would be a luxury to find here in the south."

"Not too hard. My people also have them, but they are probably different to yours." So, to Ayesha's surprise, a friendship was soon born from a discussion of differences and similarities in bathing habits.

Chapter XXI

Astrid

That night Astrid sat entranced at what Ayesha could do. *When I forget myself and lap at my drink, instead of sipping, if I look around to check, no one seems to have noticed. Ayesha has introduced me to Stefan and his friends and, in the breaks, I can happily exchange hunting stories with them. Simple ones, I don't speak much Dwarven, but at least I get to learn new words as we go. At least you don't need many words for hunting stories.* During these talks Astrid accidentally learnt of Stefan's desire to leave the town, and so Stefan and Ayesha became the first people that she mentioned to Father Anastasias the next day.

Next day Astrid joined in at archery practice. *It seems that Ayesha's people only use little bows. The girl has never seen a bow like mine before.* Astrid watched as she measured herself against it. *It is far taller than Ayesha is and, at the centre, is nearly as thick as her, admittedly slender, wrist. On foot, she cannot shoot as far as me, or as well.*

In three days, the modifications for Ayesha's saddle were finished and she then showed the others what she could do as a mounted archer. *"My people do not ride."* *I have to explain what skis and sleighs are and why canoes are more useful than horses in our cold and marshy boreal forests with their endless lakes and rivers.*

To Astrid's surprise, given how others had looked at her as she came south, the tiny Muslim girl with the veil and the tall pale blonde from the north were soon familiar to everyone in the village and, if anyone presumed on them, as unaccompanied women, Astrid just smiled at them sweetly. *Soon people are calling me the Cat. I think that is funny. I have always been known as Astrid*

Tostisdottir. I was never given a by-name at home. To have a name that is all my own is both new and good to me.

The two discovered that the inn had a rarely used room downstairs on the same level as the baths. *It is supposed to be a private eating room but is rarely used as such. Like many of the better taverns but perhaps with more it also has a quite a few books in it, perhaps thirty, some of which are from before The Burning. I am not sure why, but Ayesha is delighted and insists that we make this room our own.*

Sometimes we allow Father Christopher or Stefan to join us in our 'private room'. Some of the books are old enough to have been written for normal folk, but in High Speech and, on discovering that Ayesha could read this, a very happy Father Christopher insists that she start telling him what is in them. I like the stories.

Chapter XXII

Hulagu

When they arrived in the fields around Evilhalt, Hulagu could see some people standing around while a girl rode a horse, steering it with her knees, and shot arrows at a target. "The girl is very good, but she is not Khitan."

"How do you know that?" asked Bianca.

"She wears a veil over her face and she is dressed as the people of the Caliphate dress when they are on a horse. See—"

"I don't know how they dress," said Bianca shortly. "Remember, all that I have seen is my people, a little of yours, and what I have seen of traders coming through. Traders dress in anything as takes their fancy. Everything is strange to me. Even that big woman is. I have never seen hair like hers before and, if that is a bow, it is nearly as tall as she is instead of a proper size. Then there is that man in black. He sort of looks like a priest, but he has a beard and his clothes are all wrong."

"I have seen his sort before in the villages around the plains. He is a priest and I have been told that he worships your God, but he does it differently. Your people kill priests like him by burning when they catch them."

Bianca looked horrified at that idea. Her voice sounded dismissive. "They wouldn't do that to a person unless they were a devil worshipper or very evil. Does he worship the devil?" she finished by asking curiously.

Hulagu shrugged. *If she wants to see me as trying to avoid saying too much, she can. Religion is the one area we have difficulty with between us.*

"You are both wrong in your beliefs anyway. What does it matter who is more wrong? Make sure you are polite to him though. We are in his town, not the other way around, and I think that we need to be accepted without an argument." Bianca—*very reluctantly*—gave assent.

The rider has stopped what she is doing, recovered some arrows, and re-joined the others. They all are watching as we approach.

Ayesha

"One is Khitan," said Astrid. "The other is dressed like them, but she is a Christian."

"How do you know?" asked Father Christopher.

"She has a large crucifix around her neck," Astrid replied. "Can't you see? She looks unarmed. Perhaps she is his slave."

"Not unarmed. I can see more knives than I carry and then look at the horse she rides. It moves like a warhorse."

"You both have better eyes than I have," said Christopher. "All I can see is that she is blonde, though much more yellow than Astrid."

"You spend far too much time looking at books rather than for bears or beauties, Father," said Astrid and then added a grin. "Perhaps you should look at more of the latter."

"T'ey canna be a traders," said Stefan. "T'ey be a havin' t'ree packhorses, but only two to guard 'em. One other be a ridin' animal, although it be havin' no rider. Neither it nor one packhorse are a bein' led, but t' other two packhorses are."

"She certainly cannot be a slave. They ride side-by-side, not close enough to be lovers, but close enough to talk quietly."

"We'll find out soon enow," said Stefan, looking around. "I'm t' nearest watch member on duty, so I be askin' 'em, but I only be havin' a little Khitan. Does any speak it well?"

"I don't just sing in these tongues, I speak them as well. Mind you, Allah, the Merciful, grant that you never meet some of the people whose tongues I have been trained to speak in."

Stefan nodded for her to take the lead and they all moved off towards the road.

Hulagu

"What do they speak here?" asked Bianca.

"They are mostly Human, but they speak the Dwarven tongue. I have a little of that speech. About as much as I used to speak Latin." They both smiled at this. "I will try that anyway.

"Now we are coming among people, you need to gather up the lead ropes for your horses, instead of just letting them follow your words. We don't want your horses upsetting people." *She has done that, dug her heels in and is quickly beside me again.* Gradually they moved closer to the clump of people, trailing a small string of horses behind them.

Ayesha

*N*ow to see if I can remember my classes—I am the person on home ground, *so it is I who speaks first.* "I offer you the gift of hearth and water and may your sleep be safe and restful here. I am Ayesha of the Caliphate speaking for Stefan of Evilhalt, who lacks your words, and I am staying in this town for a time. If you do not mind, I will speak for Stefan, most noble lord of the plains."

From the expression on their faces I can see that the Khitan pair are surprised that I not only speak Khitan, but even knew the right words to say. The man recovers quickly—

"I am Hulagu of the Dire Wolves and I am on my wanderjahr, and this is Bianca of the Horse. She is from among the Latins, but she travels under my guarantee and that of my clan. I speak for her deeds and she may be spoken to. We accept your hospitality and thank you for it. May prosperity attend upon you and yours."

Of the Latins? That explains her appearance, but it raises many, many other questions.

Ayesha continued with the introductions as she kept glancing around to check reactions. *I was trained to be observant and this is good practice.*

"This is Father Christopher of Greensin, he is a priest who must travel for two years, almost like your wanderjahr, but his Abbot is making him do it and he does not wish to go." *The new pair are sharing a meaningful look over that.*

"This is Astrid the Cat from Wolfneck. She seeks to get away from a wrong marriage and an undesirable man."

Astrid, bless her, recognises her name, and smiles broadly and cheerfully, without understanding a word of what is said. The pair react to her teeth and Bianca quickly crosses herself.

Astrid frowned at the smaller girl.

It seems that Bianca realises that she may have just offended the large northern girl and now is giving a nervous smile back.

Ayesha turned to Stefan in Dwarven. "What should I ask them?"

"Simply, what be t'eir purpose here," said Stefan. Ayesha relayed the question.

The man—*Hulagu*—replied, "For me the answer is simple. I have received a prophecy that I must travel here. I will meet others and something, I do not know what, will happen that is important."

Upon translation, it is the turn of Father Christopher and Astrid to exchange looks. I wonder what that is about. I will ask her later.

"So I wish to enter this town, in order to help complete my geas. Bianca is with me of her own free will. She is the only survivor of a caravan from Freehold. The rest were slain by brigands. She seeks to see them slain and I will not answer for her actions if she finds any in your town, but she otherwise travels as she wills. We have money, but we will also seek to sell some of the items that we have gleaned from the two brigands we have already encountered and disposed of." Ayesha translated this into Dwarven for Stefan. *Father Christopher is whispering a cruder account in Darkspeech to Astrid.*

"Please be tellin' him t'at t'ey be free to enter t'village of Evilhalt an't'at I be accompanin' t'em to t'inn. T'ey also be comin'with me to see Siglevi t' Short, our Baron. If caravans are bein' attacked, it affects our town direct. Also, can you be an askin'if any of t'horses are for sale?" Ayesha translated.

"Mine aren't," said Hulagu. "I will have to ask Bianca if hers are, but I doubt it. They are her totem animals. She does not believe in totems, but they are hers, or she is theirs."

Turning to Bianca he asked—*in Hindi*—"That one, Stefan, who is of this town, wants to know if your horses are for sale. I said no."

"That is right. They came to me, I could not sell them," said Bianca.

"You be both speakin' Hindi!" said Stefan, interrupting. "Good, t'en I be a talkin' to you less clumsy. If you be peaceful t'en you be welcome to our town. Your answer to Ayesha be afar longer than 'no', bein' it?"

"Yes, Bianca does not believe in totems, but she is the first of the Horse totem and these horses came to her and follow her like a puppy does a child— even though two are battle trained. She need not hobble them. They do as she wishes. I doubt that they will ever leave her and I would hate to be the one to try and part them. The other two are from the brigands. We may sell them or Bianca may decide to add them to her dower herd as they are hers. She killed their old owners. I think it will be a large herd," he added.

Chapter XXIII

Ayesha

Stefan led them all into town and installed them in the inn, before saying that he was going off to report their arrival. *Now that I know I can talk to her, I want to know more. We should get her clean first—off to the bath while we arrange for her clothes to be washed. Astrid is naturally following. This is more what I expected. She has no idea about baths at all and is nervous about the idea of climbing into water that smells like that. Astrid is amused, but this Bianca does not find it amusing at all.*

Bianca

I am trying to be quite firm that you wash off exposed bits of your body when they get dirty and that climbing naked into a vast tub of steaming water is wrong somehow. I have heard of people taking baths, usually it is noble women showing off, but they always stay decently clothed, as I did on the plains, when they did so. Unfortunately, these girls will not let me keep anything on to preserve even a shred of my decency.

With her hands nervously hovering around her body trying to cover her nakedness, Bianca told them of her travels and how she met Hulagu. *I tried to hide how I got information out of Koyunlu, but Ayesha somehow drew the information out of me. It seemed that this Astrid shares Ayesha's thought that what I did was reasonable.*

"I had not thought that you western Christians could be so practical," the Muslim woman said.

It seems that she knows why the man broke at the threat and she has now told me and so I know why Hulagu, being a man, didn't. The Cat just laughs and speculates aloud about a few men who might be greatly improved if, like a beast, they could be tamed by a simple cut.

Ayesha snorted in amusement at that thought. *She is turning the conversation back to finding out more about me and my travels. She seems to be delighted that I can play a flute and is experienced with working in taverns.* "All the Cat can do is to kill things," she said.

Astrid smiled. *She obviously likes that name.* "I can cook them as well," she added brightly.

Bianca again saw why the pale-haired girl had gained the nickname. *By Saint Ursula, I need to be more polite. Once again, my eyes have widened and I have crossed myself.*

Astrid sighed and explained, "My people in Wolfneck are all part Kharl. It is a legacy of the wars many years ago. when we were a part of Darkreach. Some are more so than others. All I have of my heritage are these teeth and I can also lap my drinks. Others have greenish skin or have faces that look a bit like an animal. The man I was supposed to marry looked like a fat hunchbacked pig on two legs and acted far worse than one. He is one of the ones that I was thinking of who would be improved by a few strokes of a knife when you were talking."

Ayesha insists that I should bring my flute to the tavern to help with the entertaining. She is an infidel. Why is she being so nice?

"It would be nice to have more than a drummer, particularly if you can play some of the songs that I sing."

Hulagu

A bath—we never have this much hot water on the plains. It is even better than a sweat tent. Although the walls are thick, I can hear a lot of splashing and noise from next door where the girls are. It is a pity I am not there. While the northern girl looks more than a trifle intimidating, that Caliphate one is as small as Bianca, but I would like to see her without that veil. I suspect that, from what I can see, under the loose riding clothes there is a very nice body and a pretty face. I wonder if I can set up a sweat tent to find out—everyone goes to one of those.

Father Anastasias

The newcomers are off seeing the Baron, but Astrid has come to evening service to tell me all. She seems to be becoming accustomed to this. I have two more people to check. I will make sure that I will meet them in the next couple of days to see if I have a sense or feel of evil about them. I am particularly concerned about the Freehold girl, from what Astrid has told me.

I am reassured by what I feel. She is not an evil person, even if she is capable of acts that are not good.

I suspect, from the expression on her face when I refer to the matters, that she is very torn by what she has done but until she comes to me to confess, or at least talk about it, there is nothing that I can do.

I have made this Khitan repeat his prophesy to me. The more I think about it the more it seems that it is essential that Father Christopher is one of the group; with Astrid along to protect him, of course. If something important is about to happen, the Church should be represented. This is even more the case if this important matter is to be a fight against evil in any of its many guises, as other signs indicate. Perhaps the Church should even take the lead in this.

Chapter XXIV

Bianca

I have brought my flute to the night's entertainment, but the beat for Ayesha's dance is too foreign to any of the tunes that I can play. All that I can do is practice the rhythms without blowing and ask Saint Cecilia for aid. At least that way I can ignore the way the men are looking at the dancing girl. At least at home the entertainers don't have to show so much of their body to earn money, although, I have to admit, they also don't earn as much without giving out other favours as well as their songs and music.

It is lucky that Ayesha has some songs that I know or I would have felt like a proper fool just sitting here with a flute in my hands. Most of the songs have different words to those that I know, but the music seems to be the same. It is a long time since I have just enjoyed myself and the atmosphere. This is nearly the first inn that I have been in where I am not really working. Perhaps I am having a few more drinks than I am accustomed to.

Hulagu

The girl who has started the entertainment and is providing most of it is the same one who talked to us outside the village, but instead of being a horse archer, she is now dressed very differently. I can see that she does have a very nice body indeed. Instead of the leather pants of a horsewoman, she wears trousers that I can nearly see through. On her top is a tight embroidered bodice, like the women of the tents wear when doing the wedding dance, and her stomach is bare, displaying a tiny but strong waist. She does dances that are similar to those done by some of the tribeswomen, but the feeling I get from watching her is more interesting than I have ever felt before.

Perhaps—the last part of my prophecy—I wonder exactly how well she rides and can use her bow. Would my mother approve of her? Would she have me? She is very beautiful and I, while not being completely ugly, am fairly plain and no better looking than the next man. It seems that, if I want her, I will have to impress her with my deeds. It worked for my father, now it might have to work for me as well.

Ayesha

She looked out at her audience, gauging their reaction and seeing who she could get the most money from. The young Khitan man simply cannot take his eyes off me. His face is completely blank; as if he were deep in thought, but his eyes keep tracking me. Oh well, several men here do the same. At least he isn't leering, or ugly, or making lewd comments to those around him. Indeed—he has glared at some who have done that.

Bianca

This is Ayesha's second break. If I am to do something, I should do it now. I know that my songs are those of the taverns. They are far earthier than those of my predecessor, but they are going down well—particularly with the people from a small trade caravan that had just arrived from the south.

I know that my voice is not quite as good as Ayesha's either and I sing a much lower register, but that suits the songs that I sing and that I get the caravan people to sing with me. I am starting to collect a small pile of coins of my own. As she was finishing, the Caliphate girl told her that there were some songs that they could both sing—*she will teach me later. Apparently, that should gain even more gifts from the audience. To an extent, the night reminds me of home and—is it the memory or the drinks?—tears are seeping from the corners of my eyes.*

Chapter XXV

Bianca

Why did this infidel priest, Anastasias, need to meet Hulagu and I? At least Astrid gathering all of us in this private room to hear Hulagu recite his prophesy in full eventually made some sort of sense—wait—was that a very faint blush on the dark skin of his face as he glanced very quickly at the Muslim girl? He might think that no one else noticed. Well, he has eyes for the heathen girl, has he? Let us see what happens here.

Ayesha

All of them are talking about what the prophecy might mean and whether they might be the 'young people' referred to. At least I was able to get them debating if the group was complete. It was easy to suggest that it didn't seem like there are enough of us to triumph against any great odds. It helped when Father Christopher pointed out that the world is full of magic, both on the side of good and of ill. If we were to set out on a quest, then he is the only one with access to supernatural aid, and he is much better at healing than he is at killing. Everyone agreed with this. 'We' decided that each will begin to prepare to leave, but that 'we' will wait, at least a few more days, to see if anyone else arrives to join 'us'.

I hope that one of them will be Theodora and that she will want to join the others, otherwise I will have to make my excuses and not join them. In the meantime, I will still pretend to be as eager as the others. It helped to slow things down to point out that, to be complete, most lands should be represented, after all, they had a person from the north and the west and myself who is sort of from the east, but none has come from the south, and the people from the south are skilled with magic. After the meeting we disperse: Stefan to tell his parents of his decision to leave Evilhalt, while the rest of us go to the practice area.

Chapter XXVI

Ayesha

We had been expecting someone from the south, but that afternoon brought a surprise. Three people arrived from the east instead. To my relief one of them is Theodora and she already has a servant.

I have to somehow persuade the princess to travel along with the others. If she will join, the group will be fairly formidable. Theodora, given her lineage, should be a more than competent mage, even if she is travelling dressed and equipped as heavy cavalry. Anyone who looks could see the pouches at her bolt, sitting under her quiver straps, which have to hold wands. The little man travelling as her servant, from what I can see of his skin, looks to be part Kharl. He also looks and behaves as the perfect servant, but then I look like an entertainer. The third is a Dwarf, mounted on a sheep. Any of their—what do they call them—herdsmen—no, shepherds, would be more than adept at battle. She quickly introduced herself to Theodora and drew her into the bathing group—*as if she is what she was posing as*—to find out more about her.

Theodora

Here I am at Evilhalt, ready to make some money and plan what to do next, and I am stymied at the start. From what I have seen so far on my escape I thought that good entertainers were rare and that this would be an easy way for me to fund my travel, but there are two entertainers in this overgrown village already. One is from the Caliphate. She has brought me to this, admittedly very pleasant, bath and introduced me to the other. The first is an escaped slave and beautiful, and as deferential as a palace servant. The second girl is mainly an animal handler from the iconoclastic west and unremarkable in appearance. They have another girl with them, undoubtedly Insakharl, but with blue eyes, who is spectacularly built and with a stunning face, until she opens her mouth and shows her heritage. They call her 'the Cat' and with reason.

The women are trying to get me to go on some quest with them. They don't know what the quest is, or where they are going, but they do seem eager to go. As it turns out, the Muslim girl, Ayesha, isn't worried by competition. She seems delighted. I am not quite sure how these things work, but shouldn't we be competing? She wants to know what I do and is even more delighted to discover that I dance. She is insisting — very politely, but she is adamant. It is all I can do to remind myself that I am not a princess here — that we immediately get out of the bath and compare dances. As if they are not provocative enough fully clothed. Doing them wet and naked is, well, actually it feels liberating. After all, there are no men. It turns out that we know many of the same dances. The other girls beat out a time for them, although it seems the Freehold girl is trying hard not to look at us as we gyrate and our breasts wiggle and bottoms sway and she has a continual shocked expression on her face that she is trying to hide — badly.

Astrid

It turns out that I am the only one who is not a skald. Oh well, someone has to look out for these little girls. Two of them are tiny and the lack of hair on the taller golden-eyed one makes her seem younger than her build indicates. For once I am not the prettiest girl in the room. I won't be the one drawing all the attention. I can relax.

This new one, Theodora, is strange. She seems to have no hair anywhere on her at all, as if it is natural for her. She has those almost glowing golden eyes. Surely if it is normal for many of what she calls Insakharl there would be at least one person at home to have them — or at least there would be tales about someone who used to have them. What is more, she acts as if she owns the world and it will do as she tells it to. She says that she is just like me, but I think that she hides something and it is something that is very big. I wonder what it is.

Her little servant is kind of cute even if he may be younger than I am. His skin and his eyes show that, unlike her, he is like me. His skin reminds me of many of the men at home but, unlike them, he seems to be both quiet and polite. What a nice change that is in a man. Many of the people at home have his black eyes. Maybe if I get to know him better, I can find out what the mystery is about her.

Basil

Well, who would have thought that barbarians would like bathing? This Khitan is like a small child in his enjoyment, a very active and very noisy small child. Now, do I encourage her to join them or do I try and steer her somewhere safer? Mind you, if trade caravans are being destroyed by others in the middle of the Khitan plains, where is there that is safe? Let me see them in action. They want us to come and practice with them. I will see if they are amateurs. At least, from what this Khitan—Hulagu, that is right—tells me the western girl with the darker blonde hair is practical when it comes down to it.

She may be inexperienced in combat, but she did have the sense to know when to hide and she killed two enemies—one after questioning him. The giant northern girl with the teeth and the very pale hair moves like her name even in a room. Is she like that in the field? Maybe I should talk to the priest. At least he seems to be like the ones at home. They are always good for advice.

The Dwarf is a bit of a surprise in the bath. At least I now know that he really is male, but he is almost completely covered in hair from top to toe and, beneath the hair it could just be made out that he is almost completely covered in barely visible and very complex tattoos. I wonder if all Dwarves are like that?

Stefan

My parents actually seem relieved to hear that I am leaving Evilhalt—from the way they reacted they must have already talked about this and made up their mind to give my younger brother the business and are already feeling guilty about it. It is good of my father to give me the best sword and armour in the family, but they traditionally go to the eldest son anyway. That mail suit has been in the family for generations and family legend says that it had been found on the battlefield after Darkreach's defeat. It is enchanted to resist damage. I have always admired it. The sword, Smiter, has the same lineage. It has strong enchantments for added damage and ability to hit and the spells have been well maintained over the centuries.

The horse they gave me is my father's best horse, and better and far more expensive than I could afford. It is not a warhorse, being just a rouncey for riding, but then I'm not a great rider either. Like most of our forces, I am supposed to be able to ride to a battle then get off the horse fresh to fight with my spear or a sword. I can do that much at least. It looks like now my fate is decided—at least in its direction. Such uncertainties as life and death still hang around unanswered.

Christopher

Here I sit; a trifle uncomfortable in a huge bath with other men. I feel a bit swept away by forces beyond my control. I delivered the Bible and should now be free to go where I want but the forces above me, in this case called Father Anastasias and Astrid the Cat, are conspiring to find another task for me. I suppose that going with these others is as good as anything else I could be doing. I will at least have my own souls to minister to, at least four by the look of it, and perhaps I can convert the others. That would be good in the sight of God and had to be deemed worthy for me to do.

Tonight, I was actually sent to these baths. I was told that I needed to get to know these men and to learn to be more comfortable talking to them. I am not experienced with small talk. I suppose that I should start by trying to talk as I would to another novice I've just met.

Bianca

I feel lost—caught up in something beyond my control. I left the taverns of Trekvarna to perhaps eventually become a merchant. That, in itself, is a big move for a foundling. I have not only left behind Freehold, but also, I have lost my friends and am alone in the wider world—unless I accept these new people I have met. This group challenges most of what I know. The nuns taught me that most of the people outside Freehold are, at best, false Christians. One person I am considering leaving with is an out-and-out heathen, and the Dwarf and Khitan are both openly pagan. None of this seems to matter to anyone else. The others accept them as easily as they accept me. I was also taught that the people of Darkreach worship their Emperor, but the two from there seem to be heretics and defer to the priest here.

The woman had almost burst out laughing when I asked her outright if they worshipped their Emperor, and the little man had a smile on his face as if he was working at suppressing some vast amusement inside himself and was very hard pressed to do so. They don't seem evil and the older priest from the village who wanted to talk to me seemed more like a favourite uncle, or what I imagine a kindly favourite uncle would be like, than a servant of the devil. It is all so confusing. If these basic things I was taught were actually wrong, what else is?

At least Hulagu is an honest and open pagan, and my people have dealt with this, in war or peace, for a very long time. Even though he insists that I have a totem, I am sure he treats me as his sister and if I stick with him I should be safe. He will look after his sister. Besides, it looks like I can learn much from the beautiful woman with the golden eyes and no hair on her body and the almost as gorgeous heathen girl from the Caliphate. Both are far better entertainers than I am and seem willing to help me learn.

I will not learn their shameful dancing though. It looks wrong—even when it is done with only women present. I am sure the priests will not approve of it at all, and the nuns don't even like the village girls dancing around the October pole or in circles at all. However, I can still learn to sing better and to have more songs and even perhaps how to tell stories.

What is most important, none of these people have that 'smell' that I am thinking of as the smell of treachery, so at least I can trust them until I get that feeling from them. That makes me feel better at least.

Thord

I am happy. Some people may look strangely at my sheep, particularly at the stables, but that doesn't worry me. It might worry them, if they try to do anything to Hillclimber, but that is their problem. It is good to be away from home and seeing the world. There is even the meeting of other people from other lands—and it looks like several are bards. If this group keeps together, then I am happy to go wherever they go—even to the ends of the world. My dreams are coming true.

Chapter XXVII

Astrid

The next day at practice they found out their group were well supplied with missile weapons. After shooting first, Astrid looked on critically as they went one after the other. *It seems that I am neither the best shot nor do I have the longest range. It is my bow that best drives the heavy-headed arrows that punch holes straight through even iron armour at close range but Theodora is the best archer. How does the woman have so many skills? Hulagu has the longest range. No-one else could pull his short re-curved horse bow made of wood and sinew. Even Father Christopher and Bianca can use a sling to some effect, while Basil, Theodora and Ayesha could throw knives and things, the last two to a good result. None of us laugh at Bianca's efforts in this regard.*

She is clearly just learning and after she explained how she came by the motley assortment of knives, and how she felt obliged to use them against the people who had killed their owners, she has clearly impressed the others. Some of the knives she even calls by names—when she knows whose blade they were before she gained them. Basil and Ayesha have set to work teaching her. Both heartily approve of her motives.

It also seems to me that everyone is trying hard to impress the others with their efforts. It is clear that Bianca will be our weakest in battle, while Hulagu and Theodora are perhaps the strongest. I take consolation from the fact that none of the others can come near to touching me when they are on foot, and I have just my spear, while they have swords and maces and hammers and shields. I can fend off their attacks with ease. I need to show Father Christopher how to defend himself better with his staff—it is not too different from my spear when it is used just in defence.

Ayesha

It is nice, after practice and a bath, but before dinner and starting to entertain, to have a room to call our own—one to sit in and read. Theodora is browsing the shelves, picking up and putting back books. Behind us, Astrid and Bianca are sitting chatting in chairs—getting to know each other after a tentative start. Around us is the slightly dusty smell of old leather chairs and we are beginning to relax into our conversations.

"How about that book on the top?" Theodora suddenly asked.

"What book on top?"

"It is on its side, right on top of the case. Its leather is the same dark colour of the wood and there is no writing on its spine."

"Most noble, I hadn't even noticed it. You are taller than I am after all."

"Help me with this chair," ordered Theodora. They pushed a chair over against the bookcase and Theodora climbed up. Reaching past the empty shelves she came down with a small book completely covered in dust. *It has obviously lain there for some time untouched.* Theodora carefully shook the dust off the book and blew more off, to the accompaniment of several sneezes from those clustered around. Letters appeared on the cover, long hidden by dust.

"It is in High Speech," said Theodora. "*My Travels Over the Land and Beyond.* That is a strange name for a book."

"There is a beyond?" asked Bianca.

"Of course there is a beyond," said Astrid in a seeming aside. "I have been to at least a part of it."

She has me looking at her as well.

"I have," she said as she looked around at the faces looking back. Her voice sounds defensive.

It seems to me that she doesn't like being challenged when she states something.

"There is the frozen north for a start and there may well be more. The people in the north often live in houses made of snow and ice. There is a warm area, near some hot springs, like the one here but much bigger, where water sprays into the air and where they live in houses built into the hillsides, like beavers do in dams. That is where I went first. They call me Mathanharfead there. Most of them live in the snow and the ice."

Everyone is still looking at her. After a pause she sighed and continued, "They ride in boats with sails that go across the ice on runners, like our skates and they pull up the runners when they go in the water. The boats are made mainly of bone and leather as they have no trees and must buy wood from us."

"You are making that all up," stated Theodora. "I would have heard of such a land."

I am right. Astrid clearly looks quite indignant and speaks abruptly in reply. From the faces, it is a tongue that none of us have ever heard before.

"What was that language?" *I am sure I sound far too eager. I thought that I at least knew the sound of all of the tongues spoken by living men and what I have just heard is very different to anything that I have ever heard before.*

"What did you say?" said Theodora. *She was but a fraction behind me. Her voice is very puzzled.*

Astrid changed back to Hindi. "I said 'And if I was, would you know?' See, I even speak some of the Inuit tongue!"

Now she looks smug as she looks around at the expressions around her. Her voice now changes to be less defensive.

"I really only speak a little of their tongue and they try and be polite at my accent, but my town trades with them. Much of the oil, ivory and dohl that we sell in fact come from them. I am a ship-owner's daughter and I had begun to sometimes help in the trades. Their land lies far to the north, past the northern islands that none dare set foot on and past the floating mountains of ice. In winter the sun never rises there and in summer it never sets. The people only dress in fur or leather, or what we sell them. They like bright threads and embroider everything including the leather. Some of their houses are like ours in Wolfneck, but others really are made of snow and ice, but they are warm inside. They need to be. It is colder there than it is on the highest mountain. We call their home The Northern Waste. They call it The White World. We sell them lots of timber as no trees grow there."

"All right," said Bianca. "Does this book mention your White Waste?"

"Northern Waste," corrected Astrid.

Theodora brought the book over to the table and opened it. The spine was stiff and creaked faintly as it revealed its contents. The pages were of vellum, scraped thin and close written. Theodora, pointing to the right bits, announced that the front page that the book was written by Simon of Richfield and that it dated from well before The Burning.

"There is no such place as Richfield," said Bianca. "There is a Brickshield, but that is all."

"Places often change their names," said Theodora. "For instance, the town we in Darkreach know as 'Antdrudge' was once known as 'Amtrage' and 'Axepol' was called 'Erskine' so long ago. Usually only scholars and bards know of these changes." *Now she has a smug tone.*

Father Christopher then entered the room with the other males. *I can hear that he is explaining Christianity. I might be interested in one day listening to his theology, but I can see that Hulagu looks stony-faced, Thord has a very fixed smile and only Basil is paying him any real attention.*

Astrid interrupted him excitedly, "Father, you are talking and they are not hearing you. Come and look here. We have found an old book. It is about a traveller and what he did. Theodora was just about to tell us where he went. Maybe this is a sign and will tell us where we should go."

Suddenly all four men are paying attention to only one thing. Theodora started to turn the pages very carefully lest they break or tear or stick together. *I will hang back a little and move to the other side of the table so that I can watch the people and their reactions.*

"He starts from Goldentide and he states that his Metropolitan there blessed his travels."

"Metropolitan? There is a Bishop of Goldentide. Metropolitans are for the heret—" *Bianca just remembered who is here and stops herself.*

"We are not the heretics," said Father Christopher patiently. "Once there was an ecumen, a whole community of Christianity. Then one day the Metropolitan of Trekvarna, at the urging of King Roger the Third, declared himself supreme Metropolitan, and said that all others must obey him and do what he said was right. The eastern part of the ecumen refused and there was a schism. His successor now calls himself the Pope. We still hold to the original teachings, but yours have changed."

"That is not what we are taught," said Bianca stiffly.

"None the less," said Theodora, looking up, "it is true. I have studied many books from that time and they all say the same—even the ones written in Freehold."

Astrid interrupted them impatiently, "Can we get back to hearing what he wrote and you can argue about theology and old tales of who did what to whom later?"

Most nod and all of them turn back to Theodora. She is back to turning pages carefully, quickly scanning the words written on them. "He starts by travelling through Freehold."

Small maps are starting to appear and Theodora is soon showing them around. "Many of the places he went to no longer exist. He then went to, what he calls the Northern Reach—oh—it is the land of The Brotherhood."

She keeps turning pages and talking about the Dwarves of the south west. "They are still there, the Khitan, the southern towns, Haven." *She coughs and stops and pushed the book across the table to me.* "Can you continue? My throat is getting dry with this dust and I still have to entertain." *And I don't?*

Nonetheless I take up the book and continue. It is too fascinating not to. I will keep just scanning the pages. Detail can come out later if we need it. The book mentions the Swamp, Bear Land, Lake Erave and then goes on to talk of the mountains south of the Darkreach Gap.

"He went to Dwarvenholme, look, here is a map around the gate." She pointed. *This is interesting.*

"T'ere be no maps left to Dwarvenholme," said Thord. *His voice shows his excitement and he has jumped up out of the chair he has been sitting back in. He is even shifting from one foot to the other as he tries to contain himself.*

"There is now." She kept looking at the next few leaves. "The next few pages detail his journey." *I will read some of it out.* "A landslide had destroyed much of the road and we had to make a new—" She moved the book towards Theodora. "Is this word 'route'?"

Theodora nodded.

"—We came to the doors. The landslide had almost hidden the doors from the road." She turned another page. "Look, another map. This one says on the top: Our path from the old road."

"There is no indication of distances," said Theodora.

"Why should there be?" asked Hulagu. "You just look for hills and rivers. We find our way by how long it takes to ride. Two places may be the same distance apart, but one may take twice as long to reach as the other."

"Not every person moves at the same speed, even on flat ground. If you know how far away a place is, a good map will let you know how long it will take you to get there," replied Theodora.

"The map is no use anyway. We don't even know where this old road is," said Hulagu.

"No, we don't, but he says how far they were south of the Gap when they took a wrong turn in the dusk and found the road." She turned back a page and pointed at the book. "If we go along that road and follow where he says he went, then we should find it if we look. The only problem is for me. The men of the Caliphate cannot find me. If they do I will be punished."

"Such a search could take a very long time," said Father Christopher. *He sounds cautious.*

"You, at least, have a full two years of exile from the monastery ahead of you and as yet there are no plans to fill them up," pointed out Astrid dryly, and then added more cheerfully "and I have forever and no plans at all."

There is no vote, but it already seems decided. I note that Theodora has forgotten she is not a princess and has slipped out of her character and is now giving orders. She has sent Astrid and Bianca (both of whom have experience with buying and selling things) to Master Nobah to see if they can buy the book from him. Astrid took Father Christopher with her for support. They were given money to do so—quite a bit from Theodora's purse. Thord was willing to give everything that he owned including his sheep and armour and perhaps all of his future children. The others went away to start their preparations. It has been decided that we should take a few more days to prepare and then we will leave.

Personally, I think that it should have been worth a lot more than they paid, but the women must have done what they were supposed to.

A strid later confided that she was impressed that she had, with a lot of hard bargaining, just bought a book for two of the local gold talents, three gold hyperion and five silver milesaria. Apparently, that is nearly a quarter's earnings for most people with a trade around here and Astrid has never had to buy a book before. It seems that few people in her village have them.

Chapter XXVIII

Stefan

*T*his changes everything. Stefan ran excitedly to where the others were practising at the butts. "T'ere be troop of Haven cavalry approachin'. T'ey should be here in hour. I be off to t'wall now to see 'em arrive. We see lots of t'eir traders, but t'ey rare send military force up t'is far unless it be very important."

By the time everyone reached the river wall above the dock, the cavalry could be clearly seen. *From down river, where they had come from, a small plume of smoke is visible on the riverbank.* People on the wall were discussing what they may have taken their time to burn.

The troop of riders is largely clad in mail with helmets that fit close around their heads and then rise to a point. They must be coming in peace as all of them have the camails of the helms held up at the front by their sliding nasals. Green cloth is wrapped around the helms, with the point emerging from the top and with a short 'tail' of cloth coming down the back. Most of the riders have the bamboo lances of the south, the butt in a rest beside the stirrup. All of the lances are held at precisely the same angle and have small pennons flying from below the head. Among the riders is one who is dressed just in riding clothes, another with a helm, but just wearing padding and a young Orthodox priest in armour.

"Two mages," said Hulagu from beside him. "You sometimes see their patrols visiting the villages along the south coast. They always have one or two mages with them. One looks to be a man, the other, a woman. She is the one with the padding and with a bow through her saddle girth." They watched the troop approach, riding in pairs. The last pair led packhorses, one of them a giant beast.

The cavalry stopped at the ford and, after talking to the woman mage, a rider from the middle broke off and splashed though the ford to the gatehouse island. He had a short conversation with the guards there, before turning in the saddle and waving the troop forward. *They advance and splash through the ford, their horses almost in step as they move, despite the water. On one horse there is an empty saddle, and a lance is stuck through the saddle girth. Other riders show bandages. They have seen serious combat on the way here.*

They move up the ramp and entered the gate island. *The troop will cross the drawbridge into the foreshore enclosure, moving towards the actual entrance to Evilhalt. It is time to join the other onlookers in moving down the wall to the entrance courtyard to overlook them as they come in.* As the troop passed below them the female mage gave a sudden start and looked up along the row of watchers.

Rani

Sanjeev should ride over the ford to negotiate entry for us. After all, these small towns are supposed to sometimes be prickly about allowing the armed forces of their larger neighbour to gain entry.

He soon waved them over. *Many times, before now, I have seen plans of this town in classes.* Rani looked up and down the river. *What the plans do not show so well is how well it does control this crossing point, the first ford along the long river that leads down to Haven.*

Small and large ballistae are mounted on the towers and rumour has it that there are many potent magical devices in the town arsenal as well. As we ride we gradually rise from the river on a ramp that seems to have a far better footing than wet cobblestones should have. I am quite sure that this can be quickly reversed at need—at any rate, that is what I would do if I were a water or earth mage charged with defence.

A group of idlers watch us from above on the wall. She started—idlers. *One is Khitan, one is a heathen priest like Father George, another, sitting in an embrasure, is a Dwarf. A woman from the Caliphate is visible and the others could be from anywhere. One woman has hair as pale as the sand on Adeela Strand while another has raven-black. What is more my senses are prickling. Some of the onlookers carry much magic. Are these the group of strangers that the university seers mentioned?* She looked from man to man along the wall seeking to see golden eyes and was vaguely disappointed not to see them as if her prophesy had failed her. The column started to move on into the town itself, following one of the guards.

"We are being taken to see the Baron," said Sanjeev as he rejoined her.

"Once we have explained the problem of the caravans then we will go to the inn and tomorrow will say our farewells. Then you are going to be on your own. Are you still sure that this is what you wish to do?"

I nod. I need to look determined, even if inside I am full of doubt.

Stefan

*D*epending where we end up, I might be fighting people just like these in the future. As he thought about this the others offered their observations on what they had seen as they watched the cavalry enter the town and move towards the Guild Hall.

"They look serious," said Bianca, "and very disciplined. Our knights do not ride like that. They each travel with their retainers and servants, not in straight lines. I do not understand why they have one of the other Christian priests with them."

"That puzzles me as well, but the Haven cavalry are very serious," said Hulagu. "They lack bows, but they are determined and do well in a charge with those light lances. Most of their infantry are not impressive, but their cavalry, and their elephants and chariots, are very dangerous. Their mages are very, very dangerous. A Havenite battle mage is most formidable. They train to do little else but kill as a part of their army. Killing in battle is their whole life. It is unusual for a group that small to have two of them."

Father Christopher exchanged waves and smiles with the priest. "The priest is Father George from Erave Town," he said happily. "He is a little older than I, but I know him well. They must have brought him with them as a messenger of some sort. I haven't seen him for a while, so I guess that I will find out more from him later."

"Let's go back to the inn," suggested Astrid. "All travellers seem to end up there, so this lot will eventually go there and then we can find out why they are here as soon as they finish with the Baron."

With nods, they all trooped down off the wall and back to the inn.

Rani

*W*e are led through the town to a small, two-storey stone building. Rani looked around. *It is large by the standards of this place, but small according to what I am used to. It all is. After all, this whole village can fit* *onto the island the university is built on and yet have room to spare.*

"Please be stayin' here," said their guide in accented Hindi. "I be seein' if t'Baron is here."

Sanjeev has dismounted and signalled for the rest of the troop to do so as well. They do, standing by the horse's heads. Rani also dismounted, giving her reins to Amin and stood chatting to Sanjeev and Father George. Their guide came back very soon.

"Be followin' me please," he said.

They went through the door and up some stairs, along a corridor and into a room. *With a title of 'Baron', I was expecting something different, but this is a working office. Two men stand in the room near a desk. One is one of their priests, an older man with a very full beard and a penetrating stare. The other is very short and broad, several hands shorter than I am and far wider. He wears an axe at his belt, even in his office. Without something to judge his height he can easily be mistaken for a Dwarf on first glance. He moves towards us. I wonder if his shape had anything to do with his election.*

"I be Siglevi t'Short, Baron of Evilhalt," he said, "an' t'is be Father Anastasias. I believe t'at you be havin'somethin' t'at you be needin' to tell me. You may talk in front of t' Father. I would be discussin' anythin' important with him later anyway." *He smiles. It is a cold smile.*

Rani and Sanjeev looked at each other. *We did not decide who should speak—I suppose that I should start with the cover story.*

"It has come to our notice in Haven that something is happening to the trade caravans. It is a simple problem. For some time, no caravans have arrived in the south that are supposed to have come across the northern plains. As well, we think that some caravans are missing that are supposed to have come from the north coast. We are here to ask if you might know anything at all that would help us."

While I was speaking, the Baron and the priest were exchanging glances. They know something. I nudge our priest. He can be next. Father George took the hint. "Mayor Cynric and Metropolitan Cosmas send their greetings to you both. We noticed this problem near six weeks ago. We first thought the Havenites had simply arranged new routes. Our captain, Leonas, is sending out more patrols to see what can be found and I was sent with these people to add our town's voice to their concern. I'll take back any news that you may have to my town when the patrol returns to Haven."

The Baron looks at the priest as if seeking advice —The priest nods towards the door and the Baron speaks.

"One of Father Anastasias' charges may be havin' information for you." *He turns to our guide.* "Art'ur, you be goin' to t' inn an' ask t' Khitan man an' t' young Freehold girl if t'ey be pleased to join us."

238

The young man left and Father Anastasias and the Baron began to question Rani and Sanjeev about their journey. Rani left most of that to Sanjeev.

After the accounting of their trip, the Baron said, "It seems that somethin' indeed be a goin' wrong around us. We be a havin' four sets of people arrive recently. Each be a reportin' t'ey bein' attacked by more t'an t'usual menaces to travel. Several caravans be overdue, although t'ose t'at have arrived have said t'at t'eir trips be unremarkable."

Two Khitan finally arrive, a man and a woman—no, she cannot be Khitan. I can see a Christian symbol around her neck. The girl fairly glows with magic. Some of the feeling is from visible knives; more is from places where throwing knives would be kept out of sight. I recognise two of the faces on the wall. Both of them are shorter than me. The girl is also very slender and seems very young—until you look at her face. It has a certain hardness to it that speaks of pain.

The two stand close. Not close as lovers, more like soldiers from the same unit among strangers or even more as a brother and sister, and that they cannot be. The girl bobs what looks like it should be a curtsy at the local priest. It is very brief and it looks like she is not sure if she should do it and she looks sort of embarrassed about it. The priest nods back at her pleasantly.

They looked at the Baron, who spoke to them in Hindi.

"T'ese be Rani and Sanjeev of Haven and Father George from Erave Town. Sanjeev be t'Subadar, t'officer, of t'cavalry who be just arrived. Rani be a Battle Mage who be attached to 'em." He turned to the Havenites, "T'ese two be Hulagu of t'Dire Wolf Totem of t'Khitan 'n' Bianca of Freehold."

In the next few minutes Rani found out why the little girl had such a hard look on her face. *During her recitation, done in a flat and almost detached voice, I notice that the Khitan touches her shoulder a few times, just as one might soothe a nervous horse. His face allows a slight look of concern to be visible on it as she speaks. That does not fit with what I know of his people.*

When she had finished Hulagu continued, "Some of these things are now known to my people. While we were on our way here, we saw a force moving, as if in pursuit of something. We do not permit foreign attacks—" *a brief smile there* "—in the lands of the tribes. Perhaps our shamen found a way to draw aside the veil that protects these vermin and they are now dead. Bianca wants to kill them all herself, but I think that she will be content to know that they have been killed."

The girl smiles a tight smile that is not really a smile at all and I am not so sure about that statement.

She speaks again, with more passion. "Even if they are dead, they have their own village and they make slaves, or worse, of traders. They are evil and shall be brought to justice." *She turns to Hulagu.* "Before we go to our other destination, we must try and get the others to help us find and destroy the village. That may help you with your geas too. For all we know it might well be one of the tests that we are supposed to pass."

I have heard about ears pricking like horses before, but now I am sure that mine have just done that. She interjected. "You have a prophecy—a geas— upon you? I must find out more about this. I also have prophesies laid upon me and one of them mentions me finding others upon the way. I also want to hear more about this veil that you speak of that cannot be seen through."

The Baron spoke up. "But aren't you be with t'is officer's," as he waved his hand towards Sanjeev, "patrol?"

"No," *I suppose that I need to tell the rest of the story.* "They were sent along as my escort to ensure that I would reach here. We discovered this problem along the way and they must now return to Pavitra Phāṭaka with the information that we have gathered so that something can be done about it. Haven relies on trade. Now that we know of the problem, all the mages of the university and the army will be put to work on it. Between them they should be able to force aside the veil over sight."

Turning to the Baron, Hulagu asked, "What will you do now?"

"We be a patrolin' further out 'n' be a lookin' for signs of what might be a happenin'. Even more t'an Haven, trade be t'lifeblood of our town 'n' we cannot allow anythin' to be a disruptin' it."

Hulagu nodded. "The territory of the Pack-hunters lies to the west of here. They are aware of what happened to Bianca's caravan and of what we found out. I suggest that your patrols try and talk to them before they go far so that there are no mistakes over what is happening."

"It be a good idea," said the Baron. "I be a t'ankin' you." He looked around. "Now, I be t'inkin' that we be finished here." He looked at Hulagu and Bianca. "If'n you be a showin' these people to t'inn, you can be a talkin' to each other 'bout your prophesies 'n' also give t'em a chance to be a bathin', probably not in t'at order. Father George, you'll be off to t'e church now. We be givin' you a message to return with before you go a back an' we be givin' another to you, Subadar."

Bianca and Hulagu are gathering us up to head downstairs. They show the cavalry to the stables, waiting until they are done there before leading us to the inn. I hope that I am not being too obvious about wanting to question this Khitan immediately but he keeps putting me off until 'they' are all gathered together. I would have put it down to the usual Khitan reticence in discussing their affairs if he had not made it all the more tantalising when he said that there is more than one story to be told.

Now we are installed at the inn, it will be a while more before I find out the full story as Father Christopher is taking Father George away, the Khitan is leading the other men off to their bathroom, and this Bianca is leading us women to ours.

Chapter XXIX

Rani

A bath? Why are we going downstairs then? The girl has ushered Indira and I into a basement room which contains a huge pool sunk in the floor that gives off an odd chemical odour and steams slightly. It already has several people in it but I have no chance to pay any attention to them with a servant girl trying to help me undress. It seems that, like the ghats, we ignore caste here. I see now why I was told to bring clothes. At least I can hang my belt up. That is not going anywhere, although I notice that there are few other weapons hanging or leaning there.

Rani had undressed and stepped into the bath before she really noticed who was in it. *There is the pale blonde girl opposite me that I saw earlier. She is quite buxom and stunningly beautiful, until you notice her teeth. She is introduced as Astrid the Cat. No wonder.*

Next is the girl beside me, as small as Bianca, but with more curves, black hair and darker skin than the others. She will be the Caliphate girl from the wall and is introduced just as Ayesha, an entertainer.

She turned to her left and totally missed the introduction to the girl there, as her heart missed a beat and she felt something she had never felt before. *All I can take in are the eyes of the woman, which seem to expand so that I fall into them. They are golden. Not figuratively, but literally, really, truly so golden that they almost glow. As my vision expands to take in the rest of her, the girl's face and body make me feel almost plain. I feel warm, euphoric, almost drunk. I have a compulsion to lean over and embrace the stranger and kiss her.*

I was wrong. I was looking on the wall for a man—my prophesy—my grandmother said that my love is bound to the golden eyes. I realise what I feel. I am in love—and with another woman. I am samalaingika—that is why

I have never even been interested in a man before. That is not my destiny. The prophecy that the University gave me had included that I would find love and many surprises. Well, here is the first and the second, all wrapped up in one beautiful package. Any others that follow will be mild after this.

Theodora

I wonder why the Hindi woman, Rani, keeps looking at me. It is as if she has frozen in place and she seems to be quite unaware of anyone else being in the bath. She is not even noticing the woman with her—Indira, yes, that is her name—speaking to her.

She is looking at me very oddly, almost as a mouse looks at a snake that is about to strike it.

Rani

Did someone speak? Have I moved since I saw my beloved? Wake up! She shook her head. "Sorry, I just had an odd thought. Did someone say something? As well, I missed your introduction." *—my love.*

Indira piped up. "I said so much cleaner than bathing at the ghats—but nearly as crowded. Please move over."

Just like often happens at the ghats, a lower caste person can push a higher one to get space. Now Indira pushes me over until I feel my body being pressed against that of my golden-eyed love. We nearly match in size although my dear is a little shorter. Our bodies touch and it feels as if a faint tingle has run down the length of me, just like the side discharge from a lightning spell—I nearly had an orgasm just from her touch—I don't know what to do or say and I feel more awkward than I have since I first learnt how to use magic. Where do I put my hands?

"I am Theodora," said her beloved. "I am an Insakharl, a part Kharl from Darkreach and I am out to see the world."

Insakharl indeed—not if what I was told about Darkreach is right. She is only part Human, that much is certainly true, but eyes like that and from there means that my love, my Theo-dear, is one of the Imperial Family. I am in love with one of Hrothnog's descendants—yet another surprise for me. I have to find out if Theo-dear has received any prophesy connecting us.

244

Theodora

I am worried. The Hindi mage seems scared of me! When we touch, she shudders, but she does not move away, if anything she moves closer. She still hasn't answered my introduction and I am not used to this amount of contact with others unless we are making love. I wonder if this Rani girl knows who I really am. Is my family that fearsome that knowing that someone comes from it scares a person? I will have to find out. But, after all, does it really matter here? Will anyone really care who I am?

Ayesha

Something is going on between Theodora and this new woman—Rani—and I do not know what it is. They keep glancing at each other and then quickly looking away. It is unlikely that the Hindi woman is a threat, but I will have to keep my eyes open. Eventually the two start to talk about magic and about prophecies. It turns out that both are mages; one of fire and the other of air. The conversation they are having is an odd one—awkward even—there are pauses and gaps in the conversation as if the Hindi woman forgets what has been said or what is asked of her.

Astrid

I am having fun. I have never really had a group of girls, beautiful women really, to just talk to. I am neither the brightest, nor the most beautiful here. What a relief. Theodora and Rani are talking about magic, but with odd pauses. Don't they like each other?

She kept up a conversation with Bianca. *I still cannot believe that there can be the number of people that Bianca says live in the cities and towns that she describes. I had thought that Evilhalt, with its high stone walls, is important, but Bianca says that it will fit in a corner of Trekvarna or Ashvaria. On the other hand, Bianca cannot believe my descriptions of the frozen north of the Inuit or of fishing on the sea and chasing whales. Each of us comes from lands that are equally as strange, in their own way, to the others.*

Basil

The men of the Hindi cavalry dominate the men's room and some of them have to sit on the normally empty pedestal in the centre of the bath to make room. Thord has disappeared somewhere and Hulagu and I are the only others here who are not Hindi. The conversation revolves simply around two subjects: horses and the women in the next room.

However much I try to stay the quiet and unknown one, I have to field many questions. It is normally my job to be less openly intimidating than Hulagu and some saw Theodora's golden eyes when she was on the wall. Yes, I told them that many people had them east of the mountains. It is not really a lie. Many people do have them, but they are all from the Imperial Family and all of them are descendants of Hrothnog.

Hulagu

At least I have far fewer questions to field about Bianca than Basil has. Bianca is the plainest of all the girls next door, even the cavalrywoman is prettier and their mage is far more beautiful, even if scary. Their interest in her did quicken when he told them how we met and when I mentioned her horses and how they behave for her. When they ask about Ayesha I just grin and tell them to wait until tonight.

Basil

Basil smiled quietly. *At least with two dancers my mistress will have less attention focussed on her, and just wait until these men see the cute Insakharl girl from Wolfneck and her teeth!*

It is a pity she is so much taller and better looking than I am. I have a feeling that my parents would like her. I am a hunter of the streets, but she is a hunter of the forests. I am good, but I am not sure, from what little I have seen and heard, that I would be able to face her and her spear if she was in earnest. I have only faced people. She has faced bears and that full wolf pack virtually alone. The priest doesn't count. She would be a sensation in the arena, particularly if she fought, as most do who are fighting for pleasure, bare-chested or even naked. This is a sight that I would very much like to see.

After he had found out from the men as much as he could about their trip north, he allowed the conversation to settle down to one they were all happy to talk about—horses.

Chapter XXX

Hulagu

I was wondering what would happen next. It does not take long to find out. After the men had finished bathing, the servants told them that Astrid—who seems to regard the inn as her own home—had arranged that we will all eat in the meeting room. When the men arrived, the women were already there. It seems that Bianca, Ayesha and Theodora have come along with their gear, ready to eat and go straight out and perform afterwards. The girls have brought Rani with them, but Sanjeev and the woman soldier have re-joined their soldiers upstairs. Bianca told him that Rani had indicated to her escort that she wanted to talk about the prophecies that she and Hulagu had received and, perhaps even for their own safety, the other two should not hear them.

Looking around none seems ready to be the first to speak. My story is simple. "My grandfather is the chief shaman of our tuman—our totem-tribe. As I was about to set out on my wanderjahr, my year of finding myself, he revealed to me that I had to ride to a walled town on a river," he waved his hand around vaguely, "and that I might meet someone else along the way who would come with me. He said I would face problems. I set out for here and met Bianca, you know our problems. He also said that I would meet others from different lands, that we would travel together and that we would face tests. Eventually we would face something that was very dangerous and very evil and very, very, important to us all. Bianca thinks that one of our tests might be the village that is the base for the people who destroyed her caravan." *Bianca is nodding.*

"I have no proof of this, but I am inclined to agree with her." *Do I add the rest?* "I am not sure if I should mention the rest of my prophecy, but Bianca knows it already and it might be important. My grandfather also said that I might meet a woman, not of the tribes, and marry her. It isn't Bianca. I count her as my sister and she is like a Khitan and of the tribes in so many ways, despite coming from among the settled folk." *Ah yes—my rod.* "One other thing that I should have mentioned before," he dug in his pouch and handed it to Bianca, "the demons that attacked us had this." *Bianca points it at me and it obediently goes 'beep'. She swings it around to point at each other person. It stays silent the whole time. She points it again at me and it goes 'beep' again.*

"I do not know why the demons that were sent would have this to find me, but they did. That is our entire story."

I know the other stories except the new one. He looked at Rani. *Because I do that everyone turns to look at her. She started as she realised this.*

"I would like to see that rod later." She paused. "Now, I have received four foretellings so far that relate to me and I think that I should cast a new reading after we have finished talking. The first reading I did for myself. It said that I would journey to the north and find the person from the east. If I did not, then disaster would happen."

It is Theodora's turn to look startled.

Rani

That is the easy part—now to continue. I am going into uncharted territory here and I know nothing about these people or how they will react. "I was not going to mention the second prophecy until Hulagu told us about his future wife. I am not sure which of you is his wife to be, if she is here now, but it is not I. My grandmother, who is one of the greatest seers of her generation, told me that I must travel north to find my life, my love and my future with the golden eyes." She paused and looked at Theodora.

Everyone else is soon following my gaze. From the expression of confusion on my love's face, Theo-dear must be wondering why they are all looking at her. Gradually I can see the words sink in as a blush, very evident in her dancing clothes, starts to appear.

"She was right about the love at least." *Around me I can sense everyone starting to look from Theodora to me and back. I can see my love's blush deepen and she seems not to know where to look. Her mouth opens and closes a couple of times, but nothing comes out. I feel a rush of relief at having revealed my feelings. Now it is up to Theo-dear how she will react to my declaration.*

Silence fell over the group. *The big northern girl is looking worriedly at the Christian priest. Yes, that is an interesting question I did not think of, how will the priest take this? They tend to live a very sheltered life. He does look a bit flustered and he blinks a couple of times. I can see him thinking.*

Time to continue. "The third prophecy was from the Priests of Ganesh. They are the priests of knowledge. It repeated that my destiny lay to the north and added that I might never see Sacred Gate again. It also confirmed that I would find unexpected completion with another." *A glance at Theodora, who had briefly recovered from my first comment and now starts blushing all over again.* "It went on to say that I must gather a group of strangers. Presumably that means those in this room. Some would know of their destiny—" *I nod towards the Khitan and he nods back.* "—and others would not. It ended by saying that the matter was urgent."

"The fourth set of predictions was from the University. They had known of my fate for many years but could only give it to me when I was ready. Again, it said that I must go north. It mentioned that I would face trials preparing me for my life's task and that I would find love and many surprises." *I realise that my smile at my love is quite broad and, for a moment, my hand moved, briefly and of its own accord towards the Darkreach woman.*

She was able to stop it and instead moved her hand towards her belt pouch to remove a deck of cards, as if that had been her intent all along. "If it will not offend anyone I would like to make a reading now. If you will pardon my presumption, as the last to arrive, I understand that you now face choices as to what to do. You have met and you have decided to travel, but you do not know where to go."

Thord, sitting quietly in a corner was quick to speak, "They have found, perhaps, a way to find lost Dwarvenholme. Surely that is a suitable quest?"

Bianca spoke up next. "And there is the village of Dharmal and his raiders. They are evil men and we know that someone or something gives instruction to Dharmal. He does not act on his own. It would also be good to do something about all of that..." she looked around at Thord, "...and it is in the mountains and possibly on the way to Dwarvenholme."

Next it was the turn of Hulagu to speak. "We know about you and your walking bones and the arrow from the forest. Well, most of us were attacked on the way here and, in each case, by something or someone that was well beyond the normal hazards of travel. For us they were the bird demons, for those from Darkreach it was powerful undead." *Everyone is nodding.* "It seemed like someone was trying to stop us reaching here. Somehow, I don't think they will cease in their efforts to stop us now that we have joined. It is likely that they will get more insistent. As well, my grandfather told me that something was trying to stop him finding out more. Normally, when he visits the spirit world, he would be able to be much clearer about what lies ahead. This time he reported something like a fog lay over the whole future."

Rani thought for a moment. "As you said we were attacked twice. Once might have been someone acting on their own, I don't know why, but the skeletons were also unusual in their number. All of my prophecies, except the University, and their scryings were done some time ago, reported vagueness or a fog, which prevented a better reading. Now it also seems that everyone was attacked by something evil except for you, Father," *I may need to get used to that term* "Astrid told us of the wolves. Wolves aren't necessarily evil, are they? We don't have them in the south, like you have them in the north, so I don't know."

"Evil they were, but not like skeletons or other undead. That is an evil I could have at least attempted to deal with myself. I cast a miracle of protection from evil and Astrid believes that it did help us." *Beside him Astrid is nodding.* "She also tells me, and she knows more of hunting and the wild things than I do, that the wolves that attacked me are not like normal wolves and they seemed to be hunting us and not just food." *She is nodding again.*

"It seems that the village that Bianca talks of is full of very evil people." *It is Bianca's turn to nod.* "Destroying it would thus be an act of goodness. From what little I have heard Dwarvenholme was supposed to have been lost to some great evil. These storytelling ladies probably know far more than I do on this."

He *pauses and both Ayesha and Theodora start to speak, but this Father Christopher held up his hand to stop them.* "It also seems to me that we have all just met and know very little of each other, and it is likely that we have much to discover about each other, and even about ourselves." *He glanced quickly at me and Theodora. She has realised what he means and blushes again. Well, from the quick twinkle in his eye, maybe the priest is not totally oblivious to the world after all, or at least he has a robust sense of humour buried somewhere deep inside his robes and it is trying to find its way out.*

"We would learn more about our abilities if we took on lesser evils before we tackle the greater. This means to me that we should perhaps clean up the village and other evils that we find along the way, before we look to Dwarvenholme. I have no problem with you seeking guidance. In the Church we have our own methods of doing this, but I would have to go to the local church to use their copy of the Holy Word." He stopped speaking and looked around.

Bianca started and reached for her belt. "Father, pardon my ignorance, but do you use the same Bible that we use?" she asked.

"Yes, my daughter," *I can hear the amusement in his voice.* "Your people changed much when they abandoned our faith, but they did keep the True Word—or at least most of it."

"Then I can help you." Bianca pulled a book out of a large pouch. "It is only the old half, not the Gospels," she said handing it over.

Father Christopher opened it and examined the closely written pages. "This is marvellous. Whoever did this had a very fine hand. It is not a beautiful work, but then a Bible that is a work of art is not readily portable." He smiled wryly. "It is a book meant for a devout person who travels and wishes not to be far from the Holy Writ. Whoever owned this probably had a set of the Gospels with them as well. However, let us see what this lady finds out first." He handed the Bible back to Bianca.

Rani nodded and handed the cards to Theodora. "Please my beloved," *everyone is getting used to Theodora's blushes by now, but I like saying it,* "you are already tied to me and so I ask you to shuffle the pack. You have fulfilled part of my destiny, so I ask you to help work out the rest."

Theodora took the deck. *I can see that she is nervous. She nearly dropped the cards rather than touch my hand. She made a clumsy attempt to shuffle, dropping cards several times and putting them back in the pack. Eventually she has thrust the cards back at me as if they could explode. She seems almost as scared of the cards as she is of me.*

Rani took the pack and dealt cards face down onto the table. She placed a card down with another to its left, and a third to its right and finally one below the first.

"This is a simple reading and layout. I have reasons for using such a simple pattern. We shall see if we need to be more detailed later." Rani turned over the first card. *It is a picture of a woman with wind-swept hair seated on a throne coloured green, purple and yellow—as if to represent jade, amethyst and amber. The sun shines from a corner and flowers carpet the area around the throne and a bundle of sticks leans against it. Small clouds with faces representing blowing wind are in the sky.* "The Queen of Staves."

She paused and then turned over the left-hand card. *It shows a man dressed in a toga. He has golden eyes and was surrounded by piles of coins, all golden.* "The King of Talents."

She turned the right-hand card and then that underneath. *The third card is of the house of swords. It has two bare blades on it. The last card shows two persons holding hands and kissing. Above them is a woman driving a chariot pulled by doves, its archer being a chubby child with wings who is looking down.*

"This is not a reading for everybody. This is a reading for Theodora alone. I will give it to her later and, like all readings that I do for a single person, it will be done privately. I need another to shuffle the cards. How about you Father, if you do not mind? It may help if you pray to your god for guidance while you are doing the shuffling."

"Perhaps not me," said Father Christopher. "I will use sister Bianca's bible later for guidance. Perhaps she, as one who has strong feelings on the matter, would care to assist you?"

Rani nodded and handed the cards to Bianca. "Think hard about us and what lies ahead for us as a group," *a tiny smile sideways at my love*. "You should be able to focus on that. Do not get distracted by more personal questions."

Bianca took the cards gingerly. *She looks at them as if it is her who is scared of ritual contamination. Once she has overcome her reticence, however, she has taken the large parchment cards and shuffled them with a practiced ease, cutting the pack several times and reversing half of the deck each time before handing the cards back to me. She has spent too long working in taverns.*

Let us try again laying out the four top cards in front of me. She paused briefly before beginning to lay them out. She turned the centre card. *It shows a young man on an armoured horse. He wears the armour of Hind, but with wings on his helmet. A constellation of stars is in the top right and instead of a sword he holds a wand.* "The Knight of Staves."

Rani turned the next card. *It is upside down. It shows a woman standing in front of a wheel, which has depictions of twenty-two cards on it. Standing on its top is a figure and the same figure is depicted falling near the base of the wheel.* "Chance, reversed."

She turned the card on the right. *It shows a two-horse Hindi chariot with an umbrella mounted on it and under that stands an armoured man with blue skin. The charioteer is lightly armoured. One of his horses is white and the other black. Flying above the chariot is a hawk.* "The Chariot."

Finally, I turn the last card that lies underneath the others. It shows a robed and blindfolded woman who holds in one raised hand a jeweller's scale and in the other, a sword of mercy. Above her flies an owl. "And lastly we have Justice."

"This one is for all of us." *I need to concentrate and look into the cards.* She closed her eyes then tilted her face up and held her hands over the cards, with their palms downwards. She held that position for a minute and then began to speak. *I have seen and done enough readings like this to realise that my voice is now slightly different, perhaps a trifle stilted.* "The Knight of Staves stands in the position of the Enquirer, the person who asks the question. In its simplest meaning the card indicates both travellers and journeys and, I believe it stands for us. As well it also indicates both restless curiosity and a desire for change. From what I have heard these motives drive several among us.

"The card on the left stands for past history and what lies behind a question. The card of Chance, when reversed indicates strange omens and dark prophesies. There is no doubt that these have occurred and they lie behind at least some of us being here. The third card stands for the way ahead. The

Chariot is a card of turmoil and battle, but it also implies that the questioner will triumph in the end. The last card tells us the final result. The card of Justice means that right will prevail over wrong and evil will be vanquished and feel retribution.

"Taken with the other cards this is not some everyday evil, such as a stolen ring or a murder, this card means justice will come to pass over a major source of evil. These are all strong cards and their meaning is unequivocal. They offer no guidance on the direction that we should take, but given that a course of action has been discussed and I am sure that Bianca was focussed on at least the first part, we are probably headed in the right direction or else the cards would have been less certain."

I have spoken the whole time and pointed at objects with my eyes closed. Now I open them and let my shoulders slump ever so slightly. It is strange how something so simple can drain you. She looked around at the gathering. "Given the difficulty with getting meaningful readings at present, I think we have a good and very clear answer."

Father Christopher then took control over the meeting. "Can all of the Christians present please follow me in prayer, Bianca, if you wish to join in, I assure you that you will not find this offensive to your beliefs. Thord, Hulagu, Ayesha and Rani, please either clear your minds or pray silently to your own gods for me to receive guidance." *He is leading his small flock through what he calls the Lord's Prayer. He looks quickly at Bianca, and then naming it for the 'pagans and heathens present' through another joint prayer he calls the Nicene Creed.*

Bianca

*W*hy is he saying these—I can—should—join in. I am sure that these are all the same rituals that I would hear performed by the priests of the True Church if they were going to do the same thing. I have said these words enough times myself. What then are the differences? Why have I been taught that these people are heretics?

Rani

The priest is picking up Bianca's religious book and, closing his eyes, is praying aloud.

"Oh Lord, we beseech Thee for guidance. We are faced with choices as to the path that we must take and perhaps none of these are correct. We desire to do what you would have us do and so we humbly ask you to show us the way with your Divine Words. Amen."

Bianca has kissed her cross and made her sign of the cross in front of her. The others make the sign of the cross as well, although crossing themselves the other way around. I wonder why.

Without opening his eyes Father Christopher placed the book on the table and allowed it to fall open, felt for it, and placed his finger on a page. Opening his eyes, he looked down and began to read. "I have found the Psalms of Solomon, chapter fifteen and verse six. 'But they shall pursue sinners and overtake them, and they that do lawlessness shall not escape the judgement of God.'"

He stopped and looked around the table. *There is a look of awe on his face. Looking around I can see that most of the listeners have wide eyes at the directness of his answer. I am fairly certain that I look surprised as well.*

There is a note of slight shock in his voice as the priest again speaks. "It seems that the Lord has spoken to us through His Words. I think that it is fairly clear that this applies to us — very clear actually — much more so than what our seer has assayed. To me, from what this says, it is now very apparent that we should chase Bianca's bandits back to their village and so bring them to face justice. What happens after that may become clear, but I think that we will have to seek guidance again. Having said that, in my opinion, the first step for us is now absolutely certain and I will follow it — alone if need be."

As he speaks I can hear conviction creeping into his voice. When he finished he closed the book, kissed it and handed it back to Bianca, who returned it to her largest pouch.

I have heard of this method of foretelling, one that relies more on the holiness of the questioner than on any skill in foretelling, but I have never witnessed it before as it is one that is rarely used in Haven. Our texts are not as amenable to bibliomancy as that of the Christians seem to be. I am impressed. It seems to give a very direct answer that cuts right through the fog — at least in this case.

Chapter XXXI

Basil

*W*hat will happen next? He moved to place himself to keep an eye on his charge and on the Hindu mage. *I never thought to see Theodora's reserve as a noble shaken, but it is—severely. I still am not sure about this new development, but I do not see the Hindu woman as a threat. Indeed, if she is truly in love with my mistress and it is returned, and I have no problem with that—some of Hrothnog's descendants have far more odd relationships than such a straightforward pairing—then she will be fiercely protective and having a battle mage on my side will make my job far easier.*

Led by the entertainers, they all trooped upstairs, discussing what they had heard. Once there Ayesha, Theodora, Bianca and an impatiently waiting Howard start their performances. *When she starts dancing, Theodora's performance is a trifle clumsier than usual. She keeps glancing at this Rani and blushing.*

Rani is sitting entranced and with a smile on her face. She is sitting there like a Kharl from the provinces who has never seen a naked woman before and who has stumbled into the club of a high-paid hetaera. Her eyes scarcely move from the Princess. I can see from her pupils, her breathing, and her nostrils exactly how she is feeling. It is so intense it is making me feel aroused.

It takes some time before she eventually shakes herself and seems to make a conscious attempt to be less intent—and that was doomed to fail when the northern girl, who is sitting beside her, starts nudging her and pointing out Theodora's best movements, and her beauty, with a smile on her face that shows her teeth.

Bianca

I am more than a bit shocked. I thought that these heathen dances were bad enough when there were men watching lasciviously. Now there is a girl watching a girl. I am sure that the nuns will really disapprove of that and the Holy priests never countenance such lust outside marriage and there can be no marriage between women. Can I, in conscience, travel with such people? I want to ask a priest, but here I only have the wrong priests. At least Father Christopher, even if he does not know true history, uses the same Bible.

Maybe I should be relieved that Rani is just watching and not passing lewd comments as the men often do—but on the other hand the Cat is acting like men do. She is pointing out the beauty of Theodora to Rani in the broadest terms. She has a rough sense of humour suited to the sailor and hunter that she is—actually it is one I am used to in the taverns—Dear Lord—it is how I treated the trader's guards when they were rude to the Khitan I travelled with. Maybe I am not so different than the Cat after all.

Theodora

During their breaks, the entertainers join the other travellers and Stefan's friends on the front bench. *It does not matter what I do, I seem to end up beside Rani when I just take the only vacant place on the bench, which always seems to be a spot just left by either Astrid or Basil.*

I know I am being steered there. The Cat may not have been raised in Darkreach, but she certainly has the broad Insakharl sense of humour.

I give up. I am going to just head for the seat that Rani has kept ready for me. Having made her declaration, she seems content to just sit beside me, looking at me, and chatting with me, quite intelligently really, and to wait on my decision.

Damn—two things. First, we do have a lot in common and second, the dark-skinned girl is really very attractive and she even smells nice, in a very exotic and spicy fashion. Three—I wonder what she tastes like.

Basil

The Cat is steering the two together, with more than a slight grin on her face. She has drunk several drinks and is treating the whole affair between the mages as a joke. She seems to be truly enjoying the embarrassment that she is helping cause. She really is just like my sisters in so many ways, only prettier and far larger.

Seeing that I am also trying to get the two to sit together, it is natural that the Cat and I should come into contact as we both move to act. She is well muscled, but soft in just the right places and, when standing, my head rises to an interesting height that brings this softness to my attention. She is really quite spectacular in her build and her cleavage, particularly in her leather jerkin, tight laced at the bottom and undone at the top is perhaps best described as unavoidable.

Astrid

I know what I am trying to do with the mages for fun, but is Basil also trying to get to know me better? He keeps bumping into me during the breaks in such interesting ways. It is a shame he seems to be a bit embarrassed about his size. Don't men realise that everyone is the same height lying down, well except for Svein who is so fat that he would be twice my height.

Inside herself, Astrid came to a decision. *I am now my own captain. Damn it, tonight I am going to enjoy myself. I am drinking much, indeed more than I ever have in my life, but with what lies ahead, this might be my last chance to live a life that I have never had a chance at before. If we are going to die, I am damn sure that I do not want to die a virgin. I know that I am no saint. I just have not had the urge before. Tonight, watching the Darkreach woman dancing before the Havenite made me feel—well—a little warm inside. It may be time.*

Theodora

It was during the fourth set of entertainment, and the second set of dances, that Theodora realised that she really didn't mind Rani watching her. *After all, such a relationship is not unknown. My cousin Verina has a wife who is her more distant cousin Loukia, as well as two husbands between them, and I get on well with all of them. I don't love Rani, but I can afford to let Rani love me and it could be fun.*

After all, it is not as if I am a shy virgin. I have not been one of those for many, many years—over a century. Like many of the girls who live in the palace, and indeed quite a few of the men, I lost my virginity to a condemned gladiator and have taken many more since then. Once, I even took one of the giant Insak-div to bed. I only did it once and, even with healing, I was sore for weeks. Some girls crave more than normal men can give and seek them out, but I have been content with more normal pleasures. A girl can be quite gentle and, as I have already noted, Rani is very attractive and quite exotic looking. After the night's work is finished, I will let Rani give me the meaning of that reading and, if I am not too tired, we will see what happens from there.

Basil

Theodora has regained her confidence. During the last break she didn't need to be steered and she headed straight to where Rani sits. She sat and took a drink before taking Rani's hand and leaning over to whisper something in her ear. Rani's smile has broadened and became more animated. I tried to talk to her once the entertainment restarted, leaning past Astrid to do so, but she scarcely noticed me.

Astrid

I may be a bit foggy, but Basil keeps trying to talk to Rani. It is hard not to notice. Each time he has to lean across me and he keeps brushing my breasts or placing his hand on my leg. Is he really trying to get Rani to talk, or was he using it as an opportunity to get close to me? Theodora whispered something to Rani. It looks like Rani might get lucky tonight. It is the quickest seduction that I have ever seen and conducted entirely out in the open. Damn, I am feeling, well, excited, as well. I might as well try something myself. I have decided that I am not going to a possible death still a virgin when there is a cute man of my own kith, and yet not kin, available. I want a man and there is one here.

Basil

The next time that Basil leant across to try and talk with Rani and then regained his place he discovered that he was sitting within an arm that was lying innocently along the tabletop behind him. Then he found a hand on his leg. *Is Astrid trying to seduce me? Is her drinking thinking for her? I will find out.* He put a hand on her leg. *She hasn't objected or moved away and the arm that is around me on the table has left a hand on my shoulder. Her breast is pressed against me and not moving away.*

The entertainment has finished and a loud, large, and more than tipsy Astrid is leading me upstairs. I am still not sure about this openness. It goes against my nature. As we leave, I hear Hulagu make a comment about the Cat playing with the mouse and even Bianca is smiling at the jest. At least, with all eyes on us no one has noticed that Rani is also leading someone away. I will help the Cat in being conspicuous. It will better gain some privacy for my mistress. I still don't know if the Cat is helping the two women or if she has designs on me. I like her and hope that it is the latter but will be content with the former. I guess that I am about to find out. It has been a while.

Theodora

After we finished entertaining, and my servant was dragged off, Rani has brought me from the shadows and, more quietly we are headed upstairs from the warm tavern common room to the cooler second floor. It seems that the Hindi woman has engaged a larger room than the servant's quarters that the rest of us are in. It has a large bed, a chair, a chest and even a fireplace. A warm fire is burning in it, to warm me up in my entertainer's clothes on an autumn night. On the chest is a large tray with a flagon of wine and a pair of goblets.

Rani is leading me inside. I am nervous. "I am sorry," Rani said, "there is only the one chair and no table. If you wish the chair I will sit on the bed and show you the cards and what they mean. Please, can you pour us some wine?" With that Rani removed her slippers and sari, leaving herself in silk trousers and a bodice — *similar to what I have on* — and climbed up on the bed. *She has taken her cards from the, now visible, belt pouch and, sitting with her legs crossed oddly, has begun to carefully leaf through them to sort out the ones that she wants.*

This leaves me free to look at her. My first thought is that she cannot really be comfortable with her legs contorted like that. My second is that she is certainly worth looking at. Theodora poured some wine for them and, taking one goblet, sat back comfortably in the chair to continue her appraisal. *I cannot see the cards properly and Rani cannot reach the wine.* Sighing she moved the chair next to the bed, placed the tray across the arms and, removing her slippers, she climbed up on the bed herself. She sat with her legs over the edge and, for the moment, kept the cards between her and Rani. She breathed in. *Rani smells—yes exotic is right—and almost intoxicating with the spices she obviously uses on her body.* Rani finished laying out the cards and looked up, seeming to notice where Theodora was for the first time. Theodora waved towards the wine on the tray.

"Later, my love," said Rani casually. "I need a clear head." She pointed at the central card. "This is the Queen of Staves and stands in the position of the person asking the question. I was certain that this was not a reading for the whole group and that you had a different question in your heart as soon as I saw this. It stands for you, my dearest, and tells me that you are a woman of sunny disposition, accomplished and graceful who is adept in many fields." *She looks at me and her lips part a little before shaking her head and pointing at the second card.* "This is the card of your past. It is the King of Talents and this tells me that your past revolves around a very powerful man. I have the feeling that he is a ruler, but he is also very concerned with his family. Usually it means that the person is a master of the material world, but I have a feeling that this is not just the case here. Is there such a man my love? Perhaps it is your father?" *She pauses. She is waiting for the reply that I really do not want to make.* "I do know more about you than you have said. I do know exactly what the colour of your eyes means and whose family you must belong to, but I do not know how widespread the family is or how much he looks over you."

Oh my—the central part of my being anonymous is blown away as casually as that. Is what lies behind the colour of my eyes common knowledge out here as well? How many others among this group know everything that I thought I was so cleverly keeping as a secret?

"The third card is the two of swords. It indicates that the way ahead for you is between an older person and a younger. For my sake, this card worries me. My future is tied to you and I love you, but this card tells me that there must be another for you as our ages are little different. I am afraid that I cannot lie about this. I can see that this other person, who I am ready to hate as they keep me from you, will become your lover."

Rani points at the last card and continues. Her voice is sad. "With them you will find passion and consummation. You will be complete. I wish one of us was far older than the other, but it seems that my love for you may be forlorn." *She pauses.* "Even if I do not get to have you in the end, if you do not mind, I will still follow you and I will keep on loving you. I will stay as distant from you as you wish. Does any of this make sense to you, my love?" *She has finished talking; reaching for a glass of wine and, for the first time tonight, her face is fixed into a sad look.*

I now have a perfect way out if I want it. Theodora looked across at Rani. *Damn—the girl really is beautiful and, while I do not feel for her as she obviously feels for me, it had felt quite nice inside knowing that she was watching me dance and was so open in loving me as she did so. Besides, I have never managed to have a man that I am happy with for more than a night or two. Perhaps I will have better luck with a woman. I admit it, but only to myself. I am actually feeling a bit damp anticipating her embrace and her lips. Do I follow that?*

"Put away the cards and have a sip of that wine. I have something to tell you." Rani did as she was told and then sat there, nursing her goblet. *She is looking at me hopefully.* Theodora looked at Rani. *What do I say—what words to choose—what destiny to follow?*

"Your cards may well be right and they may well refer to me. I am not as young as I look. My family live very long lives and I am already well over one hundred years old. I will not change my appearance during your lifetime and it may not be fair to you, or me, for us to love each other. I just do not know—" *Her face has brightened.* "—I know that I do not love you—" *It falls.* "—but I think that I am willing to try to learn to—" *and it brightens again and her pupils have grown huge.*

With their eyes now locked on each other both women now took a long drink, then, in unison, they put their goblets down on the tray beside them. There was a pause as they each wondered what they should do next and then, acting almost as one, they reached out for each other tentatively and softly.

Chapter XXXII

Astrid

Astrid woke early in the predawn. *I am lying on my back and cradled within my arm, head on my shoulder, is a sleeping and naked man. His left hand lies across me and cups my breast. He may be only slight in build and look young, but he has experience, stamina and other attributes that are just the right size.* Astrid felt a little sore, but very happy with herself, almost smug. She leant over to kiss her little Kutsulbalik and only then noticed bite marks. *Oops, I will have to be more careful about that when we make love again...but then, what if he doesn't want me? Some men only want the next conquest. I am no longer a virgin—what if that is all he wanted?*

She lay there panicking for a little, heart racing, while looking at his small and muscular body and the smooth scaly skin on his forearms and torso. *I hope that he will still want me. I enjoyed last night a lot more than I thought I would and I don't want to give it—or him—up just yet.*

Eventually Basil awoke and stretched slightly. "My dear," he said.

Astrid breathed a sigh of relief at his first words. His hand moved on her breast. *I can feel my nipple going hard already.*

"It didn't seem right to mention it last night, but did you realise that, when you make love, you purr?"

"Do I? Really? Anyway, as you should know I have never made love before. I didn't notice and I think that you are pulling my leg for biting you. Sorry." She leant over and kissed one of the marks left by her sharp teeth. "Would you like to prove it to me?" *Was that innocent enough?*

Astrid found out two things. Firstly, Basil still wanted her and secondly, she really did purr like a very large, and in Basil's opinion, predatory cat. Eventually Basil got out of bed, limping and making mock complaints of pain and dressed to fetch Theodora's breakfast.

"Can I help?"

"No, you are the hunter, I am the servant. I might let you show me how well you can cook, but this is what I do and is a part of my job."

Rani

I am lying on my bed naked in a tangle of arms and legs and hair—did I just hear a knock? Was I dreaming? No, the door is opening and a tray is coming through it. I am sure that I locked it last night when we entered.

"Good morning mistresses."

It is the little man with the scaly skin on his arms. He seems to be ignoring the fact that we are both unclothed and exposed and, although it is my room, he acts as if he is the one with the perfect right to be here. Is he Theodora's servant? We were introduced and I am sure that I was told his role, but I had other things on my mind at the time.

"Good morning Basil." *She sounds sleepy. We didn't get much rest. She has not even raised her head, just waving a hand vaguely in the direction of the chair.* "We are very exhausted and may not get up all day. Just put the tray on the chair beside the bed."

"Yes mistress. I do not know Shri Rani's tastes yet, but I brought both extra coffee and a pot of tea with both lemon and honey here and a jug of juice." *He is looking at me.* "I have also taken the liberty to add some fruit to the pastries, which I believe is the custom in your land, Milady. Will that be sufficient?"

Rani nodded silently. I am used to servants, but I am used to female ones. This is very new. I cannot even cover myself with bedclothes. For some reason the blankets are on the floor—oh, that is right—I remember why that is. My Theo-dear doesn't even seem to notice that he is male. That hand has stayed nestled in my groin as if we are alone.

"Stop worrying dear and give me a kiss," said Theodora. *At least she sounds happy and the way she said that was laden with promise.* "Basil will look after us. He is now your servant as well. Let him know what you like and he will try and arrange things for you."

I think that I would like to arrange Basil not only out of the room but also far, far away. Is my lover always this flighty? I don't have much experience with this sort of thing, but Theo-dear seems like a young girl showing off her first love to her friends by the way, and where, that she holds her hand and by not letting me move to cover myself. Basil moved over and removed the tray that was still on the chair that had been moved back against a wall from the night before. He replaced it with the one he carried, which gave off the aroma of fresh pastry and warm liquids, moved it closer to the bed and then busied himself in straightening the room and hanging things up from where they lay in disarray on the floor.

He is leaving, not only with the tray, but also some of my travel clothes that need mending. The door has locked itself. Does he have a key now? They broke their fast, feeding small portions to each other in the fashion of new lovers, before again becoming oblivious to the world.

Astrid

Astrid was lying languid in the bed when there was a knock on the door. *Make sure that I am covered.* "Come in." *It is Basil with a tray of food and drink, some clothes and a small box.* "You don't need to knock—you have already entered." Basil stuck out his tongue at her as he was putting things down and she returned the gesture.

"I have some mending to do," said Basil "and, seeing that you have worn me out, you can feed me while I work." He started to sew, but Astrid soon took over.

"You sew just like a man. You cannot let Theodora wear something that roughly sewn." She started to unpick some stitches *These are not Theodora's clothes.* "Oh, so they did it then? Does it look as if they just had one night?" Basil shook his head. "So, you now have two ladies to work for. You poor man—now you can feed me while I do your servant work for you."

Astrid sat cross-legged like a tailor but naked, sewing the rip in Rani's clothes. As she worked they told each other about their homes.

Basil

I am revealing more than I meant to. As it is I don't want to tell her the slightest lie. The best I can do is to say that there are some things that I cannot talk about. Astrid may think this odd and gave me a look, but she has let it slide.

She finished sewing. Basil took the clothes from her and shrugged. "I will get these back. I doubt that they have noticed that I have left them, but they may choose to emerge from their room today. Can I return? Should I bring more to eat?"

Astrid

"**I**f you do not come back to thank me properly for doing your sewing for you, I will track you down. I am very good at that." *Still, I am curious.* "Theodora decided that Rani really meant it then?"

"Yes, and I think she may be starting to have feelings back. She certainly seemed very happy and, yes, I seem to now have two mistresses."

"Are you happy with me?" *I blurted that out, didn't I? I didn't mean to. At least I have asked it now.*

Basil smiled and came over, and bent to kiss her where she sat on the bed, her feet on the floor. His left hand fondled her breast as he kissed her. *He kisses well and my nipple is swiftly hardening again.* "I am not sure that happy is the right word." *I can feel my heart fall.* "More like being in grave danger of falling seriously in love for the first time in my life," he said. "I now have three mistresses. As well, I have a serious duty. Hopefully, I will one day be able to tell you more about this, but as long as I can be, I will be with you. Not just for the sex, although that is fairly good—" *that smile had better mean he is in jest* "—but for you. Is that what you wanted to hear with your fishing?"

That is exactly what I wanted to hear. "Hurry back and we will see if I can increase the danger for you." Basil, tugged his forelock in mockery at his order, picked up the tray and the clothes and hurriedly left the room.

Basil

*T*his time when I enter with a new tray and mended clothes it is to find a circle marked on the floor with chalk and Rani and Theodora sitting on the bed. Both have their hair out and Theodora is brushing Rani's long hair. I cannot help noticing that Rani is now as smooth on all of her body parts as Theodora is naturally—Mages! Basil inched around the circle. Now I have two of them to care for—so much for hoping that Rani would help me in my task.

Rani moved her hand to cover herself but Theodora stopped her. "At home," she said, "that is regarded as being a great insult to your servant. You are saying to them that you do not trust them with such a small matter. I trust Basil and so should you." *Rani has laid her hand down but, from the looks she is throwing in my direction, still looks nervous at being so very naked before a man.*

She will learn. Besides, Astrid is so much more my type—that is a thought— until last night, I had not thought that I had a 'type'. He briefly suggested that the ladies might like to retire to the bath below while he attended to the room. *Oh great—simultaneous and identical blank stares from them both.* He quickly left with the breakfast tray muttering about returning later and, after returning the tray to the kitchen and getting more food to take away with him; went back to Astrid.

Bianca

The absence of four of the group was quickly noted at training. *Father Christopher is looking around for her—that is right—he left before it all happened.* "Where is Astrid?" he finally asks.

I know well where she is—my room is right beside Astrid's. Not only did I not sleep at all well last night—but they were at it again this morning. I admit that I am torn between resentment at being kept awake by the noise of such indecent behaviour, and jealousy at the evident pleasure that is happening right next door to me. I realise that I am more than a little grumpy. "Your girl is probably still in bed—with Basil. Last I heard, they were still enjoying themselves." *Saint Mary Magdalene—now I feel guilty about being so catty about the Cat.*

Father Christopher looks surprised at what I said.

Christopher

"She is not mine, even though it seems that she looks after me. You must not look down on her. In the north, such activity is very common when people are facing danger and a high risk of death. Indeed, I believe that many of their marriages start out that way. I understand that your land is different, but in the hard lands of the north, that is the custom she is used to. I take it that the two mages are together as well?" *I see several embarrassed nods from Bianca.* "Your priests would be shocked. We are more tolerant. To us, it is more important that there is love, the greatest of the virtues. I wonder if I will get to do some marriages." He rubbed his hands together gleefully. *I am beginning to enjoy the outside world. I need to get Bianca to be less—*

rigid—I know. "Do you have anyone lined up?" He waved his hand around those standing around. "There is still Hulagu, Thord, Stefan and myself left, even if you leave aside Ayesha."

"Yourself, Father? But you are a priest!" *Bianca is evidently shocked to her core at the idea of me marrying.*

"That is right. Unless they are a widower, our priests must marry. There is a clear direction from St Paul on this. 'Choose your priests from among men with but one wife.' Not only does this imply that others may have more than one, in the manner of Ayesha's people, but it means that if I am to remain celibate, then I must become a monk."

Bianca

*H*e is smiling broadly at the horrified look on my face. Is he telling the truth or is he making mock of me? "I am guessing that you have never been read that line." *It even exists?* "I wanted to become a monk, but my Metropolitan thinks that I should marry and go out in the world as a priest. He has sent me out of the monastery for two years to find my fate. I am already starting to realise that he knows me better than I know myself and he may well be right." *He is going on in a light tone.* "You had better make up your mind if you decide that you want me. There are priests here who can perform the service but, once we are out in the wilds, I cannot perform a marriage on myself." *He has tried to hide it, but there is a smile on his face as he turns away.*

Perhaps he is joking, but I am not sure. I have never met a priest with such a broad and earthy sense of humour before. Mind you, except for in the confessional, I have not talked with many priests and I have never done so on a friendly basis as if he is just a normal person.

Ayesha

*T*he next time the four women were together was in the bath. Ayesha and Bianca entered. *She needs a lot of work with those knives—this is interesting—the other three women are already here. The body language is obvious. The Cat lies nearly submerged and her face is completely covered in a smile and, with her teeth showing, seems the epitome of feline smugness and self-satisfaction. As for the other two—the nervousness of their first time* *beside each other in the bath has disappeared and they now sit together almost as one and both of them also look very happy.*

"So, do you two need a lady's maid or is Basil or the Cat going to look after you both?" *I am rewarded with a vivid blush from Theodora. It is hard to tell with Rani. The Cat's grin has grown broader, if that is possible. That poor jest obviously appeals to her sense of humour.*

"Can we afford it?" stammered Rani.

"We haven't thought," said Theodora.

Astrid laughed. "I am already doing their sewing," she said. *The two look at her as if they are one. This they didn't know.* "Basil can sew a little, but only enough for rough repairs, and he was making a mess of it. I can sew new clothes and so I took over from him before he made a muddle of it." She looked at Rani. "I like sewing silk. It is so much nicer that the rough wool and leather I am used to."

It is Astrid's turn. "So, and how is the little man?"

"More than large enough where it counts," said Astrid archly and with a broad smile as she stretched in the water, "and he is so well muscled and athletic. He was my first," she concluded proudly. She turned to Bianca contritely. "I am sorry if we were a little too noisy last night. It is hard to stop crying out at times—so, so hard. Tonight, you must take Basil's room. It is further away. I had not realised how much fun this making love is. It is better than whipped cream with berries. Apparently, I purr," she said innocently. *Once again she sits back and looks smug. Everyone is still looking at Astrid, almost in shock at her innocent honesty. Astrid is looking around at us looking at her.* "Anyway, I am not the only one to discover new things to do with their body—am I Rani?" *This time the mage has to be blushing. Knowing about her culture it is unlikely that she is used to being addressed like that. Astrid is looking at her with a raised eyebrow and a smile.* Ayesha just looked at the mages waiting for an explanation. Rani eventually gave up, sighed, disengaged herself from her lover and stood up.

"How did you do that? Can whichever of you did it do it to just legs and underarms or is it the whole thing? How long does it last? I need to be smooth on the legs for dancing and I hate using wax. You can have me free as your lady's maid for a month if it is permanent."

"It is a new spell that I made to thank Rani," said Theodora. "I hadn't thought of that sort of thing before. I guess that we could do other spells like that. How about you, Cat? Would you like it done for you? If you are going to sew for us we will have to pay you somehow."

"No thank you," said Astrid. "My body hair is very fine and pale anyway, so I do not touch it and I think that Basil likes the rest the way it is. He says that it is like stroking a little kitten. I will gladly sew for you to give Basil more time with me."

The conversation rapidly moved off into a discussion of the cosmetic use of magic and a negotiation for Ayesha's services. *Good—another excuse to stay close.*

Basil

*I*n the men's room, my bite marks are the occasion of much ribaldry. I let the jokes flow around me. "You are all very jealous. The hunting cat is now my little kitten." *I am not giving details or being drawn on the two other women.* "They seem very happy. If you want to know any more you must ask them yourselves—if you dare."

Rani

*T*onight's entertainment seems to be going very well. I suppose it is natural that the songs are about love. The dancing even seems, somehow, more sensual. Everyone is excited. I wish that I was not almost tone deaf. I want to better appreciate the songs that are directed at me. At least we are not the only pair. It looks to me that Basil and Astrid are going to stay very close as well.

No one else has arrived to join us today. Tonight should be our last night in town.

During the night, Rani asked if Bianca still had any of the brigand's items in her possession. Bianca said that she did. "Good—keep it safe. Neither of us is the right sign to be very good at location spells and we might need all the help that we can get once we are in the mountains to find them."

During breaks in the acts, conversation, in a variety of tongues, depending on who was speaking to whom, revolved around who should lead them and who should give orders when it is needed.

It should be me. "My prophecy implied that I would take the lead and, anyway, I am a trained battle mage and so am used to giving orders to direct soldiers and thinking about how to fight as a group."

Astrid will be the only one on foot. Even Father Christopher can ride if he has to and Astrid refuses to even consider getting a horse. "I cannot ride at all, but I can run. If I were on a horse I could not use my bow or my spear and would be useless to everyone. On foot I am a stalker and a hunter. On a horse

I am baggage. If someone can take my pack," she looked directly at Basil, "I will keep up with you. In fact, you should let me go first. At home, if I am in the forest then I am mostly a scout. If I go first I can look for tracks and things that you who sit up high and have to rely on horse's feet will not see—and I can do it quietly."

I suppose that every force needs a scout. "That is good. It is best to have someone reconnoitre in a strange area. If you are fast enough—"

Astrid snorted somewhat derisively. *I will ignore the annoying lack of respect that the girl shows all of the time.* "Then this will work. We need to look for signs anyway. From what I have been told there are quite a few of these brigands. However careful they are, going in and out many times must leave some trace of their passage—even with magic to help them. If their village is in the Southern Mountains then somehow, they are getting past Evilhalt. Since this town is at the first ford that means they are crossing the Rhastaputra River somewhere to the north, bypassing Kharlsbane and the Gap and not being noticed by the Darkreach watchtowers—or at least not being recognised by them for what they are. However, they are probably still using some of the main trails for at least a little way, so we can hope that they should leave some trace of their passing."

It is a very odd night. I have been to many tactical discussions but here— well—during the entertainment I am admiring my lover's beauty while in the breaks we all huddle around the table, discussing and planning. Discussions of tactics and warfare contrast with the attire and allure of dancing girls. Coins on the table stand for people and are moved around as various tactics are discussed: how to move, what to do when attacked, who should be on watch with whom—and when—and why—all the minutiae of a battle group, admittedly a small one.

Father Christopher insisted on taking the middle watch. "Although they can come at any time, it is the most likely time for the partly resurrected—the undead—who are usually evil—to appear. The miracles that can be used in battles that I have been told how to cast are best employed on them."

In case of any other form of attack Father Christopher also volunteered to hold the horses for all of the others as he could do little else in a fight.

After the entertainment is over we all drift off for our last night in a soft bed for some time. Most are leaving to get a good night's sleep. Basil and Astrid are also leaving as a pair, much more quietly than the previous night, shyly holding hands, and hard on the heels of my lover and I. Tonight Theo-dear is almost dragging me to bed and not to sleep.

I do not know what to think now—and I cannot get to sleep. After we made love and Theo-dear was drifting off, she mused sleepily that, now she has fallen in love with a person who she will have to watch grow old and die—she means me—and all of the other people she is with are also short-lived, then she might have to change from being the aristocrat. These people that she has chosen to throw her lot in with might be as close as she would have to a family for quite a while, and perhaps she should treat them all as if that is what they are.

I wonder how that leaves me in my position. Will my lover stay with me as I age? What is more, what is happening to me with caste? Now a little worried, and despite her exhaustion, Rani took some time to drift off.

Hulagu

Tonight, for the first time, I have a dream from my grandfather—a message is on the way and has been coming to me for some time. My grandfather has been trying to contact me for several nights—but it is still hard for him to do. I wish that I could do more than say back that I have heard his words.

Chapter XXXIII

Nokaj

Even as Hulagu was leaving his encampment, Nokaj had spoken to the hetman Ordu, who started getting the tuman mobilised. *We are the emeel amidarch baigaa khümüüs, the people who live in the saddle, and we are used to this.* After he had gotten his own encampment moving he retired to his ger to send messages from shaman to shaman through the spirit world. *These deeremchin, bandits, are not only an insult to the tribes, but if they can come this far into the plains without detection, they are also a threat to us.*

Once those who could help were told, they began to gather. It took a good while, but in time he emerged to find his horses ready. *Starting first with an individual here and there, threading their way through the ger and the smoke of the fires, the warriors of the tribe gradually begin to harness their horses, and then mount, and to drift east like smoke drifting on the plains. All I see yet is an almost casual movement. No one rides hard. Most, as I am about to do, visit the ovoo before they join with the others. We need to gather.*

Time went by and the land rose and fell. Nokaj looked out from each rise at the other crests around him. *More and more riders can be seen joining. As had been done since the days of my youth and probably for many generations before that, the groups slowly merge, like the smoke from each fire in an entire camp joining overhead into one column. As we do there is a reorganisation of the riders. People leave their tuman and start to form into what passes for large units among us. Light riders with no armour move to the front and flanks, and move further and further out as their numbers grew. Soon people armed with powerful bows are scanning the ground well ahead and to the* flanks.

Nokaj joined the Tar-khan Toluy in the centre. *The heaviest armoured riders gather in the centre. Most of them ride unarmoured horses. They hold themselves ready to spread out and envelop an opponent. Those on fully armoured horses ride to the rear of the others where they will come upon an enemy as a massive armoured fist to crush them. There I see more riders with lesser armour bringing up the rear. Around everyone run packs of the Khünd Chono, the dire wolves, our üstei akh düü, totem animals, loping along and enjoying the exercise.*

Afterafewdaysofriding, scouts reported two figures off to the left watching them rather than either joining or running away. After consulting with Nokaj, Toluy gave orders to ignore the pair and the clan rode on.

Each night Nokaj led the shamen and shamenka into a conclave around a fire. Pooling their talents, they scried for a path to follow. Four mornings after they started, a small troop of scouts were sent off. They were to make contact with the tuman of the Pack-hunters and to stay with them as messengers and proof of fair intent. They were led by the Tar-khan Toluy's son Marakes and took a shaman and shamenka with them. *I am worried, even with this much help the signs are still unclear. What we have found seems to indicate that news will come from that direction and the clan should travel north.* In accord with this he had the clan head off slowly, along the border, if such a term could be used, between the land of the Khünd Chono and that of the Bagts Anchin, the Pack-hunters. *Scouts are looking for signs of passage on the ground but, try as they might, none are found beyond the normal that would be there at any time.* Days and soon weeks passed.

Still each night Nokaj assembled the seers. *We have left our territory now and are passing along the line between the Pack-hunters and the Ünee Gürvel, the Cow Lizards.* That night news came through dreams. *The Bagts Anchin is now on the move as well, headed both to the north and for the forest edge to cut off an escape. If the deeremchin are still on the plains, they will find their way blocked by one clan and with another on their heels. It is time for me to advise that the pace should pick up.*

Finally, we have found an area that we cannot see into. What is more, there are no tracks anywhere leading to this area. This is a powerful piece of magic to use, but once its nature is known, it can be negated and worked around.

Towards the end of the next day of very hard riding, even by the standards of the clans, the scouts sighted their quarry. Word came quickly back to where Nokaj rode with Toluy. *Eight hands of riders, together with heavily laden packhorses, are headed towards the forest edge.*

Hard on the heels of this was another report. *The quarry has drawn up on a rise about a hand of hundreds of paces away from the edge.* A third report told why. *A thick line of Bagts Anchin stands between deeremchin and Aguuikh Ain, the Great Forest.* As Nokaj rode forward with Toluy, he could see the outriders of the two clans exchanging greetings on each side. *The brigands are going nowhere. We are now far north of where the caravans normally go in their path across the plains, only a day or so south of the outskirts of the first assarts of Takhilch Khot, or Greensin.*

Nokaj prompted his Tar-khan. *Like our opposite are doing, we ride out to meet the other, followed by the böö, the shamen and shamenka. The totem animals are left behind.* The giant wolves and the fast-running bright-feathered two-legged lizards with the single slashing claw on each foot are natural competitors and will often fight on sight unless restrained and there is no declared truce yet. Dusk was falling as they met. The deeremchin sit on their rise. After discussion, the tribes decided to attack them as the sun cleared the horizon. Nokaj suggested that they use a well-tried device. The shamen and shamenka would all combine to enable a strong compulsion for sleep to be laid on the camp. Prisoners are to be taken for questioning before they are executed.

It is a dark night and clouds cover the moon. Guards patrol just out of bowshot. We make our preparations. This will be a powerful casting at this range and over such an area. The area that cannot be seen into is larger than we thought. It is not just the area of the deeremchin that is covered, but most of the clans are within it as well. The blanket over events lies on us thicker than ever.

In the gloom of the pre-dawn, scouts reported to the shamen that something was happening in the brigand camp. Nokaj was furious when first light revealed what it was. *In the sky, and rapidly receding, is a carpet with four passengers.* The other shamen thought about spells and incantations, but Nokaj dismissed the idea. "At this range, it is far too late without prior preparation. Although we can see it, we cannot even sense it." *It now carries the aura of non-detection with it. The carpet is headed for the south so that it will perhaps cross the river at Lake Erave, between the two towns located there. All is silent in the brigand's camp and no movement can be seen by the scouts. They must all be sleeping.*

By the time of the attack, figures had started to stir and wake others—to no avail. The attack went in. *It is a well-practiced way to take out and capture a much smaller opponent who has access to powerful magic. A screen of khuyagt morin, the heaviest cavalry, comes from both the east and the west. They feint a charge, but fire no bows. Close behind them ride scouts with lassoes and bolas in their hands. Böö of the tribes combined their mana, feeding it to their strongest. Powerful spells of sleep and inaction are launched. The result is an anti-climax. Apart from a few arrows and a few weak missiles of fire, earth and air from wands or other devices, all of which cease when the spell strikes, there is no resistance. Only a few riders have a light wound, quickly healed. The spells knock out all the deeremchin and their horses.*

Nokaj and the other shamen and shamenka now stepped back. *It is up to our Tar-khans now to enact justice. As we watch all are bound and secured. Three people are found who are not deeremchin. There are two attractive women and a grieving man, a potter, who has seen his family butchered before him. The women, once released, have to be kept away from sharp objects. All they want to do is to kill the deeremchin—slowly and starting with the single woman among them.* Being allowed to watch the questioning and to offer suggestions on how it should proceed mollified them slightly. *It is found that these suggestions, loudly voiced, make the work much easier.* Eventually it was decided that all that could be found out had been discovered and the three captives are given a dagger each and left to deal with the bound non-Khitan brigands. An initial chorus of screams and pleas slowly dwindles to stillness over the course of the day. *Now we have dealt with the non-Khitan, ten Khitan, of various clans, are left to be judged. They are already all khuulias gaduur, outlaws.*

Without word from either the spirit talkers or their leaders the two clans move towards the forest edge and foragers gathered large quantities of wood into piles that were well over half a man's height high and well over two hundred paces long at a flat area. The piles are lit. The ten have their clothes roughly cut away and, once the fires are well lit, with hands still bound they are prodded with spears, one by one, into the narrow lane of fire to regain their honour. One captive looked around him and walked into the path slowly, his head held high, his hair catching fire even as he walks, holding in his screams. *It is good. He has taken the chance to purge his soul, to be forgiven his sins and regain his honour and his name before the fire overwhelms and then consumes him.* Others ran screaming, hoping forlornly that they would make it to the end. Two men outright refused to go, despite any prodding and, when all had gone who would go, they ended their lives by being hamstrung and thrown into the fire thus gaining neither purging of their sin nor their lives. *Their screams echo loud, but not for more than a few minutes. None leave the fires alive. Justice has been done and been seen to be done.*

Once this was done the results of the interrogations were written down and sent by fast riders to Hulagu in Evilhalt, along with news of the carpet. *Somehow, all of this is connected to my grandson's geas, although it takes me many nights to contact him in his dreams to tell him that it is coming. Even though we may now suspect what is happening, we still have no idea how to act against it. No matter how hard we try it is still hard for böö to move around in the spirit world and to talk with others or even just to wander and look around as one normally does. It may have been the tiniest bit easier, but the gain is hard to see or feel. Everything is even harder if it involves my grandson. It seems that what has been done here is only a tiny start, but at least it is a beginning.*

Chapter XXXIV

Hulagu

I am ready. Who would have thought that this is what lay ahead of me? This is the morning my destiny will unfold. The others have come for different reasons, but it all brings a bustle of preparation to the day. Although we have been practicing together with our weapons, it has been practice; this is really the first time that most of us have a chance to see the others in their travel gear and outfitted for possible trouble.

He looked around. *We are very disparate in what we wear and carry. Everyone has some form of missile weapon: a bow, a sling or even just something to throw at close range. Theodora, with her warhorse, is the heaviest armoured. She could ride with the khuyagt morin. No one, looking casually at her, would suspect that she is a mage. The beautiful and exotic dancing girl, a pose for, in reality a pampered princess, has been replaced by the very grim image of the heaviest of cavalry. Unless one knew how to look, with her armour even the gender of the rider cannot be easily seen. We do not move not like a set of caravan guards, nor a troupe of travellers. With what we wear and with our horses, this group wears the visage of an assemblage headed to war. We just don't yet move as one. We have not been blooded.*

Astrid

*F*ather Christopher and I finally join the others. We have been to church. I didn't know that it was Saint Bridget's day before now. As a matter of fact, I was not really aware at all of the number of Saint's days that there are before meeting the Father. I now know, having accidentally asked a question *in frustration, that more than one in six of the days of the year are especially Holy in some way. I hope that our skalds count as poets because I prayed for them and then added more money for the poor. None of the people in our group are milkmaids or blacksmiths so I have done the best I can with Bridget's patronage of poets.*

Hulagu

*M*y sister is fussing around the horses. They have all been brought out of the stable and are lined up beside the inn waiting patiently—with the exception of Sirocco and Firestar. Both of them are now wearing heavy padded barding. Their front-pieces are further reinforced with mail. These beasts are not accustomed to patience. Wherever Bianca is, one of them will be there. The other stays with the packhorses. Bianca insists on supervising everything to do with the three packhorses—her own and those of Basil and Rani as well. The two horses from the brigands have been brought along mainly as remounts and are laden only with saddlebags of spare tack. Both Sirocco and Firestar are fully equipped, but both also have their reins looped onto the pommel of their saddles.*

I can see that this freedom given to the two battle beasts makes many nervous, particularly any passers-by who come too close and are shown teeth or have to dodge an impatient stamp of a heavy iron-clad hoof. As befits a mount that is used to riding in a large unit of similar beasts, and a mare as well, Theodora's Esther is much better behaved, except if Bianca's two come too close to her, then she will show her teeth at them. She is not slow in showing she will not take any liberties from either of the slightly smaller horses.

Astrid

*I*t is all taking too long and will take far longer yet. "I have time. We are going on a last-minute shopping trip."

See, I was right. I have more food and even more pots to be hastily stowed away. Basil also has a good woollen tunic and some long thick trews thrown over his shoulder and gloves and thick woollen knitted leggings stuck through his belt. Like a typical male, he doesn't have enough warm clothes for the winter and the mountains that lie ahead.

She turned and looked at Father Christopher. *He looks to be feeling very un-priestly standing there in the clothes that I bought him some time ago—a warm njal-bound brown cap with flaps for the ears, a good warm flannel undershirt under a coat thick-padded with cloth in vertical strips worn under a leather jerkin, and heavy stout-woven woollen trews, with woollen socks and heavy military-style hob-nailed boots. He is smiling quietly and looking back at me. He is dressed well enough.*

Hulagu

*I*can see that Rani is finally about to get on her horse and signal that it is time to mount and head out. Right on cue a boy comes running from the direction of the western wall towards the inn. He is looking at me and has the look of a messenger. Is this the news I am waiting on?

"T'ree Khitan be a ridin' hard towards t' town," the boy said. "T'ey all be havin' remounts, but t'ey be a lookin' tired. Be t'ey for you?" He continued with barely a pause, now addressing the others as well. "Anyhows, guard commander he wants you to come to t' wall—please."

"I don't know if they are for me, but they could be."

He dismounted and moved over to where Rani stood and, after looking around, quietly told her of his dream from Nokaj before running to the west gate. *Rani is following.* He arrived in time to greet the riders. *One is my cousin, Ordin, the others are Pack-hunters.* After exchanging greetings, he was handed the message from his grandfather and brought up to date on the destruction of the brigands. *Ordin is all smiles and excited about what happened until he has to admit to the escape of those on the carpet.*

"So, their leader at least, this Dharmal, and two mages escaped? One other as well? I presume the carpet was sent to them," said Rani, who had followed Hulagu, in Hindi.

"Yes," said Ordin.

Rani has not picked it up, but I can see Ordin wondering who this city dweller is and, even more, what right she has to ask or even speak to him. He waved for him to continue and he did.

"But the good news is that there are only a small number of them left. It is now a problem for the town dwellers here. We think we have found the way to the bandit village and have a copy for the town dwellers and one for Hulagu." He now looked around.

I think that he is looking at each person who is nearby to see if anyone is listening who should not be. "It is important that what we have done is kept secret. The deeremchin seem to have friends in many places, perhaps even among the tribes, who will tell them anything important, and they may be able to do so secretly."

Hulagu grunted. "It is my problem, not that of the village. I have found companions here in my quest." He gave a tiny nod of his head towards the woman beside him.

My cousin almost imperceptibly nods back.

"And we are going after them now to complete this justice. I have a geas and we leave to follow it as soon as we have finished speaking here. This river lady is a seer and the signs given to her are as strong as those I received that this is the right thing to do. I have now given my word and must keep that. Tell Nokaj that this is what I must do and why. He will understand. At least we will now know where to go instead of tracking forever in these forests, unable to see our hands in front of us. I don't think that we have said anything important where anyone can overhear, but all of the town will now know of Bianca and my arrival and what happened to her caravan. All will soon know of your tale as well. Some of them may be able to count a hand of horses, blindfold and pass this on. Our enemies may still do something before we are able to attack them."

"You will have to be careful," said Ordin. "I listened to some of the questioning. It is all in what I gave you but the road is trapped, and they have potent magic and it is sure that they will know if someone is coming after them. It will not be as easy as trapping Üzen Yaddag Düürsen, Brotherhood chariots, against Üzen Yadalt Ursgai, Sundercud Creek."

"We have our own mages. This one"—*she nods her head, but looks a trifle prickly at being mentioned like that—too bad*—"is a Haven battle mage and the other is from Darkreach. We also have a priest of the Christians, a Dwarf who knows the mountains and at least one who may be very good at hunting and staying unseen in the forest. If what Shri Rani has seen is right"— her face is looking harder—"and, from what we have seen in her own life, she seems to see the truth"—*her smile reappears*—"then we should succeed."

With this and a little more on what had been said and done during the questioning they said their farewells. Ordin and the other messengers were taken to see the Baron, while Hulagu and Rani rejoined the others.

"I have been given information by my tribe. I am sorry Bianca, but most of the brigands are dead. Most of them died at the hands of captives, so you will be pleased with that. Before they died many were helpful and we may now know the way to their village. I don't want to say any more about this where we may be overheard, so we will talk more about it tonight."

As Hulagu mounted, the rest resolved itself. Rani now nodded to them all and signalled everyone to mount up. *Astrid has consented to ride across the ford to stay drier. This could be funny.*

Thord snorted. "I will get wet anyway and will have to be almost towed across. Shepherds on sheep are not as far off the ground as horsemen and the wool on Hillstrider traps air and makes it hard for him to sink properly to the bottom of any deep water and so get a firm grip with his hooves."

I was right. Astrid, helped by Bianca, is climbing onto Firestar, a process that she conducts in a fashion that is more like climbing a tree than mounting a horse. It is something that is obviously not to the liking of either horse or rider and my sister had to speak firmly to the horse, even as she holds him. It is also obvious that both horse and rider are considerably relieved when the river has been crossed and Astrid can clamber back down to the ground. It is also just as well that I met Bianca and the priest met Astrid, not the other way around.

The northern woman regained her weapons and, with her bow in one hand and her spear in the other, headed off in a trot along the road that led to Kharlsbane, leading the party out towards their destiny.

Astrid

I am glad to be out of a town and loping through the forest again. It is an illusion of freedom, as I still have the horses plodding along behind, but I can jog ahead and have time to stop and look at tracks, to hear the woods and to listen for their denizens. It is a shame to stop this afternoon, after a pleasant, if uneventful day. Now the real fun will begin. I have found them a caravan stop for the night.

I suppose that the Khitan knows about living in the field. As for the others — after they have all gotten down and stretched, and while I get to sit — it seems that, surprise, surprise, religion will be the first order of business, as Father Christopher and Ayesha go in different directions to pray. Christopher has set up so as to include most of the party in his. He seems content to just perform a service while we all set up. Bianca seems shocked at this.

I guess that she is used to priests being more formal. At least I am used to this now. The Freehold girl checked and cared for the horses and, while still keeping alert, the others began to gather firewood to replace what they would take from the pile usually found at such places.

I enjoy sitting while my lover — I like that word — gets a fire going for me. Soon she was cooking alongside Bianca.

Once everything was going well, Theodora came over to see her, interrupting her turning some meat. "Do you have anything, perhaps some jewellery, with either copper or amethyst in it?" she asked.

What jewellery did I bring from home—oh yes. "My mother left me an old iron cloak pin. It has been inlaid with a pattern in copper and has a large amethyst mounted on it. I don't wear it much, but it is in my pack. Why do you want that?"

Theodora looks a little taken aback at being questioned. Get used to it princess. Whatever you were in Darkreach, you aren't that here.

"Because, while I am sure you are adept at hiding from animals, I am also sure that you have no skill at hiding from magic," she said a bit tersely. "Those who are watching for us will probably rely more on magic than on their eyes, particularly to set off traps. This will be more so since they have lost so many of their people. I wish to make a charm that will make you invisible to magic and create an illusion that you are not there. Seeing that I must use something that is already made, rather than casting into something that is being created as I am casting, it is best to use something that is already yours and something that has that metal and that stone. I have been thinking of this as we rode and I think that I have a good solution. I will now go and prepare. Keep cooking and, when I am ready I will call you over. It will only work a few times a day, but that should be enough." *It makes sense. Not that I am offended, but she must have realised that she was being sharp. I didn't actually expect a full explanation from a mage.*

Astrid returned to helping Basil, who had taken over while she talked. *It turns out, that he is a better cook than I am and I can just sit down again to watch. Over near the horse enclosure, Theodora, with Rani's help, is laying out her pattern rug and setting up what she needs.* It wasn't long before Rani came for Astrid. She had already dug in her pack for her mother's jewellery and found the cloak pin wrapped up with the rest of her inherited treasures in its old felted-wool pouch.

Astrid stood and went with the Havenite woman. Theodora stood Rani on the rug and then, taking the cloak pin from Astrid, placed her on another vertex opposite Rani. *Theodora has begun chanting, in a language I don't understand. It has a soft and liquid sound and I have heard Theodora sing songs in it—although it seems different now in the forest—and with an enchantment being cast, somehow more meaningful. Rani has begun to chant in the same tongue, in time with Theodora, and she points at her lover. Rani stops and drops her hand, standing still and silent.* Theodora continued for a while longer and then lowered her hands. *Her face looks smug.* She indicated that Astrid should move off the rug, which she did, carefully not standing on any lines.

"Put it on," Theodora directed, "and fetch your spear."

Astrid did as she was told.

"Can you sense her? Anything at all?" Theodora asked Rani. Rani shook her head.

Theodora continued, "No, I can't either, so we presume that it has worked then?"

Rani agreed.

It tickles. She giggled. *Both of the mages are looking at me.* "I sort of felt a little tickle feel all over when you were looking hard at me—once for each of you. Does that mean it tells me when it works?"

The two mages are looking at each other. "A useful side effect," said Theodora to Rani as if that explained everything. *Her voice also sounds a little smug,* "I had a feeling inside that the incantation worked very well. I was lucky."

"I hope it was worth it," said Rani. "Neither of us has much mana left to defend us with if we are attacked tonight."

Theodora shrugged. "Better now than later. We should be fairly safe this close to town and she will almost certainly need it." She turned to Astrid. "I hope that you can find any physical traps before we spring them—"

Astrid snorted amusedly at this. *I can keep my eyes open.*

"—But you should be safe from magical detection as long as you wear this pin."

Out of practice for a day spent running and not wishing to get a cramp, Astrid paced around the camp looking out. As the others waited for the food to finish, they all sat quietly. *Theodora combs Rani's hair and Ayesha combs hers. Hulagu stands and looks all around into the woods before bringing out the message from Nokaj. He has a sheet of parchment in his hand.*

"We have directions," he said waving it. "Several of the brigands talked freely in the hope of a quicker death. They were disappointed. It says here that there is an old trail running from where this road turns north to Kharlsbane. It runs towards the southeast and the first Darkreach watchtower in the foothills, and is almost all under the cover of trees. It passes south of the watchtower and enters the mountains turning to the south to the villages of the Bear-folk. We have to pass along it and look for a very narrow valley with a small river coming from it that splits in two around a small hill with some stones on top. Only the southern path is safe to use, but it still has some traps on it to watch out for. Once inside, the valley widens out. The village is hidden in a small second side valley inside the first. We will probably be seen and perhaps attacked, at any time, from the moment we leave this road to when we enter the valley. Every other way in when we get there is dangerous unless we are going to be very lucky."

"Not if I can help it," said Theodora. "All of my best spells deal with illusion. As we ride I will see if I can think of a way to get us in unseen."

"I am mountaineer," said Thord. "If'n others can climb, t'en I can get t'em into mountain valley without a touching any paths. I have some equipment wit' me to help. On many slopes, I can even ride Hillclimber up t' slope," he grinned broadly, "or down it, in places where your horses couldn't even be led 'n' some of you would have to crawl."

"Let everyone else think about what they can contribute," said Rani, "and let me know any ideas or skills that may be useful. Once we have worked out what we have between us, I will come up with a plan. We can discuss this over the next few nights. Now let us eat. The Holy Fish and his Cat seem eager to feed us."

From behind her Astrid stuck out her tongue. *Basil is just smiling, turning to his pots.*

*T*hose who have this first watch all speak Darkspeech—Theodora, Basil *and me. Now, near the end of it, I know that the other two are both far too used to being in the towns. Basil is far better than Theodora, but both show inexperience in the bush. They might come out to the wilds sometimes, but this is not where they are at home. These woods are not the forests I am used to, but the other two react to each little noise as if it is an attacking army. I even had to stop them waking the others when a small herd of horned plant-eating lizards wandered past the camp going south. They were very large beasts and looked fierce, but they were as anxious to avoid us as any herd of reindeer would be, steering clear of the camp and the horses, and with adults between us and the calves—all of which are bigger than the largest reindeer. They must be what Hulagu calls cow lizards. They don't live in the boreal forests. Few of the giant lizards come that far north between the tight-packed trees, although the small ones are as common there as any other small creature.*

The night air grew chilly around them and some other animals could be heard heading south—many birds had already passed overhead from the far north. Winter had begun to set in and yet they were headed towards the mountains. Soon their watch was over and Astrid handed over and dragged Basil off to where she had set up their bedrolls together. Theodora crawled into the warmth beside Rani, who briefly grumbled something indignantly about cold hands.

Bianca

Rani has set four people to the second watch: Father Christopher, Ayesha, Thord and me. My first attention goes to the horse lines. All the horses — and the sheep — are fine and secure. We only have Hindi in common and it is the first tongue for none of us. The priest wants to have Ayesha learn some Latin and Greek as well as her other tongues. She is eager to add more languages to those she already has. Tonight, they are starting with Latin. Ayesha watches out into the night as Father Christopher has her repeat softly the basic words that we will need as we travel. He has told her that grammar can come later. From his patient manner, it is obvious that he has experience as a teacher. They are murmuring away. There is much of my own language that I do not know. If the heathen woman can learn, perhaps I can get Father Christopher to teach me more as well.

He smiles at me at the change of watch when I refuse to wake the mage Rani, preferring to head for my brother instead.

Hulagu

There is the chill of the early morning, when the night is coldest. At least we can all talk Hindi. Both Stefan and I are used to the wild, although for me the horizon is uncomfortably close. I am not used to so many trees being around me. Rani wants to know more about Khitan culture and keeps asking about the tribes and their history. It is taboo to discuss much of this with outsiders. I wish she would change subject.

She wants to know more about Bianca, how I met her and her relationship with the horses. I am happy to talk about our meeting but felt that the rest is Bianca's business. It doesn't matter how I put the mage off, she comes back with another question in one or the other area. How to distract her — I know. He explained the significance of his birth and how his grandfather was a shaman and wondered, offhand, if that meant that she could teach him to be a mage in her manner.

Silence at last — she is turning it over in her mind.

It kept her silent until just before dawn. *By the Sky Spirits — she has decided that she can and wants to start me on some tests and exercises straight away to see if I have the talent. I am soon having difficulty doing a proper watch —*

now to point out that we both have to pay attention to the woods around us. I am surprised by her eagerness and wonder if I am doing the right thing and if my grandfather will be upset with me. Still—as least it stops her asking questions, even if it is going to be a waste of time for anything else.

Astrid

*A*new day dawns bright and chilly. Stefan has restarted the fire using Basil's magic rod and has heated water for washing and making kaf and tisanes. He can do breakfasts while I stretch my muscles and roll up the sleeping gear. Looking across, the mages are both very sleepy. Neither seems to be an early riser and the bed that they have slept in is obviously not what they are used to. While I wake up looking much the same as when I go to bed, both of the mages have somehow added leaves and twigs to their hair and their hair now covers half their faces in a curtain. Both peer out blearily through hanging locks. Rani's face is smeared with smudged kohl.* "Basil, is your charge always like this when she wakes?" *He nods in reply.* "Then I hope we are not attacked first thing in the morning before they have had a warm drink."

She headed over to help them. *Ayesha is doing the same with the aroma of kaf and herbal tisane following her—I can smell porridge.*

Oh dear. Neither of the mages is familiar with this form of breakfast. They move in different circles. Dubiously, they poke at it and spoon some down as the rest of us eagerly take some and pour honey on it. Theodora likes it, but it is too strange for Rani.

From the smells that are drifting through the camp Stefan next has smoked bacon and eggs and fried mushrooms ready. The mages are more used to this, but Ayesha just takes the mushrooms and eggs. Knowing her tastes Stefan has fried some in a different pan to the bacon. It is a good start to the day. He can keep doing breakfasts.

The day was uneventful. With her pack on a horse and only her weapons in hand, Astrid loped ahead, usually travelling alongside the road, rather than on it, keeping her eyes open all around but mainly looking for tracks. Occasionally she checked behind to see if the riders were having any difficulty keeping up with her. The road was wide enough for them to travel in pairs. She could see that Hulagu rode with Ayesha, then Thord was next on his outsized sheep. *No one rides beside the Dwarf. The horses don't quite like his mount.*

After the sheep, Theodora and Rani ride. They are travelling almost knee-to-knee, or would be if Rani's horse were not a few hands shorter. Then Bianca and Father Christopher come along with Bianca's other horses just following her and with the other animals on leads, tethered to Sluggard.

The girl is thawing to the priest. She stupidly asked about learning more and my priest is in full flight as a teacher. Despite what Bianca wants, Christopher thinks she should learn Greek first as she already speaks the common Latin. I can sometimes hear him from here. Bianca has to quieten him down. He might be like a fish out of water as a soldier, but it is obvious that he loves teaching.

Basil and Stefan bring up the rear. Stefan has his shield slung over his back and both keep turning around and occasionally moving behind a bush and dropping back, but there is no sign of a follower. My love exchanges 'all clear' signals with me when he notices me looking back at him.

Astrid stopped suddenly. *Now this is interesting.* She signalled them all to come closer so that she could talk quietly.

"Groups of horsemen have been joining the trail here." She pointed at the ground with her blade. "Not recently in the last few weeks, but over several months. See, they are starting to make a new path joining on to the main trail. Look. There is even the mark of a hoof."

Looking down from his mount beside her, Hulagu nodded. "You are right. These bushes all have broken twigs. All of the breaks are old, at least a few weeks, and some point onto the road and others away from it. If we follow these to the north, I'll bet we will find a ford somewhere above Evilhalt where they are crossing unobserved."

My turn to nod—he is right. Among the others only Thord can see what we are talking about. The rest just have to accept our word.

Hulagu continued. "Now see if you can find where they left the road. Do you want to make a bet?"

Astrid shook her head and grinned broadly before setting off again, this time moving to the right-hand side of the roadway. "It would be unfair to take your money."

There it is. Towards the end of the day, Astrid again signalled for them to stop and then to draw nearer. "I told you it would be unfair to take your bet. They left the road here. They tried to conceal where they turned on and off, but not very well. The bandits are armsmen and soldiers, not scouts and hunters. This time they used an old road, not one that they were making." She cleared away some undergrowth and dirt so that the others could see and pointed to where some large flattish stones lay near the surface on the right. "My turn to make a wager. I'll bet that these are Dwarven work. Are there any takers?"

No one ventured to say anything.

"I think we may have found what we are looking for."

Thord

*L*et us look at this. Thord climbed off Hillclimber. He felt the rough stone and looked at the edges. *I am not that great an expert on the subject of stonework and cannot tell whose work it is, but if it is Dwarven, and it could be, it is very, very old. It was once well laid, but now plants force their way between the slabs. What is more, it is a hard rock that has been used for the slabs and cobbles and, despite that, the edges show signs of weathering and the flat surfaces reveal signs of wear from long use.*

Astrid

*W*e were travelling on the road that leads to Kharlsbane and the Darkreach Gap, the one that Basil said that they came down on. Now we are going east on this concealed old road. Day is starting to follow day as we travel along in a growing routine.

Despite winter coming on, there are still enough trees with leaves that I can scarce see much of the sky. Some of the trees I know from hunting or patrolling to the south of home. Tall celery-top pines and even taller myrtle beeches are all around them. Leatherwoods grow alongside the path and we often have to force our way through a green embrace, as trees and spiky dragon heaths reach across the stone surface.

Buried deep in the understorey, straggling laurel bushes are in their autumn flowering, their flowers pale cream from the lack of sunlight in the thick bush. When I can see above, the blue sky is largely obscured by low cloud and I feel continually damp as we go through occasional showers and far less frequent sunshine. The air has a damp smell. The ground under the trees has very little grass except in rare clearings where a tree has come down in the past and the forest has not yet reclaimed the sky. Even then there are more ferns than grass.

Chapter XXXV

Astrid

Although I grew up in a very different forest, I am starting to understand these southern woods. Looking through a wall of leatherwoods, some still with the last white flowers of summer on them, I can see a gap in the trees over a hundred paces ahead of me. The road is headed south-east and faintly through the leaves I can make out what looks like a bridge crossing a stream, cutting across it almost at a right angle. The bridge looks to be in a clearing where one of the giant gums has come down during a storm. I can see its roots still largely intact and high in the air.

The sun is nearly overhead and the resultant shadows are short, so the whole clearing lies open and revealed in the midday light. All that can be seen are some ferns larger than a tall man and some small shrubs and other smaller ferns. *The fallen tree, over the height of three of me at the base and scarce smaller in scale as far as I can see, spans the creek bed. Overhead perched high in one of its companions, a massive Bunya pine, a mob of black cockatoos is making the day raucous eating its nuts.* Suddenly a small mob of perhaps four hands of hoppers burst past her at speed. They swerved to the right upon seeing the horses and riders behind her. *My senses prickle and I feel the short hairs on the back of my neck start to rise as if I am truly my namesake animal. Something is not right.*

Something has scared the hoppers, and scared them badly and, try as I might, I can hear nothing chasing them. She put her spear down and held up her hand in a motion to stop the others and propped herself behind a tree while she assessed what lay ahead. *This is the largest cleared area we have seen for days. The feeling I have may mean nothing, but when I look at the lay of the land, this is an ideal place to set an ambush. I will take a little extra caution here.*

Astrid turned and looked back at her people. *They have stopped and now are all sitting there on their horses just looking at me.* She waved her hands trying to make them think about spreading out so that they did not invite incoming fire. *Hopefully they will get the idea.* She could see that, at the rear, Stefan has already hopped off his horse and he is tying it up off the trail and muttering to the others. *One by one they dismount and Father Christopher has begun gathering horses and leading them back. Only Hulagu stays mounted and he is readying his bow. He has already tucked his lance from a trail position to where he can grab it more readily. Gradually, and with varying degrees of proficiency, the others begin to disappear into the brush and ready themselves for an attack.* Astrid winced at the lack of stealth in their movement as she heard a twig break under someone's foot.

She moved back behind a tree and pointed at Stefan and waved for him to come closer, turning back to the front and peering around the tree as she did so. He was soon up with her. *He isn't too bad out in the field, for a town dweller. I can hear him moving, but most won't—the wind was coming to me from just a little east of north. I cannot smell anything if it is coming from the bridge area, but on the other hand, whoever or whatever may be there cannot smell anything from us either.*

From where I lie nothing can be seen. Nothing seems out of place. It is just quiet—far too quiet.

Why were the hoppers in such a hurry? Normally they move slowly. There is still no sign of movement from the leaves ahead of me. Looking up I can see the now almost-silent cockatoos. They move uneasily around in the upper branches and it seems that they want to crack into some of the pine cones lower down on the tree, but don't seem to want to move. They seem to be looking down the tree at the other side of the stream, upstream of the bridge and on the other side of the road to the fallen forest giant.

Stefan was now beside her. *He has the sense to remain silent and wait for me to say something.* She looked ahead again. *If I were setting an ambush, trapping people in the open where an accident has provided a clear line of fire with over forty or so paces to the target area, enough ground that you could get off four or five shots while someone covered it and, at the same time where their line of retreat is part-blocked by a hundred paces of fallen tree, would have to rate very highly.* She wiggled back a bit again and turned to Stefan.

"I am not sure, but someone may be waiting for us ahead." She looked back at the group and thought for a moment. "See if you can bring the others, except the Father and, I suppose, the Princess, she cannot move quietly off her horse, up here one by one. Keep them behind either this tree or that log." She pointed at a lesser fallen tree close beside her—one only a pace and a half high. "Make sure none even try and look over. Make them stay quiet and still until I come back—even if it takes the rest of the day. Send the mages back down the track if they cannot hold their bladders."

She looked back at the rest of their group. *I really don't know their strengths and weaknesses and that is a problem. This could be life of death or it could be a waste of time.* "Once you are back to them, I am going to head upstream and I will try and see what I can see. I cannot see anything from here. Now, have a quick look ahead so you can describe to them what is there."

Leaving his spear and shield behind, Stefan wriggled his way around the trunk, although not as silently as Astrid. He is obviously less skilled as a hunter. While he was away, Astrid pulled her woollen njal-bound hat out of a pouch and jammed it on her head. *It is a bit warm for the day but its grey-green colour hides a little of my pale blonde hair and breaks up the shape of my head. My people always wear hats when stalking game and stalking people should need the same.*

Once Stefan was forward he went still for a couple of minutes as he surveyed the scene ahead of him. After a while he wriggled back around the tree slowly. "You are right," he said. "It is too still there. No finches or robins anywhere. There are even no honey-eaters flying around and the edge of the trees along that creek is thick with laurel flowers pink in the sun. The honey-eaters may love the bush laurels but they are also very shy around people."

He regained his shield and spear and, staying low and watching where he trod, he moved back to the others. When he had reached them, Astrid took off anything she was carrying that was unneeded and started moving upstream and to the left, staying low as she did so, her spear in one hand and her bow on her back.

She had chosen to stay out of sight of the creek bed while she moved. *If there is an ambush set for us it will most likely be placed on the other side of the river, but someone could have been left this side to cut off anyone moving up the bank—there could even be a trap to catch the unwary.* Her attention moved around from the possibility of a trap to looking for a person, or signs of people. Astrid let her instinct guide her up the creek bed without really thinking of the direction. Her senses were concentrating on those more important things. *Is that a hint of the smell of a spice—the hot spices that Rani likes—curry?*

My senses are far better than those of other people, perhaps a legacy of my cat-Kharl past, but I also know that people believe what they want to believe and smell is possibly my weakest talent. She sorted through the sights and the sounds and the smells. *Even just the feelings I am getting—those most of all.*

Something is telling me of danger—of people lurking. That faint smell may be the first confirmation, or it may not. It is safer to say that it is.

She moved forward on her hands and knees towards the creek. She had taken her bow off her back and before she moved her hand, she picked up each in turn, her spear and her bow and moved them forward a little at a time. Like a stalking cat, she inched into the denser bush near the creek line, stopping frozen at the slightest sound and after each move. Her eyes probed ahead.

She was eventually rewarded—*that is an arrowhead that just moved on the other side of the creek. It seems that someone has decided that their arm is sore and has lowered their bow to a more comfortable waiting position. He has an arrow nocked, but not drawn. No one would keep that up for long and it is asking a lot just to have it permanently nocked.* She looked at where it was placed. *Yes—the bridge is well covered from where the archer is hidden. There is a bend in the creek. It allows a small stretch of bank to face the bridge directly instead of at a slant. Anyone reacting to being shot at would either have to move along the thick scrub of the opposite bank or charge over the clearing and then cross the creek.*

Now, if I was doing this—is that a rope? It is—I am sure. That will probably drop something to make it hard to ride straight through the ambush. Now, where will other people be? One to pull the rope—

It may be going behind the Bunya pine—it is broad enough at the base to shelter a couple of people behind it, but the fallen leaves under it will be spiky and uncomfortable to move around on. Still, it is the only tree large enough and in the right place, at any rate. I will assume that there is someone hiding there. It will explain the cockatoos.

Now I see the arrowhead, I am able to vaguely make out the rest of the person, but no more than that. He looks like any trader's guard in chain, and with a conical helm with a nasal. Much like Stefan looks, actually.

There will be more than two people here. Where are the others?

With the patience of her namesake, she held herself still, ignoring the ants that were starting to crawl over her hand. She was rewarded by hearing a slap from a bush only a few paces away directly across the creek. *Leaves sway. Someone with less control than me does not like the insects and now they are muttering quietly to themselves.*

No one else betrayed themselves by moving, but now I can draw a line between the closest bush and the Bunya pine. I may have worked out only where three of them are placed, but there is more than enough room for half a dozen people to be hidden along that line or even more if a couple of those trees have two behind them and not one. Suddenly she felt that odd tickling all over her body. *It could be my own mages, but someone, somewhere, is trying to sense magic. It might be time to extricate myself from here and go back and report. I am the scout and hunter. I have done my job — now to see if one of the mages can work out how to deal with it.* With as much care as she had taken getting into place, she started moving out of it.

Stefan

How well will we cope with our first fight as a war party? Rani is already moving towards me. At least her padded silk is a dull green colour and that will partly make up for her complete lack of skill in moving silently or in a stealthy fashion. She may be naturally graceful and move smoothly in a tavern, but when she is in the field she has no idea where to put her hands and feet and her exaggerated crouch is a caricature of stealth. Her sword even hits bushes as she moves. It is just luck that nothing breaks or makes more than the softest of noise. I have at least practiced some of these sorts of engagements, ambushes and raids, in the militia. I suspect that Rani is more used to practicing for large battles where hiding is impossible and the officers ride horses or elephants without dismounting.

"What is happening?" Rani asked him. "Where has Astrid gone and why did she stop us?"

"She thinks there may be an ambush ahead of us. Stay back!" He had to grab at the mage to stop her standing up and looking ahead. Softly but urgently he continued, "She has done what she is supposed to do and has gone to find out. I think she may be right, but she is better at hunting than I am. Pardon me for saying it, but you are almost useless in the bush. If you try and find anything out you will be seen straight away. If there is a mage there, you may sense him, but he will surely know that we are here as well. Our knowing that they are ahead of us, and not knowing about us, is surely our only advantage at present. They know the ground, they may have traps in place — " he petered out what he was saying as Rani stopped resisting and sat with her back against the thick trunk of the tree.

Most of my people are unused to this business. Basil is hard to see and is very still. Hulagu can be seen sitting quiet on his horse on the path, his eyes scanning all around. His horse just stands there quietly. Further back I can see Thord's sheep taking a chance to eat some of the vegetation while its rider sits with it in the shade. Behind them Bianca is being restive. At the rear of them all are Father Christopher and the horses. Occasionally the priest sat up and peered ahead, but most of the time he seems to be sunk in prayer. Ayesha has disappeared into the bush near the Darkreach mage. I can see where

297

Theodora stands inadequately sheltering behind a bush and she turns to talk to someone who stays out of sight.

I can feel a little pleased with myself that I saw the Cat coming back from a good way away. The sun has moved well away from the vertical. It is nearing the middle of the afternoon and some clouds are starting to come in, still only light, but they lead to changes in the play of light and shade around them on the leaves and ground. Astrid came in behind the same tree she had left by and sat down beside Rani while picking up her leather water bottle from where she had left it and taking a drink.

"Well, there are at least three of them waiting for us on the other side of the creek and most likely at least a hand of them." she said quietly to Rani and Stefan. She turned to the mage. "Did you try and detect any magic while I was away?" she asked directly.

Rani shakes her head.

"Did your lover?"

"I don't think so," was the reply. "I didn't see her make any preparations and she has no wands or devices that will do that. Why?"

"Because my cloak pin made me all tingly and that should mean that someone missed me if Theodora's spell worked as we think it does. I hope you were behind this tree and that a tree is enough to stop you being picked up, because there is someone out there looking for magic." *Quickly she has cleared a patch of dirt and, with a stick, drawn out and explained what she saw ahead of us and what she thinks is likely.*

Rani may not be experienced in this sort of fight, but at least she has the sense to be silent and listen to the scout and only ask questions at the end to clear things up. What is more—Astrid knows what to look for.

Rani

W hat do I have available? I have never actually been in a real battle before and this isn't even a battle. It is more of a raid—the sort of thing a battle mage who is part of a line unit practices for. It is ironic that Amin would probably better know what to do here than I do, even though I am far superior as a mage. I can plan out a battle, but not a skirmish. Still, the other two are looking at me. She looked again at the map that the Cat had drawn on the ground. *My group are strong on archery or at least missile fire if you count martobulli and slings. We have two very strong mages, even if one of them does not have much in the way of offensive spells. We probably have the advantage of surprise. Can we outflank our opponents? What would happen if Astrid took the hunters up the creek to behind the enemy and then—*

She thought on the problem for a little more time and hoped for some inspiration. *I can see Astrid wants to say something.* Rani nodded at her. *The officer seeking input.*

"How about I take Hulagu, even if you take his horse away he is far better as a hunter than the rest of you, and we go up behind them. Can your girlfriend make an illusion of us coming along the track? If she can, the rest of you can try and get into position; they will probably look at the obvious sight and miss you moving—"

Astrid went on to outline a plan as she drew on the ground. At least it sounds functional and Stefan is nodding with what looks like approval. I hope Theodora can do that sort of spell. It sounds like the sort of illusion she should be able to cast. Now is the time to find out. Following Astrid, she headed back to the others while Stefan took lookout.

Theodora

I *have just come from being shriven by my priest, now I sit and make notes on my wax tablet.* Theodora looked up at Astrid.

"Remember, this is something I have never tried before. I will have at least an hour then? You will make a raven sound first?" *I probably sound worried—I am. I have never had to make up an enchantment and then use it straight away without someone checking it beforehand and this enchantment is a complex one. It is far more complex than the Cat girl realises—even Rani doesn't appreciate how complex it will be.*

I still haven't fixed all the details, but I will possibly have to drain my storage to do it. I could probably just use any images for it, instead of copies of us, but I cannot be sure about that and I want to get it right. I already have something from each of us, and each of the animals, and I should be able to build a simulation that is good. The illusion will need to act as I direct, seeming to fall and take damage.

"I have only seen crows this far south. You are sure you can tell the difference?" Astrid asked, seeking confirmation from her. *Is the Insakharl girl nervous as well? I am sure that she isn't.*

"You will be there," Theodora pointed where Astrid had indicated. Astrid nodded. "I am sure there won't be a crow coincidentally in exactly the right place—and we haven't even heard one of them today. I will wait until I hear the raven call three times from the same place before I start doing anything."

Astrid nodded in confirmation and then went over to Basil and gave him a kiss. Theodora heard him respond in a low tone, she didn't hear what he said, but Astrid had responded with, "I will see you soon."

I can see that Basil is nervous as well, but for Astrid, not himself.

Astrid turned to Hulagu. "Ready?"

The plainsman nodded. Astrid looked up at the sky. *She is confirming what time it is before returning her gaze to the Khitan.* "Then let's go." The two immediately bent over and, again using the smaller fallen tree as cover, moved off along the path that Astrid had previously followed.

With that Theodora went to start her own preparations.

Astrid

This time, with the advantage of knowing where she was headed, Astrid stayed further away from the creek as she moved. *I want to be at least slightly behind our opponents to make their position of strength a trap. When I start shooting, I need them with the creek at their back doing exactly as I plan. For all I know we could be greatly outnumbered and, regardless of that, there are only two of us out here and we have no spells. We will be relying on the speed and accuracy of our bows once our opponents reveal themselves. Hopefully we can target the mage first. There will be at least one of them. I can count on that.*

It did not take long before they had gone far enough upstream. *It is time to head towards the creek. It is time to start to move slowly, very, very slowly. It is evident that each of us is in stalking mode.* She almost giggled. *I have returned to my cat-like pose while Hulagu moves almost like a hunting dog.*

While I stay on all fours and freeze, Hulagu moves and then lies down, scanning ahead for a while before moving again. When he is stationary he is almost always lying down unless something is under him. Sometimes, if he thinks he has heard something he will freeze in place. The two stalkers moved beside each other only a hand of paces apart. Constantly, they checked on each other and their progress. *I am not worried. We have plenty of time. I deliberately said it will take longer to get in position than I think that it will, just in case.*

It took more than twice as long to cover the distance to the creek than it had to move double the distance upstream. Eventually, they were rewarded by coming to the last screen of laurels before the water. *The coarse, serrated leaves provide more shade than cover and, with the advancing afternoon, that dappled shadow is what we want.* Astrid looked ahead of her. *The new position, about a hand of hands of paces upstream of where I was before, is ideal. I have a tree to hide behind while waiting and, peering around, I can clearly see four of our opponents. More importantly I can see two people behind the Bunya pine and one of them, from what he is wearing and the way he is leaning back against the tree root and staring at the sky, has to be a mage. He is as useless in the bush as my two are.*

She looked to the left. *Hulagu is examining the scene ahead of him as well.* After a while he slowly moved his head and looked at her before showing five fingers. She showed four back. *It looks like his view is better than mine.* She checked the sky. *There is still a little bit of time to go.* She retreated slightly to behind the trunk of the tree she was beside and started to prepare arrows to fire. *Looking upstream I can see that Hulagu is doing the same.*

Theodora

I feel sure that I have the spell worked out now. At least I hope that I do. As soon as she had worked out the ideas on how to do it on the tablet, she pulled out a notebook and wrote it all down and checked it several times. *Basil can hold the book for me when it comes time to cast.*

Now, for it to work, I have to move to where I can see the bridge and yet still have flat ground to set up my casting position. A little closer than two hands by a score of paces will be all I need. I am creating the spell to sound as if the illusion is at least that far from me for it to be convincing. It will have to gradually become audible to the ambushers over the creek and only later visible.

Basil is nervous, but it seems that they did not see me move. However, it probably is as well that he made me take my armour off. I nearly tripped once as it was. I hate this tip-toeing around. In my experience, princesses don't do that sort of thing. We glide around and others comment favourably on our grace and poise.

Rani

I am nervous sitting behind the tree where Stefan insists that I stay. I can see my casting pattern in the open pegged out and ready for me to step into if

I need to do more than use a wand or fire an arrow. Ayesha took it from me and quietly put it in its place and, although I don't like others touching my equipment, I have to admit that the Muslim slave girl has done it far quieter than I would have been able to. To my left and right I can see Stefan, Bianca and Thord also sitting behind trees ready to come out once the trap is sprung. Only Stefan has even an idea where any of our opponents are located, but hopefully they will reveal themselves once Astrid and Hulagu start shooting and I tell them all to come out and fire. I just hope that I will know when it is time to do that. I don't want everyone just standing around looking for targets.

Kartikeya forgive me. I could have ensured that everyone could have followed what is happening by giving Astrid some of my explosive shafts. Next time we are going into battle, I will have to make sure I do that. Agni aid me—I am new at this. What else have I forgotten to do? I suppose that I will find out in time. I hope that none of the omissions will be fatal for my people. Pleading that it is my first real battle will not be much consolation if someone dies.

Astrid

The shadow of the branch that Astrid was tracking had now moved across the ground to touch the twig she had placed in the ground. *It now denotes the time that I have marked in my head as being when I will start things off.* She looked to Hulagu. *He has his arrows ready as well.*

She raised her head and made the loud cry of a raven. *I hope that, by calling up, it will make it sound like the bird is placed up in the trees. Although the birds will move along the ground, they rarely call out when they do so.* After a pause, she called out again and then, after a pause of similar length, again. Cautiously, Astrid peered around the trunk of the tree as she waited to see what would happen next. *On the other side of the creek nothing moves.*

Theodora

Basil is nudging me. Theodora started. *The raven is calling! I nearly missed it.* She stood up and started her incantation. *It is not a short spell.* She said it all slowly and deliberately so as to not make an error. *As I told him to, Basil has everything ready each time I nod. I hope that the smell of burning rose incense in the woods will not alarm anyone and will only make people think of a mage approaching.*

I have not added aroma to the illusion. Sight and sound are more than expensive enough and adding a touch of solidity to cause any magic to detonate means that, although I have not told my lover this, I will not be casting anything else today or for the next day either. It had better all work properly.

Basil

*M*y mistress is making mage-like motions and waving her hands around *in a fashion very similar to her dance moves. All she needs are the bells to make it complete.* He handed her pouches containing hair from each of them and from the horses and even wool from the sheep when she nods and places a hand out. *She places these around her as she softly speaks what I presume are words of power, but could be a laundry list as far as I know. At least she is reading them out from the book I hold with one hand so I suppose they are the right things for her to say.*

Finally, she stops moving and points back down the road. I can hear what sounds like the incautious approach of a group of riders. We are moving and making far more noise than we usually do. I can see Astrid strolling along the path towards me. It cannot be her though. My girl is never that clumsy and the illusion hardly looks around. It is just walking along with a spear over her shoulder and her bow on her back.

Basil looked closer. *The illusion is how Theodora sees Astrid rather than the way Astrid is herself. I wonder if the princess is jealous of the size of the Cat's breasts. She has emphasised them more than a little and my lover never wears her jacket open like that in the field.*

The image of Astrid is where the princess is pointing. She raises her other hand and points with that and, one after the other the rest of our group come into view. I can even make out soft conversation—or a murmuring at any rate, as I cannot distinguish any words at all. The image of Astrid has moved up to the creek and, following Theodora's hand movements, has stopped. Theodora's little finger has cocked up and the image raises its hand and looks around. The princess' other hand now stops moving and the other images stop. It is very odd to see how someone else sees me. I think that I look more like one of my nephews than like myself and my swords are not that large. Fingers wiggled and horses stomped and made noises.

Theodora is now looking carefully ahead and her right hand starts moving slowly again. Astrid's image moves slowly onto the bridge and, obeying the fingers, looks up and down the creek. Surely no one would be that blatant?

She moves a little further across and then the little finger wiggles again and her image waves back to the other images.

Now the left hand again begins to move without the right shifting. They are all being bunched up to make a better target. He looked ahead at the rest of their group. *Rani is staring at her own image. My mistress really does love the Hindi woman. I have never seen a real woman project so much sexuality as the mage's projected image does.* Quickly he looked at the others. *The princess thinks she is that plain; does she? Ayesha and Bianca are almost plain as well.* He tore his eyes back to the front and put the book away. *I won't need it now. I have to get my weapons out and ready. It looks like everyone else is preparing. We are all hoping that our opponents' gaze will be fixed on the illusion. The archers are already rising behind their trees and putting shafts to strings. The Astrid image is just about to step off the bridge—and there is an arrow from up the creek.*

Theodora

*T*he arrow exploded. It is just as well I worked out how to include that *cantrip for solidity.* She wiggled a finger and the image of Astrid toppled screaming into the water. *Learning how to make each digit move on its own was one of the hardest things of my training in illusion. My hands move like someone playing a hurdy-gurdy with both hands as the images all do different things. I really have to concentrate on what is happening as arrow after arrow and blasts that have to be from a wand come in one after another. The ambushers will see through the illusion soon, but I have to prolong that point as long as I can.*

Astrid

*S*eeing myself die is not an easy thing to have happen. It makes me queasy. *That archer will be my first target.*

She looked at the backs and sides of the ambushers. "Now," she hissed to Hulagu as she stood, drew and released in one fluid movement. *My targets are now all at least partly visible. I don't know when they will realise the trap and return fire so I need to fire fast and accurate. At ten hands or less, that is not hard. My archer has a cap like Stefan's with a nasal and a chain coif under it.* The first shaft went under the back of the helm and straight through the mail, opening it up easily with the heavy war heads she had chosen to use. *They don't travel as far as a normal shaft, but they hit hard. Already the man is dying. His bow has been flung clear as his spine is severed and, at least temporarily, until its weight proves too much for the shaft, his body is pinned to the tree he was sheltering behind.* As she turned to her next target she saw her first already start to slide towards the ground. *He hasn't even made a noise, and my actions have been covered by the sounds coming from where Theodora's illusions are battered by spells and shafts, and themselves fall and die.*

My next target is the mage. He must have some sort of protection up. My shafts are missing the man. The first hits above his head—the second in the tree a scant hand in front of his eyes. He has nearly fallen over as he realises his danger and cries out. He ran around the tree to try and get it between him and her. *The fact that he did that tells me that the protection is not perfect, but he is too hard for me to hit now anyway. He is now a problem for the main group.*

She turned to the next man she could see. *He has reacted to the mage's call and has been looking around for a target. He seems to have found Hulagu. I fire a fraction before he does and his arrow goes off target as my long-shafted arrow takes him through the chest. Luckily it shoots away wildly. He is one who is using enchanted shafts and a large whitey-wood bush, between the Khitan and I, explodes in flame when it is hit—my shaft has not killed him instantly—the man has dropped his bow, slumped to his knees, and is reaching for something at his belt as he stares down at the next arrow that sprouts from his chest—he has a bemused look on his face as his hands rise and began to tug at it. He may just not know that he is dead yet.* She followed it up with another couple of shafts to be sure and he finally fell and stopped moving.

Thord

*N*ice trap. A Human appeared in front of him a bare hand of hands away. *No attention is being paid to my side of the river at all. It is time to make them pay for that. I did not like seeing an image of myself burst into flame and beat at itself as my sheep and I headed for the water on the other side of the bridge. It wasn't perfect and I noticed that the image floated far too high in the water, but the ambushers hadn't and that is all that is important. The man has a wand in his hand. He will be first.*

Rani

You are not really supposed to do this. She stood there with a wand in each hand. *It is slightly more inaccurate, even if it is fun.* Flame burst from each as she aimed at the one she thought was the mage. *That the first blast only just caught him and the second missed, confirmed that likely he has some form of protection. I now have his full attention and he is turns to face me with a wand of his own and his back pressed to the tree. He is calling something.* An arrow someone fired went into his open mouth and pinned him to the tree. *It must have passed straight through—there is a look of surprise on his face as he begins to topple forward.* His head slid along the shaft as he did so until the feathers went into his mouth and he fell to the ground.

She kept up firing at him and was rewarded as the mage's body shuddered. *As most mages do, even me, there is a contingent cure spell set to be triggered if he passes a certain level of sustained damage. That arrow could have done that on its own, a good or a lucky shot. Who cares? The mage's mind is already trying to get his body back under control as it returns to some degree of health and it is my job to stop that.* She fired twice, three times more. *Whichever of my archers fired the first arrow has realised what would happen just as I did and has kept firing as well. Soon the body is lying twitching on the ground as a few more shafts thud into it one after another to make sure the mage is not trying to be cunning.*

I am convinced. He has no more cures in operation. Now, who is left among our attackers? She scanned along the creek ahead of her. *There is no movement apart from an archer from Haven wearing just a kilt, his long sword still sheathed on his back. The man lies half in the water screaming, twitching and obviously dying. Another shaft hits him and he gives a last wail and expires.*

Theodora

Trying to manipulate this many images is hard. My teachers tried to make me push myself and I used to think that I had—at the time. Now I realise that they were easy on me. I have to watch what is happening and react to it. I am bending my hand and sending my puppets in different directions—the images of the packhorses are galloping over the water. She moved to pull them back to the road. *My opponents don't seem to see that mistake—thankfully. I have been reduced to making random noises and screams instead of tailoring them—it is getting too hard to try and match them to the people. Once hit and on the ground, I am leaving the images alone and uncontrolled. That makes things a little easier, but it also leaves the image repeating its actions on a loop. Have the arrows stopped coming in?*

She paused and looked, unaware that her own image, the only one still on its horse and intact had also stopped now that her fingers had. *I haven't been able to bring myself to kill, or even seriously hurt, my own image and I am not happy about hurting my lover's image either. I settled for just leaving her lying still and possibly just unconscious. Basil's avatar is surprisingly hard for me to hurt as well. It now lies in the water behind the bridge.*

At least things seem to be in hand as far as the combat is concerned. It has all worked as a stratagem. Good. Now it is time for me to relax—I am suddenly feeling very tired and very thirsty. Theodora took a step out of her pattern towards Basil and went to ask for something to drink.

Basil

I will bet she is so drained that she will be asleep for a day. Theodora is stepping towards me. Her eyes are already glazing over as she falls towards me. Hopefully that is all she has done and she has not taken any permanent harm. I have seen mages do this before, using so much mana that they are completely drained and as limp as a dishrag after it had been used in the washing up for a whole tagma. Sometimes they go too far and are never able to cast again or even are un-minded. I don't think that is likely. She was in control right up until everything just stopped or kept looping. As he lowered her to the ground, he looked up and saw that the images ahead of him were slowly becoming transparent and misty.

He looked along the line. *Rani is firing wands with pauses between blasts. Thord, Stefan and Ayesha are all still shooting. None of them seem harmed at all.* He turned to see Father Christopher hurrying up towards where he crouched over his charge. *Behind the priest, Bianca is already bringing the horses up, her own two openly getting in the way as they stand on each side of her.*

Rani

I can hear my people all around me. From somewhere invisible up the creek comes Astrid's voice.

"All clear this side."

After a short pause, from beside me and making me almost wince, comes Stefan's call. "They are all dead here," he yelled.

Around me the others can be heard celebrating in their own way. Caution seems to have been thrown away for at least an instant. It has to be Hulagu up near Astrid who just let out a yell that is almost the howl of a wolf. It will be Ayesha who ululates in elation. She looked around. *Theodora lies on the ground behind me, her head on Basil's lap, and the priest bent over her. What has happened?* Quickly she launched herself in that direction. *Basil doesn't seem concerned and the priest is already standing up.*

"She seems fine," Christopher said, as he raised a hand palm forward to slow her rush. "She is asleep and probably exhausted, but her breathing is even and her pulse strong. You may not know, but priests can also often sense life force, and hers is strong. Leave her with Basil and organise the rest."

Rani turned to do that. *It is already in hand. Stefan has people already crossing the bridge.* She came out into the open. *Astrid and Hulagu must have crossed through the creek as they are already recovering arrows.*

Stefan

Stefan looked at faces. *Damn—I know these people. Two are from Evilhalt itself, another two from assarts to the west, and the rest are ones I have seen with various caravans. As far as I can remember all of the locals are single men and related.*

A pair of brothers and the others are cousins—he tried hard to remember anything about them—*parents dead, and none of them with a real trade or good at much except what would suit them to an easy life of being guards for traders—certainly not good enough for cadre. I even recognise the mage and the two Hindi men. Somewhere there will be horses. It seems that whoever does not like the people I have attached myself to, has either hired themselves people who don't have many scruples or else they have a local group working for them and helping the bandits.*

It had all seemed like just an exciting story to me before this. It doesn't seem like just a story now. I wonder how much more there is waiting for us and what our enemies have found out about our destination. It is indeed a pity that none of our ambushers are still alive. From what I have heard, we could have given them to Bianca to find out more about what is happening and why.

Glossary

Adeela Strand: a legendary beachside holiday spot in the south for the rich of Haven with flawless white sand.

Adversary: a term used in various religions and traditions to denote the evil side of theology.

Agni: Hindu God of Fire.

Aguuikh Ain: Khitan for the Great Forest.

Aissa Flow: a major river starting in the plains and ending in the sea in Freehold. It is navigable by sailing ships to the town of Brickshield. Known to the Khitan as Aisi Darya. It ends near Glengate.

Alat-kharl: one of the races of Kharl. They live (where possible) in heavy forests and jungles where they enjoy clearing forest and building things. They are found in the trade quarters of most towns as well. These are the artisan Kharl; although they are just as happy to enjoy close combat as others. They are usually coloured in an unattractive green-brown mottling pattern. They enjoy embellishing their tusks with gold and silver inlay.

Alhambra: Palace / fortress of the Caliph in Dimashq.

Al-jihad al-Akbar: the Great Struggle against Satan or evil or the attempt to convert everyone to Islam, depending on context.

Al-kīmiyā: the Arabic word from which we get the word 'chemical'.

Allāhu akbar: an Arabic phrase that means 'God is the Greatest'.

Antdrudge: A major town, once known as Amtrage (in Old Speech), it is located on an island near the mouth of the Butsin River in the far north-west of Darkreach. It is a major site of manufacturing.

Antikataskopeía: a part of the Army who are also police. Sometimes they are in uniform and sometimes they are not. The term may be translated as 'secret police,' for they are responsible for looking for subversion, spies and treason as much as normal criminals.

Ardlark: Capital of the Empire of Darkreach and near the furthest east in The Land. It is by far the largest city known (twice the size of Ashvaria and four times that of Sacred Gate and Trekvarna) with several walls and many outlying settlements.

Ashvaria: the capital of Freehold and its largest city. The Queen resides there and it is the home of the Pope.

Asperser: a pierced metal ball on a stick, often made of silver or gold, which is used to cast Holy Water.

Assarts: small clearings and farms, sometimes these will stay as just a single farm, but some will grow to become hamlets and then villages.

Axebeak: These birds are one of the greatest menaces on the plains, in forests and in swamps. They are large (2.5 metres tall) and flightless with a large bite and two large claws. They give their name to one of the clans of the Kara-Khitan.

Axepol: Once called Erskine, it is a large manufacturing town located on the sea at the mouth of the Sasar River at the west of the Great Plain. Home of the Metropolitan of The Plains.

Babu: Hindi for a clerk or servant.

Baerami River: a tributary of the Aissa Flow that curls back towards the north-west.

Bagts Anchin: Khitan for 'Pack Hunter', both the animal and the clan.

Baklava: a common sweet dessert delicacy in the Caliphate and Darkreach.

Battle Mage: A Fire mage of the Kshatya or Brahmin caste in Haven is a battle mage. They are an army officer and well paid even when studying. They learn spells of destruction and combat as well as military tactics and weapons use.

Bear-folk: supposedly a reclusive group of alleged shape-shifters, or maybe they just keep bears as totem animals. They live in the foothills of the Southern Mountains.

Betterberries: This is a species of small shrub (up to one metre tall) with dark green leaves and small spikes. It occurs in northern and southern forests. It has small white flowers. If its berries are picked in autumn, they can be used to magically cure a minor amount of damage when they are eaten.

Bison: a plains animal and they are a clan of the Kara-Khitan.

Bodhran: a small round and flat drum usually played with a two-ended beater.

Böö: Khitan word that means both shamen and shamenka, the male and female 'priests' of the Khitan.

Boyuk-Kharl: Once only another kharl tribe, the Boyuk-kharl are now a completely separate species being larger, stronger and smarter than other kharl. They also cope better with strong light, being on the same level as Humans. Although sometimes used as officers for other Kharl units, inherent Boyuk-kharl racism often leads to conflict and tension within their command. Boyuk-kharl units are often the Kharl who are given isolated and independent commands, although in battle they are the vanguard. They are fond of water and can often be found in ships.

Brahmins: the religious caste of Haven.

Brickshield: a large village and castle on the Baerami River in Freehold. Once known as Richfield, it exists mainly for defence and is the seat of the Earl of the Marches and has a substantial agricultural area with sheep and grain production, a market each week day and an annual fair around St Cuthbert's Day. It is the main setting off point for traders across the plains and the head of navigation on the Aissa/Baerami river system.

Bridget, Saint: Holy day 10th Sixtus, Patron of dairymaids, compassion to the poor, blacksmiths and poets.

Brotherhood, the: The Brotherhood of All Believers is a schismatic sect of neo-Calvinists who have set up a theocratic state in the north-west of The Land.

Burning, the: Also called The Plague by some cultures, this was a great plague that ravaged The Land for over a hundred years. There have been no known outbreaks for nearly twenty years. Victims have a fever and gradually develop a mania that forces them to burn and destroy anything that they can. It is thought that only a tenth of the people survived the disease and the devastation caused by its sufferers. Many towns and other settlements were lost or abandoned.

Camail: a piece of mail hanging from the helmet and protecting the neck and shoulders.

Cantrip: another name for a spell

Caravanserai: an Arabic term for a place that is mainly for an overnight stay rather than local food and drink.

Cecilia, Saint: Holy Day 23rd Undecim, a Patron of Bards and Entertainers.

Christopher, Saint: Holy Day 25th September, Patron of travellers and sovereign against water, tempest and sudden death.

Circus, the: A large construction in many Darkreach towns where public combat takes place, either exhibition matches or fights to the death among criminals. That in Ardlark holds a significant proportion of the city.

Circus Maximus, the: an oval area for racing horses and other beasts.

Cold Keep: the most northerly settlement of Darkreach in the arboreal forests east of the mountains on the coast.

Cow Lizard: This is the prototypical ceratopsian that lives in the plains and forests. They have two large and one small horn. Although largely herbivorous, they will eat carrion. They travel in herds. They are also the totem beast of a clan of the Kara-Khitan.

Dar al-salaam: The House of Peace, an Arabic expression for the whole group of Believers.

Dagh Ordu: Khitan term for a large monolith in the southern plains. It is known as The Rock to others. It is forbidden for non-Khitan to go near it. A dragon lives inside the top.

Darkreach: a multi-racial Empire that takes up the east of The Land. Ruled by Hrothnog it most closely resembles the Roman Empire of Constantinople at its best.

Darkreach Gap: Also known just as the Gap. It is the only pass through the mountains and runs from Nameless Keep to Mouthguard. The Methul River starts in it.

Darkspeech (half-Kharl): the most commonly used tongue in Darkreach.

Dating: Years run over a 48-year cycle with the twelve zodiacal signs used on Vhast and the elements of Earth, Air, Fire and Water. There are twelve months of equal length, each having six weeks of six days. The first parts of the story take part in the Year of the Water Dog.

Deathguard Tower: a strongly fortified village with a large garrison that watches over the burial mounds that cover the Funereal Hills.

Deeremchin: Khitan word for a bandit or brigand

Delver, The: a tavern in Kharlsbane.

Deodanth: The deodanth are a feared race that is spread throughout The Land. They only live in small family groups consisting of a bonded pair and up to four children. Children leave the family upon reaching puberty and will generally roam around either on their own or with one or two others of the same gender until they bond. Deodanth are like large Humans with black skin—not Negroid but black. Their eyes also have black pupils. They are almost exclusively carnivores and particularly like Human flesh. Their teeth are therefore adapted more for rending than chewing, being long and pointy.

Denarii: plural of denarius, a gold coin of Darkreach that weighs 4.5g and is worth 450 nummus.

Dimashq: the capital of the Caliphate on the shores of the lake called Buhairet Tabariyya in the fertile mountain plain known as the Rãhit. It is a very large town rather than a full city.

Dire wolf: A large canine, with several sub-species, which is found on the plains, in mountains and one variety is even found underground. It is the largest of the wolves. The animal also gives its name to one of the clans of the Kara-Khitan.

Dochra: it is located on the shore of the Nu-I Lake to the southwest of Ardlark in the Great Plain. There is an artesian spring leading down to a small wet section of the lake. It has an oasis around it for growing dates and other crops.

Doumbec: a small hand drum.

Duvel River: a tributary of the Methul River near the Darkreach Gap.

Dwarf (Dwarves/Dwarven): a race of humanoids that tend to live below ground. Most people cannot tell if there are any female dwarves, as all of them are bearded and similar in appearance. They are skilled miners and artisans. Dwarves are one of the few races that are not fertile with Humans.

Dwarvenholme: the long-lost capital of the Dwarves. Many people regard its existence as a myth.

Eagle: not only the bird, but also a clan of the Kara-Khitan.

Ecumen: a collective name for one Christian Church expressing the same beliefs.

Elder Race or Eldar: Legends abound about the Elder Race. Some of them are correct. They are taller and generally more slender than Humans, very attractive in appearance and dominating in aspect. They are often seen as implacable and iron-willed. They have eyes with purple irises and epicanthic folds. The Elder Race take extra damage from iron weapons. The Elder Race fought alongside humanity against Darkreach. Having helped in this victory, none were to be found within the Land within a few months. Several legends say that they sailed away from southern ports leaving behind their language, High Speech, which is still much used by mages, and still found in many artefacts and gravesites. The Elder Race could interbreed with humans and some families claim descent from them.

Elephant: not only the animal, but also the totem beast of a Kara-Khitan Clan.

Elephant Island: see Hāthī Dvīpa.

Emeel amidarch baigaa khümüüs: Khitan phrase used to describe themselves, literally 'people who live in the saddle'.

Erave Town: a town on the southern end of Lake Erave. Its culture is strongly influenced by Haven and the families of many of its inhabitants were originally from there.

Evilhalt: a town at the northern edge of Lake Erave nearly in the middle of The Land. It is the northern limit of navigation for an ocean-going ship up the Rhastaputra River and is strongly fortified. The people there speak Dwarven among themselves.

Faen: the language of the people of The Swamp.

Festival of the Dragon: an annual Khitan ceremony where the dragon of Dagh Ordu is fed and appeased. It is secret (or at least not believed) outside the tribes.

Firestar: one of Bianca's warhorses. He used to belong to Paulo.

Fisherman's Arms, The: a tavern in Erave Town.

Follis: the standard coin of the independent villages, a value will be given in these. They are made of tin and weigh 20g.

Francis, Saint: Holy Day 4th October, Patron of Animals.

Freehold: A Kingdom in the South-west of The Land. It covers most of the southwest between the Aissa / Baerami system, in the south, and the No-iu flow in the north. Between these are the Trekvarna and Oban Rivers. There is dispute with the Khitan over much of the inter-river plains areas. The capital is at Ashvaria and the Queen is Daphne IV Acer. As a culture, it most closely approaches early 1500s Western Europe.

Funereal Hills: a plateau in Darkreach covered in burial tumuli and mounds from an unknown race. Some of these are large enough to be thought of as hills. Many of them contain undead of various sorts: wights, wraiths, shadows, and simple skeletons.

Ganesh: Havenite elephant-headed god of wisdom and knowledge. This includes foretelling. He is often depicted riding on a mouse. He is one of the more popular gods.

Gap, the: see Darkreach Gap.

Garthang Keep: The most northerly part of Haven. It is an ancient and large fortress meant to control the Rhastaputra and the major tributary that leads from the Swamp.

George, Saint: Holy Day 23rd Quartos, Patron of those who fight dragons and demons, also of cavalry.

Ger: the domed tent of the Kara-Khitan made of leather over a frame work of flexible light timber. Usually these are on the ground and set up each time the group stops, but for important people they may be on a huge wheeled platform drawn by oxen or cow lizards.

Ghats: long shelves forming a series of steps which lead down to the Rhastaputra River. These mark ritual bathing places in Haven.

Ghazi: a holy warrior of the Caliphate. Often referred to as Assassins by the rest of the world, their true function is almost always as guards, scouts and spies. They are faithful even if it involves their own death. Some are also minor priests.

Glare-wraps: thin sheets of scraped mica bound in leather that act in snow or ice to polarise light and allow vision instead to just 'seeing white'.

Glengate: A large village in the Great Forest at the head of the Aisi Darya or Aissa Flow on the shorter, more southern and most usual path from Lake Erave to Freehold across the plains.

Gnolls: one of the wild races of the Mountains, they are related to Kharl (whom they hate). It is thought that they rarely form groups of more than a family.

Goldentide: a coastal town in Freehold and site of a Bishopric. It is held personally by the Queen as Baroness Goldentide. Its wealth comes from fishing.

Grey Doe, the: an inn in Ardlark catering only for female customers.

Granmer: a term used for any female of the Imperial family of Darkreach who is at least two generations older than the speaker.

Granther: a term used for any male of the Imperial family of Darkreach who is at least two generations older than the speaker.

Granther, the: specifically refers to the head of the Imperial line, the Emperor Hrothnog.

Great Bitter Lake: an almost always dry salt-lake west of Ardlark. It is north of Deathguard Tower on the other side of the road to the Funereal Hills.

Great Chain of Being, the: The pre-Reformation church placed Man only half-way towards God in a framework of Creation.

Great Plain, the: Also known as the Dry Plains it is a peninsula which makes up a large proportion of Darkreach west of Ardlark.

Greek: main language used by the Orthodox Church, it is also used by several of the independent villages of the plains and as a tribal tongue by one group of Humans in Darkreach.

Greensin: a large village or small town on the Ogunbil River just west of the Great Forest in the north. It is the seat of an Orthodox Metropolitan and he rules the town. There is also the monastery of Saints Cyril and Methodius. It is known as Takhilch Khot to the Khitan.

Greydkharl: are the most underground of the Kharl races. They have eyes that can see in poorer light conditions and thus are easily blinded by bright light. They are seldom seen above ground except in sieges and at night. Almost all Kharl siege engineers are Greydkharl. Their skin is a paler coloured green than other Kharl and they are usually noticeable as their eyes are much larger than most. They have many tattoo designs that are common among them & they enjoy this art form.

Gulama: Hindi for a slave.

Guthog's Blessing: This is a small species of grass (up to 30 centimetres) found on the plains. A wash can be made from the leaves. It rids all Humans and animals of ticks and mites and relieves any itchiness they have caused.

Half Kharl: see Insakharl

Hāthī Dvīpa: or Elephant Island. It is one of the islands of Sacred Gate. It has mainly wealthy upper caste residents but also houses other facilities like the Royal Armouries.

Hand: everyone has five fingers and a thumb so a normal unit of measurement is a hand of six. A hand of hands (or hand filled) is thirty-six.

Haven: a nation at the mouth of the Rhastaputra River. Although small, it is a densely populated area with a population at least as great as Freehold.

Hesperinos: The beginning of the Orthodox liturgical day, it occurs at sundown. To the Catholics it is known as Vespers.

Hetaera: a skilled courtesan in Darkreach. They are often also entertainers of note.

High Speech: the language of the Eldar. It has soft and melodious tones and is used mainly by mages.

Hindi: the language of Haven.

Hobgoblins: Hobgoblins are far larger than Goblins and even Kharl or most Humans, but are similar to Goblins in appearance although they have grey skin and even more prominent teeth. There are a few small tribes of Hobgoblins in the mountains. Hobgoblins do not like strong light but can stand daylight if it is not too bright. They use scimitars and medium shields (which they generally trade for with the Goblins) & prefer long bows. They are feared warriors who are more likely to kill than talk.

Hoppers: there are many species of this common animal in the Land. Here we would call them wallabies and kangaroos.

Houppelande: a large garment worn by men and women west of the mountains. It is used to extravagantly show wealth with the amount of cloth used in it and often the richness of the cloth.

Hugon pir: a petroleum product that most closely resembles napalm. It is used by the armies of Darkreach and exported with permission.

Hyperion: Coin of the independent villages made of gold and weighs 4.5g. It is worth 450 tin follis.

Ibrik: a small pot of an odd shape that is used for brewing kaf.

Imperial: a Darkreach coin made of gold and weighing 20g. It is worth 2,000 nummus.

Insak-div: Often referred to as 'dark trolls', Insak-div are not related to trolls in any way. They speak their own tongue. There are no Insak-div mages and very few clerics. Insak-div are ugly, not very intelligent, and lack any concept of stealth or subtlety (indeed their own language lacks words even related to these concepts). They make up for this in increased size, strength and endurance, and a thicker skin. Insak-div are very dark-green and almost black in colour. Despite their fearsome appearance, they are usually very happy and jovial unless provoked. Unfortunately, they are very easily provoked. Insak-div enjoy drinking and singing—really simple songs—especially rounds and additive drinking songs, which they will continue for hours. A common cause of their fights is brawling over mistakes in these. An Insak-div bar fight will reduce a normal bar room to matchsticks very quickly. Bars catering for their needs lack seats (other than built in benches on walls) and tables. Insak-div are usually happy to sit on the floor.

Insakharl: Also known as half-Kharl, all persons who are not fully Human or fully Kharl in ancestry regardless of proportion.

Isci-kharl: One of the Kharl races, they are large, less intelligent and lazy, but also strong. Their skin is thick and rough and dark in colour—ranging from very dark green to almost black. Isci-kharl are the shock troops. They are tolerant of daylight but prefer darker days and fighting at night as they have eyes that are more light sensitive than Humans. Despite this, a farmer Kharl, or one who is a general labourer, will most likely come from this tribe.

Jade Mountain: a region near Ardlark where a series of steep misty hills produce large quantities of jade of different shades.

Kaf: This is any one of four species of evergreen shrub that grows to 5m in the north and south mountains. Leaves are dark green and glossy around 15cm long and 6cm wide. The flowers stem from the leaf axils in white clusters with five petals in early spring. The seeds ripen by late autumn and start green then go to yellow, crimson and finally black. Fruit is green when picked for a stimulating beverage. Coffee.

Kāfirūn: Arabic for the unbelievers, those who do not follow the Prophet.

Kapok: This is a prolific jungle vine that climbs trees. It produces seedpods that can be harvested and processed to produce a warm and soft cloth. These pods can be in very dense growth and are often quite high up and difficult to harvest. It is an important cloth for some mages.

Kara-Khitan: collective term for the tribes of the plains.

Kartikeya: Hindu God of War.

Kataphract or Kataphractoi: a heavy cavalryman (or woman) from Darkreach. They ride an armoured horse and are themselves armoured. They employ a variety of weapons depending on range and target. They charge with their knees touching.

Kentarchkos: a Darkreach officer usually placed in charge of a Century, ten companies (or tourma if cavalry) of around one hundred and forty-four troops each. They may have a smaller independent command.

Kha-Khan: the head of the Kara-Khitan.

Kharl: According to most reliable histories, Hrothnog created the Kharl several thousand years ago. Kharl are usually quite ugly. Their faces usually resemble those of a pig, complete with tusks. Their skin is usually greenish in colour and has a scaly texture. Kharl are hardier than Humans, able to eat a wider range of foods and to drink more polluted water. They are not good leaders. Kharl usually enjoy violence. They have ritualised violence into a game called 'ball' which is played on a field with teams. Kharl are devoted followers of their (racially coherent) teams. They also love watching condemned prisoners fight in gladiatorial combat. All Kharl will speak Darkspeech. In addition, they will speak their own tribal language. Although all will marry and breed with Humans, the tribes rarely interbreed and may be on the way to speciation. There are five tribes of Kharl in the Land, Kichic-kharl, Alat-kharl, Isci-kharl, Greydkharl, and Boyuk-kharl.

Kharlsbane: A settlement of the Dwarves in the Northern Mountains. It is a largely above-ground town carved direct from the rock it is built on.

Khitan: language of the Kara-Khitan

Khünd Chono: Khitan for 'Dire Wolf' (both the animal and the clan)

Khuulias gaduur: Khitan for an outlaw.

Khuyagt morin: Khitan for the heaviest cavalry, full armoured riders on armoured horses, what Darkreach call 'kataphractoi'.

Kichic-kharl: These are the smallest and brightest Kharl. They excel at tracking. Their colour is a light forest green and Kichic-kharl often blend in with outside vegetation. Their units are lightly equipped, often concentrating on missile fire and they wear little armour. They are the best adapted of the Kharl to full daylight. If you see a Kharl mage, it is likely to be of the Kichic-kharl.

Köle: Khitan word for a person captured in battle and owned by their captor, alternate words are slave, thrall, or gulama (Hindi).

Kshatya: one of the five castes of Haven society, the caste of warriors (including most mages) and rulers.

Kynigoi: Darkreach light cavalry, they can be on horses or camels and they skirmish and use missile fire rather than close for close combat.

Lake Erave: the largest lake in The Land, it is at the northern navigable point of the Rhastaputra River with Erave town in the south where the river leaves the lake and Evilhalt in the north where it enters.

Latin: the language of Freehold.

Law of Contagion: a magical law that says that if something used to belong to or be a part of a person or thing then it still has a spooky connection over distance with the original.

Law of Similarity: a magical law that says that if two items are similar then one can be used to better affect the other. It is on this basis that incense, cloths, gems, numbers, and shapes are used in castings.

Leman: acknowledged sexual partner.

Lion: not only the animal, but also a Clan of the Kara-Khitan.

Logothetēs tou trapeza basilikē: the chief of the Palace accounts in Darkreach, a high official and combination bookkeeper and cashier.

Mahr: Money paid by a man or his family to a woman's family in Darkreach when she is given in marriage as a compensation for the loss of her services.

Mandira Dvīpa: or Temple Island. This is an island in Sacred Gate that has the main temples of almost all of the gods on it.

Martobulli: a throwing dart weighing a bit less than half a kilogram. They can be thrown for a long distance and, particularly when used en-masse, can be quite deadly.

Mary Magdalene, Saint: Holy day 4th Quinque, Patron sinners and those hoping for redemption.

Metal Hill: a hill outside Ardlark in Darkreach that is almost entirely made of iron ore.

Methul River: a river that starts in the Darkreach Gap and end in the north at Wolfneck. It drains the western side of the mountains in the north.

Metropolitan: a rank in the Orthodox Church which means the same as a Bishopric in Freehold.

Milesaria: a coin of the independent villages made of silver and copper alloy that weighs 2.5g and is worth 15 follis.

Mouthguard Keep: a fortress and growing village in the Methul River at the western end of the Darkreach Gap.

Mundu: a Havenite garment consisting of a single length of cloth draped around the body and over the shoulder. It is similar to a Roman toga. They are almost always worn by holy men and are usually orange in colour.

Muslims: both the inhabitants of the Caliphate and one of the tribes of Humans in Darkreach.

Nameless Keep: a massive fortification at the eastern end of the Darkreach Gap that is carved out of a ridge of basalt and has major magical enhancements.

Nekulturny: a word in the Darkspeech of Wolfneck. It is a word that roughly means 'uncultured' but is far more derogatory.

Njal-bound: a way of making clothing similar to knitting.

Northern Ocean: the water between The Land and the lands of the Arctic.

Northern Waste, the: see White World.

Nu-I Lake: a large salty lake west of Ardlark. Dochra is on its shore.

Numismata: a coin of Darkreach made of silver and weighing 2.5g. It is worth 15 nummus.

Nummus: the base coin of Darkreach, it is made of tin and weighs 20g.

Order of St Ursula: a militant female Catholic Order. Some of its members are ordained as Deacons and can perform services. It is known for its missionary outreach and good works.

Ogres: Despite some legends, these are the intellectuals of the non-Humans. Ogre-mages are well known and feared. They are common and powerful. Ogres have dark-yellow to dark-green and (rarely) black skin and black hair, often worn long and either loose or in a pony-tail. They have prominent functional incisors and all males have a small horn growing from the centre of their forehead. Ogres will also eat anything that is not an ogre.

Old Lobster, the: an inn in Dochra.

Ovoo: a shrine of the Kara-Khitan and one of the few things they build. It consists of a pile of rocks. Weighted down in the pile are all sorts of blue items, from flowers to clothing or scraps of cloth, left behind by people engaging in a long journey.

Orthodox: the dominant religion outside Freehold. Its followers are scattered in villages and lack numbers outside Darkreach.

Orthros: the first service of the morning for the Orthodox. It usually starts before sunrise. The Catholic equivalent is matins.

Oxys Dromos: the Darkreach Imperial messenger service. Using relay chains and magic, they expect to move a messenger as well as up to 20kg of mail a distance of 360km in a day.
Pack-hunter: These are similar to the now extinct raptors. They are fast-moving and intelligent. Pack hunters can be found in jungles, swamps, forests, in the mountains, and on the plains. Their classic attack is a leap using their large rear claw in a slashing attack. They can also use a bite. They are brightly feathered and also give their name to one of the clans of the Kara-Khitan.
Panic: the smaller moon of Vhast. It orbits in 28 days.
Pavitra Phāṭaka: capital and largest city of Haven. It is made up of the riverbanks at the wide mouth of the Rhastaputra River and many islands in the river. The islands are connected by bridges and ferries. It also houses the University, which is the premier magical training site west of the mountains.
Peelfall: a large town in Haven on the Rhastaputra. It is the most northerly of the major settlements and separated from Garthang Keep by forest. The riverbank south of it has been cleared and is dense with people.
Pope: head of the Catholic Church.
Plague, the: see Burning, the.
Platys Dromos: The Imperial Freight service of Darkreach. They shift heavy loads of important materials and cover 32km in a day in flat terrain.
Pūrvī Taṭa: the eastern shore of the Rhastaputra River at Pavitra Phāṭaka.
Rakis lacoum: a sweet jelly-like confection common in the Caliphate and Darkreach. In English, a version of it is called Turkish Delight.
Recorder: a senior University official in Haven in charge of all the staff and students at the University.
Rhastaputra River: the largest river in The Land. It drains from the North-West Hills down to Haven along the base of the Southern Mountains and so provides drainage to much of the wettest areas. It is navigable for most of its length to Evilhalt.
Richfield: see Brickshield
Riq: a small finger drum.
Roving Insakharl, the: an inn at Mouthguard.
Samalaingika: Hindi for a lesbian.
Sacred Gate: see Pavitra Phāṭaka
Sasar: a mining town on the west of the Great Plain. They mine iron ore and the town is covered in dust from the mine.
'sblood: an expletive contraction of 'God's Blood'
Scholars Isle: see Vidvānōṁ Dvīpa
Sesterces: A silver coin from Darkreach that weighs 25g and is worth 150 nummus.

Seven: Hobgoblin legends maintain that there are seven old Gods and an unknown number of Eldest ones.

Seytanyi: depending on context this Arabic term may mean Satan or any of the major demons.

Shamen / shamenka: mages and religious leaders of the Kara-Khitan.

Shelike: a large town in Haven upstream of the capital. It is the centre of the elephant trade.

Silentochre: This is a large town at the head of the Oirmt Reach and the mouth of the Oirmt River in Darkreach.

Simon, Father: the chief Orthodox priest of Wolfneck.

Sirocco: one of Bianca's warhorses. He used to belong to Antonio.

Slain Enemy, the: the newly renamed tavern in Evilhalt.

Snake: not only the animal, but also a Clan of the Kara-Khitan

Somniofulgio: A pernicious vine found in the jungles. It has climbing claws and will attach to anything. If its leaves are collected at night they may be dried and smoked as a mild hallucinogen. The smoke is aromatic and has a sweet smell.

Southern Mountains: the entire mountain chain from the Darkreach Gap to the southern seas. This is over two-thirds of its length.

Southpoint: The most southerly settlement in Darkreach, usually reached only by sea. It is on the Demaresque Creek at the head of a small bay with a fairly narrow but deep inlet.

Spearleaf: This is a plains herb. A potion may be made from its roots, which is a poison. A second potion may be made from its leaves, which cures sleeping sickness. Its berries may also be eaten and they are a strong hallucinogen.

Strategos: A Darkreach military rank. It can be thought of as General or Admiral.

Subadar: the lowest Havenite Officer rank.

Sundercud Creek: a watercourse in the north-west that marks the southern boundary of The Brotherhood.

Superhumeral: a detachable collar used in Darkreach formal costume and by priests of both Catholic and Orthodox Churches. It is at least embroidered and is often heavily jewelled.

Swamp, the: known to its inhabitants as The Confederation of the Free, this is an area of jungle and swamp filled with tangled rivers. It lies between Haven and the Southern Mountains. Its inhabitants have a notoriously light-fingered approach to other people's property.

Tagmata: In Darkreach the basic unit of the land-based military is a patrol of 12 men (or women). Twelve of these form a company (or tourma if cavalry) with one of them as a command element. Ten companies or tourma make a kentarkhion or century. A tagma is made up of ten Centuries or Kentarkion.

Four Tagmata make up a Regiment. A Tagma may contain cavalry, infantry and/or engineers.

Tahlin: This is a small species of jungle shrub. Its leaves produce a waxy substance that is compounded to make a yellow depilatory cream. It also acts as a skin balm and can sometimes clear up rashes, acne and similar. It has mild antiseptic properties and can be compounded with other herbs for a mixed effect. It smells similar to roses.

Takhilch Khot: Khitan for Greensin. It literally means 'Settlement of Priests'.

Talent: a coin of the independent villages, it is made of gold and weighs 20g. It is worth 2,000 follis.

Tar-khan: the leader of a Clan.

Temple Island: see Mandira Dvīpa

Terror: the larger moon of Vhast. It has an orbit of 36 days and determines the months.

Thrall: One of the terms used to denote a slave, a thrall has different rights and duties in different cultures. In Freehold it is for life, in the Brotherhood for many generations, and in Wolfneck for a fixed term.

Toppuddle: This is a small town of several thousand on the Oban River in Freehold. It is ruled by Archibald Neville, Baron Toppuddle, who has some Royal troops in addition to garrison. It is the seat of a Bishopric at the cathedral of St Basil the Great. It owes its existence to agriculture and the manufacture of anything that needs water and water power.

Tuman: a part of a Kara-Khitan Clan and ruled by a Su-Khan. It will generally have around a hundred effective combatants.

Vinice: a very large Havenite town on the Rhastputra between Peelfall and Shelike.

Ünee Gürvel: Khitan for 'Cow-Lizard', both the animal and the clan.

Unguent: an ointment.

University of Pavitra Phāṭaka: the main site for mage training outside Dark-reach.

Ursula, Saint: Holy Day 6th September, Patron of virgins and strength through faith.

Üstei akh düü: Khitan for totem animals (literally 'fur siblings')

Üzen Yadalt Ursgai: Khitan for Sundercud Creek on the border of the Brotherhood, literally 'Stream of Hate'.

Üzen Yaddag Düürsen: Khitan for the Brotherhood of All Believers, literally 'Hate-Filled'

Vidvānōṁ Dvīpa: or Scholar's Isle, site of the University and home to many mages and people who work in that area.

Walla: any cloth made from the wool of llamas, alpacas, or similar animals. It is significant to some mages.

Wanderjahr: The Year of Discovery for the Kara-Khitan. A person about to become an adult will take a year to travel where they will to help find their destiny. They wear special marks to show that they are above normal violence and feud. Most stay within the land of the clans, but there is no restriction. This is one of the most important Rites of Passage for that society.

Westway: a small hamlet being built to the west of Evilhalt.

White World, the: The Arctic lands of Vhast. Most people are unaware of its existence. It is called the Northern Waste by the people of Wolfneck.

Wolfneck: A small town with a wooden palisade on an earthen rampart in the forest at the mouth of the Methul River. The forests around it produce furs in abundance and much fishing and whaling take place in the waters around here. Unusual in that the main language used is Darkspeech (with a distinct local accent) due to it once having belonged to Darkreach. All of the population are part Kharl.

Wootz: a form of steel that creates an effect like Damascening or pattern-welding. It makes a superior weapon or piece of armour that is very resistant to breaking or penetration and keeps a good edge.

Yāqūsa: This is a small town on the Khābūr Rūdh (or river). It is the most northerly settlement in the Caliphate.

Yuggel River: a river leading from the northern mountains to the Methul. The Dwarf village of Kharlsbane is near it.

Zils: small cymbals attached to the fingers and used by dancers.